Between Sisters

ALSO BY CATHY KELLY
FROM CLIPPER LARGE PRINT

It Started With Paris

Between Sisters

Cathy Kelly

W F HOWES LTD

This large print edition published in 2016 by
W F Howes Ltd
Unit 5, St George's House, Rearsby Business Park,
Gaddesby Lane, Rearsby, Leicester LE7 4YH

1 3 5 7 9 10 8 6 4 2

First published in the United Kingdom in 2015
by Orion Books

A CIP catalogue record for this book is available
from the British Library

ISBN 978 1 51004 378 7

Typeset by Palimpsest Book Production Limited,

Print ... in
by TJ In... ...rnwall

For Dylan, Murray and John, as always.

PROLOGUE

LONDON

Dr Elsa de Marco sat in the television studio make-up room and closed her eyes to allow the make-up artist to begin the slow task of airbrushing her with foundation. It was a fabulous gizmo, Elsa often said to people who marvelled at her youthful screen self – despite the HD screens – and her not-so-youthful self in the flesh.

One moment she was pale with the wrinkles and uneven pigment of a sixty-year-old woman, and the next, she was sandblasted with television-quality beige, fluffed up with peachy, illuminating blusher to create cheekbones, and the majority of her wrinkles were expertly hidden with special magic pens.

Even her eyes, hooded now from age, shone out of her face the way they used to all those years ago: bright, a little too knowing, eyes that had seen it all, now lined with expert gel liner to give her gravitas along with a hint of sex appeal.

The thinking man's TV psychoanalyst crumpet, a newspaper supplement had once called her.

Tanya, the presenter of *The Casebook*, had not been pleased. Tanya liked all attention on herself.

1

'I hate the press interviews,' Elsa had pointed out with the calm, even tones she found worked with highly strung, highly jealous people like Tanya.

'That's right, you don't,' said Tanya, looking curious. *Why would anyone not want to be in the newspapers?*

'You're better at that sort of thing,' Elsa added before Tanya got thinking as to *why* any reasonable person would pass up lifelong exposure to media scrutiny, which was Tanya's dream.

If Tanya had ever asked her this, Elsa would say that psychoanalysts liked to stay in the background and let the stars shine, which would be handily manipulative – and not entirely honest.

In truth, Elsa didn't want anyone delving too deeply into her life. Being in the background was her speciality.

Elsa's close friends still teased her about the 'thinking man's TV psychoanalyst crumpet' comment. But her psychoanalyst friends, who thought their profession should stick to small rooms, couches and comfy chairs instead of television shows, didn't mention it, apart from the odd comment about how nice it must be not having to worry about money.

Either way, Elsa didn't mind. She'd learned that she could not change how other people thought of her. And having money, after many years of playing catch-up, *was* nice.

Still, she didn't look too bad for a woman her age, Elsa had to admit, staring at herself in the mirror.

'Where could I get one of those foundation spray-on machines?' her tactless, young, new upstairs neighbour had asked only the previous weekend, catching Elsa about to leave the house and exclaiming again that television make-up was: 'science-fiction brilliant because, honestly, look at your skin now compared to when you're on the telly!'

The Elsa of thirty years ago might have snapped that, yes, she was an aged harridan compared to the twenty-something in front of her, and she had a polymer mask that they glued on in the TV studio. But the Elsa who'd spent most of the past twenty-four years praying for peace and acceptance at great personal cost smiled benignly at her neighbour and said, 'They're available on the internet, I think.'

'Oh, gosh, thank you. My skin . . .' The young woman touched her face, and Elsa, who hadn't been wearing her glasses, finally noticed the acne marks. 'It's so hard to find the right foundation for coverage,' she said awkwardly.

'This is great, but you're too young and beautiful to need it,' Elsa said kindly.

The young woman grinned.

'I've seen you on TV – you're always the nicest one to people. My mum's dead impressed I'm living above you. If she comes up to London, could she get your autograph?'

'Of course,' said Elsa, but the knot was in her chest again. Incredible how few words could do it.

She'd learned how to deal with the knot. Repeating her words to live by helped: *the wisdom you've learned was worth the journey*. That's what she told herself every single morning.

But it didn't always help.

All of these thoughts were rippling around in Elsa's mind as she was being beautified that morning in the busy make-up room in OTV, where a rising boy band with degrees in hotness were being cooed over in one corner and a Miss World-lookalike newsreader with a degree in English Lit was being stared at by the boy band. Just your average morning in make-up.

Amid the buzz, Gigi chatted to Elsa. 'What's the topic this morning?' she asked.

Elsa liked it when Gigi was the artist working on her face. She was young, calming and concentrated on her work. Their conversations about the show centred Elsa, took her into the space of thinking about the guests and what she was going to say.

'Grandparents' rights in the first show, and then plastic surgery and the danger of unrealistic expectations about it,' said Elsa.

'Interesting,' said Gigi, standing back to check if Elsa's eyes were evenly shadowed. 'So not to expect a nose job will change your life – it'll only change your nose.'

'Exactly,' said Elsa, thinking of precisely how painful a nose job actually was, because she'd had one. It had hurt like hell and she'd looked like

4

she'd been in a fist fight for two weeks. 'You could be doing my job.'

Gigi laughed. 'You've got the qualifications, Doc,' she said. 'I'd just be talking common sense but you really know what you're talking about.'

Elsa smiled good-naturedly. A degree was a wonderful thing to hide behind. A doctorate was even better.

Dr Elsa de Marco was an expert and nobody asked experts how they knew what they did. It had all been learned in dry, dusty lecture halls and over endless hours of listening to people spill out their pain as they lay on the analyst's couch. People never expected academics to have learned most of their wisdom the hard way.

Still, Elsa had found college a joy: learning why people were made the way they were was like finding the key to the puzzle of everyone she had ever known.

Gigi went back to her work, instructing Elsa to close her eyelids again. Under the black nylon make-up cape, Elsa's hand strayed to her left armpit, as it had so often these past few days.

Stop it, she told herself.

She'd palpated the lump so many times it would be impossible now to know if she'd created this swelling with its dull ache or if it really was something sinister. Probably nothing. That's what she said at night when her fingers touched it lightly, an innocent little nodule that could be so many things.

Sign of an infection, for a start. Plus she was run-down. Filming twenty shows in a ten-day schedule was insane.

'Budgets,' was the answer of the production company and the show's constantly beleaguered producer, Stanley. Cheaper to get the team in for a full day and work them to the bone filming two shows in a row. Get the guests up for one night in a London hotel – not as good as the old hotels used to be, now cheaper chains with no mini-bar so vast drinks bills could not be rung up with after-show relief. Have make-up do everyone in one high-speed swoop. So what if the afternoon guests' minimal make-up was sliding off their faces after lunch in the canteen? Nobody wanted to see the guests looking too glamorous: real life in all its normal, reddened or aged skin was what was called for. The talent – the show's host, Tanya, plus Elsa and Malik, the child psychologist – all had the services of a make-up artist on set so that by the second show, they were still unshiny and with no thread veins peeking through.

Suddenly Tanya breezed in, a cloud of heavy perfume behind her along with a nervous PA wielding a cup of coffee and an iPad. Everyone with eyes closed for eyeliner opened them to see the vision.

Today, Tanya was encased in some sort of bandage dress that Elsa knew her fashion-conscious friend, Mari, would be able to identify. In it, Tanya's forty-five-year-old body looked like a rather sexy mummy straight out of the sarcophagus, having torn her bandages to mid-thigh and rather low on the bosom.

'Tanya knows about the pain of cosmetic surgery,' Gigi murmured quietly to Elsa.

Elsa smothered a laugh. Tanya's bosoms had miraculously increased in size one summer and she'd had the gall to say she planned to be the face/bosom of an entirely natural breast-increasing cream.

'They're going to pay me a fortune!' she'd said gleefully.

Stanley, a man with great sad eyes like a Bassett hound and an entirely bald head from tearing his hair out over budgets, had taken her aside and muttered that she might be accused of false advertising.

'Any, er . . . cosmetic help would count against you if you implied the, er . . . increase was due to creams alone,' he'd said, desperately trying not to look at Tanya's breasts, which perched high on her chest as if they were a TV drama heroine's and had been stuffed into a corset by Wardrobe.

When Tanya had subsequently taken two days off 'sick' as proof of her rage, Stanley had been heard to say he should have kept shtum and let her be sued.

'You're ready to go, Elsa,' said Gigi cheerfully five minutes later, admiring her handiwork and sliding the cape off Elsa's shoulders.

'Thank you,' said Elsa with the genuine warmth that had made her a star.

'If you can fake warmth, you can do anything,' Tanya liked to say, a bastardisation of the old W. C. Fields joke about being able to fake sincerity. Tanya's warmth was skin-deep and most of the time she shimmered with malice. Tanya hated that Elsa was beloved of the viewers.

For a moment, Elsa thought about what would happen if the lump under her armpit turned out to be more than her being a bit run-down. Tanya would tonelessly say, 'Oh dear,' and then turn to Stanley and the director to discuss Elsa's replacement in a heartbeat. Tanya's reputation for being as hard as nails was entirely deserved.

The lump was bound to be nothing, Elsa assured herself. Nine out of ten breast lumps were not cancerous. *Use your training. Calm yourself. Do not catastrophise. Give it a few weeks and see if it calms down.*

She remembered a doctor once telling her that if you heard hoofbeats, you shouldn't always assume zebras were coming. Breast cancer was a herd of zebras, or whatever the collective noun was. This was probably nothing.

She climbed down from the make-up chair and went back into her dressing room where she made, purely for want of something to do, another cup of lemon and ginger tea.

She sat in the stiff armchair she'd made comfortable over the years with some cushions, trying to run over the details of the first show. But her mind was betraying her, slipping and sliding all over the place, refusing to deal with the case of grandparents trying to persuade an angry former daughter-in-law that her children would benefit from seeing them.

The Casebook was supposed to be a cut above the ordinary 'let's open the DNA-test envelope and see who the father is' morning show. Elsa was proud of the work she'd done on it over its ten-year run. It was the achievement she was second most proud of in her life. The list of things she regretted was far longer, but time and help had taught her to forgive herself for her failings.

Yet she couldn't forgive herself for them all. Sometimes it was impossible to close the door on the past.

Again her hand slipped under her silk blouse to the painful lump. If it was cancer, what would she do? Did she have the courage to confront things the way she made people on the show or in her practice confront things? She'd confronted so much herself, but now she was out of energy.

Physician heal thyself.

No, she was fed up with dealing with things. She'd let this wait. She'd know if it was serious, wouldn't she?

CHAPTER 1

DUBLIN

Dark hair plastered to her head with rain, Cassie Reynolds stood in the weary queue in Starbucks at five past eight in the morning and half-listened to the conversations going on around her.

'The kids won't get up for school. Do you think it's easy for me, I asked them?' demanded a forty-something woman laden down with laptop bag, handbag and light raincoat for the unseasonable downpour outside.

'They won't go to bed on time,' agreed her friend, equally laden down.

Cassie, mother-of-two, and carrying just as much equipment in the way of laptop, overstuffed handbag and rain gear as the two women, understood their pain. Her daughters Lily and Beth, thirteen and fifteen respectively, seemed to think it was *her* fault that they had to get up for school in the morning.

'It's inhuman. Teenagers have rights too,' Beth had taken to saying when 6.45 rolled around each morning and Cassie woke the household up.

Cassie wondered if she could go into the school

Amnesty International group – which Beth had just joined – and point out that they were supposed to be explaining to the kids in class about basic human rights, and that this didn't include moaning about their own first-world problems.

'I'm sooo tired,' Lily complained every day. 'Can I have five more minutes, pleeease?'

'I don't want to get up either,' Cassie wanted to say when she was poleaxed with exhaustion. 'But we have to. You need to go to school or I'll go to jail for keeping you out, and I need to earn money. Simples?'

She hadn't said it so far – she knew she'd sound unhinged if she did. Unhinged was bad parenting, apparently. Or so it said in the women's magazines she occasionally had the energy to skim through at night in bed.

Trying to get everyone to bed earlier didn't work, nor did dire threats to remove electronic equipment for weeks. The only possible power she had left was turning off the Wi-Fi but she quite liked going on Pinterest herself in the evenings. She liked meandering in and out of photos of lovely holiday destinations and photos of adorable animals, pinning them on her wall of 'Places I'd Like to Visit' or 'Cute!' boards.

All of this activity was avoidance of setting up a 'Why Are Teenagers So Tricky?' or 'Am I a Bad Mother?' board, which would be far more to the point.

She pondered this as she stood in the queue.

Was it the girls' ages that made her feel so stressed lately?

Yes, that was it: being a parent of modern teenage daughters was the equivalent of running the Government or the health service. No matter what you did, you were always in trouble. Nobody apologised for yelling at you, nobody hugged you, and no matter what sort of fabulous meal you conjured out of thin air after a full day of work, nobody ever said thanks.

The years of being 'fabulous Mummy' had morphed into slamming doors to a chorus of 'You're horrible and I hate you!'

It broke Cassie's heart.

She'd tried so hard to make her family into all the things she'd missed as a child: the perfect nuclear family with a cat, home-cooked food, camping holidays and Cassie doing her best to help with homework even though she worked full-time. And it had worked, until about two years ago when her daughters had hit hormone city one after the other and, suddenly, they weren't a nuclear family – they'd just become nuclear.

Making scones or healthy oat and raisin cookies on Sundays for the girls' lunches at school the following week didn't cut any ice when someone was sulking up a storm over not being allowed to go to a party where Cassie knew the parents would think it perfectly fine to let teenagers bring their own beer.

Saturday night was no longer a cosy movie-and-take-away family night because the girls spent the whole evening ignoring the movie and texting, despite dire warnings about phone confiscation. Now Beth could officially watch 15 movies, she wanted to watch 18 ones.

'I'm not a kid anymore so why do I have to watch kids' movies?' she'd say in outrage at the sign of any sort of family movie.

Beth now mooched around the house wearing low-slung pyjama-type joggers with her slim teenage belly visible. She had made hints about getting a belly ring, comments which made her father go green and made Cassie say 'over my dead body' in the manner of a Victorian parent.

She wore coal-black eyeliner, sky-blue nail varnish and had posters of shirtless young male singers with six-packs on display Blu-Tacked to her walls.

Lily, once a sweet little poppet prone to hugs and drawing kittens, had thrown out all her fluffy, fairy-style tutu skirts and insisted on jeans so skinny her mother worried about Lily's circulation. Her once-beloved Lalaloopsy dolls were in a box under the bed and Lily kept rushing into her big sister's room to watch things on YouTube. More reason to ban Wi-Fi for the next ten years.

Any comment on either sister's clothes was followed by the refrain, 'But everyone's wearing these now, Mum!'

And, being infatuated with her cool, older sister,

Lily now wanted to paint *her* nails blue and had begun shrugging off any type of hug.

The only thing Beth and Lily tried to hug with any regularity was the family cat, Fluffikins, who was not a touchy-feely animal and protested loudly at being picked up and dragged out of rooms after rows. Cassie thought the cat might possibly go deaf, what with all the slamming doors he was exposed to.

'It's a phase; the girls will grow out of it,' Grammy Pearl said whenever they discussed it. 'You did.'

'Please tell me I wasn't that bad or that hormonally difficult,' Cassie begged her grandmother.

'The times were different and you were different,' Grammy said diplomatically. 'You had a lot of hard things to deal with, Cassie. Teenage girls need to fight with their mothers and you didn't have one. You only had me. I'm not easy to argue with – having your Great-Aunt Edie as a sister had taught me how to avoid arguments, because Edie could start one in an empty room.'

Grammy Pearl mentioning Cassie's lack of a mother was the closest they ever came to discussing the great pain of the Keneally family – how Cassie and her younger sister Coco's mother had left them when Cassie was seven years old and Coco had just turned one. How the pain had eventually killed their father ten years ago, destroyed by grief.

Jim Keneally had floated on the edges of the all-women household in Delaney Gardens, letting his mother sort out arguments and sign school letters. When Cassie thought of her father, she could see him bent with his head in a book, retreating from life because it hurt too much.

There had been happiness and love too – Pearl had made sure of that. But their family had never been the sort of normal family Cassie used to dream about – the ones in books or the ones her school friends had. Like a child peering in at a happy family at Christmastime, Cassie often felt that she'd spent much of her childhood peering through the glass windows at the homes of happy families she knew, watching as people made jokes and giggled, as mothers dropped kisses on father's heads, as fathers were teased for hopeless anniversary bouquets for their wives.

Despite the happiness in hers and Coco's childhood, they were different from their peers. Motherless.

That had made Cassie utterly determined to create the perfect family with Shay and her daughters, to make up for the one she'd never quite had. Her daughters would never be the ones with their faces pressed up against the glass windows, peeping in.

Except lately, it had all fallen apart.

'One day they'll come around and they'll be hugging you, saying you're the best mum ever,' Grammy said. 'Mark my words, it'll happen.'

'Any date in mind for this miraculous event?' Cassie asked, laughing without mirth. 'I want to mark it off in my diary and then see if I can get tranquillisers to keep me going until it happens.'

Worse was her marriage, because the most united thing she and Shay did now was to discuss their daughters and have rows about belly rings, clothes and unsuitable videos on YouTube, where male singers sang about sex and barely dressed girls who got called 'hos' danced around them.

She and Shay never scheduled the apparently vitally important 'date nights'. Without date nights, your marriage was as dead as a dodo, and their version of a date night were nights when both she and Shay were too tired to cook – he really did his best to help, although he wasn't a natural chef – and they got a takeaway with which the whole family slumped in front of the TV and hostilities were temporarily suspended.

Did that qualify as date night? Nobody fighting? Surely there was kudos for that?

Besides, if Cassie felt the spark had gone out of their marriage, then wasn't that what happened to people with kids and busy lives, stuck on the mortgage hamster wheel, endlessly trying to make it all fit together? Shay worked in an engineering firm and these days – thankfully – he was as busy as she was.

Time was what they needed, and one day they'd get it. Well, they might if only Shay's mother, Antoinette, let them.

Cassie, who had no real mother, had married a man who was joined at the hip to his. There were three people in their marriage, as the Princess of Wales had once said.

Three years ago, Shay's father had died, and since then his mother had permanently attached herself to Shay like a barnacle to a whale. She rang constantly, asking Shay to come fix plugs, change light bulbs and open the jammed washing machine door.

'*I* wouldn't ask him to fix those things,' Cassie said in outrage to Coco.

'She's grieving,' said her sister, always the peacemaker. 'She'll get it out of her system. Remember that sweet lady who used to come into the shop all the time when her husband died, in every second day, always with some little trinket? She could have brought it all in in one fell swoop to sell but she wanted the company. It's like that. Then she got involved with the bingo crowd and now I never see her. She just needed to find her place in the world again.'

'It's not like that with Antoinette,' said Cassie, sighing. 'It's like she wants a replacement husband.'

'Don't be freaky,' said Coco, laughing.

Then Cassie had laughed and said she wasn't being freaky, but honestly, Antoinette lived forty-five minutes away: it wasn't as if she was around the corner. She had two daughters into the bargain, and 'Could she not learn to change a plug herself?'

'She will,' soothed Coco. 'She'll adjust and find a new life.'

Except Antoinette hadn't. Three years on and

Shay still drove to his mother's house like a good little boy whenever she phoned.

Cassie had explained to Shay that he was spending a lot of time in his mother's house and might it not be a better plan to talk to his sisters, Miriam and Ruth, and say that they could all club together to afford handymen to help her do the odd jobs, and perhaps to share visiting her all the time?

'Oh, Cass, she needs me now my father's gone. Don't you understand that?' Shay had said crossly when she'd made this suggestion, so that Cassie had felt as if she was being selfish and horrible by wanting her husband to spend some time around their house at the weekend.

Worse, what Cassie couldn't say to her sister – because it sounded stupid and melodramatic – was that she didn't feel loved when Shay put his mother first every time. He kept choosing his mother over his wife.

Cassie had been too scarred by this happening when she was seven to want it to ever happen again. But how could she say this? It would sound ludicrous and childish.

Antoinette was older and alone; she needed Shay more.

Cassie tried so very hard to adjust to this and yet everything in her life was shifting. She'd relied on Shay to be the one constant in this teenage maelstrom but even he had shifted off course and was dedicating himself to his mother. Cassie was supposed to not be even vaguely upset by any of this. She was 'good old Cassie' who kept the home fires burning and required no love or affection at all.

Cassie could tell nobody, but this withdrawal of Shay's presence – and, to Cassie's mind, his love – was the most frightening thing of all.

The Starbucks queue shuffled forwards and Cassie let her attention wander to scan the customers, eyes paying particular attention to women in their late fifties and sixties. She'd been doing it for so many years that she didn't notice she was doing it: always looking.

The woman she was looking for could be dead now for all Cassie knew. She might live somewhere else entirely; she might be living on a street dressed in blankets and begging for a few coins so she could buy something more to drink. Or would she have moved on to harder stuff? Heroin? Meth? Wasn't that what happened to women like her mother?

Who knew?

Thirty years since she'd last seen her, yet Cassie couldn't stop herself looking out for her mother. Despite the fact that she'd told everyone – Coco, their father, their grandmother, her husband, her friends – that she'd long since got used to the fact that her mother was a loser and had abandoned her without a second thought, Cassie still looked. And hoped.

She had no idea what she'd say to Marguerite

– she would never call her mother or mum – but she was sure she'd know what to say if the chance ever came.

Why did you leave? Why did you never come back? Was it my fault? Was I not lovable enough?

The voice in her head when she spoke those words was never that of the always calm, mature Cassie Reynolds, née Keneally; it was the voice of a heartbroken seven-year-old who'd never forgotten the day she'd come home from school to hear that her mother had just left.

Her father had picked her up from school, not Grammy or Rita from next door, who did it when Mum couldn't. Dad never picked her up. It was always Mum, except the day before they'd had the crash. Maybe Mum was upset about it, even though she'd laughed at the time and said it was all fine. Just a teeny little mistake.

Mum liked to do fun things when she came. She'd have Coco all bundled up in her car seat and she'd have a plan.

'Let's go to the cafe for tea and buns!' she'd say, looking all shiny and pretty with her hair curled and her woolly coat – Mum said it was fake fur and she looked like a snuggly and glamorous bear, Cassie thought, with it wrapped around her.

Mum never talked much to the other mums.

'They're boring,' she'd whisper to Cassie, except Mum didn't whisper quietly enough and people heard her.

Cassie knew she should feel bad at the stares people gave them, but Mum didn't care. She shook her streaky dark hair and beamed back at everyone.

In the car, Cassie got to pick what music to play and they'd sing along loudly as they sped down the road, laughing and talking. Mum's perfume was everywhere in the car: flowers, spices and something else Cassie didn't recognise, something uniquely Mum.

She loved her mum more than anyone else in the world but sometimes, only sometimes, late at night, Mum got angry and shouted. Her voice sounded funny too, not like Mum at all. Cassie had heard her, heard Dad shouting back, heard Coco's cry as she woke up.

Those nights gave her a pain in her tummy and she had it now when she saw Dad waiting for her at the school gates with all the mothers. He looked sick, sort of pale, like he might fall over if he wasn't leaning on the gate pillar.

He took her hand in his and led her over to the car, with the big dent in it where Mum had banged it.

'Only a teeny bang,' Mum had said happily.

'Teeny,' Cassie had agreed, giggling.

'We could cover over where the paint came off with nail varnish! Pink or red?'

Cassie had giggled some more. The car was pale blue. Pink bits would be so funny – a special car, for a special mum.

As she got into the car, Cassie didn't ask Dad

why he was there. Coco wasn't in the back seat. She was at Grammy's, Dad said. It was the only thing he said on the whole journey. His hands were really shaky the way Mum's sometimes were – 'Silly Mummy with her shaky hands!' – and Cassie didn't ask why they were driving to Grammy Pearl's house with the pretty green and the old tree in front instead of to their home around the corner.

Grammy was at the door, reassuringly normal and calm, and she hugged Cassie and said she had made butterfly cakes. 'Your favourite. I had to stop Basil and Sybil from nibbling them all,' she added, as the pugs, both black and shiny with fat pink tongues, panted up to Cassie for kisses and licks.

On the ground, encircled by soft fur, squashy bellies and adoring dogs, Cassie felt a moment of safety. Grammy would tell her what was going on. Grammy had been the one who'd said Mum and Coco had to stay in hospital for a bit when Coco was a teeny baby and had been sick. Grammy was good at minding her when things went wrong.

But Grammy said nothing all day. Not when Cassie was doing her homework, not when they were watching *Scooby Doo* and Coco was asleep in her carrycot. Not that evening when Grammy brought Cassie up to the spare bedroom that was decorated in sunflower yellows and had all Cassie's things magically in it – her teddies, her nightlight, her jammies with the rabbit on the front, and her books.

Cassie had to ask.

'Where's Mum?' she said in her quietest voice, so Coco wouldn't hear. She didn't want Coco to get upset, even though she was a baby and everything. She might get upset and cry again. Coco was special because she'd been so sick and Mum called her 'my little angel'. Cassie felt a powerful need inside her to take care of Coco. She was the big sister, after all.

Grammy muttered that the pillowcase looked unironed and went to find a new one. She didn't look at Cassie as she changed it. 'There, all nice and ironed now.' She paused. 'Your mum isn't well, Cassie, and she had to go away to get better.'

'Go away? Without me and Coco?'

The pain in her tummy had never felt this bad: it was like something ripping her tummy into two bits, carving a hole the way the people on the television had carved a pumpkin once for Hallowe'en to show how it was done.

Grammy Pearl sat heavily on the bed.

'It's the best thing, Cassie.'

'No,' wailed Cassie, not caring about the noise. 'It's not the best thing! I need her. Coco needs her. Somebody made her go! She was kidnapped! She wouldn't go, she loves us!'

Grammy Pearl hauled Cassie on to her lap and held her like she was a baby.

'Of course she loves you; that's why she went. Because she's not well and she wants to be a better mum to you both.'

'She's the best mum!'

'I know, I know,' crooned Pearl as Cassie sobbed. 'It's the best thing, really. I promise.'

A day had gone by and Mum hadn't come home, hadn't even phoned. Then another day. Then a week.

Grammy said Mum would come home but Dad hadn't. Once, only once, he'd stared at Cassie with those sad eyes and had told her the worst thing in the whole world: 'Your mother doesn't want us anymore, Cass – that's the truth of it. She's not coming home. We can be happy without her, can't we?'

He'd hugged her then and Cassie had been afraid to cry, afraid to say 'Noooo', afraid to do anything but hug her father back and pretend that everything was fine, like there wasn't this hole in her life.

Eventually nobody even talked about Mum anymore. The photo of Mum and Dad on their wedding day disappeared but Cassie found it in Dad's room, hidden on his dressing table behind a school one of her in her grey pinafore.

She began to worry about baby Coco. What if she went too? So Cassie decided that she would never allow that to happen. Coco was her sister and if they took her, they'd have to take Cassie too. Coco was hers to mind, whatever happened. Nobody would ever hurt her or take her away.

A skinny double-shot cappuccino in one hand, Cassie entered Larousse Events via the revolving door and made her way to the lifts, drinking some of her coffee, hoping it would work its magic. She'd been awake in the middle of the night due to thirteen-year-old Lily having a nightmare, and Cassie had ended up spending an hour in her younger daughter's bed, hugging her until the night terror was over.

'There are no monsters, honey,' she'd said, holding Lily tightly until the shaking stopped. 'Mummy's here with you; you're safe, Lily.'

The holding always worked. Like swaddling an infant, Cassie thought. It had taken a while to work out what seemed to calm Lily.

'I used to put a cool cloth on your arms and legs and the cold gently took you out of it without really waking you up,' Grammy Pearl had explained when Lily first started the nightmares.

Nightmares in children could be genetic but Cassie couldn't remember having them until her mother had left. Maybe she was wrong. Her memory of those days was hazy now. She didn't remember what from that time was the truth anymore.

But she knew one thing for certain: she couldn't imagine what would ever make her leave her children.

There had to have been something wrong with her mother, hadn't there? Not just the addiction. That's what Pearl had finally, grudgingly, told her about when Cassie had begged to know – the drinking and the drunk driving. There had to be something more. Because any mother who really loved her kids would sober up and come home. No mother could leave her kids forever.

Except for Cassie and Coco's mother, Marguerite Keneally, who'd had a family and a home and who'd packed her bags one day and had never returned.

There were no photos of her in the house in Delaney Gardens where Pearl lived alone with her darling pug; no memories whatsoever. It was as if Pearl, who talked and laughed about everything, had done her best to remove Marguerite from her granddaughters' memories because she thought the memory of a long-lost mother would break them. It was enough that their father had died permanently mourning his wife. Pearl had decided that Marguerite could do less damage if she were forgotten.

In the office lift, Cassie tried to summon up her game face. Broken sleep seemed to be worse than no sleep at all. Shay and Beth had slept through it all. The double shot in her cappuccino might help and she hoped she'd get a few moments in the office to let her hair dry and let the caffeine sink in before the phone started.

Larousse Events – 'We Make Your Imagination a Reality' – had a quarter of a floor to themselves in an office block in the financial district. One half was executive offices and an imposing reception that had been designed to look like the lobby of an expensive boutique hotel and which was beloved of the company boss and owner, Loren Larousse.

'First impressions are vital,' she intoned as the staff worked out how much the original art on the walls cost and wondered how the cost of it had affected Loren's decision to cut bonuses that year.

The rest of their part of the fifth floor was a warren of tiny offices and cubicles where the work actually went on.

Cassie, as a senior organiser, had her own office close to the huge meeting room which Cassie's friend Belinda called 'the place where ideas went to die'.

Loren Larousse – which had to be a made-up name for a girl from Dublin, but nobody had ever managed to get their eyes on her passport as ultimate proof – had set up Larousse Events twenty years ago and viewed the company not so much as her baby but as her own private fiefdom.

In the media, she was much vaunted as a female entrepreneur who loved to hire women. In private and within the tight-knit industry, she was an equal opportunities employer: capable of being a complete bitch to both men and women.

Whenever she sat at a meeting in the huge boardroom with its vast ceiling-to-floor windows, Cassie dreamed of pushing Loren out.

'We all think you're a witch, so let's see if you can fly!' she'd say gleefully.

But that was bolshie Cassie speaking, the

nineteen-year-old girl who'd been full of who's-going-to-make-me attitude. Modern Cassie, who was tying herself in knots to be the perfect mother, perfect wife and perfect career woman, would never say such a thing.

It was now 8.15 and the Larousse Events staff were just getting in, hanging up coats, checking how many zillion emails had uploaded in the night, hoping for a few penile enlargement ones or lonely girls with unlikely names who wanted to be their best friends because they could happily be deleted.

Cassie's head ached as she thought of the day ahead. Her workload today included the final stages of setting up a conference in a large hotel west of the city, where it transpired the spa was going to be out of order during the three-day conference the following week.

'They'll be too busy to be in the spa,' blustered the hotel's manager the day before, a new hire who made Cassie long for his predecessor, who'd made everything run smoothly.

'Theoretically they might be too tired to use the mini-bar, but it will be stocked in every room, won't it?' Cassie had replied. 'We need this sorted out or we'll have to discuss pulling the conference,' she added.

That was utterly last resort stuff. Everywhere would be booked. The company needed a big hotel and really big conference hotels in Dublin were short on the ground.

She was thinking how she'd call him first thing

to see if he'd come up with a solution, and knew she'd have to drive out there to talk in person, when she spotted Belinda, her closest work colleague and possibly second-best friend on the planet, walking back from the ladies' room, handbag in hand.

Belinda was ying to Cassie's yang – a tall, cool blonde, keen on silk T-shirts, sharp skirts and *Vogue*-editor heels, as well as done-every-month highlights and blood-red manicures. Cassie was petite, had dark curly hair like her sister Coco, and taming it into work mode was easier when she could corral it back into a loose knot without actually doing much in the way of brushing it. Brushing caused lethal 220-volts frizz.

While Coco was the sister who wore vintage and lived in fifties cinched-in dresses, Cassie's wardrobe veered towards the androgynous, with loose modern jackets and trousers. Never skirts. Never heels. Heels were girlie and Cassie was not. Being her sister's protector from the age of seven meant Cassie had been the ultimate tomboy and she still was, she sometimes thought.

Instead, Coco was the girlie one with the bow-shaped lips and dimple on one side. Cassie had a strong chin, deep-set grave eyes and a serious problem with freckles: cute on kids, but not so cute on late-thirty-something career women.

Sometimes she wondered if she'd got those freckles from her mother because nobody else in the family had them except Beth, but because there were almost no photos of Marguerite, she'd never know. Her memories of her mother had faded to that memory of perfume in the car, something spicy she'd never been able to identify because it wasn't there fully in her consciousness, just hidden beneath the surface.

When she closed her eyes, though, Cassie was sure she could smell it: something exotic, reminding her of a Moroccan souk with spices, heady oud and vanilla.

'What do you think?' Belinda asked in a murmur as they fell into step beside each other. 'It's a new foundation,' she continued, gesturing to her perfect skin. 'Said to last forever and make me young and dewy. Or something along those lines. I don't know why I believe that crap, actually, but they sucker me in every time. Advertising works.'

Cassie smiled.

At forty-one, Belinda was three years older than Cassie, but had one older son who was unlikely to have woken her in the night since he was away at college. She actually did look pretty dewy but that was down to facials, IPL lasers and a new thing called jet flushing that cost as much as a week's food shop, and apparently you needed six in a row to get any result at all. Cassie knew she would never be getting flushed unless her numbers on the lottery came up.

'You look fabulous,' she told her friend truthfully. 'Are you still using that magic concealer pen to get rid of under-eye circles?'

'Yup. Fakes eight hours' sleep.' Belinda was

31

single and liked her own space, but not all the time. Gentlemen callers were welcome as long as they knew when to go home. Men messed up the towels.

Cassie used to wonder if Belinda was lonely. But then she realised that these days, *she* was sometimes lonely, and she was married with kids. Maybe those date-night people were onto something.

'Can I borrow the magic concealer pen?' Cassie asked.

'Lily had a nightmare?'

'Yes. Can't you tell? I'm trying to eradicate it with caffeination before Loren sees me and rips me in two for appearing in the office looking less than perfect.'

'Yeah, well, we can't all have a professional blow-dry every morning and get dressed from a wardrobe set up by a personal shopper,' Belinda replied.

She briefly gazed at her friend's pale face, the bruised smudges beneath her brown eyes and the wet hair. With amazing sleight of hand, Belinda took Cassie's coat and laptop bag, handed over her own handbag, and muttered: 'Go. Let the under-eye thing do its magic. Use the highlighter/sculptor thing too. Charlotte Tilbury. Ludicrous price but worth it. Does actually make you look like you've been on holiday and have cheekbones like a supermodel. We should have gone into the beauty products business years ago, honey. That's where the money is today. Then we wouldn't have to be prostituting ourselves working for the Wicked Witch of the West.'

'Isn't it the Witch of East?' said Cassie.

'She was the good one, wasn't she? Nah, West. Loren had all the good sucked out of her on her last liposuction procedure.'

Cassie had her first laugh of the day and, juggling her coffee and Belinda's handbag, headed for the loo.

The ladies was large and full of chatter as women from the various companies on the floor talked while they brushed their hair and slicked on lipstick. Usually a hotbed of rumours, the current one was about the US event company, Prestige, taking over Larousse Events.

Cassie still hadn't found out if it was true or not but that didn't stop the gossip. From what she could ascertain, Prestige was a much leaner affair than their own company. Friendly takeovers were just like hostile ones but with more smiles: many people would still lose their jobs. The thought sent a little shiver through Cassie. More change, and she hated change. She hoped that rumour was just a rumour.

She went to work with Belinda's magic products, dried her hair with some paper towels and listened.

The other gossip was that Denise, from the small accountancy firm on their floor, had left her husband after an affair with one of the personal trainer guys in the gym on floor ten. As Cassie applied Belinda's brilliant concealing pen to the dark shadows under her eyes, she heard how Denise had been sick of her workaholic husband and how he had no time for her.

'Nothing in the bedroom department,' the girl with all the news informed her avid listeners.

'Do you think yer woman with the Rolling Stones fella was right about how to keep a man?' someone said. 'Cook in the kitchen and hooker in the bedroom?'

Everyone was silent as they thought about this. At least half of the women on the fifth floor had kids and really needed a wife to keep the show on the road. Bedroom antics were way down the list.

'I wouldn't be into yer man from the Stones,' said Gladys, senior supervisor from the insurance company, as if Mick Jagger was waiting outside for her command to have him washed and sent to her tent. 'The mouth on him.' She shuddered. 'Now, that nice Michael Bublé, if he was around . . . Well, you wouldn't kick him out of bed for getting crumbs on the sheets, would you?'

Everyone laughed, breaking the tension.

But Cassie didn't laugh. Instead, she thought of how long it was since she and Shay had made love. True, she was perpetually too tired for sex. Arguing with the girls gave her tension headaches too, but it was months now and Shay hadn't made a single move to make love to her. She tried to remember the dates but couldn't, yet she realised that it was a long time since Shay had reached out in the bed towards the wall of her back, stroking, telling her he wanted her.

She put down the magic concealer pen, no longer really caring about how she looked. Was her husband going off her? *Had* he gone off her? The ripple of anxiety over abandonment she'd never truly been able to shake began to hit earthquake status.

'Cassie.' A voice interrupted this terrible thought. 'Do you have a moment?'

It was Karen, a junior in Cassie's department: a sweet girl in her twenties who was going out with the boyfriend from hell.

Desperate to talk, Karen just blurted it out: 'I told him what I was thinking and he walked out. Just walked out, Cassie. I don't know what I'm going to do. I thought we'd talk about our relationship but he didn't. He got his stuff, said I was too high-maintenance with my talk about our plans for the future, and then he went. My brother's wedding is next weekend and we were going together, but now I'll be there on my own.' Karen's crying sounding like howling. 'Cassie, what do I do?'

Cassie managed to put an arm around Karen and let her howl.

As ever, it was a supreme irony that Karen had come to her for help. People had been coming to Cassie for help and support all her life. People told her things. She didn't know why.

'You have an open face; we have open faces,' Coco had said years before. 'We look like we can keep secrets and that we don't judge.'

Coco had been born looking as if she was interested in everyone, with sparkling brown eyes that could turn almost black with emotion and feeling, and made the person talking to her feel as if nobody else on the planet existed but them and their problems. She exuded warmth, caring and kindness. And she didn't mind.

Cassie had been born looking as if she was the woman who could sort out every problem, starting with the Middle East. And she did mind.

Tell me and I will fix it was the unspoken message on her face, and although Cassie had spent hours looking at herself in the mirror trying to figure out why people felt this about her, she was at a loss. She only saw a woman with dark eyes, winged brows, those darn freckles and a too-wide mouth that possibly smiled too much because smiling was safer, she'd learned over the years. Smiling stopped people asking 'are you all right?'

Since she'd been seven, though, she'd understood pain. Was that the secret? Did people see pain in her eyes and think *she'll understand?*

Either way, Cassie fervently wished she hadn't been born with this look on her face. She knew the secrets of half the people in her office, many of the mothers in the girls' school and, when Coco was busy, her friends turned to Cassie for advice. It was exhausting.

36

Grammy Pearl had the same gift. People loved to talk to Grammy and total strangers flung themselves at her at parties, telling her their life stories while searching for tissues in their pockets or handbags.

Weird how genetics worked. They'd got this unasked-for gift from Pearl.

It could hardly have come from Marguerite.

Still, Cassie summoned up the strength she'd been summoning up since she was seven, closed off her own problems deep inside her, and began to calm Karen down.

She might text Coco later and see if she could come round for supper that evening. Coco always cheered her up. And Coco never, ever let her down.

CHAPTER 2

Coco Keneally liked to think that her vintage shop, The Twentieth Century Boutique, was a bit of a mysterious jewel: bijou-looking on the outside, a slightly shabby Tardis on the inside because it hadn't been painted in a few years, and yet filled with sparkle. Set on the main shopping street in Silver Bay, a once down-at-heel but now up-and-coming part of Dublin Bay's outer reaches, it stood out among a trail of shops that included two competing hairdressing salons, a small jewellers there since the year dot, a convenience store and a new coffee shop that had made the local pubs up their game in terms of morning coffee and cakes. There was a sprawling pet shop, a small strange establishment that never seemed to be open but had clocks, toasters, screwdrivers and the odd power tool in the dusty window, and a glamorous chemist where a quick trip for tissues could result in a haul of nail varnish, things for removing hard skin from feet and an essential oil known to cure all ailments if rubbed on every day.

Coco had been running her shop for five years

and the premises covered two shop fronts and a large upstairs, where the more expensively labelled clothes and accessories were: the rare and valuable Diors, Chanels, original Halstons, the tiny YSL Le Smoking nobody could fit into but which Coco found herself loath to sell via the internet on the grounds that, one day, the right person would come into the shop and Coco would *know* it.

She couldn't get so much as a leg into the suit – not without major amputation of a limb. Le Smoking suits had been made with svelte, tiny-boned women in mind and Coco was more of a pocket-sized Gina Lollobrigida: big hips, a DD bra to keep her breasts firmly in place, and the ability to put on weight by so much as looking at a bar of chocolate. So she went for a fifties look herself – sleek dark eyebrows *à la* Elizabeth Taylor, dark eyes emphasised with a cat flick, ruby red lipstick that suited her full mouth with its finely arched upper lip – and idly waited for the day when a woman walked into her store to befit the exquisite YSL suit.

Vintage store was perhaps the wrong description for the place, Coco often thought. It was a treasure trove of the past, mysteries bound up in clothes, handbags and costume jewellery, memories of other lives.

Coco loved the past. 'Who knew what sort of life this nightgown has seen?' she might say, holding up a crêpe de Chine garment when she was in Grammy Pearl's house around the corner going through a cache of clothes, searching for special pieces.

If Great-Aunt Edie, Grammy's younger sister, was visiting at the same time, she'd sniff disparagingly and say something about how she couldn't understand people buying second-hand clothes.

'If faded old nighties from the thirties are vintage, then I'm from the moon,' Edie would add. 'Vintage is just other people's old stuff, smelly and stained . . .'

Edie disapproved of people working in shops that sold other people's old clothes. She'd wanted Coco to go to college to study law or something . . . well, *suitable*.

'I'm the oldest vintage here, Edie, and calm down,' Pearl would say warningly. Nobody was allowed to criticise Coco or Cassie when Pearl was around. 'Play nice or no cakes with the tea. I've got almond Danishes.'

Grammy Pearl had encouraged Coco every step of the way with her shop but, strangely, she didn't seem as keen on the past history of garments in the way Coco was. Grammy Pearl didn't even like talking about the past. She was more of a looking-forward person; astonishing for someone of seventy-eight, Coco thought.

But then, helping to raise your granddaughters kept a person young, as Grammy Pearl often said. She looked quite like Great-Aunt Edie in many respects: same strong chin, good bones, high forehead. But where Edie was all angles and wrinkles

40

around her mouth from pursing it up in near-constant disapproval, Pearl's face had the softness of the finest silk, Coco thought. Edie dyed her hair a rich and unlikely shade of brown, while Pearl's was white as snow and clustered around her face the way it did in photos going way back. Pearl's eyes gleamed with fun and enthusiasm, and she used face powder, lipstick and a hint of mascara every day.

Pearl was proud of everything Coco did, even if she didn't wear vintage herself. But Coco loved to watch the expressions on her grandmother's face on those times she visited the shop, fingering everything from recent, pre-loved things to garments that had last graced skin when the Second World War was raging through Europe.

The stocking pile was top of Coco's agenda when she opened up that September morning. Silk stockings from that era didn't last in any meaningful way but there were places where you could order honey silk stockings with the all-important seam up the back.

A lollipop-pink-haired fashion stylist on a mission had ransacked the stocking display the previous evening and after Coco had run an eye over her empire, she did some quick spritzing of some of the new stock to make sure it all smelled OK, then took the lock off the door to proclaim that they were open, and settled down to reorganise her stockings.

Normally she went online first thing, to Facebook

and her blog, to pin up photos of her latest finds, but she needed Adriana doing front of house when she was in the back office on her laptop, and Adriana was late.

The internet was what made The Twentieth Century Boutique a success. Neither the suburban village that was Silver Bay, nor the city of Dublin itself, were big enough markets for a shop like Coco's with its wildly diverse and often high-end stock, but with one click of a mouse, a buyer in Melbourne, Memphis or Mysore could pick up an alligator handbag, an original Biba coat or a highly sought-after Rifat Ozbek bone-decorated jacket.

Coco loved the internet and the conversations with her regulars – people who didn't buy all the time but loved to talk about what was up or something glorious they'd seen. At the moment, someone was trying to track down a strapless DVF sheath dress with an African pattern and all Coco's efforts had come to naught. And then there was a kooky Japanese girl named Asako – a regular customer who was studying in Ireland and loved the forties – who had found a cache of cashmere twinsets but they were seriously moth-injured.

'Time for DEFCON 4,' posted Coco. 'Nothing you can do except get them out of your house now before they infect everything else.'

There had been another email from Asako in her inbox the week before; somehow she had decided that Coco knew the answers to all the questions of the universe, including men.

'He asked me to meet his parents,' Asako wrote in her perfect English. 'This is good, yes?'

'Very good,' emailed Coco. 'Say in advance what you don't eat, though, or else you might get a big Irish meat dinner and I know you don't eat meat.'

She knew Asako would email to tell her how it had all gone and Coco looked forward to that. Unlike Cassie, who was so busy she didn't really have the time for the people who thought the Keneally sisters knew the answers to everything, Coco liked being needed.

This morning, Coco listed her latest finds on her site and was just logging off when Jo, her oldest and closest friend, appeared at the door.

'Ready for our coffee date?'

Jo worked in the secondary school around the corner and if she had a few free periods and no marking to catch up on, she sometimes dropped into Twentieth Century for a speedy coffee date. She was a tall, slim, no-nonsense woman with short hair who looked like she might possibly teach games. Instead, she was the school's French teacher.

Coco winced. 'Adriana got a flat tyre,' she said, speaking of her part-time sales assistant who was finishing a Masters in film studies at night and working by day. 'She's due soon.' Coco consulted her watch. It was already twenty past ten and Adriana, who'd been due at half nine, had phoned at twenty past to say she'd be a bit late. Coco pondered the fact that Adriana's car/phone/house keys had had several mishaps during the past few months, making her very late for work, and hated herself for wondering if ill relatives would soon follow suit as excuses. It was all a bit 'the dog ate my homework' for Coco's taste, but Coco was also not the sort of person who'd do anything about it.

'Could we have coffee here?' she asked Jo apologetically. 'I can brew us up some but I can't close the shop.'

'No, I'll rush out to the café. After fourth year French, I need something chocolatey with cream on top. Everyone has forgotten every single verb they knew before the summer holidays, nobody has settled back in yet, and there's a lot of staring out the window and sighing. That's just me. Do you have any decent biscuits?'

'Gosh, don't know. Go and look.'

As Coco worked on the stockings, Jo went in behind the counter to the office, where organised chaos reigned and a faint scent of alcohol lingered in the air.

'Jeez, it's like a brewery in here and it's only half ten in the morning.'

'I just vodka-spritzed some dresses,' Coco explained. 'Theoretically gross and does make the place stink in a dirty-stop-out sort of way, but it can really get rid of old smells. You spray, then leave them to air. They're upstairs in the hall, hopefully getting infused with rose potpourri sachets, but I keep the spritzer stuff in the office.'

'Rose potpourri sounds better than vodka

sachets. I can't go back to school smelling like I've been spending my free period in the pub. Can we light a candle or spray some perfume?'

'Candles are too dangerous,' Coco said, 'and perfume contains oils which ruin the clothes.'

'Are there hidden dangers in takeaway coffee since you can't leave the shop this morning?' Jo said.

'No hidden dangers and safer for you, actually. I drink coffee for the safety of my customers. Without coffee, I'm dangerous.' Coco made a vampire face and bared her small, white teeth.

Jo laughed. With that warm, engaging smile, Coco was the least vampiric person she knew. 'As if I don't already know, Ms Caffeine Addict. The usual? Skinny latte, two shots, one sugar, smallest cup?'

'Yup.'

When Jo had gone, Coco dusted the counter, and then turned to pricing and listing some new stock.

Jo was her oldest friend, the one in school who'd been there the first time she'd heard about her mother.

'Your ma left you because you were a crybaby,' said Paula Dunne, possessor of wild, curly hair and a streak of toothpaste on her uniform. Much taller than Coco, she was already at home in the class after just a week.

Weird how you could forget vast parts of life and remember others with such clarity, Coco thought. But then, hearing that your mother had left you was the sort of thing a person remembered, no matter how small you were.

Coco had been just four: young for junior infants. She knew she didn't have a mother but that was fine because she had Dada, Grammy Pearl and Cassie. Cassie, who was eleven, was in the big kids' part of the school, upstairs in the final class before heading to secondary school.

'I'll be here for you, Squirt, if you need me,' Cassie had said when she waved goodbye to Coco each morning outside Miss Rosen's class, where butterflies and flowers decorated the walls and picture books filled the shelves.

But Cassie wasn't there when Paula said those hateful words.

Coco felt her bottom lip wobble. *Don't cry. Don't be a crybaby.* Mummy was sick, that was why she'd gone away, and one day, Grammy said, she might be better. In the comfort of home, in the small box bedroom with the Minnie Mouse bedside light, smells of Grammy cleaning her face with that lavender cream in the next bedroom, and Cassie's *Famous Five* books beside her bed waiting for when Cassie came up to bed, all that was security and love enough for Coco.

And now Paula was taking all that away. Coco couldn't help it: the tears came.

'Told you: crybaby,' said Paula. 'Coco's a crybaby!' she shouted. 'That's why her ma left her.'

Coco cried even harder.

Then Jo was beside her. Josephine, as she was called in those days, with a sister called Attracta and a brother named Xavier by overly religious parents. Josephine was the youngest and Attracta and Xavier were a lot older, and they'd shown her how to stand up for herself against the likes of Paula Dunne.

'Go away, Paula!' she shouted, hands planted on her hips the way Attracta did when she was cross.

Josephine had the best hair in the class: long and fair, held in a single Valkyrie-like plait. Everyone admired it but even the roughest boys knew it would be a mistake to pull it. Standing there, tall and strong, she looked fierce. Josephine could thump just like a boy.

Paula Dunne knew it too.

'I was only sayin',' she muttered.

'Say sorry, then,' ordered Josephine, judge and jury.

Paula's face screwed up with anger.

'Say it,' said Josephine.

Attracta had explained that some people needed to be told how to behave and the trick was to stare them down.

'Sorry, Coco,' muttered Paula with bad grace.

She stomped off and Coco was left alone with Josephine, who'd never so much as looked at her until then.

'Thank you,' mumbled Coco with a still-trembling voice.

'Would you like to come to my house to play sometime?' Josephine asked. She might be only young but she knew they didn't have people home to their house much: they had no telly, the

47

radio was only on for the news and religious programmes, and there was never any sweet cake like you got in other people's houses. But still, Coco wouldn't mind.

Coco looked at her saviour with slavish admiration. She nodded, her dark curls bobbing. She wasn't up to actual speaking just yet.

Jo had been there, along with Coco's beloved sister, Cassie, for the other big disaster in her life – the one with Red. But Coco tried not to think about Red too often. There was no point going over past dating disasters, her latest self-help book said. 'Move on!'

Coco was doing her best to move on, although it was tricky, even after four years.

'Move on!' She repeated her mantra.

She'd certainly managed to move on with regards to her mother, she congratulated herself. *She* wasn't ever coming back. People didn't leave like that and never even so much as write a note afterwards if they were coming back.

But Red . . . He came to Dublin often to see his mother, a woman who glared at Coco if she so much as spotted her, and he'd never come back to see her since. Which proved she'd been right about him. Red, like her mother, hadn't planned to be around forever.

Pricing done, Coco went to the iPod dock and switched on her current favourite music – her namesake, Coco Emerald. Forties-style, big band and almost burlesque with Miss Emerald's sassy tones singing that she was coming back as a man, it suited Coco's mood today and the shop.

She wondered what Coco Emerald had been christened. Coco had been baptised as Coraline Patricia Keneally but nobody had ever called her Coraline.

'Little Coco' everyone had called her from the get-go and the name had stuck. Now people wondered if she'd changed her name because of a certain Gabrielle Chanel but Coco said that would be like changing your name midlife to Missoni because you liked the classic Italian design brand.

'I was Coco from when I was little,' she always said. Coraline was a bit of a mouthful. So too was Cassiopeia, which was Cassie's true name.

She'd asked Dad once why they had such unusual names. He'd prevaricated. 'Must have been something from the TV,' he'd said eventually, scratching what was left of his hair because he'd been bald from as long as Coco could remember.

Coco hadn't believed him. It was her mother, she knew it. Her mother had liked unusual names. But nobody talked about her mother. Asking her father used to result in his going into a dark place where he spoke to nobody for hours. It was simpler to let it go.

She sniffed the air. Jo was right: there was a certain pub-after-hours smell to the place. Hastily she sprayed some room spray on the mat inside the front door and wedged it open with a little rubber wedge to let some air in.

49

Jo returned a few minutes later carrying takeaway cups and a box containing two iced cupcakes.

'We need the energy,' said Jo.

Coco eyed her one mournfully – a perfectly miniature carrot cake with a teeny iced carrot on top. Jo knew it was her favourite.

'I was thinking of doing a juice diet,' Coco said, thinking of how tight the belt felt on her classic swing skirt.

'Think about it tomorrow,' advised Jo. 'People need pleasure in their lives.'

Despite the fact that she regularly stroked soft marabou, sleek velvets and exquisite silks, the way her friend said the word 'pleasure' pierced Coco like a sneaky, minuscule arrow as she realised how little pleasure there was in her life. Pleasure made her think of Red and she was never thinking of him again. He meant nothing but pain and heartbreak and she'd had enough of that to last a lifetime.

They were silent for a while as they ate and drank, then Jo talked about work and how she ought to be getting back.

Coco loved chat from the school. School life was so crammed with incident and people: funny teachers; the handsome new geography guy who had half the staffroom and most of the girls staring at him in awe; how the transition years were working on some Machiavellian plan to have TY turned into a non-uniform year.

'Anything new with you?' Jo asked, after she'd

binned her debris and washed her hands in the shop's tiny loo.

'Only the possibility that Adriana is taking the mickey out of me by never being on time. She said she had a flat tyre today and, you know what, I don't believe her. Is that mean of me?' Coco asked anxiously.

Jo, not as soft as her friend and possibly a better judge of character, laughed.

'Coco, you need to harden up, babe. Adriana has you totally figured out. She knows she can come in late and you won't do a thing. You deserve better. Fire her.'

'I couldn't!'

'Fine. Get Cassie to do it.'

Coco didn't reply and watched as Jo made a beeline for a fifties prom dress in polka dot chiffon yellow.

Jo had absolutely no eye for colour; never had, never would. And she would never wear the prom dress, either.

'Step away from the yellow,' Coco said in a mock-stern voice, relieved to be able to change the subject. 'You wearing yellow will frighten the heck out of your next class. Yellow is for people with warm complexions, ideally exquisite Indian girls with silken, mocha skin. Or people from the Caribbean. You and I with our milk-bottle-blue skin look like we're about to die of consumption when we wear it.'

Coco grinned at her best friend to lessen the blow.

51

'And you are successful at selling clothes *how*, exactly?' demanded Jo, moving down the rail.

'By being truthful and not allowing either customers or best friends to buy things they will never wear,' Coco said. 'You know I put all my efforts into you and for that reason, I can't let you buy yellow, lovie. You'll never wear it and it will stare at you reproachfully from your wardrobe. Do you know we wear only twenty per cent of our wardrobes—'

'Yeah, eighty per cent of the time,' finished Jo with a sigh. 'That's people like me, boring worker ants of thirty-one. People like my daughter wear one hundred per cent of their clothes over the course of one weekend. She changed four times on Sunday. Fairy at breakfast, princess in the park, a fish – *don't ask*, something to do with a science project – all afternoon and then, when it was time for bed, she went into serious dress-up mode and wanted a fashion show wearing my shoes, which are pretty boring, it has to be said. She wanted to know why I didn't have cool shoes like you.'

Coco glanced down at her red patent Mary Janes fondly. She was afraid they gave her fat ankles but she loved them so much.

'Her energy levels rise just before bed. Why?' asked Jo. 'Nobody can tell me. Unless it's competitive parenting, every other nine-year-old I know is apparently asleep by eight. Whereas Fi's gearing up for fun. She's just like you were about clothes.'

Coco laughed at the thought of her beloved goddaughter tearing through her wardrobe, flinging what she didn't want on the bed until she found the perfect outfit.

Unlike her mother, nine-year-old Fi had an innate sense of personal style and the determination to carry it off. Fi was petite by comparison with her mother's tallness, with skinny legs, a mischievous smile and hair as dark as Coco's. All a debt owed to her father, who'd been handsome and dark-haired as well as cavalier with other people's lives.

Looking at how happy Jo and Fiona were, Fiona didn't seen damaged by not having a father in her life.

But then, Coco worried – as did Jo – that one day, Fiona would demand to see her long-gone father and insist that his absence had destroyed her. It was the great fear of Jo's life because how could you tell a child that a man simply hadn't had it in him to stay around to be a dad?

Coco hoped Fiona wouldn't go through what she and Cassie had. After all, Fiona's father had simply never been there at all, while Marguerite had – and had *then* abandoned them.

Coco loved having Fiona as a goddaughter: it was almost like having her own child but without any of the responsibility that went with it. Coco was never having children herself.

Never.

To distract herself from having landed on this

horrible thought, she asked, 'Have you thought of asking Mr Geography out for coffee?'

Jo snorted. She'd been put off romance for life when Fiona's father had run a mile as soon as she got pregnant.

'I'm saving myself for someone perfect,' she said sarcastically.

'Oh, me too,' joked Coco. 'Let's say that next time we get asked why two such lovely girls are on our own.'

'The people who ask that are always married and want everyone else to be paired up too,' Jo said. 'Dating and bringing up a small child on your own are mutually exclusive.'

'At least you have an excuse,' Coco said. 'I think I'll start saying I'm gay.'

'People will simply start introducing you to their lovely *female* next-door neighbours and workmates instead of the male ones,' Jo pointed out. 'No, celibacy is the only way. That and a diet of sexy novels where men are men and women are never too tired or hormonal.'

'Yeah, I suppose,' murmured Coco thoughtfully.

Two customers came in and Jo waved goodbye, making an *I'll phone you* gesture as she left.

It was a wonderfully busy morning in the shop. Coco sold a small frame handbag with a tortoise-shell clasp, a set of diamanté drop earrings and a matching brooch to a bride-to-be, and a 1930s astrakhan and velvet coat in Chinese lacquer red to a tall, dramatically dark-haired woman who slipped it on, looked at herself in the mirror and then beamed. 'I'm not taking this one off.'

Coco was thrilled.

Adriana made it in by eleven, dressed in a flowing floral dress she'd got with her staff discount, and not looking as if she'd been frantic-ally wrestling with the car jack as she changed her tyre. Instead, she looked soothed and happy, with the relaxed face of a woman who'd just spent the morning in bed with her boyfriend. Coco didn't have a shred of evidence except there was no stress on Adriana's face from the trauma of the flat tyre, plus Adriana's blonde hair looked so very bed-head, and Coco knew for a fact that Adriana possessed very fine hair that flopped no matter what products Adriana used. In that case, there was a pretty good chance that bed-head hair meant actual *bed*-head hair.

Within five minutes, Adriana had made herself tea, had ignored the duster Coco had left out on the counter for her, and was on the phone, whispering.

'You too? I feel wonderful . . . What a start to the day . . . Sooo sexy . . .'

Coco raged: she'd been *right!*

She watched with irritation as her single staff member slipped past a customer to drift over to the stairs where she sighed and whispered some more sweet nothings into her phone. Adriana only worked part-time to help fund her college work, but she'd missed an hour and a half of her shift and yet would expect to be paid for it. When Adriana had been late before, Coco had paid her full wages without question, but this was now the fourth time in a few weeks that Adriana had been late.

Plus – and Coco felt annoyed with herself over any irritation about this – it was clear that Adriana, for all her slacker lifestyle, had a healthy, wonderful sex life with her boyfriend, while the only things to keep Coco in bed late were either her phone alarm clock not going off or a vomiting virus.

She hadn't had a date since her last blind date, which had turned into a disaster of epic proportions and had made her decide, finally, that men were a waste of time.

By half one, Coco was tired and looking out on to the street where the September sunshine shone down, and thought a quick walk down at the sea wall might blow the cobwebs away. She'd grab a sandwich on the way back and let Adriana take her lunch then.

'Adriana,' she began, as she got her purse, 'I'm going for a walk and then—'

'Oh, Coco,' said Adriana, twirling a strand of bleached blonde hair. 'Er, remember I said I had to go early today for, er, that essay I'm finishing for college? If I could go now, as I did ask . . .'

Coco, who never lost her temper and who knew she was a complete pushover when it came to both staff and people haggling in the shop, suddenly lost it.

'You want to leave at half one instead of half three, when you didn't get here till eleven?' she said furiously. 'And you no doubt expect me to pay you for six hours when you'll have worked two and a half? Am I correct?'

'Well, it's only fair. I got a flat,' Adriana said, looking injured.

'I don't believe you,' said Coco.

There, she'd said it.

'This is your fourth time late since the last week in August. Do you want this job or not? Because I need someone I can rely on, not someone who waltzes in late and leaves early.'

'That's not fair!'

'Adriana, it's totally fair. I pay you to be here working, not spend hours on the phone to your boyfriend!'

The burst dam inside Coco was pumping out a flood, but Adriana brought out the ultimate weapon: tears.

'I'm so sorry, Coco. You're so good to me, like a big sister, and I never had a sister, and I love you, you know that.'

'Hush.' Without almost knowing what she was doing, Coco instinctively put an arm around the sobbing Adriana.

'It's fine, you can go early now.' Coco cringed inwardly, wondering if she could discuss not paying Adriana for the missed hours. No, she decided. Cassie would be able to do it. Cassie could take on anyone and did, but Coco wasn't built that way.

57

'Please don't let it happen again. I need you, Adriana.'

'Course, I understand,' snuffled Adriana. 'It won't happen again. I promise.'

It took five minutes and an emergency chocolate biscuit to get Adriana smiling and out of the shop, after which Coco began to wonder if she'd done the right thing.

It was just hard to be tough with people you worked closely with . . . Yes, that was it. Adriana would buck up. Coco knew it.

As for now, she'd have to shut the shop to grab a sandwich and she hated doing that. The success of the shop rested entirely on her shoulders and though the place was doing pretty well on the internet, a random person shopping on her lunch break and encountering a 'closed' sign on the door might assume Twentieth Century was always closed and never come this way again.

Coco took off her heels, put on a pair of flats, grabbed the keys and her purse, stuck a 'back in five minutes' sign on the door and ran out into the September day, racing to the café where she could grab a ready-made sandwich.

Maybe she should have done what Great-Aunt Edie wanted and done something boring in college, instead of Fine Arts, she thought, panting as she ran. But then she wouldn't be her own boss. And Coco loved that more than anything.

Life was too full of twists and turns, decisions taken out of your hands, people leaving and never coming back. Her mother and Red came to mind.

No, if you were your own boss, you were in charge and nothing happened if you didn't like it. Because when random things happened, people got hurt and nobody recovered from the hurt. That was what Coco feared most of all.

Coco always said she'd never minded not having a mother.

'You don't miss what you never had,' she'd told her new girlfriends at college when they were on their second night out at the college bar and had moved on to sharing mother stories – the fabulous mother who was the kindest woman on the planet; the mother who behaved as though men were all raging sex maniacs and had sent her daughter to a convent lest one of the said maniacs got his paws on her; the mother who had a narcissistic streak and couldn't hold a conversation for longer than two minutes without dragging it back to herself.

The other three had been silent for a beat when Coco Keneally mentioned that she'd never known her mother.

'She left home when I was one. I don't even remember her,' Coco said lightly, because it was easier to tell this story in such a manner rather than imply it had hurt in any way.

'But a *mother* . . . You need a mother,' said Janet with great sadness – Janet who was the youngest of the four new students and had been explaining how she had the kindest mother *ever*.

Beers had been consumed and a level of honesty had been reached between the four women who'd been strangers until a month ago when they'd met on registration day for First Arts: four eighteen- and nineteen-year-olds, anxious but hiding it, madly trying to appear cool.

Even then, Coco's love of vintage clothing had been obvious: she'd worn Grammy's felted wool swing skirt with the kick pleat at the back, a red fake leather trench coat, and a black beret over her long, insanely curly dark hair.

'Coco,' Janet went on, 'how can you bear it?'

'Lots of people don't have mothers. I had my older sister, Cassie,' said Coco simply. 'I had Dad when he was alive, and Grammy. Between them they made it not matter that my mother had left.'

'I've just realised: you won't have a mum to help you buy your wedding dress!' hiccupped Lorraine from the convent, where it appeared that, despite reports to the contrary, convent girls were not wild and were certainly not able to hold their drink. On her second beer, Lorraine was already well beyond the tipsy stage. 'That's so sad.'

'Look on the bright side: your mother will never want to upstage your wedding,' added Carla (narcissistic mum) cheerfully. 'At my brother's twenty-first birthday party, my mother wore a leather mini skirt, a crop top that showed off her belly bar, and flirted with all my brother's friends.'

'Midlife crisis?' said Janet hopefully.

'Ah no, just my mother,' shrugged Carla, with a glitter in her eyes.

'That's so sad—' began Janet, tears at the ready.

'Thirty's a nice age to get married,' Coco said, wanting to cut off Janet before she really started to cry at the thought of mothers unlike her own fabulous one and *how had people coped?*

'Yeah, thirty,' said Carla.

'Twenty-seven,' insisted Lorraine. 'Still in your twenties; any older and you seem sad.'

An argument started on the wisdom/sadness of getting married in your thirties and Coco never got around to saying that she knew she'd have her sister and her grandmother by her side when it was her turn. And who needed a mother they couldn't remember, anyway? Little kids didn't remember that far back.

When she got married, she thought, allowing herself to imagine this event with all the talk of weddings, the pretty green in Delaney Gardens would be the venue. Cassie would plan it all like a military campaign: a hundred tea lights lit by 3 p.m., sir! Cassie could organise anything: her two tiny daughters, her husband, her job, even the newly purchased semi-detached house a mile from Delaney Gardens where the previous tenants had left it looking like a squat and had somehow removed all the grouting from the bathroom tiles.

A small marquee would fit in the patch of glorious green in Delaney Gardens between the gnarled crab apple trees, the bluebells and the huge old fig tree. Grammy would source food from all her cooking pals, so no fortune would have to be spent on four courses or sorbets or any of that nonsense.

Coco wanted the music of The Andrews Sisters and Glenn Miller, with a hint of the seventies thrown in to get people up dancing.

'You'll need disco music,' said Cassie, shocked, when Coco had explained how she and the girls from college had been talking about weddings. 'You can't get married without Abba, at least.'

And the sisters had giggled at the thought of this lovely imaginary event to plan, and had discussed how it was handy Coco was waiting for several years, because right now, Beth would be a very bad flower girl as she was going through a stomping phase in nursery school.

Had she really been that naïve? Coco thought now. Thinking thirty was the right age to get married – as if it were something you had the slightest control over.

Coco had grown more and more accustomed to the concept that life rippled along in its own way no matter what you did to intercept it, but she was still shocked by how powerless she was about it all.

She was thirty-one now, and her last serious relationship had been with Red, four years ago. Since then she'd had a couple of dates and then, for a whole year, nothing. Nada. Zip. Until last month and the disastrous blind date at a friend's dinner party with a recently separated guy who'd muttered endlessly about his ex-wife and her new man, and then grabbed Coco as she tried to leave and slobbered drunkenly on her in a manner he clearly thought was kissing. Nice.

'Sorry,' said her friend who'd set it up. 'I thought he was over it. I shouldn't have made Brandy Alexanders . . .'

'No,' said Coco, and she'd nearly said, *It's me. I am catnip to the wrong men and the right men run from me.*

Red had run from me, the man I wanted to marry, was what she'd thought, but she never told people things like that.

Instead, she'd said, 'He was drunk. Hardly your fault. You didn't pour it down his throat. But no more blind dates and dinner parties, please? They make me feel hopeless and pitied. Trips to the cinema and things like that, lovely. But dinner parties with other couples just make it worse.'

In the years since Cassie and Coco had planned the perfect wedding, Cassie and Shay had long since renovated their house on the cheap and Coco's nieces were now thirteen and fifteen. Beth had gone back into a stomping phase, Cassie pointed out miserably.

And still no need to set up any type of marquee in Delaney Gardens for Coco.

Was there something wrong with her? Was nobody in her family telling her the truth because

63

they loved her? Would therapy help? No, cross that off the list, Coco thought gloomily. She couldn't afford therapy. The electricity bill from the shop alone made her wince every two months. Who knew what professional therapists charged for their services?

No, perhaps she was simply one of those women who were destined to be alone.

CHAPTER 3

That afternoon, Pearl Keneally stood in her red and white themed kitchen with Ritchie Valens singing in the background and toyed with the idea of putting the salted peanuts out in her small, hot-pink and blue dishes from Ios, but then thought better of it.

Liam's blood pressure was high enough: he didn't need the salt. Plus Gloria was back in diet club for a winter wedding and would stab Pearl if she saw needless temptation. Pearl snagged a handful of peanuts for herself, then put them in the back of the treat cupboard. Daisy, an oyster pug who needed to be on a diet herself, sat at Pearl's feet, smiling and watching with delight. For Daisy, her mistress's weekly events meant treats.

Snacks and drinks was what they'd agreed when they set up the Thursday night club all those years ago. The group, who all lived in Delaney Gardens, had between them seen children grow up, grandchildren grow up, had experienced death, illness: you name it, they'd seen it. And still they came together once a week, rain, hail or shine. The rules hadn't changed: no proper dinners or cheese squashed into shapes on crackers, or it would soon become a huge effort when all they wanted were a few card games and the company.

Now that over forty years had passed, people's varying ill health meant the snacks had to be wildly healthy, not dangerous for anyone on anti-stroke medication and suitable for Annette, who was diabetic. Pearl found the low-cal, low-salt, low-taste nibbles and put them out with some trail mix, along with diabetic chocolate near the seat where Annette usually sat.

Some members of the club were gone to wherever it was people went. There were six of them now instead of the initial nine: Loretta and Dai were dead, Louis in the mysterious and painful land of dementia.

Annette's husband, Dai, had had a heart attack when he was sixty and, years later, Annette insisted that she'd never have survived without her Thursday nights.

'I couldn't fall in love with anyone else,' she said. 'Dai was the love of my life. Thursday nights saved me. I had somewhere to go.'

Gloria's husband, Louis, was in a nursing home with advanced dementia. He no longer recognised Gloria or any of his family, and sat whispering fearfully about 'going home', by which he meant his birth home.

Gloria had stayed away from the Thursday night club for a year when Louis had first gone into the nursing home.

'The guilt kills me,' she'd told Pearl the night Pearl had gone over to Gloria's to beg her to come back to the poker club. '*I* should be taking care of him, not someone else, someone who doesn't know what he likes!'

'And what would you do if he got run over by a car when he escaped from the house again, looking for the way back to his mother's house, Gloria? You'd feel twice as guilty then,' Pearl had said, knowing she had to be cruel to be kind. 'What Louis needs now is something you can't physically give him. He needs people who are rested and expert, people who aren't so worn out with emotion that they want to cry when he won't eat and sob with exhaustion as they try to change his clothes. You can't do that, Gloria.'

'I know.' Gloria sat with her face in her hands. 'But I feel guilty.'

'You will if you sit at home and brood. You need a few hours every week where you forget it all, where you can laugh and know nobody's judging you and that we love you. We all miss Louis, he was a part of our lives too, but he wouldn't want you killing yourself with pain because he has this bloody disease.'

'He was a great poker player, wasn't he?' Gloria remembered proudly.

'Better than the rest of us put together,' Pearl agreed. 'He loved the tradition of it all, the fun. I'm not just saying what I think you need to hear, Gloria,' Pearl went on, 'but I knew the real Louis.

He was good and kind and loved you with all his heart. He would hate to see you in this much pain.'

Gloria let the tears flow. 'I am so lonely, Pearl.' She almost breathed the words out, she spoke so slowly. 'We had fifty years and now it's all over, gone. How can it be gone when he's still actually here? It would feel like cheating on him to have fun when he isn't.'

'If *you* were in the home, if places were reversed, what would you want for Louis? Endless pain and guilt, or a life with friends who helped you?' Pearl delivered the final bit of her argument.

That was a year ago, and Louis was going steadily downhill, getting thinner and having more and more chest infections he couldn't shake, but Gloria was somehow coping. Joining the diet club was a huge step, Pearl knew. The Gloria of a year ago was so numb that she didn't care if she was five stone or fifty.

Ritchie Valens was singing 'Bluebirds Over the Mountains'. Whisking around the living room with Daisy panting at her heels, Pearl admired her house and thought how pretty it all looked now: one person – her younger sister, Edie, who'd been born with a bitter taste in her mouth – had said it was ludicrous having a Mediterranean-themed house in a northern European city, but Pearl pointed out that when there wasn't always enough sun outside, you had to generate it *somewhere*. Plus, the house was very near the sea after all. The sea wall of Silver Bay was only half a mile away, so a maritime theme worked. And people needed vitamin D.

Her walls were primrose yellow, her couch was a faded turquoise with rainbow crochet cushions, she had a heated fish tank for a sense of the ocean, a jungle of stretching, gleaming cacti plants on the low windowsill, and the pictures on the walls were of Santorini, Thessaloniki and Crete.

All the people whom Pearl loved, loved her home. Coco, Cassie, Shay, Lily and Beth adored it. The Thursday night club loved it. Edie could go hang, with her beige carpet, beige velvet couch and OCD-inspired overuse of hand sanitiser.

'Pearl, it's like being on holidays,' Lily liked to say, lying on the couch and looking up at the Greek pictures.

When she was little, Beth hadn't been able to say Great-Grammy but had liked saying 'Grammy Pearl' in her breathy, little girl's voice, and so Grammy Pearl it had remained for both of Pearl's great-granddaughters.

'I think I'm on holidays when I'm in this room too, Lily,' Pearl would reply happily.

Pearl had always loved Greece and for years now, sturdy, white-haired but nut brown from a summer spent outside in her tiny garden coaxing tomatoes and baby strawberries to grow, she'd chosen to wear gleaming whites and Grecian blues, and had her toenails painted coral by Coco who lived just up the street – ten minutes at Coco's fast pace.

The nice new young doctor in the local practice

had said it was incredible that Pearl was up to so much gardening, had only had a hint of arthritis and was a supple as she was at her age.

'Not many seventy-eight-year-olds have your energy or stamina,' he'd said. 'You have great genes, Mrs Keneally. Or is there another secret to it?'

'I raised my granddaughters,' Pearl said simply. 'I couldn't be old because they needed a mother; theirs was gone. Love is a powerful thing.'

Automatically she turned to the photos of the girls on the old upright piano. Cassie on her wedding day, radiant in a brand-new dress, despite Coco's attempts to get her into something old and romantic.

Pearl's son, Jimmy, had been alive then and he stood tall and proud in the photos, but with that hint of sadness around his eyes. That had never gone. Pearl loved Jimmy with all her heart but she'd never been able to help him recover from his wife's departure. You *could* die of a broken heart, Pearl thought, even if it was a slow death.

She'd done her best when Marguerite had left them all those years ago. She'd insisted that Jimmy and the girls move in with her to the small narrow house in Delaney Gardens and had been a mother to all three of them: devastated Jimmy, Cassie, who was seven and had coped with a combination of bewilderment and, later, of acting out, and little Coco, just one and the most adaptable of the three.

Despite it all – dire warnings from Edie, sympathetic glances from neighbours, concern from Cassie's schoolteachers during her particularly difficult teenage years – they'd managed.

'You'll go straight to heaven for all you've done,' Edie used to sniff when it turned out that Cassie *wasn't* planning a life smoking dope and living in a squat as she'd grimly foreseen when Cassie was seventeen and had a wardrobe entirely made up of tight jeans, T-shirts with rude slogans on them, a studded leather jacket and Doc Marten boots.

'I'm not planning on going anywhere anytime soon, Edie,' Pearl said in exasperation. 'Stop shuffling me off this mortal coil.'

Yet Edie's words left unease in Pearl. She wasn't a saint – far from it. She'd played her part in their family drama in more ways than raising the girls Marguerite had left behind.

Over three decades since her daughter-in-law had left and Pearl still felt the raising wasn't finished. That, she could have told the young GP, kept her alive to be a mother to them.

At seventy-eight, she knew in her heart that she ought to be able to enjoy her card-playing nights in peace, but she wasn't. Her girls weren't settled, for all that they looked perfectly happy from the outside.

There was Coco, who, despite all her early romance, had no man in her life. Lots of first and second dates but nothing more. Once a man got close, Coco shoved him off the way she discarded tatty fake designer stuff for her shop. Red – Pearl usually hated men who were known by nicknames and not their given names, but Red was different – was gone now and Pearl had been so sure that Coco would go through with it this time: marriage, babies, settling down. But no.

Red and Coco had broken up four years before and since then Coco had thrown herself even more into her vintage clothes shop. Work was all well and good but it didn't keep you warm at night, did it?

While Cassie . . . Pearl sighed.

Cassie was good on paper. It *looked* as if Cassie had it all: those two lovely girls, a good husband, a job, and yet Pearl could see something not quite right these days. It was more than the nightmare of the teenage years. Pearl suspected it was something to do with Shay, but Cassie hadn't confided in her.

Despite how close they'd once been, there was a firm boundary around Cassie since she'd grown up – as if all those years of wishing her mother would come home had hardened something inside her, and made her feel that a castle wall to protect her was the safest way to cope with life.

Pearl could see how her granddaughter tried so hard to be the perfect mother to her two daughters. Indeed, how she tried so hard to be perfect at everything: perfect mother, perfect wife, perfect employee. Even perfect baker. Most Sundays Cassie spent at least three hours in the kitchen making dinners and cakes for the week. It was what she thought a good mother would do. And Cassie was, without knowing it, desperately trying to be the good mother she'd been denied.

Pearl, who'd been just fifty when Marguerite had left, was no baker. Pearl had done her best to fill in all the motherhood gaps but she still wasn't the real thing.

Never would be.

And now Cassie was desperately trying to recreate something she'd never quite had as a child and Pearl wasn't sure if her granddaughter was even aware she was doing it.

'Guilt keeps me alive,' Pearl would have liked to have said to that young doctor if she was speaking frankly. 'Guilt at what I did do, what I didn't do, and how it's too late to change it all. Guilt at how I shouldn't have let Marguerite leave, guilt at how I should have helped her more when she was here, guilt at thinking that one day she would come back.'

At night when she couldn't sleep, Pearl sometimes sat in the window of the small house on Delaney Gardens, a house that had once squeezed two girls, their father and grandmother into it, and she stared unseeing over the garden and its huge fig tree. It wasn't really what anyone interested in planning would have called a square. More a patch of square grass around which the houses were ranged on three sides: once state-owned houses that most people now owned. Built in the thirties as part of a social housing project, they were sturdy and compact with long back gardens, perfect for vegetable growing, which was how people fed themselves in those days.

In the centre of the actual Delaney garden was the old fig tree, bigger than the one Pearl had in her back garden. This one was a gnarled, twisted old beauty that had withstood many lovers' initials scraped into it, small folk climbing its branches, and harsh storms that rattled windows long before double-glazing was invented.

The tree was allegedly a relative of the famous Australian Moreton Bay Fig, and now roots from the branches grew down into the ground, creating a safe enclosure of roots around the centre of its massive trunk. To small children, it was like a kindly grandparent leaning down to hug them.

'Isn't it a fabulous specimen?' strangers always said in fascination. 'I've never seen a fig tree like that before.'

'And it grows fruit?' others would ask.

Fruit galore. Fruit for jams, chutneys, desserts, and when Pearl had been young and had lived in Delaney Gardens with her husband, Bernard, fruit dripping down their chins as they sat on their threadbare, third-hand old seats in front of the fire, laughing and planning for their future.

'It never turns out the way we plan, Bernie,' she said to him. He was now long gone, his kind smile and ever-present pipe smoke drifting around somewhere else. She hoped he was on a divine cloud somewhere looking down, but not seeing the mess she'd made.

No, Pearl told herself, even if her sister had been planning Pearl's funeral since Pearl had hit seventy-five, there would be no going anywhere, no letting go of the reins of the family until she'd sorted it all out.

She had so many regrets, and now she thought it was time to do something about them all. Too many lives had been hurt and she'd been a part of it. The family circle needed to be complete. Pearl had thought that keeping quiet would help her beloved girls, but missing someone hadn't helped her, had it?

And if she told them the truth, she'd have to tell them the whole truth. And they might look at her with loathing if she did that. Cassie was always saying Pearl was an amazing woman. If the truth came out, about what she *hadn't* done for their poor mother, Cassie certainly wouldn't believe that anymore.

Flat shoes were useful for big hotels, Cassie knew, as she parked as close as she could to the enormous Springfield Hotel.

The Springfield was like a giant E block set down in the middle of a field that had been landscaped to death and now had walks, little streams and bridges dotted all over the place. To get to any one place you had to walk miles, and guests at weddings had been known to spend hours wandering tipsily around in the wee small hours, wielding hotel keys and saying, 'It's over here, near this statue, I know it is!' until rescued by the concierge staff.

Billed as a spa hotel, it was, in fact, a major conference and wedding hotel because it had four hundred rooms, three giant conference rooms and a ballroom you could play ice hockey in, if you so wished.

Leo Quirke, the new manager, kept Cassie waiting when she arrived at half two to discuss the problems for the conference starting on Thursday. She sat in the outer room of Leo's office and thought how she'd never had to wait for his predecessor, who had gone on to run a department of a luxury hotel in Boca Raton and who was, no doubt, delirious to have washed his hands of the Springfield, which had been beset with so many teething problems the joke in the trade was that it needed its own dentist.

Too big, built too quickly, and with too many corners cut, there were always problems with the hotel. But Fiachra – Leo's predecessor – had sorted them out. Leo seemed to be more of an *ah, sure, whatever* type of manager. The type who'd give you a shove on the shoulder to imply a matey we're-all-in-this-together.

'Cassie, sorry to keep you waiting.' Leo, who was forty-something, bank managerial in a navy chalk-striped suit he was clearly no longer able to button, smiled urbanely and held out a hand. 'You are looking lovely, if I may say so,' he added, doing some eyebrow lifting.

Cassie gave him the *you may not say so* stare she'd perfected over many years in the events management business, shook his hand briefly and said crisply: 'Can we go into your office and sort this out, Leo? I'm pressed for time.'

She walked in ahead of him, sat down at the desk and quickly spread her papers in front of her. Larousse had a watertight contract for the event and it was very specific on deal-breakers. Facilities not working were top of a long list that went over many issues.

Leo leapt into the fray. 'Obviously we are doing all we can from this end,' he said. He did the eyebrow thing again.

Was that flirting? Cassie had no idea. It was millions of years since anyone had flirted with her. She didn't give out any signals, did she?

Right now she had a headache, her hair had dried strangely after that morning's rain, so she'd had to pull it into a tight bun, and despite the application of Belinda's make-up, she wasn't sure how she looked. She knew how she *felt*, though: tired, headachey – probably the tautness of the darn bun – and worried about what she'd do if she had to pull a conference for a hundred and twenty-five people two days before it was due to go ahead.

Flirting? Did Leo have any idea how close to the edge she was?

77

The set-up crew were due into the hotel first thing on Thursday with the company's logo boards, presenters and goodie bags, and Cassie herself was due there by twelve to go over the final checks for the meals, drinks and entertainment for Thursday and Friday night. The paraphernalia for the Saturday golfing match was being handled by Jason and his crew from Larousse, who specialised in sports events. Jason was a dab hand with golf events and had several professional players' managers' numbers on his personal mobile. Yet secretly he hated golf and only liked golfers for the glory of those shifting shoulder muscles when they hit a fabulous drive; but then nobody needed to know that.

'You were a little unclear on the phone,' Cassie began in her discussion with Leo. Saying you figured someone had been downright lying on the phone never started a conversation well. 'What exactly is the problem with the spa, Leo, and what is being done to fix it?'

'We're doing everything,' Leo said gravely. 'You know how tricky spas can be . . . The hammam has a problem and there's something wrong with the pool filters . . .'

The pool had been refitted at vast expense only last year, Cassie thought, instincts prickling.

'Let's take a look,' said Cassie suddenly.

He hesitated.

'I love the spa here,' Cassie said, standing up and making for the door.

He had no choice but to follow her.

Whatever the question, flat shoes were the answer, she thought, as she walked down endless corridors with Leo scurrying to keep up, arriving finally at the spa.

Instead of the familiar spa scent of essential oils, non-stop burning of candles and the inevitable hint of chlorine, she smelled paint. Bestowing a glittering and dangerous smile on her companion, Cassie pushed open the double doors to find that the Springfield spa and health club was being repainted.

'Water leakage,' tried Leo weakly.

'Show me.'

'Well, you know, all over the place . . .'

Cassie marched around, pushing into every changing room, checking the hammam – stone cold and it took *forever* to heat up – and the pool area.

Painters wandered around with cans of paint, and nobody looked to be in any sort of rush. There was a mañana atmosphere, helped along with the hotel's jazzy Muzak. All they needed were a few cocktails and the whole thing might turn into a party at the drop of a baseball cap.

'Is anything actually *not* working apart from it all being turned off so you can paint?' Cassie asked Leo.

He took a deep breath and then said, 'No.'

Cassie smothered the desire to stab him. Shay would undoubtedly be wildly busy at work and therefore not available to bail her out if she was

79

arrested for the said stabbing. She put her game face on again.

'Right. Get them all finished and out of here tonight, spend tomorrow eradicating the smell of paint, heating the pool and the hammam, and we have a deal. I'll be here tomorrow first thing to check. Otherwise I will be cancelling and you'll be getting a call from Loren Larousse about the financial implications of breaking a contract with us. Morally or legally correct or not, I can tell you that Loren will waste no time telling other event management people about this and it will not be good for the Springfield's future conference bookings. You can phone me on the mobile to discuss in an hour.' Cassie delivered the final blow. 'I need to get back to the office to check out where else we can hold the conference. If we have to pay more for a higher quality hotel or for travelling down the country, we will – and trust me, I know that from past experience – Loren *will* take you to court for breach of contract.'

At that, Leo paled.

There were times, Cassie thought, when her boss's tough reputation within the industry came in useful. In reality, court cases took forever and helped neither side professionally, but still, nobody who knew what Loren Larousse was really like wanted to cross her in business.

'I'm sorry, it's just that . . .' began Leo, blustering.

Cassie felt momentarily sorry for him, but then

thought of all the work involved if she had to even attempt to co-ordinate another hotel, undoubtedly not one in Dublin, and how she'd explain all of this to the conference people themselves. Loren would blame her for not literally camping down in the hotel because there was a new and untried manager around, and she would end up spending Thursday and Friday night stuck in the inevitable room beside the lift, overseeing everything personally in an attempt to make it all up to everyone.

At these thoughts, her feelings of sympathy withered and died.

'Leo, we are in business. We don't arrange conferences in hotels where the facilities get closed for redecoration on a whim. I have one hundred and twenty-five important guests coming on Thursday to stay with you for a convention booked six months ago, and you think it's OK to repaint the spa while they're here so they can't use it?'

'Well, you know . . .'

More bluster. What was wrong with saying, 'Sorry, I screwed up'?

'Leo, I will keep my boss from phoning up your chief executive and serving you as Thursday's banquet main course if you can sort this out. *Capisce?*'

Then she turned on her heel and walked out.

It took twenty minutes to get out of the hotel and find her car, by which time it had started raining again and Cassie's hair and clothes were wet through. Shivering, she sat in the car with the heater jacked up and thought of how nice it might be to text someone she loved. The girls were in school with their phones, hopefully turned to silent. Coco was always busy during shop opening hours and her speciality was returning texts three hours later by saying:

Sorry! Busy! Didn't see phone!

And she and Shay rarely rang each other at work anymore. So she sent Coco a text instead:

Hi, honey. Come to lunch at the weekend?
C xxxx

CHAPTER 4

Her grandmother really had been an amazing woman, Cassie thought as she unlocked the front door, weak with pure exhaustion, and Lily and Beth hurried into the house ahead of her. Grammy Pearl had raised two kids who weren't even her own and Cassie wondered if she and Coco had been as annoyingly teenager-ish as her own daughters were.

From the moment she'd picked them up from school, there had been squabbling, a heated debate over why they had less pocket money than anyone else in their year (Beth), and a mutinous murmur over how her phone was totally crappy and why didn't she have a really cool phone like everyone else (Lily).

Inside their painstakingly renovated house, the girls dumped their rucksacks full of books and their coats on the floor at the bottom of the stairs, shrugging off the detritus of school. Nobody moved to help their mother with the shopping she'd raced around the supermarket to purchase before she'd collected them.

Eighteen months ago they'd been mother's

little helpers; now they were hormones on legs – happy one minute, gloomy the next, worrying about how they'd ever be rich and famous singers after that.

'I need a bath before I finish my homework,' announced Beth, who was tall like her father but with her mother's dark and unmanageable curly hair. 'I got a whack of the ball in netball today. There's already a bruise. Honestly, Mum, do I have to do it? I'm never going to be any good at it . . .' And then she was gone up the stairs, trailing her school tie and shoes after her, coat still on the floor.

Beth was mercurial, definitely like Shay, but she could be funny and sparkly when she felt like it.

Cassie looked at the coats on the floor, which would miraculously move themselves via Mother Power, which was a well-known family phenomenon. Like the laundry fairy and the answer to the 'where are my trainers/black jeans/pink long-sleeved T-shirt?' question. Mother Power could do it all and knew where every lost item was.

Breathe, Cassie told herself as she shouldered her way through the door with the shopping. *Breathe.* Think of that mindfulness book she had on the floor by the bed and occasionally actually read. *Be in the now, feel your feet touching the earth, rooting you . . .'*

'Mum, there's a message on the phone. I listened and it's Gran,' roared Lily from the kitchen.

The very notion of calm breathing and being rooted in the earth vanished to be replaced by the wild irritation she was accustomed to.

It could not be good for the body, this irritation.

In the kitchen. Lily's skinny body was half in the fridge. Her appetite was mythic. Nobody could believe that somebody so small could consume so much and be so endlessly hungry. She could eat a trencherman's dinner, and half an hour after, amble over to the cupboard, pull out the cereal and start gulping handfuls from the box. Where precisely it all went, Cassie didn't know.

Lily was slender and short, like her mother, but Cassie's slenderness came from watching what she ate and occasionally, just occasionally, going for a walk with Coco where they talked about most things. Not everything, but most things.

Lily appeared to do as little exercise as possible, despite the school system, and just ate.

'Fast metabolism?' Shay would say absently, when queried about this. 'Great for sports, though. She likes tennis. Should she have tennis coaching?'

'Who,' Cassie wanted to screech, 'would drive her to this extra tennis coaching? Not you, because you are never here anymore!'

But she couldn't say that because it was the unsayable. She would not count how many times he'd been at his mother's lately. She would not.

Breathe.

She put the bags on the counter still messy with the morning's breakfast dishes and pressed the answerphone button as she watched her younger daughter plundering the fridge.

The frail-sounding voice of Antoinette, her mother-in-law, whispered through the kitchen.

'Shay, pet, the hot water's not working. I don't know what to do and you know I'm scared of messing with the controls. Your father always did it. Could you come round?'

If Lily hadn't been there, Cassie might have sworn out loud, something long and filthy that would necessitate serious paper money in the swear jar, but as it was, she consoled herself with a silent curse. Somewhere deep inside, it made her feel marginally better.

Then she opened the fridge and took out the half-full bottle of white wine chilling inside. She banished the thought that she'd only opened it the night before and that Shay hadn't drunk any because he didn't believe in drinking mid-week. She needed this, needed something to help cool and calm her down. What harm was there in a glass of wine?

Shay's mother, Antoinette, had always said she wasn't good with the phone and could never remember which one to ring, so she had a system of leaving messages all over the place. She'd have left one on Shay's phone and probably in his office too. *Just in case.* By now, Shay and the entire northern hemisphere would know he was needed in his mother's house and he would have obediently gone there, to his former home on the other side of the city instead of to his current one.

He wouldn't be late for dinner with Cassie and the girls because he wouldn't be eating with them at all. Antoinette would have 'something small in the oven, pet, seeing as you've come all this way'.

To add to this, Shay might not even text or phone to explain where he was and Cassie's blood would boil all evening. 'But sure, you knew I'd be with Ma, didn't you?' he'd say in bewilderment when he'd roll up at half ten or eleven, fed and happy after an evening with his mother. He wouldn't have had to put away groceries, organise the next day's dinner, put on washing, drag the recycling bin to the gate or do any of the normal jobs associated with family life.

Nobody could castigate a man for taking care of his widowed mother. Cassie certainly wouldn't have done so until over three years ago when her father-in-law had died.

Arthur had been like Shay: a big man, fair-haired and freckled, larger than life, great fun and endlessly practical. Like his son, he worked in engineering and, consequently, both men knew their way around a tool kit and could put together flat pack furniture with good-humoured expertise.

Then a massive heart attack had taken Arthur away and Antoinette's life had changed. Shattered, Antoinette had not been able to cope and Cassie had felt enormous pity for her fragile mother-in-law.

Despite her clothes being modern and fashionable, the internal Antoinette was like a woman from another time, one of the timorous gentle ladies from eighteenth century novels who had fits of the vapours at all aspects of painful modern life. It would be difficult for her to live on her own, Cassie thought, but at least Antoinette had two daughters as well as Shay. Three grown children to be there for her.

Ruth was single, worked in television production and lived in an all-white apartment not too far from her mother, while Miriam was married with one teenage son, worked part-time and lived about four miles from Antoinette's Clontarf home.

Unfortunately, Miriam and Ruth weren't on Antoinette's emotional radar at all. Only Shay could fill his beloved father's shoes. And Shay, to Cassie's astonishment, was filling those shoes with vigour. Antoinette's emergencies were twice-weekly events at least.

'Doesn't she ever phone Miriam or Ruth?' Cassie had asked once, six months on from her father-in-law's death, when Antoinette's frantic phone calls were still coming fast and loose, and Shay appeared to be half living with his mother.

'Ah, the girls are hopeless with house stuff, you know that, Cass,' said Shay. 'Miriam never answers her phone and Ruth's so busy.'

'Busy?' Cassie heard the rage in her voice but was too angry to quell it. 'And you're not busy? You have a family and a job. Ruth only has one of those. It wouldn't kill her to phone her mother once in a blue moon, and I don't know why Miriam doesn't answer her bloody phone. Push the button, say, "*Hello, Mum, yes, I'll come round.*" It's not rocket science. You are not your mother's only child.'

'Ma needs me right now,' Shay said, managing to look a combination of irritated and hurt. 'I don't know how you can't understand that, Cass. She'll adjust. She's lonely, that's all. We live five minutes away from your grandmother, so it's no big deal if you need to drop in. It's only because Mum lives on the other side of the city that it seems like I'm gone for ages. I'm not. It'll pass.'

But over the past three years, Antoinette hadn't become any less lonely.

Other than the time aspect of it all, what hurt was the never coming first. Never. Shay had a list of important people in his head and after almost four years of his dropping everything to see to his mother's emergencies, Cassie felt she was right at the bottom of it.

In her darker moments, she decided that if she drove off a bridge and Antoinette phoned simultaneously with a message about having pranged her car on the garden gate, Shay would throw Cassie a lifebuoy, roar, 'I know you'll be able to sort yourself out, love, you're so capable,' and he'd be gone. Gone to his mother who was too fragile for life.

Cassie, who prized herself on her ability to cope with anything, was seen as strong enough to manage on her own.

'What's for dinner, Mum?' asked Lily, looking at the shopping.

'Fish pie,' said Cassie, putting an arm around her younger daughter and hugging. Sometimes a person needed a hug and Beth had become very unhuggy these days. Something to do with her animal instincts making her pushed loved ones away before they pushed her away: defensive tactics in the evolution of a teenager. It still hurt like hell.

Lily, in a moment of respite from the hormonal dark side, embraced her mother, snuggling in for a hug the way she used to.

She was like a little sprite in school uniform: dark hair growing out of a pixie cut, with knowing blue eyes that saw everything, a ready smile when the hormones weren't torturing her, and a fondness for teenage fiction set in dystopian worlds.

'Yum,' she said now, blue eyes lighting up. 'Is there any Chunky Monkey left for afters?'

'Did you eat it all last night? If so, it's just ordinary supermarket vanilla.'

'Think I did,' Lily said, sighing. 'Can I melt Nutella on to the vanilla, then?'

'Sure.' Burying her head into the soft cloud of Lily's hair and breathing in the scent of flowery girl perfume, Cassie closed her eyes and wished everything was as simple as what to have for dessert.

Don't grow up anymore, she wanted to beg Lily. *Please go back to being my little girl for a bit longer. Let just one thing stay the same . . .*

Lily wriggled out of her mother's embrace and skipped out the door.

'Take your coat and put it in the cupboard,' Cassie begged.

''K,' said Lily.

At least Lily still did what she was told. Telling Beth to do anything was akin to co-ordinating a rocket launch and hoping nothing exploded.

Although Cassie firmly believed that people, even teenagers, had to clean up after themselves, it was sometimes easier to put Beth's stuff away herself rather than wait for a missile strike from hormone central.

It had been an exhausting day. She'd been drenched twice, had to deal with the whole Springfield Hotel crisis, and then being balled at on the phone by Loren, who'd shrieked – as if Cassie didn't already know – that one messed-up conference would have a hugely negative impact on their reputation.

'You are supposed to let that moron know that I will rip his guts out through his nostrils if he screws this up,' had been Loren's grim advice when Cassie had phoned in. In a chaotic world, one could always rely on her boss to be enraged about something.

And it seemed as though one could always rely upon her husband to be at his mother's house, Cassie thought.

She glumly surveyed the shopping. She had picked the groceries off the shelves, put them into the trolley, loaded them on the conveyor belt, packed them into bags, hauled it all in a wonky trolley to the car, and now she had to put them all away again.

At least dinner was ready to go. All it needed was reheating in the oven, which she switched on now. She clicked on the radio and found something with a pumping beat to keep her energy up so she could force herself to begin unpacking. As she listened to the music and drank her wine, she tried to keep the tears from her eyes. Crying and drinking: she was like a student in a flat, she reflected grimly. And then that thought shifted on to girls and tattoos.

She might get a tattoo.

Too long a sacrifice can make a stone of the heart.

She'd always loved W. B. Yeats. She'd get it somewhere secret so nobody would see it or need know what it meant, because she would. That was enough.

By twenty to eleven, Cassie had all the washing done, some of it dried, and had ironed the girls' school blouses for the next day. She'd taken out the next day's dinner from the freezer but that was the last of her stash; tomorrow she'd have to cook up a few meals for the rest of the week. The wine was long gone and Cassie had, with great difficulty, stopped herself opening another bottle. She'd had too much already.

Upstairs, Beth was in bed reading her history textbook and listening to music at the same time. Cassie had switched off Lily's light twice already.

'Just one more chapter! They're about to get into the time reactor to try and switch everything back to the previous month before the invasion,' wheedled Lily at ten, when Cassie crept upstairs with her ironing to find that Lily was reading again despite the 9.30 school night lights-out rule.

'No,' Cassie said firmly, but patted her daughter's hand in case she sounded irritable. 'You need your sleep, darling.'

'Here are your shirts,' Cassie said quietly, entering Beth's domain.

In bed, with the eye make-up off and in her fleecy pyjamas, Beth looked more like the fifteen-year-old she was and less like the seventeen-year-old she seemed desperate to turn into. She had her aunt Coco's heart-shaped face and perfect eyebrows, and her father's eyes with those unusual striations of amber in the centre. All in all, it made for a pretty amazing package and Cassie worried endlessly about her daughter's effect on the male population and the tangles a young girl could get herself into.

Sighing because she knew wine made her maudlin, Cassie put a few things in the laundry basket and then sat on the side of Beth's bed, angling her head so she could see the title of the textbook: *European History from 1000AD to the Glory of the Renaissance*.

'That's a nice small area of research to get through,' she joked.

'I know, *nightmare*, right?' said Beth. 'It's very

brutal, too: everyone killing everyone else, or else they died from poverty or disease. Yeuch. And women were like objects, just things, almost not people at all. It was so horrible, I flicked ahead to the Inquisition.' She shuddered. 'That was way worse, the things they did to people.'

Her eyes filled with tears.

Knowing she could have her arm shrugged off but risking it anyway, Cassie leaned in and put an arm around her older daughter.

'Honey, that's probably not a good thing to read before bed. Some people can read about the most horrendous periods in history and it doesn't affect them, but you and I – and darling Lily, as well – are not among them. When I read about how they treated witches, who were most likely just midwives or healing women, I couldn't sleep for weeks. The thought of it all just stayed with me.'

'Really, Mum?' Beth looked surprised. 'I didn't know that.'

'Hard to imagine,' joked Cassie, 'but I was a bit sensitive when I was at school.'

She still was, Cassie reflected ruefully, thinking of how upset Shay's continued defection could make her. But kids seemed to function better when they saw their parents coping fabulously, so she tried not to let it show.

She rapidly moved off that subject. 'Your aunt Coco couldn't read Anne Frank's diary. She kept trying to but she'd sob so much that Grammy Pearl went into the school and said she didn't care if it was on the course or not, Coco wasn't going to read it.'

'Go Pearl!' laughed Beth.

'Now, how about you pack up the history, flick through a magazine for five minutes to see what new band are in or out, and then try to sleep, because it's really late, darling. I could bring you some hot chocolate?'

Beth smiled at her mother. 'Yeah, that would be nice.'

Cassie almost bounced downstairs, so happy to have had a positive conversation with Beth.

By half eleven, Cassie was in bed herself, not reading, just mindlessly flicking through the TV which was turned to low, trying to find something mind-numbing to send her off to sleep and get her mind off the fact that Shay still wasn't home.

His 8 p.m. text—

Gone to Ma's, won't be late

—was plainly untrue and Cassie found herself simmering at the lack of any further texts.

Blast Shay for having the sensitivity of a ten-tonne truck, she thought, and switched out the light forcefully.

Cassie would kill him, Shay Reynolds thought as he sped through the darkened streets in his car, weariness overtaking him. He hadn't noticed how late it had got. Once he'd sorted out the water heater problem, Mam had wanted to watch this old documentary on the TV about the building of Knock airport in the west of Ireland, and he'd said he'd sit with her for a bit of the programme. But she was so persuasive, and he'd made them another cup of tea – hers in the special china mug with the roses on it – and suddenly the show was over, it was after eleven and he'd been there for far longer than he'd meant to.

All the same, he felt so sorry every time he left his mother alone in the house he and his sisters had grown up in. He swore her face got smaller and sadder each time when she stood at the door to kiss him goodbye.

The routine was the same every time: Mam standing there wearing one of her soft woollen sweaters because she really suffered with the cold, and her wedding ring on a chain around her neck because her fingers were too misshapen from arthritis to wear it anymore. She hated that. His mother prized herself on looking youthful and pretty. She'd never been the sort of mother to slouch around the house and had always dressed up, wearing the pastel colours that suited her blonde-streaked hair.

'Drive safely, love,' she'd say at the door. 'Give the girls my love, and Cassie. I hope she's not working too hard. And you, love.' At this, she'd reach up to hug him. Shay was six foot and his mother was almost a foot smaller. 'You take care because nobody can replace my wonderful son.'

She'd never been much for make-up, but he associated the goodbye hugs with the scent of something flowery from his childhood, vastly different from the perfumes Cassie wore. Cassie's were sharper, cut with citrus, modern; Mam's was old and familiar, comforting, the scent of flowers of the past. It made him think of a time when life was simpler, when the office wasn't such a jungle, when the girls had been younger and weren't like tinder just waiting for a spark to set them off. When Cassie had seemed happier with him.

Simpler, that was it. Life had been so much simpler.

The sea wall raced by as he got closer to home and Shay made himself slow down as he reached the Silver Bay area. He was tired, although he'd have to deny it to Cassie and imply that he had loads of energy. But driving while tired could be fatal.

He looked briefly up at the road to Delaney Gardens as he passed it, thought of the redoubtable Pearl, and reflected that a huge part of the problem was that Cassie had no experience of a woman like his mother. Pearl was seventy-eight, acted like a woman three quarters of her age, and didn't consider being within grasping reach of eighty to be any barrier to having a full life. Shay was pretty sure she and Peter from her poker club were lovers – it was the way Peter smiled and touched her face gently when Cassie and Coco were out of the room – but Shay had never shared this notion with his wife. Kids were weird about their mothers having sex and no doubt about it, Pearl had more or less been his wife's mother.

Perhaps if she'd had her real mother, she might have understood his own mother more. He'd often thought this.

The bits he'd heard about Marguerite implied she was a fragile sort of person – well, she'd been a drinker, hadn't she, and who knew what else – and sounded a million miles away from the strong Pearl. Edie was the one who'd filled him in on Marguerite. Edie was a mine of information about the past and was always delighted to reveal it.

'No better than she should have been,' had been her verdict on his long-gone mother-in-law, which was clearly Edie-speak for some sort of wild/trollopy/insane woman.

Pearl never mentioned her one-time daughter-in-law, and neither did Cassie. It was as if she'd vanished from all their minds, never to be thought of or spoken of again.

He drove slowly in the gate of their drive, parked beside Cassie's small and now ageing Golf, and wondered how she'd react if he told her what his mother had been discussing with him tonight: selling both their houses and buying something bigger, with a granny flat for her.

'Then you won't be out all the time and we can be beside each other,' Antoinette had said cosily.

Shay was smiling as he got out of the car. This would solve all their problems. He wouldn't be racing off all the time to his mother's because

98

she'd be there. There would be no more rows. Result! Cassie would come round to it once she saw how it would work in all their favour. Just getting her to agree would be the problem. Cassie could be stubborn and she loved their house, but he knew how to work around her. It was a matter of picking the right time to tell her, that was all.

There were some nice new builds coming on to the market near the sea wall, which would be slightly closer to Delaney Gardens than their current house. Cassie would be closer to both Pearl and Coco with this plan, and Mam would be looked after. Everyone would be happy.

CHAPTER 5

It was a week of excitement, Vera, from across the square, told Pearl. A new family had possibly bought number twelve, which had been vacant for so long – although it was riddled with damp, God love them – and a special charity meeting was to be held in St Fintan's church hall on Friday night.

At least sweet Father Alex had the sense to have his meeting at six, Pearl thought, as she and some of her Thursday-nighters made their way slowly up the back lane, through the mock-Georgian Ashleigh Estate and into the church grounds. If all was over by seven, people would still be home in time for the soaps and she'd get a bit of September sun in her back garden.

At this time of year, the verandah Bernie had built all those years ago – utilising old furniture and packing boxes because they hadn't money for anything else – came into its own. Once he'd sanded it all down and painted it a pale south-of-France blue, nobody noticed that it was made from a hodgepodge of wood.

With the tangle of climbing roses and wisteria,

not to mention the scent of nicotiana that drove the bees half crazy, the verandah was the perfect place to soak up the heat before the cool of October arrived and got into Pearl's bones, making getting out of bed so hard in the morning.

'How are things, Madame Pearl?' asked Peter, slowing his long-legged pace to walk with her. Peter was a year younger, a lot taller and would give Gandalf a run for his money when it came to the long white silky beard and wise, smiling face.

'I'm wondering what we are to be charitable about tonight,' Pearl murmured. 'It's early for the Vincent de Paul Christmas drive.'

Peter considered this. 'The old church needs work but someone will have to win the lottery to do that.'

'Maybe it's a papal message about selling a few Michelangelos,' Pearl said wickedly. 'That would fix up the church and do a bit for charity – quite a few things for charity.'

Peter laughed. 'Don't say it to poor Alex: he's got enough on his plate as it is. And why—' Peter lowered his face so it was very close to Pearl's and she could smell that woodsy cologne he wore – 'did Edie come along? Is her broomstick in for a service and she can't get home?'

'You are so bad,' whispered Pearl. 'She's just lonely, you know that.'

'I can't drop round when she's there,' Peter murmured. 'Can't she be lonely in her own house?'

It was Pearl's turn to laugh gently.

'What's so funny?' said Edie, marching along and trying to keep up even though she was wearing her mink jacket and was roasting with heat.

Edie liked her furs and she had so little chance to wear them nowadays. It was a bit warm for the jacket but it was her favourite and surely there would be none of those mad, paint-throwing animal rights people in the church hall?

Mrs Maguire from The Pines had forgotten her hearing aid and Father Alex Wiersbowski, curate of St Fintan's, couldn't get the microphone to work.

'Plug it in,' said someone helpfully.

'Batteries?' shouted another kind soul.

Father Wiersbowski, who'd done a degree in fine art before his vocation, and who daily lamented the fact that men of religion were supposed to be brilliant at everything from comforting the dying to encouraging small children through the sacraments, twiddled the on and off buttons on the microphone with irritation. He was not a techie person.

He felt the eyes of the crowd on him. The church hall, cold even in high summer but warming up now due to some magic that had gone on in the boiler room thanks to Tom, the sacristan, was half-full with the older members of his congregation. Half full was good for the hall, better than the attendance at the actual church, where sometimes Father Wiersbowski wondered why he even went through the motions for a handful of the faithful.

Tonight, the Thursday night poker club people were here, which was a relief, because they were helpful, enthusiastic and blissfully funny. Unfortunately, Pearl's sister was also there. Mrs DeVere had to be handled carefully, like an unexploded bomb, a thought that made Alex Wiersbowski say a small prayer of contrition with guilt.

The thing was, Edie didn't approve of the modern Mass, wanted priests to talk permanently in Latin, and believed all young people – possibly himself included because he was only forty – were dangerous hoodlums hellbent on destroying society.

No point in explaining that the local secondary school – no doubt a hotbed of hoodlumism in Edie's eyes – had come up with the idea for the fundraising drive for the school that St Fintan's Church sponsored in Africa, and that the transition year students, all sixteen- and seventeen-year-olds, had pledged that they'd raise twenty thousand euros for the school.

They were doing sponsored walks, bag-packing in supermarkets, twenty-four-hour fasts: anything to raise the funds.

'Any chance the parish could match the money so we could send a grand total of forty thousand euros out when the students make their trip in March?' the principal of Parnell Avenue Secondary School had asked.

Poor Alex Wiersbowski had been caught between a rock and a hard place.

The school principal was another person to add

to the list of people he couldn't manage: the bishop; the bishop's private secretary; a frightening woman who ran the Legion of Mary; Pearl's sister, Edie DeVere; and now the school principal, Ms Wilson, who said 'Call me Maggie,' and rumbled some long-buried part of his brain where life before celibacy lurked.

'Well, I do not know,' he stammered, his Podkarpackie accent unleashing itself through the English he'd spoken for twenty years now as he thought about how he'd get out of this one.

The church needed repainting. He was worn out from travelling to three churches and two nursing homes every weekend trying to say Mass, bring Communion, organise funerals, weddings and baptisms, and keep old Father McGinty from blowing up the parochial house because he kept forgetting to turn off the gas burners on the cooker. Plus, Alex's car had ninety thousand miles on it and Lorcan, the mechanic, had said: 'Father Alex, I'd start praying to your boss, the Man Above, for a miracle, if I were you. That thing's barely roadworthy and one day she'll stop dead in the middle of the road and trust me, there won't be any coming back to life like that Lazarus fella.'

Alex didn't feel he had a flock so much as a small stampede of wildly diverse creatures to control, and now this principal was giving him another impossible job to complete.

'Ms Wilson,' he'd begun when she'd ambushed

him about the fundraising. He had to haul this back before it got out of hand.

'Call me Maggie,' said the principal again, with a smile. 'No need for Ms Wilson or Father Wiersbowski,' she'd added smoothly.

Alex closed his eyes as he remembered the meeting.

All this temptation, hard work and a car on the verge of death. And now this woman wanted him to get his parish – not a wealthy one, by any means – to come together to raise more money for the school in Africa, which had been his pet project all along, even though the parish had only managed small donations before. He could hardly say no.

His loyal parishioners had raised funds for the local poor and the homeless, but there were few houses in the St Fintan's parish where money wasn't an issue. How was he going to manage this? Where would the money come from?

He looked up at the hall roof with its telltale signs of damp: another crisis waiting to happen.

Maybe he should have gone on the Missions. Converting people to Christianity was more what he thought being a priest was going to be than this – this non-stop careful handling of people's moods and trying to be intuitive and prayerful on days when he felt tired and like going back to bed with a box set.

There was no joy to be had with the microphone. 'Shout,' advised the sacristan. 'You'll only have to say it all twice so Greta Maguire can hear you, otherwise. I don't think she knows how to work that hearing aid yoke, to be honest.'

Alex thought it might be nice to have a hearing aid himself so he could turn it off when he didn't want to hear what was being said.

Raising his voice, he explained about the school's plan to raise the money and how it would be wonderful 'if we can come up with some way to match the school's donation,' he finished up lamely, knowing that most of the people in the hall were living on pensions, worrying about their own health, worrying about children and grand-children and *their* futures.

'Say that again,' roared Mrs Maguire.

Her companion took it upon herself to loudly repeat the whole thing.

'Haven't we enough poor of our own here without helping other countries?' said Edie DeVere crossly, rearranging her fur jacket as if she was going to drop dead with cold.

Father Alex suppressed the ignoble thought that St Fintan's wasn't even Edie's parish and that selling the diamond eardrops attached to her earlobes might cut the fundraising total in half.

And what was it with the fur in September? Along the Carpathians, which ran to the west of his homeland, many people wore fur, but that was when the temperature dropped to minus twenty. There was no need for such a coat on an autumn evening in Ireland, especially now the sacristan had blasted the hall with heating.

Pearl was mightily sorry she'd allowed Edie to come along, and she glared at her sister. She was too long in the tooth to be embarrassed by anything Edie said. Lord knew she'd heard enough clangers from her sister's mouth over the past seventy-odd years to be used to them by now, but still Edie came up with them.

To put a stop to whatever next Edie was about to say, Pearl heard herself speaking. 'Father Alex, what a wonderful idea,' she said loudly, shooting Edie with a glance so acidic it would peel paint from a door.

Edie, used to it, didn't even appear to notice.

Pearl rolled her eyes. 'We will all help, won't we?' she went on, looking around at her friends and neighbours. '"When you open your heart to giving, angels fly to your door",' she quoted. 'I don't know who said that – it's of unknown origin.'

'What's this fascination with angels?' grizzled Edie. 'There's angels all over the place these days. Used to be hippies and hallucinogenic drugs, now everyone's seeing angels. There's even an angel shop opening up near me. What's wrong with saints and the like? Take Saint Philomena – I have a special devotion to her, myself.'

Peter and Pearl exchanged a glance. This was the first Pearl had heard of a 'special devotion' to St Philomena. Edie was just stirring it.

'What could we do?' Peter said calmly, to soothe the atmosphere.

Bingo nights were suggested. A raffle. This was considered. Raffles could make a lot of money.

'But what would we raffle?' asked Edie crossly.

'A loan of your fur for a week, Edie,' teased Peter, who was rewarded with a scowl.

The poker club all laughed, Gloria loudest of all.

'I'll bid for that,' said Liam cheerfully. 'I fancy myself in fur. Is there a hat to go with it? One of those little round furry Russian ones?' And the club were off giggling again.

A mad idea came into Pearl's head. Almost before she'd had a chance to try it out properly in her mind to see if it made any sense, she blurted it out. 'How about a week of fundraising, a festival of fundraising? We can have things on the green and down at the seafront.'

'Like what?' asked Adrienne.

'A sale of work and jumble sale one night,' Peter suggested. 'Those of us who paint could sell our canvases. Lord knows our friends and families would be glad not to have to take any more of them.'

There was a ripple of laughter at this. At least eight people in the parish painted. None expertly, but all with great joy. A local course had got them all started, and in fine weather they hauled easels and watercolours along to the sea wall, where they held up thumbs for hours at the sea or at the sugared-almond-coloured houses behind them, and then spent a lot of time sitting down, having a rest with flasks of tea and biscuits.

'A fashion show,' said Pearl suddenly. 'All the local clothes shops could do it. The Seaview Hotel would surely help out. My granddaughters would love to be involved too, I'm sure.'

Everyone knew Coco ran that pretty vintage clothes store and Cassie's company was in the papers all the time, running this event and that. With them on board, things would be organised, proper.

'I love the sound of that,' said Adrienne, her tired face perking up.

The poker wasn't enough, Pearl knew. Since Adrienne's daughter had gone off to London for work, she was like half a person, living for calls on Skype, so lonely without her grandkids. Her arthritis didn't help; it had got so bad she couldn't while away hours in her gardens, pretending to be busy. There was a hole in all their lives and a bit of chat around her fire once a week wasn't enough for it.

Edie made a noise like a warthog snorting, and then Gloria said something about how her great-granddaughter wanted to be a model and wasn't this just the chance to start her off on her great career.

Greta Maguire had a second cousin who had a son who made hats. 'Mad yokes. None of us would wear them, obviously. They're all made to look like UFOs or strange square things with feathers on, but sure, they'd be perfect for a fashion show.

Strange, you know. That's what the fashion crowd like.'

'Let's make a list, Father Alex,' said Pearl loudly and, as usual, everyone obeyed and started hunting around in pockets and handbags for bits of paper and pens.

Father Alex beamed with relief. At least he'd have help. There was no way in hell they'd make twenty thousand euros but they could do something, and the principal – Maggie – would get off his back. Pearl really was an amazing woman, no doubt about it.

Later that night, when Edie had been coaxed off in the direction of her own home in her ancient Mercedes, Peter and Pearl lay in her comfortable bed, with Peter twisted to one side as he smoked one of the rare cigarettes he allowed himself.

'Sorry,' he said as a plume of smoke drifted over towards Pearl, snug within the covers and her soft white sheets pulled up around shoulders tanned from summer in the garden.

'It's all right,' Pearl said. 'I don't mind after all these years. As long as you make the tea afterwards.'

'Don't I always?'

Peter turned to her and grinned, his long silver beard glittering in the candlelight.

He'd been marvellous-looking and charismatic in his youth and those looks had transformed into elegance and handsomeness all mixed in with an air of great wisdom as he'd aged.

'Uncle Peter was a real stunner,' Coco had said once, looking at old photos of Delaney Gardens from forty years ago when they held picnics on the lawn at midsummer and the Fourth of July, in honour of Peter's American wife, Loretta.

Still is, Pearl had thought to herself. She'd never told her granddaughters about her and Peter. Not that she was ashamed of it. They'd never so much as exchanged an illicit glance when Loretta was alive, had never for a moment thought of each other that way, but they were people with needs and had both ended up alone. One poker night Peter had stayed to help clean up and had stayed longer than he'd meant to.

It had been years since Pearl had felt a man's hands on her naked body: Jim's father, Bernie, was long dead, and raising the two girls kept her too busy to think of finding love again. She'd been in her sixties when Peter had come into her life and they'd had to be careful because of Coco and Cassie. It was easier now she lived alone, and yet her and Peter's love had been clandestine for so long, they'd thought: *why change it?* They brought each other joy and comfort.

Peter had no children. Loretta had suffered from some malady inexplicable in the early sixties, and she'd had three late miscarriages until, despite the exhortations from blithe male doctors to 'Keep trying, pet', they'd given up. There had been no groups for people denied parenthood then and

Loretta had never recovered from the loss of those three tiny babies.

Nobody had ever agreed with Peter that the heart attack that had killed his wife in her early fifties was the result of her poor, broken heart. Except for Pearl.

Slowly, years after they were both on their own, their friendship had turned to love. Love and kindness: the best combination of all, Pearl always reminded herself, feeling so lucky.

'I feel sorry for poor Father Alex,' Peter said, cigarette extinguished as he settled himself back into the bed, moving carefully because of his dodgy hip. He spooned his long body around Pearl's smaller, softer one, and stroked her shoulder gently. 'He'll never have this.'

'I know,' said Pearl. 'Crazy. We need all the love we can get.'

Inevitably, her thoughts ran to her grand-daughters. Coco had nobody to love in her life. And as for Cassie – Pearl could see that all was not well with that marriage. Yet it wasn't her place to interfere. She'd probably interfered enough long ago.

'Will you stay the night?' she asked Peter.

He didn't stay often. There were plenty of people up early in Delaney Gardens and not all of them understood the meaning of the word 'discretion'.

Peter held her to him. He'd catch the moon for Pearl.

'Of course,' he murmured.

CHAPTER 6

The second-to-last Sunday in September was Pearl's seventy-ninth birthday and an outdoor party in Delaney Square was planned, so when Cassie woke at half past six that morning to see the sun peeking in through a gap in the floral curtains in her and Shay's bedroom, she was delighted.

Pearl loved the sun and Cassie had so many memories of her grandmother sitting in her tiny garden soaking up the rays, knitting up a sweater or peeling apples for fruit pies – never just sitting doing nothing.

Beside her in the bed, Shay lay deeply asleep, one big hand flung out towards her as if reaching for her in a dream. It had been hot the previous night and he'd worn only boxers to bed, so his large, strong body was naked from the waist up, stretched out like a man from an underwear advert.

She'd fallen in love with that body first, she used to tease him. He'd been in the college football team, a 'jock', Cassie's friends had said dreamily, but he'd been smart too: an engineering student determined to do a PhD when he was finished his degree.

Cassie was studying business and their paths wouldn't have crossed except that Cassie and some friends had gone along to an after-game party and she had found herself being chatted up by the type of tall, muscular guy she'd never normally look at. He was freckled and fair-haired, a strawberry blond with hints of sun-kissed blond streaks. She knew without asking anyone that he'd have a stream of female fans after him.

'Haven't seen you at one of these crazy nights before, have I?' he said, a bruise developing nicely over one eye, remnant of the tough game. He was good-looking, no doubt about it, and knew it, Cassie decided. Guys who knew they were cute should come with health warnings.

'I like to stay in the library and talk to the geeky guys,' she'd replied with mock innocence. She might be wearing a pretty conservative student outfit of jeans and a white shirt, but once she'd been a wilder kid, the girl who liked her old studded leather jacket, and she'd had plenty of practice verbal fencing with equally wild boys.

Shay had leaned against the wall, and those eyes, blue with the same amber striation their daughter Beth had inherited, were almost hypnotic. He seemed to see through her with those eyes. 'I don't believe you,' he said. 'You look all buttoned up on the outside, but inside . . .'

Cassie had felt a strange leap of inner excitement

that neither the nerdy guys nor the wild ones had incited in her. Maybe he wasn't a dumb jock after all. Maybe he was smart.

'Inside you're something else. Want a drink, Library Girl?'

'Something soft, a lemonade or juice, Jock Boy,' she teased back. 'Us Library Girls don't want men taking advantage of us.'

'Damn,' he'd said. 'You just foiled my evil plan.'

Cassie stood on her tiptoes so she was closer to his ear. He was tall, she wasn't, and she lowered her voice to a breathy sexiness: 'We could always . . . talk.'

And they had. All evening. They'd eventually left the craziness of the party to find somewhere they could share a few slices of pizza and keep talking without being interrupted by someone turning the music up to eardrum-popping levels. After that, they'd been inseparable, and even though Shay had still called her Library Girl, by then he knew Library Girls were anything but boring.

It was a long time since he'd called her that, Cassie reflected. Years?

Having children had been such a wonderful step for them, yet grown-up life, work, and now having his mother permanently on the phone had turned the glorious romance between two students into something else entirely: a relationship held together by different strands, with what felt like all of the original attraction lost somewhere along the way.

Jock Boy had turned into a serious man with

weighty work issues in the engineering company where he worked, and as for Library Girl: she seemed like a creature from aeons ago, a figment of Cassie's imagination.

Shay stirred in his sleep, and briefly Cassie allowed herself to think of how once she'd have woken him up so they could take advantage of this quiet time to make love. She might have wriggled back under the covers and arched herself against him, rubbed her body against his muscular one. He cycled and ran, still keen on keeping in shape, and he still loved the feel of her body. Or at least he used to, she thought with a pang.

The great chasm of loneliness ached in her chest. She felt so unloved.

Why couldn't Shay understand he was pushing her away by giving all his attention to his mother?

She'd never explained her fear of abandonment but she was sure he understood. She was terrified of being left . . .

Suddenly, the thought became too frightening and a shiver of fear ran through her.

He could leave her.

Men left, the way mothers left.

Her heart palpitating, she thought of how much she loved Shay. They had two daughters together. Wasn't that enough?

They'd get through this because only dreadful mothers broke their families up. Mothers who didn't care who they hurt. Mothers who walked out and never came back.

Imagine a father who'd do the same if he was pushed too hard . . . No, they'd make it work. They had to.

Her chest tight with both remembered and current pain, Cassie slipped from the bed and quietly went downstairs to make a morning cup of calming herbal tea to bring back to bed.

It was rare to feel so alone in their house. There was always noise, her family pootling around, someone on the phone, the radio blasting loud modern music she never recognised anymore. But this morning she was blissfully alone and she walked in her bare feet along the wooden floors into the peppermint-green kitchen, where Fluffikins lay on the windowsill, luxuriating in the morning sun.

Once a tiny and indeed fluffy white kitten, Fluffikins had been named by Beth when she was nine and had since grown into a giant, grumpy moggy who should, by rights, have been named Lord Albert the Fifty-Sixth or something equally grand from the stately way he progressed around the house, barely deigning to sit on anyone's lap.

Fluffikins gave Cassie a cool stare and then closed his eyes again.

'Morning, your lordship,' Cassie said, but was ignored.

Animals were so simple – what you saw was what you got. There was no subtle subtext. She liked that, although sometimes, when she read about how animals could lower your blood pressure, she wished Fluffikins wasn't quite so lordly and would occasionally snuggle up to one of them. The person he liked most was Shay, who didn't like cats. Knowing Fluffikins, this made sense.

'Can't we get a dog?' Shay liked to say plaintively when Fluffikins had settled on his master's lap, calmly grooming and shedding white fur all over Shay's sweater.

'We could get a pug, like Pearl's Daisy! I love Daisy,' said Lily joyfully.

'But who'd walk the pug and take care of it during the day?' Cassie felt like the voice of doom but someone had to be reasonable around here. Her every nerve was already stretched, although she'd always loved dogs and had adored her Grammy's velvety-soft little dogs with their huge, happy eyes. Those dogs had helped her through so much. She could remember sitting with Basil and Sybil when her mother left, their shiny black fur pressed against her body as if they could comfort her with pure squishing . . .

'You're up early.'

She jumped, shocked, as two strong arms encircled her as she stood in the kitchen.

'I thought you were asleep,' she said, leaning back into her husband instinctively. He'd brushed his teeth before coming downstairs, she realised, and he nuzzled into her neck and shoulders from behind, planting delicate kisses on her skin.

Her body had missed his and she leaned further into him, reaching to grab his forearms and tangle her fingers with his. And then he'd turned her and Cassie was touching his fair head, pulling it down to hers.

It wasn't only women who needed sex to make them think they were loved, she thought briefly as they kissed, and she felt the tension drain away from her body. They could talk about his mother another time. *This* was something only they could share; this love could make their marriage strong so there would be no question of anyone leaving.

Edie planned to wear her good cream waffle-print dress, along with the diamond pin that Harry had given her on their twenty-fifth anniversary, to Pearl's birthday party. Harry might not have been the most faithful of men – not that she'd tell anyone that, especially not her sister – but he'd had wonderful taste in jewellery.

One of Edie's friends had told her over lunch that she should leave him that time in the early seventies when he'd taken up with the shop girl from the department store. The shop girl wasn't like the others: she was scheming, Edie's friend said. Scheming enough to see herself installed in Edie's house, and to heck with what people said.

'Why would I leave him?' Edie had replied, splendid in her favourite lunch outfit, an apple-green Jackie Kennedy-style suit – Jackie had such *style* – nicely accessorised with her Harry Winston bracelet, product of a holiday where Harry had done a lot of guilt-purchasing.

'What about your dignity, Edie?' the friend had cried.

'My dignity won't give him permission to live with a little floozy, spending our money and leaving me to wilt at home,' Edie had snapped back. 'Women on their own don't get asked out to the races or parties; they don't get diamond pins; they don't go on holidays unless they can hitch up with some widows or spinsters or other deserted women. There's no life for you if you don't have a man. No, I'm staying married, thank you very much. Harry will get over this; he always does.'

He had, eventually. Edie had a floor-length sable in her wardrobe from that one. Not that she went out of the house in it much. Pearl said she'd be mugged if she wore it.

'Robbers will take one look at you, know you've a few bob in your handbag, Edie, and you'll be lying on the ground in a flash, handbag gone, wrist broken, probably, and scared out of your mind. For goodness' sake, don't borrow trouble.'

Pearl, unconventional and all as she was, had never been stupid. She had a point. The young pups today who mugged elderly people – well, locking up wasn't good enough for them. Hard labour or even a go on that island surrounded by mangrove trees – what was it called? – Devil's Island. Yes, that was the ticket. None of this namby-pamby letting them out on bail to rob another poor person. If Edie was in charge of the criminal justice system, it would all be very different.

She adjusted the diamond pin on her dress. Her diamond drop earrings were too long to go with the pin: one had to be tasteful. The cluster ones would be fine today. Plus somebody had to be properly dressed for this shindig. Pearl wouldn't be. She wore those flowy cotton things, had her toenails painted deranged colours, and went around in strange sandals.

'They're Birkenstocks,' Pearl had informed her. 'You'd love them. So comfortable.'

'Style is not about comfort,' Edie had informed her in return, determined never to give up her beloved patent shoes with the low but elegant heels. She'd die before she wore anything flat and comfortable.

Of course, she was the only one with standards. Cassie would undoubtedly arrive wearing trousers and a long tunic-style thing over them; while Coco – Edie had a soft spot for Coco – would wear something old and although she'd look marvellous, as Edie kept explaining to her, men were wary of eccentric women and wearing old clothes was certainly eccentric. What that girl needed to do was get a husband and stop with all this career business. She'd had that Red O'Neill on the hook and somehow it had all gone wrong, and now look at him: always in the papers talking about that big business of his.

It wasn't that Coco wasn't pretty enough – she was. Took after her mother, actually, with that dark hair, the mischievous dark eyes and the wide, animated mouth. Cassie's daughters looked quite like her too, except for the eyes: Lily and Beth both had Shay's eyes. Not that Edie could ever say such a thing about the girls looking like Marguerite. Pearl had banned her from so much as mentioning their mother.

Coco had sex appeal too, or SA as they used to call it in Edie's day. Not that she seemed aware of it, goodness, no. It was Pearl's fault, Edie felt. Marguerite, for all her faults, had been sexy too and would have shown her daughters what to do with it, how to use it to get a husband. Cassie, who'd been sexy once, had managed to get the husband but Edie was sure she'd lose him. Cassie wasn't the practical type who'd be able to let Shay go off on the odd romp, and if she didn't buck up and start dressing nicely, she'd lose him to some young one for sure. Edie had seen it happen before.

Plenty of women thought their marriage was safe, but men had needs. Edie knew all about men and their needs, she thought darkly as she fingered her diamonds.

Pearl and Daisy were putting the last-minute touches to the flowers. Pearl had always favoured unusual vases, and today she'd found her old, cracked crimson and white Japanese teacups at the back of a cupboard, and was arranging some of the wildflowers Coco had brought from the florist.

Daisy, who liked to be in on the action, sat on the arm of the couch snuffling the flowers with her little black nose while Pearl sat at the dining room table, snipped stem lengths and tied teeny bouquets with string so they wouldn't fall apart once placed in the cups.

'Grammy,' said Coco, coming in with a platter of cakes covered with kitchen paper towels. 'You're supposed to be upstairs beautifying yourself. I said I'd do that—'

'I can do flowers,' interrupted Fiona, following on Coco's heels, carefully carrying a much smaller plate. She was dressed for the party in embroidered jeans, a pretty broderie anglaise top and a kaleidoscope of her home-made loom bracelets. Jo had put her daughter's hair up in a high ponytail, while Coco had supplied a flowery clip from the 1960s.

'Ms Doherty said I made the May altar look very pretty in school when it was my week to do it. Coco, I think we need more sparkles on the fairy cakes. They're not sparkly enough. Look.'

Fiona pulled the kitchen towel off her plate, which contained cakes decorated with sparkles, icing dust and multi-coloured sprinkles to within an inch of their lives. Fiona had even added some of the tiny hard silver balls, which looked glorious but nearly always made Pearl fear for her dentures when she mistakenly bit into them.

Pearl and Coco admired the little cakes.

'I don't know about you, Coco, but I think they're sparkly enough and very pretty,' Pearl said gravely.

Fiona pursed her delicate bow mouth. 'Mummy said that but Mummy doesn't understand cakes and sparkles. Not like you, Coco,' said Fiona innocently.

Pearl grinned as she watched her granddaughter being expertly manipulated by a nine-year-old.

'Well . . .' Entirely hooked, Coco considered it. 'If you think we need more . . .'

'Pearl has a box of sugar flowers in her cupboard,' Fiona revealed, blinking like a newly born fawn to take away from the fact that she'd been rummaging wildly in Pearl's cupboards looking for more things to stick on the cakes. 'They would help.' There was more fawn blinking.

Pearl reckoned that the sugar flowers were left over from a long-ago baking party with Lily and Beth, so would be as hard as rocks by now. Time for a cupboard clear-out.

'I'm not sure you can eat those, Fiona, because they're a bit old, so remember to tell people the flowers are for decoration only, OK, darling?' she said, and went back to her flowers.

Coco and Fiona headed off with the cakes again and Pearl kept smiling at the thought of her darling granddaughter's relationship with Fiona. If only Coco would see, really see, how glorious it would be to have her *own* children, then she might think more about settling down. There was no sign of Coco dating anyone, and the odd date she went on invariably turned into disaster.

'All the good men are gone,' Coco would say with an air of good humour, if asked about this.

But Pearl wondered if the problem ran deeper. Was Coco so afraid of being abandoned that she ran away from relationships?

No, Pearl decided. She'd been with Red for a long time. Two years, although it was nearly twice that since he'd left her.

There had to be something else. Perhaps she simply wasn't meeting the right ones.

Or was it fear of being in a relationship and then, eventually, being a mother?

That thought made Pearl feel weak with misery and guilt all at once.

She'd talk to Jo about it later. Coco's best friend had always had her head screwed on correctly. If anyone could make Coco see that love was a fundamental part of human happiness, it was Jo. No matter that Jo didn't have the love of her life in the form of a man – she had it in her precious daughter. She'd want Coco to have that too. A husband, a child, some precious family of her very own.

CHAPTER 7

'I am not ticking "bubbly",' said Coco fiercely, staring at the ForeverInLove.com website as Jo logged on to it. 'That's code for people like me: not too tall but could lose a few pounds – or more than a few pounds.'

'You don't need to lose any weight,' said Jo automatically. 'And there's no box for bubbly. A lot of them work by psychometric testing. You answer a whole series of questions and they set you up with a group of guys. You don't list your vital statistics. This whole dating thing has changed. It's more scientific, less of the "GSOH, loves hamsters and old movies". Although they do use photos.'

Yeah, right, huge change there, Coco thought miserably, remembering how fat her calves had looked that morning when she'd put on her favourite swing skirt and had twirled to see it from behind. How had she not noticed this before? Thirty years of living and her ginormous calves had hidden themselves from her, hiding in plain sight. Another flaw.

No, she and her flaws weren't ready for this.

Using a dating site was asking for trouble. Meeting friends of friends was less complicated – often tricky but not impossible – but strangers, *total strangers,* on websites looked at photos and read the information looking for clues. Looks were vital, no matter how many psychometric tests you did.

And some sites did make space for 'describe yourself'. 'Petite' was undoubtedly website code for a short, too-rounded piglet who lived entirely on chocolate and wore fifties clothes to hide this fact.

How she regretted that five-minute dating conversation now. Jo had found her at a weak moment at Grammy's birthday party, when everyone had been happy, and the house and green had been full of merry people, chatting, hugging and being lovely. Under those circumstances, it was easy to think the whole world was just as welcoming. She'd momentarily let her guard down and agreed with Jo that it *might* be nice to have a man in her life, and Jo had instantly said they had to go online to search for suitable men before Coco changed her mind.

'It is different for me, kiddo,' Jo had said. 'I've got Fiona. I don't think I could fit a man in my life, to be frank. Unless he was brilliant at cooking, because you know how useless I am. I mean, that might work . . . but really, I'd . . .' Jo had paused. They were sitting on the green, enjoying the evening sun beside the fig tree and watching Fiona playing cards with Peter and Pearl, who were being taken to the cleaners.

'I'd love you to experience motherhood, Coco. It's incredible. I've never said that before because I didn't want to do the whole *you know nothing because you're not a mother* shtick. I hate women who do that. Also, I know how complex a subject parenting is for you because of . . . you know, your own mother. But it's incredible.' Jo's eyes were misty as she stared at her daughter laughing riotously as she collected up all the Monopoly money she'd won at snap, and Coco had wanted to cry too.

'It's love like nothing else, Coco,' Jo had finished.

'Yeah, I know,' Coco mumbled, then managed to say something about getting more sandwiches because there were still some left in the fridge and the party would be winding up soon.

As she ran towards the safety of Pearl's home, she breathed deeply so she wouldn't let herself down and cry in front of everyone.

The subject of motherhood was like a flare with a short fuse in her mind. Mothers were not reliable. They never came home. Grammy Pearl had been an incredible substitute but she hadn't been Coco's real mother.

She'd gone.

Despite Jo's interruption all those years ago, Coco could still hear the schoolroom taunts from Paula: 'She's a crybaby who made her ma leave.'

Maybe she had. Maybe her mother had been

incapable of being a mother and Coco's birth had pushed her over the edge. Maybe Coco herself had been to blame. Maybe it was genetic. No matter what, Coco couldn't bear to go down that route. She might be just like her mother and want to run as soon as she'd had her children. She would not subject a child to what she'd gone through.

Cassie had got it out of her system by being a wild child when she was a teenager, but Coco had repressed all the pain until she'd been with Red.

Then it had come out, and look what had happened.

But Jo had kept the subject alive.

'Let's look at dating sites,' she'd said cheerfully on Friday evening when Coco, Jo and Fiona were in Coco's apartment after having a quick pasta supper, which was something they did every few weeks. Coco was a marvellous cook and Fiona loved going to her quirky apartment two streets away from Delaney Gardens, where the walls were covered with art deco gallery prints Coco had picked up over the years, and the faded amethyst couch was a vast velvet nest of embroidered cushions and squishiness. Fiona was sitting cross-legged on the fluffy violet rug, playing at the low coffee table, and inventing a new hat with an old sunhat and bits and bobs from Coco's always replenished 'things to be repaired' box from the shop.

After a while of registering on one site and

looking at pictures of wildly attractive men that had Coco reconsider her point that 'you can't choose someone to love from their photo', they were at the knotty part of agreeing what Coco was really looking for in a man.

'Let's see what we can agree on,' said Jo, looking at the dating website. 'We'll think of your dream list and write it down so you can pick guys who fulfil those ideals. Handsome?'

'Hell, yes. Definitely handsome,' said Coco wearily, giving in. She might as well give it one last go. Couldn't hurt – apart from how awful it would be if she and her calves were rejected. And she *was* lonely, not that she'd admit it to anyone.

'No, that's wrong to look for handsome,' she said suddenly. Here she was worrying over fat calves and yet she was ready to pick a mate based entirely on looks.

'OK, let's not look for handsome. Taller than you, though?'

Coco agreed. On the list of prospective male requirements, this one wasn't hard to achieve. Most men were taller than her. The Seven Dwarfs were taller than her. Coco insisted she was five two, but had embroidered on that last inch. Red had been six foot exactly. He'd been able to lift her up effortlessly. Nobody would ever be able to do that again.

'You need to be looking for solvent,' Jo went on. 'You've got to be realistic.'

Coco nodded grudgingly. She'd been out with

a few non-solvents over the years when she had dated and it was always expensive. They had the best taste in wine, the most romantic ideas for weekends away, but funds ran out at the most inopportune moments and Coco always had to cough up. Paying for your own flowers/wine/birthday gifts did tend to pall. But, after Red, she hadn't wanted a career man; she'd wanted someone entirely different from him. Unfortunately, this tended to mean men with no money and less ambition than sloths.

'You need solvent, Coco. Even half a job,' Jo said sternly. 'Apart from Red, you've been going for broke men in bands or performance artists living with their mothers and getting rent allowance. You need a guy who doesn't think jobs are for the little people. Now, you can figure them out pretty quickly on most of the sites – "searching for his passion in life" means he's failed at ten things and is trying to figure out what number eleven is. Also means you will be footing every bill.'

Coco still hadn't exhaled after the mention of Red's name. She hated people even mentioning him. He was handsome, solvent, all the things on every woman's top-ten list on every dating website, but he'd left her. It had all been his fault.

Besides, it had been a lucky escape, when she thought about it – as she had, endlessly. He'd been too Type A and demanding.

So there would be no more go-getters, no more high-achievers for Coco. They could deliver a killer heart blow in a way that dreamy non-solvents never could.

'I like artists and musicians,' Coco began, nose in the air.

Jo gave her a harsh look. 'That's playing the romantic card, as if you're a terrible romantic who's still looking for Mr Darcy, and we both know he does not exist.'

Jo used to be a romantic until she became pregnant with Fiona, whereupon romance was knocked clean out of her mind with the knotty problem of a boyfriend who had decided this baby lark wasn't for him as soon as the pregnancy test showed the two blue lines. Fiona's father apparently now lived in the Philippines with a wife and young family, and had never met his daughter. Coco was listed as Fiona's guardian because Jo's family situation was complex.

'Jane Austen has a lot to answer for,' Jo remarked, as she had many times before. 'How many handsome, rich, single men are there out there who own an estate like Pemberley, know how to apologise for a messed-up proposal and save your sister from disaster – tell me that?'

Coco and Jo laughed. 'If one does exist, he doesn't need to be on ForeverInLurve dot com,' Coco said. 'He's probably beating women off with a stick.'

The TV was tuned to a children's channel but both Jo and Coco knew Fi was listening breathlessly to the conversation.

'A dog,' said Fiona. 'He needs a dog. Can you say Coco wants a man with a dog, Mum?'

'You're probably right, Fi,' said Coco humbly. 'Men who like animals are nice. Do you think that nice vet on Bondi Beach is available?'

'Sadly, I doubt it,' Jo said, with genuine regret. 'Another man who looks as if he needs a stick to keep the women away. Should we say you like opera? Do you think you'd get a more interesting type of guy if he likes opera as well as playing air guitar?'

The women gazed at each other.

'I like listening to opera,' conceded Coco. '*Madame Butterfly* makes me cry. But I don't know if I could sit through a whole one. And I like guys who adore rock music.'

She typed some more.

'No opera,' she muttered. 'Honesty is the best policy.'

'We *have* said I'm five two,' Coco pointed out.

'We should make you taller. You can wear heels. There's probably a subsection of men who only like short women. You know, like there are men who only go for bigger girls or women with huge . . .' She glanced meaningfully down at Coco's large breasts.

'I've met all of them,' Coco said. 'Those guys only see 38DD.'

'What's 38DD?' asked Fi, on cue.

'The bus from Blackrock into the city,' said her mother.

Fiona, nine and a quarter, possessor of the steely mind of a German chancellor, pondered this for a moment. 'That's a fib,' she said.

'Fiona McGowan, are you accusing me of telling fibs?' demanded her mother with fake shock.

Fiona giggled. 'She tells them all the time, Coco. You don't get sick if you don't eat green things every day: Louise in school told me. All mums say that and it's not true. Chocolate cereal is good for you too, and you say it's not a proper breakfast.'

'I always feel that the milk's the healthiest bit,' agreed Coco, who was secretly very fond of chocolate cereal herself.

'Milk is really good for you,' Fiona said, as if that made the whole thing all right. 'Chocolate milk is a food group, Mum, isn't it?'

'We have work to do on our food issues,' Jo sighed. 'Tomato ketchup is not a vegetable, by the way, Fi.'

Fiona's eyes twinkled as she went back to her hat-making. 'I know,' she said. 'But chips are.'

Jo and Coco controlled their laughter and looked at the website again.

'Right, do you want to do this or not?' asked Jo.

'Sign me up,' Coco said with an air of resignation.

When Jo and Fiona had gone home, Coco double-locked the apartment front door and tidied up the kitchen. Then she sat down on the couch again and flicked through the evening TV schedules to see if there was anything to amuse her for another hour before bed. She used to be keen on social media and had kept up with all her old pals from college, but since Red and the broken engagement she'd stopped and rarely went back on again.

All those months of chatting with people who'd seen her changed status: *Engaged! To the most wonderful man in the world!*

These giddy words of love were followed by photos of herself and Red doing things that were ultra-ordinary but were gilded with excitement because it was the two of them together, in their glorious bubble of love. They'd walked the pier in Dun Laoghaire, with Red taking pictures of them waltzing around the Victorian bandstand, eating ice creams in the park, hiking up to Mahon Falls on a blissful summer weekend in Waterford, marvelling at the sheer scale of the Giant's Causeway and how the smooth basalt rocks looked as if a giant had indeed placed them there.

And her favourite photo of all, one she'd never put on Facebook, was of them together in her bed, just a close-up of their faces against the creamy pillows, blissfully happy with love, a sheen on their skin from lovemaking, smiling as Coco held the phone up to capture the sheer power of their happiness.

She'd loved that photo; used to look at it when Red was out of the country on business, phoning from airports and conferences, muttering softly about how much he missed her and what he'd do to her when he got back. When she forgot herself and let the photo get into her head, Coco could still feel her body cuddled up to Red's long, strong one, his heat against her. He was the only man who'd ever made her feel fragile and pretty; the only man who'd never made her worry about her little pot belly or how curvy her legs were instead of the long slim ones she'd prayed for since she was a teenager.

They'd probably looked ludicrous together, she told herself when it was over: her short, verging on the pocket siren, and him tall and with a broad chest like the heroes in the books her girlfriends used to read in school. Big hands and long, mobile fingers that could do things to her body that made her laugh and gasp all at the same time . . .

On her couch, TV remote in hand, Coco felt the familiar misery well up in her. She'd never told anyone how it had really ended, not even Cassie, and they were as close as it was possible to be. Some things you couldn't tell anyone.

She could still see the anger in his face that last day. Red was never angry with her. He cherished her, Pearl used to say, like she was a precious jewel.

'The way that man looks at you . . .' Pearl said happily. 'He's a keeper.'

It had been raining, needles of rain that had left the streets puddled with water.

Coco had avoided all Red's phone calls since the night before.

She'd raced home after the horrible scene in the restaurant, grabbed a few things, and had driven off at high speed to stay with Jo, whom she'd ordered not to let Red in, even if he turned up.

He hadn't.

He'd phoned. Nine times, nine messages, pleading in eight of them, until he'd ended with one cold message: 'If you want to talk, I'll see you tomorrow at one outside Bellamy's. We can sort this out then. Bye, Coco.'

Not even an 'I love you, Coco' like in all the other messages.

Bellamy's was the city centre restaurant where they'd met, even though they'd grown up only streets from each other.

Coco hadn't opened the shop that morning because she'd kept crying and having to repair her make-up. But she got to the restaurant on time, wearing Jo's raincoat, which was too big for her, and a pair of black trousers, also Jo's, because she felt so fat and ugly, and she thought they might be slimming.

Red was sitting outside at one of the black cast-iron tables, menu ignored in front of him.

'Why didn't you wait for me or even listen to me?' he said instantly, and Coco was astonished to see how angry he was.

He had the most amazing colouring: that dark red hair and the skin that tanned so easily, now darkened with anger.

'I'm not waiting if that's how you're going to talk to me,' said Coco shakily.

She didn't move towards him so Red shoved the extra chairs out of his way to join her on the street, the screeching of cast-iron chairs alarming the two women sitting at the next table dithering over what to have for lunch.

'You have to trust me, and if you can't, Coco, what sort of future do we have?' he said. 'I can't believe you'd rush off like that. As if I'd hurt you like that, as if I'd cheat on you . . .' He stopped, as if he couldn't manage to say anything else because the notion of his cheating was so incomprehensible.

But Coco had seen him with the other woman. That was her proof.

'But I *saw* you! I saw you with her. She's everything I'm not. How do I know she's not what you want all along?'

The other woman had been tall, Bikram-yoga-lean, with well-behaved long blonde hair: the exact opposite of Coco. She surely was a model, even if Red had said she was someone he'd been asked to get a job for, and that night she'd looked like the sort of suited-and-spike-heel-booted woman who never needed to diet, never worried if her bum looked big in anything. The sort of woman who could take another woman's man away from her.

'I told you what happened,' Red said fiercely. 'I would never cheat on you, Coco. How can you not believe me?'

His hair was spiked up from his running his

fingers through it and the rich mahogany red that had given him his nickname when he was a kid was darker now, the colour of beech leaves.

His voice was hard. 'You either believe me, Coco, or you don't.'

It had started to rain again then, a crazy monsoon-like autumn downpour, and still they had stood there, the rain making Coco's borrowed coat cling to her and turning Red's navy business suit to black.

'I need you to believe me, Coco. Hell, we're getting married in a month.'

'I don't believe you,' she said in a whisper.

How could she? She'd seen what she had seen.

She tried to wriggle the antique ring off her finger. They'd bought it in Gray's, the lovely family-run shop in Johnson's Court off Grafton Street. It was an art deco-inspired square Ceylon sapphire of the palest blue in a princess cut surrounded by eight little diamonds. It felt tight so she had to pull, while Red watched her stone-faced.

'*I* don't want it,' he said grimly.

Finally she wrenched the ring off and she reached out to hand it to him. He didn't move.

'I don't want it,' he said, his face harder than she thought it could ever be. 'Don't you hear anything I say? You don't hear that I love you. You don't hear that I'd never ever cheat on you.'

She dropped it at his feet, tears and rain combining as they ran down her face.

'I don't want it either. Give it to *her*.'

She turned and ran, blindly at first, because in her grief she wasn't sure where she was anymore. When she reached the corner she looked back and he was standing there like a statue, as if he hadn't moved or even picked up the ring.

Four years ago. Four years and she could still remember it as if it was yesterday. Coco rubbed away her tears with the sleeve of her beloved pink and moss-green Fair Isle cardigan and flicked the TV remote until she found the grisliest crime show she could bear.

That's why she liked crime shows on TV: the bad people got caught and punished no matter what. In a crazy world, at least you could rely on that.

CHAPTER 8

On Saturday morning, on a small hill farm in Wicklow, Phoebe McLoughlin surveyed the duck house and sighed. Giorgio, number one duck and the chattiest of the bunch, stood beside her.

'It's not your fault, Giorgio, I know,' Phoebe told him. 'Toilet training isn't in your genetic code.'

Giorgio made his gentle murmur. He didn't quack like the other ten ducks. He had an entire selection of noises and this one was his version of: *Sorry, nothing I can do about it, Phoebe.*

'You know you can't come in with me when I'm cleaning your house,' Phoebe told him kindly.

Giorgio protested and gazed up at her.

'No, really, you might be flattened. You know what I'm like when I'm going hell for leather. Go off, find Rocha and de-slug the garden. It rained so much last night, there must be a million slugs and snails in the lilies.'

She shoved the cap down on her head and bent enough to enter the duck house, a small stone-built shed with a galvanised roof. The ducks had low comfortable nests made of hay and the floor was scattered with fresh hay once a week. First, Phoebe had to clean it out, of course, which meant shovelling out the droppings, washing the whole place down and cleaning the nesting boxes. Her favourite part of the entire event was when it was over for another week.

Sighing, she began shovelling, doing her best to ignore the smell and send her mind off to where she liked to go when she had to clean out all the animal sheds: into the world of fashion.

Today's daydream involved a phone call to her fabulous studio in . . . Phoebe's shovel caught on the old sticking-up bit of stone floor. Caught her out every time.

In Paris, yes. Not that she'd *been* to Paris, but she'd read so much about it, had seen films about it, although she wasn't sure that the Matt Damon one where he was an amnesiac assassin would be much help in that it showed a lot of the actual city but none of the glorious women with Gallic chic and amazing heels. Phoebe was no good with heels herself. It was the wellington boots, she thought grimly, shovelling more duck shit. Your average nineteen-year-old girl got to practise in heels but she spent much of her life in either the old clogs her mother used to wear or in wellies. Farm life in Dromolach, a small town in the Wicklow Hills, didn't mean either the money or the opportunity for Manolo Blahniks.

But no point dwelling on the negatives. Paris . . .
Yes, Miss Gaga, Phoebe would be delighted to

design a dress for you. She won't work in meat,
though. She's a vegetarian. Her closest friends are
cows, ducks and chickens, you know. Silk crêpe de
Chine and Vionnet bias cut is more her style . . .
She's working on a series of designs inspired by
Russian Orthodox iconography. You'd like that? Oh
yes? Phoebe will start working on the gown straight
away . . .

The duck shed took her forty-five minutes because she was doing a thorough job. She wouldn't be home again for two weeks and Ma wouldn't have time to do it. There was no way she and the kids were going to suffer because Phoebe was going to college in the city. If she had to get the bus home every weekend, then so be it. The city lights would have to burn brightly without Phoebe McLoughlin. The McLoughlin clan stuck together – had done ever since Dad had died.

A gentle and inquiring clucking at the door made Phoebe rub her eyes and look up.

'Donna, pet, what's wrong?'

If Giorgio was her favourite duck, Donna Karan was her most beloved hen. Half Silkie, half Rhode Island Red, she looked like a child's auburn knitted pompom brought to life. Sweet, wildly bossed over by the other hens, and entirely Phoebe's pet, Donna liked to follow Phoebe around as she did her chores.

'Did you get thrown out of the henhouse?'

Donna clucked mournfully.

'Honestly, girl, what are you going to do when you don't have me to stand up for you?' Phoebe said. She bent to stroke Donna, who cooed happily. 'Things are going to be different and if you let the girls boss you, you'll be miserable. I won't be here, you know . . .'

Donna did a few more mournful clucks and began poking around on the floor for something edible. 'You'll be fine,' Phoebe informed her firmly. 'Everyone will be fine without me. I'll be home in ten days and then every weekend. You won't know I'm gone.'

'You won't know I'm gone,' Phoebe said to her family as she stood, rucksack on one shoulder and her cross body messenger bag weighing her down in the kitchen the next day – leaving day. September wild flowers that her little sister, Mary-Kate, had collected for Phoebe's special going-away dinner still sat on the scrubbed wooden table, and Prince, the sheepdog, lay under the table with his nose burrowed in his paws, canine senses registering off-the-scale human misery.

Nobody was to come to the bus station with Phoebe.

'Tommy Joe will drive me,' she'd said briskly, as if briskness would ward off any tears. 'He'll be glad of the business now the tourists are nearly gone.'

Phoebe wasn't sure whose tears she was trying to ward off: hers or everyone else's.

'Mind yourself, Mary-Kate, and look after Donna

for me, will you? Check her every day when you collect the eggs. She's still getting pecked sometimes.'

Mary-Kate lifted the freckled chin that was so like her older sister's and nodded. Her eyes, the same colour as the autumn beech leaves, were wet with tears.

'I'll install close circuit TV while you're gone,' she said with a hint of her usual sparkiness. 'Hen TV. For those nights when there's nothing else on the box.'

Phoebe bit her lip. 'Brilliant idea. Don't know why I didn't think of it, MK,' she said, wondering if she'd been as brave and funny at sixteen. 'You could do that for the Young Scientist competition.'

'Nah,' said Ethan – fourteen, gangly and wearing the precious Man United football shirt that was too big for him. 'She's doing nuclear fusion. Or cooking, as she calls it.'

Mary-Kate managed a quick punch on the arm before Ethan bounced away, grinning.

'Obviously no killing each other when I'm gone,' Phoebe said. 'Killing can only happen when I'm here to referee.'

Everyone held their breath. She wouldn't be back for two weeks. Phoebe had never been away that long before, even when she'd gone to Dublin to show her portfolio to the fashion college. That had been two days and two nights and it had seemed to last forever.

Her being gone for two weeks didn't seem right.

The McLoughlin family were closer than a four-some of Siamese twins – everyone said so. They had been since the accident had taken Dan McLoughlin. The whole family never fought, always looking out for each other.

'You're in charge of the ducks, Ethan,' Phoebe told her brother, moving on swiftly.

Ethan sniffed.

'And Prince,' Phoebe went on. 'You're in charge of dog food and his water bowl.'

None of this was entirely necessary because Ethan loved the sheepdog more than anyone else in the family and would have Prince sleeping in his bed, if possible. Phoebe and her mother had decided that Ethan needed to feel he was looking after someone else, and making it official that he was Prince-Minder-in-Chief was part of this plan.

'Give him more than the ducks, Phoebs,' Mum had said. 'He doesn't love the ducks the way you do. Let's put him in charge of Prince.'

Phoebe had smiled. That was classic Mum; rearing three children single-handedly had taught her skills that would put Dr Phil to shame.

'You're guilty about leaving us and you shouldn't be,' Mum went on. 'I lean on you too much. It's my fault.'

Phoebe hugged her mother. She was taller now, even though Kate McLoughlin was a tall woman. Phoebe was nearly six feet in her socks and she prayed she stopped growing soon or she'd get into the *Guinness Book of Records* for something other than being the most successful fashion designer ever.

'It's not your fault. You don't lean on me,' lied Phoebe. 'I wouldn't be going if it wasn't for you.'

She wouldn't have applied to the design college if her mother hadn't insisted.

'You all need me,' she'd argued. 'Lots of people go into fashion without qualifications. I can do it over the internet and work on my pattern cutting here. I can do it—'

'Not you, Phoebe,' her mother said. 'What would your dad think if he looked down now and saw me stopping you from fulfilling your potential? He'd think I'd failed, that's what.'

Kate was flushed from playing her ace. Now she only talked about their dad on birthdays and at Christmas. Three and a half years ago, when he'd died after a tractor accident, she'd talked about him all the time.

'Your dad would want us to get on and be happy,' she'd say determinedly, not realising they could all see the tears about to leak down her face. Kate McLoughlin had worked hard to talk about her husband. Kids did better when they were able to face their grief, not hide it away from a distraught parent. No matter how much it hurt her, she made sure their father was still alive in their hearts even if he wasn't there physically.

'He'd never think you failed us, Mum,' Phoebe said now, knowing she was beaten.

★   ★   ★

Tommy Joe's taxi smelled strongly of car freshener in a scent that was allegedly pine. Having grown up with woods surrounding her home, the little green smelly Christmas tree hanging from the mirror smelled like nothing coniferous Phoebe had ever encountered.

'Off to the big smoke,' said Tommy Joe congenially, as he rattled the old Cortina at breakneck speed down the mountain lanes. 'You're back at the weekends, though, your mother says. Ah sure, they'll be lost without you.'

'They'll be grand,' said Phoebe, determined to stop her lip quivering. 'They won't know I'm gone.'

'Well, if the snow comes, you won't be able to get through the Sally Gap and you'll have to stay in town,' Tommy Joe went on. 'It's great living on the mountain until the bad weather comes in. Remember when that Sky television team got stuck up the mountain with their big jeep and they had to be rescued? When it snows up here, Phoebe, nothing gets through. A tractor, now . . .' Tommy Joe added thoughtfully. 'That would be your only man, but you might lose it in a ditch and then where would you be?'

Phoebe turned up the radio, tuned as ever to something country. A man with a soulful voice was singing about how his heart was broken and it would never be fixed again.

'Now that's a man who can sing,' said Tommy Joe with satisfaction and all conversation stopped.

It never occurred to him that his passenger's father had died in a tractor accident.

Phoebe kept staring out the window but she wasn't seeing anything anymore. If she reached into her bag for a tissue, Tommy Joe might notice. They had enough time for the journey to the train station for the tears to have dried on her face.

'You don't have much stuff, do you?'

The landlady, a stout woman in a housecoat who said her name was Mrs Costello, stared suspiciously at Phoebe's rucksack and the cross body messenger bag. 'I hope you won't be skipping out without paying the rent?'

'No,' said Phoebe, trying to be upbeat with only a chocolate bar, a muffin and a strong coffee inside her. Her tears from earlier were gone. Here, in a small, dingy house in Delaney Gardens, was her new home, and just because Mrs Costello had clearly had bad experiences before with students didn't mean that they should get off to a bad start.

Mrs Costello's son, a fellow student, had shown Phoebe around the bedsit the first time in June when she'd snapped it up – despite the general air of decrepitude and the loud gurgling of the water heater in the corner.

'Bedsits are going like flies,' he'd informed her.

And Phoebe, who read the papers and knew that September was like the first day of the sales when it came to rented accommodation for students, had put a deposit down even though bedsit number four was hardly a palace. The clincher for her was the location: Delaney Gardens was about ten minutes' walk from Larkin College of Art and Design, and the square itself was like a little oasis of country flowers in the middle of the city, which had made Phoebe sigh with pleasure.

The square was made up of small two-storey workers' houses dating from the 1930s, she reckoned, with long front and back gardens and all manner of fascinating plants and shrubs. Across from this house there was a home painted an almost peppermint green with the crimson of Virginia Creeper clustering around its walls; another with cerulean windowpanes and what looked like a Venus de Milo dressed languidly in moss staring out at the central garden area, where shrubs and plants were abundant. Phoebe was sure that was a fig tree in the centre of the handkerchief-sized green. She'd never had fresh figs, never seen them grown, and couldn't imagine they would in Ireland. Surely they were for tropical countries? But her father could have grown them: her father had had green fingers.

She dragged her gaze from the window to listen to her new landlady, who was explaining the rules, of which there were many. No men friends over. Nobody staying over at night. No parties.

Phoebe looked at the small room, where there was just enough space for a tiny old two-seater couch, a defiantly single bed, a kitchenette and an afterthought of a shower room with a toilet, all of which was jammed into a corner and cobbled together with cheap wood. The bathroom was the other bonus for her: privacy.

'No parties, right,' she said gravely to Mrs Costello.

It was a squeeze with the two of them in there. Phoebe was sure that if more than three people were gathered in the room, the fire brigade would have to cut one of them out.

Perhaps she might meet a troupe of acrobats and have parties with them draped in odd positions on the curtain rails. Otherwise, she was destined to sit here alone.

'Hmm,' said Mrs Costello, giving Phoebe the sort of look practised by suspicious customs officials scenting blocks of cocaine in people's suitcases. 'See you do understand,' she said. 'There's no house phone,' she went on. 'You all have those mobiles now. Used to cost me a fortune in the old days and the phone in the hall never stopped. Nurses . . .' Mrs Costello's face went red. 'Nurses were the worst. Always organising parties.'

Phoebe thought she might possibly giggle at this point. One of her best school friends, Carla, was in nursing training college. Carla had lost half a stone in her first year from sheer exhaustion, was shattered every night and wanted to know why the entire population believed that young nurses were wild, untethered creatures who needed to dance all night, every night.

'When evening comes, all I have the energy for is sleep!' Carla said crossly.

151

Phoebe looked once more out the window at the square towards the pretty houses on the other side. 'It's so beautiful here,' she said, trying to drag the conversation back to something less contentious.

'Humph,' said Mrs Costello, following her gaze. 'Some foreigners moved in last year. Not that they're noisy yet but you don't know when it'll start. Gloria O'Brien lives in that house. Her husband's gone gaga, in a home. And that's Pearl Keneally's house over there. Always a crowd in there on a Thursday,' she added grimly. 'Playing poker, I hear.'

'That sounds like fun,' said Phoebe. She could remember many evenings at home with her father teaching her the card games he'd learned as a kid in County Clare: twenty-five; its more complex cousin, forty-fives; pontoon; and gin rummy. In the remote countryside where he'd been brought up, his mother had cycled off on her bike many a night to different houses, where they'd play for hours to win a goose or a duck.

'There's a washer and dryer in the utility room. Coin-operated,' Mrs Costello continued, taking a look at Phoebe's very plain outfit. 'What did you say you were studying?'

'Fashion.'

'You wouldn't know it,' were Mrs Costello's final words as she departed, with a last look at the bedsit as if she were leaving a room of valuable antiques and sets of Sevres china to a couple of bulls.

Phoebe giggled to herself as the door shut loudly behind her and began to unpack. She wasn't sure what she could do to make bedsit number four, painted a bilious green, look homely, but she'd try.

Once she'd unpacked and laid her possessions out in the bedsit to make it feel more like her own place, Phoebe stared, as she had so many times before, at her wardrobe. In Wicklow, living in a farm in the hills, there had not been much call for high fashion. Even though Phoebe had lived and dreamed clothes since she was nine, had collected *Vogue* with her pocket money, and had fantasies about cutting exquisite garments and draping them straight on to model's bodies, her own wardrobe was somehow less than fashionista. Tall, strong girls looked ridiculous in modern cream tulle with a felted bodice: the outfit Phoebe was sure had finally won her a place in the prestigious Larkin College of Art and Design.

Phoebe had made the outfit for Lizette, a platinum-haired hair-dresser from the village, and she'd modelled it for the photos. But Lizzy was small and slender-boned, while Phoebe had no slender bones anywhere and had been a star netball player all during school. Finding jeans to fit her long legs was a nightmare. The best thing she'd ever made for herself was a heavy wool coat, slightly eighteenth century in design with a long, sweeping tail to it, but since then she'd been too busy with school, the farm and her portfolio to make much else.

She'd been trying to make a new wardrobe for herself since she'd heard she'd got the place in Larkin in June, but there was so rarely any time. The sheep needed to be taken care of, the hens and ducks needed to be fed and their houses cleaned out. Phoebe had her part-time job at The Anvil, the nearest pub where farmers went for their few pints, and where a complicated system of designated drivers had been set up to cope with the drink-driving laws. Not that everyone went along with it.

Due to her height, Phoebe was considered a good woman for taking the keys off recalcitrant men who'd decided that imbibing six pints meant they were perfectly fine to drive the pick-up truck home that night.

'You'll thank me in the morning,' Phoebe used to say, and earned herself a few extra quid in her pay packet and a smile from the owner, a small woman who could pull a great pint but was no good when it came to playing car-key tag with drunk customers.

The job meant she had the money for her college fees, her books and her rent in Mrs Costello's dream bedsit, but she'd have to get work in Dublin too or she'd never cope.

No time like the present to start looking, Phoebe thought, mustering up her courage. She walked quietly downstairs and was sure she heard a door in Mrs Costello's apartments open. At least there was no need for an alarm system, she told herself.

154

Mrs Costello would have any burglar whacked over the head with a frying pan before he'd got so much as a leg over a window frame.

She'll grow on me, Mum, Phoebe thought to herself, deciding that dictating a letter to her mother would help her cope with the loneliness.

All her life she'd been part of a family, with people and animals. Now she was alone and it was the one part of this giant adventure she was terrified of. No Mum, no Mary-Kate, no Ethan, no Prince, no beloved farm animals.

She was so used to talking to the farm birds that perhaps talking to herself was the answer.

The square is not quite a square, Mam – more a rectangle – but you wouldn't believe the plants here. All sorts of things and a fig tree . . . I'm not sure if I'm allowed into the garden but oh, a man with a terrier has just gone in, so I must be.

The man and the dog were both old and they did a slow perambulation of the tiny park, with the dog lifting his leg on a few bushes, before both shuffled off again.

Phoebe smiled at the man, who smiled back, and she felt more human to have smiled at another person. Not everyone around here could be as standoffish and suspicious as Mrs Costello.

But perhaps it wasn't really her landlady's fault, Phoebe tried to think charitably. Maybe poor Mrs Costello had been overrun by mad tenants who'd graffitied the house with spray paint, phoned Mars on the house telephone, and blocked all the toilets before scarpering without paying their rent? Who knew?

Phoebe looked wistfully over at the pretty house with the cerulean blue windowsills and the riotous garden and wished *they'd* been looking for tenants and not Mrs Costello. She liked the look of the upstairs room, which faced the square and had the branches of a beech tree tapping lazily against it. But she was in Mrs Costello's, and if Dad's death had taught her anything, it was that there was no point in wishing for what wasn't true.

Think the best of people, Mam liked to say.

I will, Mam.

Twice a week after Mass, Antoinette and her girl-friends went for coffee.

'No point going every day; it wouldn't be special,' Dilys said. Dilys was the oldest, the mammy of the group, and was celebrating because she was driving again since she'd had her second hip replaced.

'I am the Six Million Dollar Woman,' she liked to joke. 'They have rebuilt me!'

She still had the walker because the left hip wasn't totally healed, plus she liked the walker because it got her to the front of the queue in sales.

'Nobody can afford to go for coffee every day,' said Josette, who was the youngest at fifty-nine, and was addicted to clothes shopping.

Antoinette, who was sixty-four and felt every one

of those years despite her determination to hold on to her looks, loved their coffee mornings.

Sometimes they went to the coffee shop beside the church, and other times they went to the big shopping centre where Josette and Dilys could indulge in their fierce passion for shopping, albeit different types. Dilys was a bits-'n'-bobs shopper, ever searching for the best deal: the cheapest and yet most expensive-*looking* toilet roll holder; the new tights that kept you warm or cold, whichever your body needed; any number of tchotchkes that might cheer up her already wildly cheered-up house.

'I hate those hoarder shows,' she sometimes said mournfully. 'They make me feel like I'm one step away from being buried alive by stuff. I have to stop buying things. I mean, imagine years from now and I'm stuck in the house without room to move, suffocated by cushions, nice floral storage boxes I never use or blasted china pigs.'

She liked collecting pigs.

'I think my mother started me off,' she said, 'but it could have been Nana Reilly. With the knitting, you know. Great knitter, she was. I have an old pig she knitted for me when I was a child, so that could have been it. But now I see them and I have to have them. This feeling comes over me and it's no use, my self-restraint goes out the window and I'm at the till in five seconds.'

Dilys' house, quiet now that the kids were grown and Bob had died, was a shrine to pigs in every form: embroidered tablecloths with piglet faces; china ornaments in every porcine design; pink, satin-edged hand towels with piglets embroidered on them; mugs that oinked when you picked them up.

'I beg of you, don't get me anything with a pig on it,' she'd say at Christmas and her birthday. And then they'd be out for a day, would wander into a shop and Dilys would shriek at the sight of a pen with a plastic pig hanging off the end, or a handbag hook with a piglet painted on it.

'It's a bargain! I know I shouldn't but . . .'

Josette was more of a clothes bargain sort of woman. Show her a blouse with a button missing on the sale rail, and she was in heaven.

'I'm sure I have a button like those in my button box!' she'd say delightedly, and both Dilys and Antoinette wouldn't dream of pointing out that anaemic peach wasn't her colour and that they'd yet to see her wear the last blouse she'd bought that only needed a button to finish it off.

Antoinette didn't shop much on those days out. She liked younger boutiques than her two friends, whereas they seemed content to settle into what Antoinette called old-ladyness with acrylic cardigans and flat, lumpy shoes that she couldn't have borne to wear. She might feel old sometimes – certainly she did since Arthur died – but she didn't want to *look* old. Old wasn't beautiful, old wasn't pretty, and Antoinette had always been pretty.

She often wanted to say, to Josette in particular, 'Stop with the flat shoes!' But she said nothing.

Instead, she got her hair highlighted at a salon filled with young, trendy girls and boys who had asymmetric cuts, odd earrings and fluffed up her hair with expensive product, saying things like: 'This is young and trendy, Antoinette, and very modern.'

Antoinette wore slim jeans, watched her weight and saw no need to look old, no matter that she had to use a special jaropener thing in the kitchen because of how stiff her hands got. She had nicer clothes than her daughter-in-law, she thought with some pride. Really, Cassie hadn't a clue. If Cassie wasn't so pretty – and she was, Antoinette knew, with a hint of the jealously she was ashamed of – she'd look like a man with those boring suit jackets and trousers she always wore.

Cassie was one of those capable women: the sort who could change a plug as easily as wash the car. Men hated that in a woman, Antoinette felt. Arthur had loved her femininity and the fact that she'd needed him so much.

This reliance on each other had formed the bedrock of their marriage: Arthur Reynolds had a beautiful, ladylike wife who wouldn't put a pearly-polished fingernail on a screwdriver if you paid her to; and Antoinette had a big, strong husband who treated her like a princess and brought her flowers home every Friday night. Glorious red tulips for true love; richly scented blue hyacinths for constancy; and flowering jasmine for sweet love.

'Did you get the washing machine sorted?' Dilys asked her as they stopped for the inevitable second cup of tea and cakes – chocolate rice cakes for Antoinette, who was careful with carbs.

'Shay came round to sort it out,' said Antoinette. 'Had it fixed in no time.'

She was busy pouring her tea and didn't see the searching look that passed between her two friends.

'Shay? When was that?' asked Josette conversationally.

'After work. I phoned and he dropped on his way home.'

'Not easy to drop into this side of the city when you live and work on the other side,' Josette went on.

'I don't know anything about washing machines,' Antoinette said airily. 'That's a man thing, isn't it? Besides, that's something I have to talk to you about,' she added happily. 'It's a plan Shay has for me to move over with them. You know, sell my place so he and Cassie can buy a bigger house and I can have my own place attached. Not a granny flat, though – definitely not.' She laughed as if that notion was entirely ridiculous. Antoinette Reynolds was not a *granny* sort of person, even though she had three grandchildren. 'But close to Shay so I have someone to do all those difficult things.' She beamed at her friends. 'Solves lots of problems in one fell swoop, except how I'm going to get to see you pair all the time. I wouldn't be up to driving over here . . .'

'Why not?' demanded Josette, who had an old Mini and drove it like she was about to go on to the grand prix track at Monaco, waving merrily at anyone she cut across and blowing kisses if anyone honked their horn at her.

'It's a long way,' said Antoinette.

'That's not the point,' Josette said, vexed. 'You drive a Micra, Antoinette – it's not as if you'll be manhandling a ten-tonne truck over the East-Link bridge. And besides—' Josette was warming to her theme now – 'you have your life here in Clontarf. What do you want to be ending all that for to live with Shay and Cassie? Who came up with that notion?'

'I did,' admitted Antoinette. 'It makes perfect sense.'

'Ah now, Antoinette,' said Dilys, 'would you have liked your mother or your mother-in-law moving in with you when you were married?'

'My mother never had a chance,' Antoinette said, stung. 'Poor woman died in her fifties. I'm only seven years older than her, you know. I have to take care of myself. A woman needs her family around her.'

'Quick, Dilys, phone the undertaker,' teased Josette. 'If you're about to drop dead, what about poor Dilys here, with her dodgy arteries and her metal hips that set off airport scanners at fifty

161

paces? You don't see her desperate to move in with her family to look after her, do you?'

'Heaven forbid! I'd kill my Lorraine if we had to live together,' admitted Dilys, speaking of her eldest daughter. 'But even if she was a saint, I wouldn't move in with her. Roots and wings, girls: that's what we give our children. Not us turning up with incontinence pads and all our misery. Besides, you're only sixty-four, Antoinette. When I was your age, I was still going to the Argentine tango nights. I'd be going now if it wasn't for my second hip not being totally healed yet. Hard for Vincenzo to twirl me on one leg, under the circumstances.'

'I'm not you, Dilys,' Antoinette said stiffly. She'd never been a dancer: the one ladylike thing she'd never quite mastered. 'I'm hardly moving in with incontinence pads. It's just that I need family close to me. I need Shay.'

They all sat in silence, the noise of the café going on around them.

In the end, Dilys signalled to Josette that she, through virtue of age, would be the one to say it.

'Is this great plan fair to Shay, or Cassie, or your grandkids?' asked Dilys. 'Antoinette, you're the youngest of us in so many ways – the clothes, how you look after yourself, even those blasted rice cakes.' She gestured to the plate with its remains of dark chocolate and a few scraps that resembled polystyrene, as far as Dilys could tell. 'You're the last one to be behaving like you're the dowager and need taking care of . . .'

162

'What's wrong with wanting to have my son be around for me?' demanded Antoinette, going red under her layers of Estée Lauder. 'I brought him up and, now his father's dead, I am due something!'

'Listen, love, the day we say our kids owe us something, we're in trouble,' Dilys replied. 'You had your life and they have theirs. Don't forget that. You could simply move closer to the girls. They're both only down the road, so you'd be close to us too. What do they have to say about this plan?'

At this mention of Ruth and Miriam, Antoinette's face tautened.

Ruth was spectacularly annoying when Antoinette phoned about problems in the house.

'Get a man in to fix it,' was always her answer. The subtext being: *Don't bother me with this rubbish, Ma.*

Miriam was so tied up with her son and husband, some school rota she was involved in for study carpooling and a charity sports thing she'd started organising, you'd swear she was running a giant social media corporation. She never had time to listen. *That* was what was lovely about Shay – he made time to listen.

'I haven't told them. I'm going to go,' she added, rattling her cup loudly back on to the saucer. 'I'm hurt you don't understand but I don't need your approval for how I live my life. I need my family.'

★   ★   ★

'Were we too hard on her, do you think?' Josette asked anxiously when Antoinette was gone.

'I don't know.' Dilys drank her tea, looking every inch her seventy-five years. 'But Antoinette's finding it hard to find her place in the world since Arthur died. Antoinette needs to be loved. I don't know why she doesn't join a dating agency: she needs another man and not to be the dowager around poor Shay's house. It's not fair on him or his family either.'

'Cassie and Antoinette get on, though, don't they? It's not like they dislike each other, is it?' asked Josette.

Dilys shot a knowing glance at her friend. 'It's one thing to get on well with your mother-in-law, Josette; it's another thing entirely to live with her every day. Maybe they'll have room for us all and we'll start a commune. You know, find a nice man to share between us, have a different person to cook dinner every night, grow wacky baccy in the back garden beside the parsley, have a hot tub put in, that type of carry on.'

The two women giggled until Dilys said she had to stop or she'd wet herself laughing.

'Would you have let your mother-in-law move in, Josie?' she asked.

'Lord,' she said, looking upwards and making a quick sign of the cross, 'I'm sorry.' She turned to her friend. 'That woman was the nearest thing to a living devil as you'd find on this earth. Always on at me about having something wrong with my inner workings because I couldn't give her grand-children. Not that we didn't try. She had the whole family terrified of her. If she came to live with us, I'd have been out the back door with my suitcase and over the garden wall.'

They giggled again.

'I do feel sorry for Antoinette,' Dilys said after a few moments. 'She was always the most beau-tiful woman on the road, all glam and with the husbands running around to fill her wine glass. Now she's older the parties with nice men have dried up and she doesn't know where she fits into the world. Widowhood's not easy, no matter what age it happens, but there's no running and hiding from it.'

'No running and hiding from anything,' agreed Josette, who'd seen her husband die painfully from cancer. She had no children to run to, no daughter-in-law to get on with or not, as the case might be. She'd got through the first few years of her widowhood one painful day at a time.

'I feel sorry for Cassie,' Dilys said. 'When Antoinette gets an idea into her mind, there's no shifting it. But I feel sorriest for Shay. Talk about being stuck in the middle.'

CHAPTER 9

'I've gone off pizza,' announced Fiona on Monday evening, making her blue eyes very big to emphasise that this was a serious matter. She was sitting on one of Coco's two stools at the breakfast bar in Coco's minuscule kitchen, even though Coco had expressly forbidden her to sit on them until her feet reached the ground. Fiona was a great believer in pushing the envelope.

'Totally gone off?' asked Coco, thinking of the fridge with the two margarita pizzas residing in it, waiting to be heated up, along with oven chips. She even had ketchup and garlic dough balls. All the major food groups.

'Yup,' said Fiona, swinging her legs. 'Totally.'

Earlier, Jo had said pizza was fine.

'Parent/teacher nights are enough of a night-mare without hassling over food,' she'd said when she dropped her daughter off at Coco's flat at half five that evening.

'I've chocolate biscuit cake for dessert, we're going to watch half of one of her Disney movies, and then bed at eight because tomorrow's a school day,' Coco recited.

'Did you hear that, Fiona?' said her mother. 'Bed at eight.'

Fiona had done that thing with the big, blinky eyes again. It was her current look, a sort of *trust-me-I'm-sweet* look that made Coco anxious. Jo seemed used to it. It was clearly a look designed to make babysitting godmothers sweat.

At nine and a half, Fiona was frighteningly grown-up. Coco was quite sure she had nothing like Fiona's self-possession when she was the same age.

Fiona could narrow her eyes when her mother and Coco were discussing something she wasn't supposed to understand and hiss 'explain' in her best menacing voice, which was a growl she'd copied from watching *Beauty and the Beast* too often, and which made Jo and Coco laugh.

Ever since the night they'd discussed Coco joining a dating website, they'd become very wary of letting Fiona hear anything.

'Not so much little pitchers have big ears but more the type of child that spy agencies will be signing up because of her ability to hear and analyse the information with total accuracy.' Jo had sighed. 'Just as well I am never dating again because I'd hate to try to do anything naughty on the couch with a man. I can just see Fiona emerging from her bedroom wearing her outraged expression and wielding some sort of weapon. Probably a gun she'd figured out how to print on a 3-D printer.'

'She's innovative,' Coco agreed.

Now Coco contemplated Fiona's new-found dislike of pizza.

Fiona was staying the night because of Jo's parent/teacher meeting. They went on for hours. She and Coco had decided it was better for Fiona to stay over at Coco's and for Jo to drop in first thing in the morning to take her daughter to school.

Jo had just left and Fiona was already setting the ground rules, which was Coco's job.

Coco gazed at her goddaughter and thought that being a headmistress or boss of a large company might be more in Fiona's line than anything in hairdressing – her current favourite thing if the number of cropped-head Barbies were anything to go by.

'How about a compromise?' Coco said, wise to children's wiles after spending many holidays and weekends with both her nieces, and Jo and Fiona. 'You eat the pizza and afterwards, if you eat enough slices, you get to have some chocolate biscuit cake – the one from the cake shop, not one I made myself.'

Fiona looked at her beadily.

'I can dress up in your clothes as well?'

Coco gave in. It was important to know when you were beaten.

'Deal.'

That evening, Cassie was running late.

Loren, boss/bitch extraordinaire, had decided on an impromptu late management meeting and even though Belinda had pointed out that she had an appointment at half six, which she'd have to cancel, Loren had been firm.

'It's a battleground out there. If you want to hold on to your jobs, see you in the boardroom at six,' she'd snarled as she stalked out, leaving her small management team looking at each other miserably.

'Bet she's been dumped and she wants someone to take it out on,' said Kenny, who'd worked with Loren since the start-up and knew her better than anyone. Not that it meant she was nicer to him than to anyone else. Just that he had a head start on them as to her moods.

'You mean guys actually date her?' asked Belinda sardonically, dialling to cancel her appointment.

'I know, incredible, but yeah,' Kenny said. 'They see the whole vision—' he impersonated Loren, explaining to new staffers how important a person's look was: a look which included perfectly blow-dried hair, manicured nails and designer clothes, in Loren's case – 'and they fall for it. Straight men are idiots,' he added.

Cassie stepped into the hall, phoned Shay and got his voicemail.

'Honey, can you phone me as soon as you can,' she said. 'I've got to work late and I need you to pick up the girls from afterschool.'

She sent a text message too and waited for him to reply.

After ten minutes, she texted Beth:

**Running late at work. Can't get Dad. Can
you get a lift with Mel's mum?**

Since Lily had started first year, Cassie had been
relying on the school's after-hours programme
where homework classes were held until six.
Previously she'd got both girls picked up by a
neighbour who worked as a childminder. So far
it had worked out, but then neither girl had been
sick. Nessa, the childminder, said she'd step in
if absolutely necessary, but Cassie knew it was
a big ask.

Mel's gone already. Dentist apt.

Beth replied.
'Damn,' said Cassie out loud.
She phoned Shay again and again, but his phone
went straight to voicemail. In her irritation, Cassie
bit a nail – unmanicured, as Loren would be
displeased to see.
There was only one other place he could be,
but Cassie couldn't quite believe it. After Saturday
she'd got the sense that she had her husband
back. They'd both been more affectionate towards
each other: it was like a real marriage again.
She'd felt, without him saying it, that he'd try to
offload some of his mother's demands on to his
sisters.
Still, just in case, she'd phone her mother-in-law . . .
'Cassie!' said Antoinette in obvious delight when

she picked up the phone. 'How lovely to hear from you. Shay's been such a pet with the washing machine. I knew all it needed was the filter cleaned but I can't do things like that . . .'

Cassie hadn't known she was grimacing until she caught a passing member of staff looking at her strangely, so she quickly adjusted her expression.

'He's very handy with washing machines,' she lied, thinking that Beth – who treated the utility room as a luxury hotel laundry facility where things dropped off that morning were returned, dry and ironed that night – actually knew *more* about the washing machine than her father. He never used it, to her knowledge, but some part of her was damned if she'd let Antoinette know this.

'He's with you, then?' she asked brightly.

It was five forty-five on a Monday evening, Shay had left the office to be with his mother, and who cared how many frantic phone calls he missed while he was there. Work, family – who cared? Mummy dearest had called.

'Yes. Well, he's at a delicate bit . . .' Antoinette said, and Cassie wondered had her mother-in-law always sounded so croaky and fragile. It was as if widowhood had made her frailer, or at least made her sound frailer.

Antoinette went on: 'He's trying to reach in behind the machine to unplug it, you see, and I can't find the torch. Goodness, I know it's here somewhere . . .'

'Never mind,' said Cassie, managing to summon up a bit of kindness from the depths of her bile. 'Ask him to look at his phone messages, would you, Antoinette? Must dash. Bye.'

She stalked into the office kitchen, found a squashed-up chamomile teabag in the corner of a herbal tea box, and dashed hot water on it. She hated chamomile tea, thought it tasted like lawnmower dust, but it might help. Because without something vaguely calming, there was a possibility that she would race out and thump the first person she saw.

She picked up her phone again.

Coco answered straight off.

'Thank God,' breathed her sister. 'I have an emergency. I won't even go into it but let's just say, Shay is unavailable. I have to work late so is there any way you can you pick up the girls from school now, take them to yours and feed them?'

'Sure,' said Coco, thinking that she could pick up more margarita pizzas in the shop on the way back. She hadn't even put hers and Fiona's in the oven yet. And there was enough chocolate biscuit cake for all. 'You sound harassed. Should I text Beth and tell her about the change of plan?'

Cassie took a deep breath. 'Yes,' she said. 'If you don't hear from her—'

'I know what to do,' Coco said. 'Stop worrying. I'll take care of Lily and Beth. I've got Fiona here, so we can have a teenage girls' night in.'

Fiona, who was listening, beamed at both being

called a teenager and the thought of spending time with Lily and Beth, whom she idolised.

'Right,' said Coco, flicking off the oven and grabbing her keys once she'd hung up, 'we've got to get Lily and Beth from school, buy more food and we need to set out now.'

'Ready!' said Fiona, racing eagerly to the door.

No mention of where Shay was, Coco thought, as she locked the front door and hurried down the stairs after Fiona. *Strange.*

Pearl was on the verandah with a cup of tea, enjoying the last of the evening sun and wondering if she could afford a winter holiday this year, because the heat did help her bones. She and some of the Thursday night poker club had gone away to Ibiza the year before. They'd rented a small villa, nothing fancy, just a little place in the hills close enough for taxis to decant them all into the local village, where they'd feasted on local seafood and good wine.

She and Peter had shared a room and nobody had so much as mentioned it.

'They all know anyway,' Peter had said as he put her suitcase on the bed so she could unpack it when they'd arrived. 'They see the way I undress you with my eyes.'

Pearl had laughed and thrown a cushion at him.

'That's not undressing me with your eyes, you crazy man; that's you trying to see if I have the fourth ace or not,' she teased.

'Oh no, undressing, definitely,' Peter went on. 'I love the heat in Ibiza.' He nuzzled the soft place between her neck and shoulder. 'Makes me feel younger. Not so achy.'

Pearl leaned into his kiss, knowing how lucky they were to have this wonderful second chance of love at their time in life. 'But let's be thoughtful, honey,' she said. 'Poor Gloria will never be kissed by Louis again and we don't want to rub her face in it.'

'Yes,' said Peter, straightening up, instantly serious. 'It wouldn't be easy for Annette, either.'

'I think Annette's in a better place,' Pearl pointed out. 'She's chosen to be alone after Dai's death. Gloria's in the never-never land. People like Edie would be shocked if Gloria so much as smiled at another man with poor Louis in a nursing home.'

'Why is it that the Edies of this world are judge-mental when it comes to other people's happiness?' asked Peter. 'Louis and I were the best of friends, but he's in a different place now. Alive and yet not here. If he could choose, he'd never choose this life for him or Gloria. He'd truly want her to be happy. Who could judge Gloria if she did meet someone and get a bit of happiness after so many years of pain?'

'Lots of people would judge,' sighed Pearl, thinking of her sister's firmly held views on just about everything.

On her verandah now, she deadheaded a few roses with her ever-present secateurs and tied up a few trailing stems of violet-tinged Rhapsody clematis with green wire. The garden needed a big makeover but she no longer had the energy for it. Neither did Peter. He had his own garden to look after, although he said he was planning to turn it into a Zen shrine so he'd have gravel and no lawn-mowing to do.

Perhaps they should have married years ago, when it would have made more sense. She'd been so busy trying to keep all the balls in the air and protect the girls from more change that she'd refused Peter when he'd asked her.

And now they were both old, living apart, and who knew why?

Daisy panted and dropped on to Pearl's feet, making Pearl smile. It was hard to feel anxious around a pug, she thought, as she had thought so many times in the past.

A warm drop of rain fell on her face and she looked up to see a dark cloud had settled over the house. A dark cloud full of heavy September rain. Even the temperature had suddenly dropped. Pearl shivered. She felt anxious, as if the cloud held some dark portent.

Jo Kinsella sat at her desk in the big sports hall in St Fintan's school and looked past Mrs Boyne to the line of parents waiting beyond. The parent/teacher meeting system in St Fintan's was haphazard and Jo longed for a time when people would get specifically allocated ten-minute slots instead of wandering frantically and randomly from desk to desk, lining up to meet teachers and getting more and more annoyed as every moment passed. Jo had a dull nagging headache at the back of her skull, slightly to the right. She never got headaches. Must be her neck from leaning over doing all the correcting of French verbs, she thought.

By Jo's calculation, she wouldn't be home before eleven. At the back of the line she could see the parents of a sweet child who was being forced to study higher-level French by her pushy mother and who really would be better off in the lower-level class.

It was the living vicariously problem. The teachers talked about it in the staffroom all the time: parents who'd been hopeless at sports and who now stood on the sidelines at school matches and screamed themselves hoarse, wanting, *insisting upon*, championship performances from wildly unsporty kids.

Or the parents with delusional memories who insisted that they'd been fabulous mathematicians themselves and wanted their children studying physics, applied maths and higher-level maths when said children were clearly far more right-brain than left-brain, suited to happy hours being creative in art class or writing essays in English.

'Martha loves French but she worries a bit,' Mrs Boyne was saying. 'I don't want her to worry; I just want her to be happy.'

Jo beamed at Mrs Boyne: a woman after her

own heart. Who cared what Fiona did in school as long as she was happy? Children were gifts, not puppets whereby parents got to correct all their own mistakes and make their kids do what *they'd* always wanted to do.

She thought of her parents and the rigid upbringing she and her siblings had undergone. It wasn't the prayers that had been hard, but the fierce moralising, the hypocritical denouncing of everyone who didn't follow their creed; and finally the screeching that her brother Xavier was wicked and needed to be saved, because 'God couldn't stand the very thought of homosexuality'. They'd actually tried to have him visit a retreat where his gayness could be 'cured'. Devastated, poor Xav had eventually left the country and settled in Paris. Jo doubted if he'd ever come home. He was happy now, with a partner called Thomas and with friends who loved him for himself.

'Ms Kinsella, are you all right?'

Jo was conscious of Mrs Boyne suddenly staring at her. The headache coalesced from dull and aching into something more – something sharper and intense. In an instant, Jo was conscious that her arms had slumped down to her lap and that her head was lolling to one side. Very strange. Her face felt funny, the left side – was that the right word? Left . . .? Yes, the left part felt odd and . . . and . . . *darkness*.

Jo knew no more. She didn't hear Mrs Boyne scream or grab her, she didn't hear someone shouting for the school nurse, or another person yell for an ambulance. She was gone, into another world . . .

The margarita pizzas went down a treat and by half seven, Beth, Lily and Fiona were all dressed up in Coco's clothes, having consumed the entire container of chocolate biscuit cake. All homework had been done, Beth promised.

Coco, having been styled by Fiona, now sat in a white flouncy 1970s dress from the shop, wearing Fiona-applied lipstick (heavy pink gloss) and with a diamanté necklace attached to her head like a headpiece, with the help of many painful hair clips. Her eyebrows were Frida Kahlo dark and all she needed was a striped shawl, a few necklaces and some major art talent to complete the look.

Beth's phone was playing her favourite Taylor Swift album as Beth herself, clad in tight black, tried on every pair of Coco's high heels. Lily was experimenting with a 1940s dress with a fitted bodice and huge cartwheel skirt with acres of tulle underneath. She kept twirling to enjoy the effect of the underskirts of tulle.

'Fashion show time,' announced Fiona, done up like a little queen in a far-too-big red spotty dress with perilous heels, a giant black hat, and wearing black suede gloves that Coco had never been able to sell in the shop because of a big orange mark on one of them.

'You have to fix the room afterwards,' Coco

said weakly, because she knew she'd be doing it all herself later. Clothes were flung all over the place, her en suite bathroom looked like the chorus line of Le Crazy Horse Saloon had just got made up in there, and the scent of perfume and pizza mingled in the air.

Cassie hadn't phoned yet but Coco hoped she'd laugh when she did turn up. Whatever disaster had gone on at work, nobody could fail to laugh when they arrived at the door to see Coco's normally pristine apartment in such hilarious disarray.

Taylor was just singing about how the game was played when the doorbell rang.

Cassie must have forgotten her key, Coco thought, relieved that the noise level was going to go down once her nieces went home.

She opened the door, not caring that Cassie would see her looking ridiculous. But it wasn't Cassie at the door: it was a tall, older woman, accompanied by a young woman Coco was vaguely aware of knowing.

Then it came to her: the younger woman was a friend of Jo's from school. They looked grim and instantly, her stomach lurched. Why would Jo's colleagues turn up at her door unless they had bad news to impart.

Stepping into the hall and shielding everyone inside from the sight of the visitors, she leaned against the doorjamb and said: 'What's happened? Is it Cassie?'

Please, no, please not Cassie. And the girls . . .

How would she tell her nieces something had happened to their mother? *Lord, please let it not be serious . . .*

'Coco, we met once,' said the young woman. 'I teach at St Fintan's too. It's Josephine . . .' The woman bit her lip as if she couldn't speak.

'I'm Ellen Barrett, headmistress of St Fintan's,' said the older woman, reaching out for Coco's hand. 'I am so sorry to come here with such bad news, Coco, but Josephine has been rushed to hospital—'

'Has she had an accident?' interrupted Coco, trying to make sense of it all.

The younger woman found her voice. 'She just went unconscious at the parent/teacher meeting. Nobody knows why . . .'

'You're listed as her next of kin on her personal details,' the headmistress said. 'Does she have no other family?'

Coco thought of the long answer, the one that encapsulated the strange religious fervour of Jo's parents, the fervour that had made all their three children distance themselves from them. Jo had long since made peace with the fact that her parents were locked in their own harsh, judgemental world.

Jo had gone through several legal hoops to have Coco listed as her next of kin and make Coco Fiona's legal guardian.

'Me, a guardian?' Coco had said at the time, honoured. 'Can you trust me?' she'd joked.

'You have to think of these things when you have

kids,' Jo had said, 'and yes, I do trust you. Better than those poor God freaks who would have Fiona in a hair shirt, confessing all sorts of insane sins, and on her knees saying the rosary ten times a day. They've got worse as they've got older, Coco. It's just not normal, honestly. It breaks my heart to do it but no way my daughter is having anything to do with them. It's like they're in a cult that makes them wild-eyed and unhappy. I do not want that for my daughter.'

'She has family but she's estranged from her parents,' Coco said to Ellen Barrett. 'I'm her next of kin and her daughter's guardian.' Mentally she ran through how she was going to tell Fiona what had happened.

Your mum is sick in hospital. No, how could she do it?

She said goodbye to the two women, said she'd rush to the hospital, but first she needed to sort out the children, including Jo's daughter, who were inside.

The headmistress clasped Coco's hand again. 'Tell us if there is anything we can do,' she urged.

Back in the apartment, great giggling was going on. Coco closed her eyes at the notion of inter-rupting it all with what seemed like tragedy.

She looked around for Beth. At fifteen, she was the oldest person present other than Coco, and for a second Coco had a vision of what it must have been like for Cassie and herself when their mother had left home. Cassie had been just seven, a kid, and yet she'd taken care of Coco in her own way all their lives. Whenever she could, Cassie had fought Coco's battles.

Jo was unconscious, had been when the ambulance had taken her to the hospital, and Fiona had no older sister to take care of her. Instead she had Coco.

'Beth,' she said quietly, 'can I talk to you for a moment?'

Briefly she filled Beth in on what was going on.

'I don't think I can take Fiona with me to the hospital,' Coco said anxiously. 'But what if Jo wakes up and wants her. Or what—' she could barely think of it – 'if Jo doesn't wake up?'

'Mum will know,' said Beth confidently. 'She always knows what to do.'

In the meeting, Cassie heard her phone buzz discreetly under the table in her handbag. Carefully, she reached down to see who was phoning her, thinking it might possibly be Shay phoning to apologise. But it wasn't, it was Coco. Normally she might not have bothered answering, assuming it wasn't anything important, but the girls were with Coco and some strange instinct made her answer it, get out of her seat and leave the room in one swift movement. She was aware of Loren looking at her angrily but she ignored it.

'Yes, Coco,' she said. 'What's wrong?'

'Oh Cassie,' breathed Coco, and Cassie felt her heartbeat shoot up. 'It's not the girls; they're fine.

It's Jo. She's . . . I don't know how to say this but she collapsed at the parent/teacher meeting. She's unconscious and an ambulance is taking her to hospital.'

'Unconscious, for no reason?'

Cassie was momentarily rendered dumb. She thought rapidly of all the terrible things that could strike younger people. Sudden cardiac death came to mind, and her own heart lurched.

'I'm here with the girls, but I need to get to the hospital quickly and I don't know what to do. I've told Beth and she's been absolutely brilliant, she's amusing Fiona because I don't think I can look at Fiona right now, to be honest—'

'Calm down, honey,' said Cassie. 'It's OK. We'll figure this out.'

Her mind was still processing this shocking information. Right now, though, she had to think of a plan. She had to be the big sister in charge.

'OK, this is what you're going to do. Ring Pearl and ask her to come over to sit with the girls until I can get back, OK? You can't leave them there on their own. Beth is brilliant but she's too young to handle this, and Fiona will want to know where you've gone when you're supposed to be minding her, so get Pearl over. Better still, I'll phone Pearl—'

'Yes,' interrupted Coco, sounding panicked, 'but where do I tell Fiona I'm going?'

There was a pause while Cassie ran over the options in her mind.

'If she was older we could tell her that her mum's sick and they've taken her to hospital, but she's too young—'

'I couldn't do that,' said Coco, interrupting again. 'She'll want to come and the other teacher from the school said it was bad. Who knows what's happened. I can't bring her to casualty. I need to know what's happening before I can tell her.'

'Right,' said Cassie, 'just lie then. I hate lying to the children but perhaps it's the right thing to do in this case. Say . . . say you've got to come and see me, and that Pearl's going to drop in and stay with them for a few minutes. Oh, yes!' Inspiration struck. Small girls loved sleepovers. 'Say that we had this brilliant idea that she comes over to my house with the girls; we'll say it's a special sleepover. She idolises Beth and Lily.'

'That sounds better,' Coco said. 'The thing is, Cassie, Jo is all she has. I mean, she has me too, but I'm just a part of her life; Jo is *everything* to her. I just wouldn't be able to tell her something had happened to Jo. I'm not qualified for that.'

Cassie breathed out slowly.

'I don't think anyone's ready for that, ever,' she said. 'I'll leave the meeting now and I'll come and meet you in the hospital, OK?'

'No, it's probably best if you're there when the girls come home to your place,' Coco said. 'That seems more normal. We can tell her in the morning.'

'Are you sure you don't need me there for moral support?'

184

'I'm fine,' said Coco. 'I can do it. Love you.'

'Love you back,' said Cassie and hung up.

She stuck her phone into her pocket and walked back into the room, where Loren stopped speaking and looked up at her enquiringly.

'Family business?' said Loren, investing the words with sarcasm. Loren thought all family business involved children – small creatures she actively disliked because she saw them as a serious threat to productivity.

'Yes, family business,' said Cassie, an edge to her voice. Suddenly she wasn't in the mood to pander to her boss's moods anymore. 'A family emergency, actually, Loren. I'm afraid I have to go.'

She collected her things.

'Everything OK?' whispered Belinda.

'No, my sister's best friend's just collapsed and went unconscious at a parent/teacher meeting. She's a teacher and she's only thirty, thirty-one max.'

Belinda blanched. 'You hear about that but you never think it's going to happen to someone you know.'

Cassie nodded. She'd felt like that a lot as a teenager – weird stuff happened to some families, and hers just happened to be one of them. But she and Coco had managed. The Keneally sisters had battled through. They'd make it through this, too. Whatever Coco had to deal with, Cassie would be behind her.

CHAPTER 10

It was 12.45 on Monday night – no, it was now Tuesday morning, Coco thought wearily, as she tapped on the door of Cassie's house.

Cassie let her sister in quietly.

'Well?' she said, knowing that things couldn't be good from the white, shattered look on Coco's face.

'The consultant neurologist said it's a haemorrhagic stroke,' Coco said, looking as tired as a person would after spending several hours in accident and emergency. 'Which apparently means an artery leaked in the brain. A nurse told me it's lucky he was there because it's so easy for medical staff to first think of options like drug reactions instead of diagnosing a stroke. I've heard that type of thing before. For example, if you're young and you go to A and E with a heart issue, everyone assumes it's a cocaine problem until the toxicology results come back. So we were lucky that guy was there.

'They did CT scans and neurological tests, you name it, and they're pretty sure. They gave her anti-clotting meds and the doctor said that if patients get these within forty-five minutes to an hour, it hugely improves their chances of recovery. The golden hour, they call it. What nobody's telling me is how somebody of Jo's age can have a stroke. They say it happens, but why? How? It makes no sense.'

Coco walked into Cassie's kitchen and went automatically to the kettle to boil it.

'The good news is that they don't think she needs surgery, but we will have to wait and see. I got to sit with her during some of it and she's so out of it, and when she talks, it's like she's drunk because her words are so slurred. One junior doctor came in and told me she'd probably be brain-damaged for life. Luckily another, older, doctor heard him and said they know nothing of the sort. How do they let people say those sort of things to you?' she asked. 'And then, before I left, she started crying. The nurse says stroke victims do that but I felt so helpless—'

Coco started to cry herself. Fluffikins jumped silently on to a countertop, shocking them both. To Cassie's complete surprise, the cat made his way surefootedly over to Coco and rubbed his head against her arm.

'You have the four-leaf clover,' Cassie told her sister. 'He actually hates people.'

'He might hate happy people,' said Coco, 'but obviously feels at home with devastated, confused people.' She bent her head to croon at the cat, letting tears drop on to the countertop as she did so. She hadn't cried once in the hospital, not even when she'd seen darling Jo for the first time, all wired up, seemingly asleep, face drooped on one side, looking like a victim instead of the survivor she was. Tears were wrong in the hospital, even when the young doctor had blandly said Jo was going to be damaged forever, but here in Cassie's presence, Coco could finally cry.

'He could be a healing cat, for all you know,' she said, snuffling.

'First I've seen of it,' said Cassie, knowing that Coco needed a little bit of peace to cry. She'd been the same as a teenager: hated to be looked at when she was upset. 'He's normally a grumpy, leave-me-alone cat. Sit, honey, I'll make the tea.'

Coco gathered the cat up in her arms and sat on the old, worn, fake suede couch, which was shoved up against the wall. Behind it was a huge photomontage of the family, including Coco, in all sorts of happy poses and places. Beth and Lily used to do their homework there but now they worked upstairs in their rooms, while Cassie roared up occasionally about loud music and how could anybody work with that noise?

Coco had spent many happy evenings in this room while babysitting, her nieces snuggled up against her as they watched family movies on the small kitchen TV. The couch felt homely and comforting.

Fluffikins sat patiently on her as if waiting to be helpful: a warm, soft bundle of love.

Making a pot of tea, Cassie kept looking over at this vision. It added to the strangeness of the night. Upstairs in the spare bedroom, little Fiona lay fast asleep on a 'sleepover', while her mother – her thirty-one-year-old mother – was in hospital after suffering from a stroke. In the midst of these happenings, Cassie's cat behaving oddly was probably not that odd after all.

'They told me to go home. Said they'd phone if there was any change. That there was nothing I could do.'

'Was there hassle over you being her next of kin?'

'Not really. At first everyone assumed I was her sister, but someone from the school emailed in the details the school had about me being first of kin and Fiona's guardian, so that sort of nailed it. Now they think I'm her girlfriend. I phoned Attracta in Australia and she couldn't believe it. Kept saying, "Are you sure?" and then said to call her again later when I knew more. Didn't sound like she's coming home, though. Xavier's phone went to voicemail. I hated saying it was an emergency with Jo to a stupid voicemail, but I had to say something. I feel strange, though, as I should phone her parents . . .'

'Well, I suppose you have to,' Cassie said reluctantly. 'They're her mum and dad, after all. It's the right thing to do. But as long as they don't upset Fiona.'

Cassie had known Jo as long as her sister had, and had seen how Jo's parents had gone from devout to over-the-edge religious hysteria. It was not beyond reason that the Kinsellas would march in and declare that their daughter's illness was divine retribution for some transgression.

She brought the tea and some biscuits, which Coco tried not to eat, over to the small table in front of the couch. Now was no time to worry about calories.

Both sisters sat together and suddenly Fluffikins leapt off Coco's lap, as if the sense of anxiety and fear emanating from both of them had frightened him. Separately he could manage their anxieties; together, the scent of sheer stress coming from the sisters was too much.

'Not a healing cat, then,' commented Coco, polishing off her first biscuit.

'Never has been before. So, what's next?'

'I don't know,' said Coco. 'If she hadn't lost consciousness where she did, who knows? It could have happened in her sleep and she could be dead. Or really badly affected. Remember Pearl's friend who had a stroke and ended up in a nursing home, in a wheelchair, not able to communicate? Pearl used to take us to talk to her and we hated it, remember?'

The sisters sat and hugged silently while the cat watched them.

'That's got to be the extreme version, doesn't it?' Cassie said, trying to find hope. 'She was an old lady then and I'm sure there are different levels of stroke. Plus, they saw Jo early and gave her the magic meds, which probably weren't around all those years ago with Pearl's friend. And if it's a brain injury, she can have rehab and recover . . .'

'Maybe,' said Coco. 'I don't know.' She gazed off into the middle distance.

'So, how are we going to tell Fiona?' Cassie asked, and Coco sighed inside with relief.

It was the use of the word 'we'. With her sister on her side, Coco would try anything, but taking care of a frightened young girl, mothering her . . . How could she ever do that? And yet it was what she'd signed up for.

How easy it had been to say she'd be there in case anything happened to her best friend, but how hard it would be in practice. What did she really know about taking care of a child? But there was nobody else and she wouldn't want Fiona going to anyone else. She loved Fiona like a daughter.

'I kept thinking, as I looked at Jo, that I was going to have to tell Fiona what's happened, yet how do I do that? She's a child. How is she going to understand that her mother can't speak properly right now, that she doesn't even look like her mother normally looks? That she'll need rehabilitation, that she might never speak properly again, that she might use a wheelchair and be silent, just like Pearl's friend.'

Even the words seemed strange: *Jo* and *rehabilitation* together.

'I have no idea how to tell her,' Coco said sadly. 'No idea at all.'

191

She'd said as much to one of the casualty doctors, who'd looked at her blankly and then sighed. 'I don't know,' the doctor said, her face weary and pale from night shifts. 'How do you tell anyone this? It's not my area of expertise. I don't have kids.'

'Neither do I!' Coco wanted to say frantically, but for now, she sort of did have kids. One kid. With Jo in a hospital bed seriously ill, Coco was technically acting as Fiona's mother.

She simply wasn't equipped to impart this sort of information.

'If I sleep on the floor and maybe try to tell her in the morning . . .' Coco broke off.

All through the terrible time in hospital, she'd thought of Fiona's little face when she would finally see her mother. Jo was surrounded by monitors, clamped to a narrow hospital bed, and with the paralysis of her face and her inability to speak except in a weird slurred voice, she didn't look or sound anything like herself, and when Coco had left, she'd been crying for the past half an hour. How exactly could Coco explain *this* to a nine-year-old?

'We have to tell her that her mum's going to get better, that she still loves Fiona even though she's in hospital, that you and I are going to take care of her, and we'll all be there when her mum gets out. Children need to know they're loved, that none of this is their fault, and that the adults are taking care of it all,' Cassie explained.

Coco stopped drinking her tea. 'Is that what you used to tell me when I was small? That it wasn't my fault Mum had left?'

Cassie felt the breath leave her body as fully as if she'd been punched in the stomach. It was like having something she'd been avoiding thinking about for years suddenly emerge in front of her like a giant stone wall.

'It wasn't your fault she left,' she said, inhaling shakily. 'It was mine.' She corrected herself. 'I *thought* it was mine. Kids do, you see. They think they made their parents split up or they made everyone upset.'

Saying 'kids' think that made it sound as if Cassie hadn't felt that it was entirely her fault that their mother had left. Although she had. Totally.

Somewhere inside, she still did.

If she'd been different, better, maybe her mum might not have gone. And even if she had gone, maybe if Cassie had been the sort of child she'd wanted, maybe her mother would have come back. It all came down to those simple details. Simple and devastating enough to last a lifetime.

'I thought my being born had made her want to go because I wasn't right or something,' Coco said slowly. 'I know, silly when you're a grown-up and look back at it, but I thought it was me. She'd loved you, she didn't go when *you* were a baby, but she went when I came along. It had to be me, you see.'

'Nobody wanted to talk about it, did they?' Cassie said slowly, trying very hard to hide her own shock and devastation. Her heartbeat was racing now. Was this a panic attack? She had to cover it up; Coco had enough going on without Cassie going into a meltdown about their personal thirty-year-old tragedy.

What was *wrong* with her? She should have gotten over this by now. It had been thirty years ago, for heaven's sake!

'I always felt Pearl could have told us more but didn't want to hurt us,' Coco went on, in between drinking her tea.

'Yes,' said her sister absently.

Shay. She needed Shay. They'd barely spoken since he'd come home that evening – she'd been so irritated that he'd been busy with his mother when she'd needed him. He'd gone to bed without hugging her. Was that her fault or his mother's? Was Antoinette trying to drag him back to the family home . . .? Was he going to leave too?

The sisters sat in silence for a while, watching the cat stalking around the room until he found where he wanted to sit.

Coco reflected that their mother's absence was the elephant in the room for so much of their childhood. Nobody else talked about it, and quickly the subject had became clouded with the patina of silence. Sometimes, late at night in the room they shared in Delaney Gardens, the sisters could speak of it, in the moonlight, and with nobody else around. It had an ephemeral quality, talking about the mother who'd gone; outside that room, they never discussed her.

'She left Dad too,' said Coco. 'Looking back, I think that killed him. Do you ever think that? That he fell apart and never got fixed?'

It was that thought that finally broke Cassie's calm self-control. Watching a happy, entirely unaware nine-year-old going to sleep had brought it all back to her: what would happen to Fiona in the morning when she learned the truth? The way Cassie had learned the truth. In her case, that people left and never came back.

And it was the ones left behind who fell apart.

Mothers could leave. Mothers left. Wives left. People left. Everything was precarious.

Coco touched her sister's hand with the lightest of touches, as if she was reading her thoughts.

Coco had never known Dad any other way but sad. She could see him now: the bald head with the tonsure of grey, and the sad eyes that could perk up into a smile but never really went into full-blown happiness. Pearl had made up for it. Pearl had had enough *joie de vivre* for three people – she'd had to.

'We don't know why she went, Cassie,' said Coco. 'We still don't know why. We know it's not us, whatever really sent her off. We were kids. If you left Lily and Beth now, would it be their fault? No, it wouldn't.'

But Cassie wasn't really listening anymore. It was as if she had gone to some other place in the past. 'I can sort of remember her perfume,' she said mistily, 'but it eludes me whenever I'm in a department store and I sniff at the older perfumes. Some of them sort of smell right, but are not quite hers. Her hair was long, like yours more than mine – richer, darker, all tumbling curls. She had your sense of style: different, cooler than everyone else. She used to come to pick me up from school in this fun fur coat, golden and shaggy, like a lioness's, and she looked more glamorous than all the other mothers.'

Cassie turned brimming eyes to her sister, who was staring at her sadly because Coco had seen none of this. 'I loved her so much and she left me. She left us. It still makes me scared that other people will leave.'

Coco, who had no memory of perfumes or the softness of a furry coat any more than she had memories of a happy father, held her sister and wished she could remember something about the mother who'd gone so long ago. She'd always said to people that she'd never missed having a mother because she hadn't known one, but Cassie had. Cassie had known what it was and she'd suffered the loss the most.

Cassie had worn herself out trying to make life perfect for them all: for Coco, for Shay, for Lily and Beth. And all the while, there was still this hole inside her.

Maybe it was inside both of them. A mother-shaped jigsaw piece that had been lost and still needed to be found.

When Coco had gone to bed, Cassie opened the fridge with shaking hands.

She tried so hard not to think about her mother, but sometimes the thought of being abandoned just came and poleaxed her out of nowhere. But this – this was huge: like the imaginary stone wall crushing her.

She'd bought a box of wine (so much more convenient than a bottle), and poured herself a large glass. This might help her sleep, might numb the feelings. More than anything else, Cassie didn't want to think about the past.

Shay was driving into work, shattered after sharing a bed with a wildly distressed Cassie, who didn't appear to have slept a wink, even though she'd clearly had a few glasses of wine, and he knew that normally knocked her out because she wasn't much of a drinker. His wife was incredibly upset about the news of Jo's stroke – it was pretty shocking, Shay admitted. It made you think of your own family and want to protect them all like a caveman.

What would he do if something like that happened to Cassie or, God forbid, the girls? He simply didn't know.

He used to think that women were better at

dealing with all this sort of stuff but, after last night, he wasn't so sure. His cool, calm Cassie seemed to have disappeared to be replaced by this slightly wild-eyed woman who'd been about to leave the house wearing two wrong shoes until Beth had told her in a voice heavily laced with irony.

'Mum, like, the fashion police are going to arrest you,' Beth had said, pointing down to her mother's feet.

Shay thought Beth might give Cassie a break, given the night before, but no. Weirder, Cassie didn't even appear to register the faintest hint of irritation over her daughter's sarcasm-fest.

She seemed almost blank. 'Oh, right,' was all she'd said as she'd looked at her unmatching shoes and went slowly upstairs to put on matching ones.

Coco and Fiona were still asleep when Shay left, and he was sort of glad. Coco he could handle, but he wasn't sure he could face Fiona after she'd heard her mum was in hospital. He didn't envy his sister-in-law the task of breaking the news to the little girl.

His car phone rang as he got nearer the office and he pulled in to answer it.

'Hello love,' said his mother. 'Isn't it a lovely day? Lifts your spirits. I've been looking at the property supplements, you know . . .'

'Mum, we've had a bad night at our end,' Shay began, and filled her in on the details.

Antoinette sounded suitably upset, but she

198

quickly rallied. 'This is more proof of how our plan will work brilliantly, love,' she said triumphantly. 'I could have taken care of the children and Cassie wouldn't have had to race home from work in a tizzy after all!'

'Er, Mum, let's keep this under our hats for the moment,' Shay said quickly. 'I still haven't exactly mentioned it to Cassie and she's very upset right now. Let's wait a while before I raise the subject with her.'

On her end of the phone, Antoinette beamed. 'Darling, you know I'm the very soul of discretion!'

Coco watched Fiona sleep and wished everyone in the Reynolds household would stop making noise so the child would not wake up. Because when she did, Coco would have to tell her that her mother wasn't at home but was in hospital.

Coco had already phoned in twice that morning – once at six and again at half eight when the nursing shift changed over – to see how Jo was, but there appeared to be little change.

'She's stable,' said one nurse, while another offered the information that Jo was more alert this morning.

'I can't come in yet,' Coco said. 'I have to tell her daughter what's happened.'

'How old is she?'

'Nine.'

Fiona slept peacefully, exhausted by the late-night fun Beth had managed to conjure up out of nowhere.

Coco had hugged her niece that morning and said a huge thank you.

'It was the least I could do,' Beth said, leaning deeply into her aunt and hugging her back. 'Poor Fi. I don't know what I'd do if it was me. I can come home early and play with her, you know.'

'I'll text you if I need you, Beth,' Coco said seriously, because she simply had no idea how she was going to impart this news and how she'd deal with Fiona afterwards.

Cassie had silently left a cup of coffee beside Coco and tiptoed out until, finally, they were alone in the house. Still Fiona slept on.

Coco sipped her coffee and planned. 'Honey, everything's going to be fine,' she whispered.

'Coco! Why am I still here? It's school time!' Fiona sat bolt upright on the bed, eyes wide and startled. Beth's clock, a giant Dali-esque thing, hung on the wall, clearly proclaiming that it was half nine.

All intelligent thoughts left Coco's head and she stared at her goddaughter anxiously.

'Why didn't you wake me for school? Mum will be so cross with you!'

Coco didn't think her face had changed that much, but it must have.

'Coco, what's wrong? You look all funny and sad.'

'Your mum had an accident, darling. She's fine,' Coco said, trying to be reassuring, 'but she's in hospital. That's where I was last night. I didn't want you to be upset until I saw she was OK, and she is . . .' *Huge lie, there.* 'But she is fine now and we can see her later today . . .'

She got no further. Fiona's little mouth closed, her small face paled until it looked as if she was as ghostly as the heroine in her favourite ghost school storybooks, and her big blue eyes brimmed.

'Is she going to be dead?' she asked tremulously.

'No, no!' Coco hugged Fiona to her. 'She's not, honestly. She had a thing that went a bit wonky in her brain and she's talking a bit funny, but they gave her special medicine and she is fine, really. We can go and see her now.'

She held Fiona tightly, knowing she'd screwed up it somehow, not having explained properly that Mummy wasn't quite the same, but being desperate to reassure her that Jo was going to live. Because she was.

'Mummy wants me to mind you until she's better, so let's get some clothes from your house and then we can go to the hospital,' Coco said, wishing she'd found someone last night in the hospital who knew how to break such horrible news to children.

'I want to see her now,' sobbed Fiona.

'You can,' said Coco.

'Now! Mummy!'

Coco could do nothing but hold on to her darling goddaughter for dear life because, right now, she was the nearest thing to a parent that Fiona had.

★　　★　　★

On Tuesday morning, Phoebe stood a few yards away from the door of Larkin College and watched the beautiful people roaming in as if they hadn't a care in the world. Clutching takeaway coffees, or weird-coloured juices, smartphones stuck to their ears, wearing wildly fashionable clothes and wildly fashion-of-tomorrow clothes, they sauntered in, bouncing to their own beat, utterly sure of themselves. There were girls with actual designer handbags, rucksacks customised exquisitely, small elegant feet in Converse, Keds and a variety of other cool shoes. One girl wore the beautiful Missoni Converse Phoebe had lusted after but hadn't been able to afford. *She* looked like a fashion person: tiny, interesting hair dyed blonde with a hint of pink, perfect eyebrows and a rattle of cool bracelets jangling on her slim, tanned arms.

There were perhaps slightly more girls than boys walking in, all terrifying in their determination and couldn't-care-less-ness.

Phoebe, in the skinny jeans that ended in slightly the wrong spot on her ankles, wearing the non-Converse shoes she'd customised, and her old (made three years ago) green silk parka not entirely right for among these birds of paradise, held on to her takeaway coffee cup as if it were a lifeline. She wouldn't be able to afford this sort of coffee every morning. Not until she'd got a job, anyway.

Registration started at ten. Incredibly late, by her standards. She thought of the hens clucking their disapproval loudly about wanting to get out from about 5 a.m. on summer mornings. Maybe she could get an early waitressing job somewhere, but a four-hour shift? Nobody hired people for that length. Cleaning might be an option. A contract cleaners rather than house cleaning, which was more random. She could do late night or early morning office cleaning. Or else waitressing or pub work.

'I want you to get the best out of college,' Mam had said on the phone that morning when they'd all rung to wish her good luck. 'Don't get too much work, lovie. You can't be too tired to get your college work done.'

'You know how bored I'll be without all of you if I don't work! So I've left my CV all over the place,' Phoebe said, longing for home with all her heart and trying to sound cheerful. 'I'll find something good, you know me. Keep me out of mischief till I can get home again.'

'And no sending money back to us, you promised. We can manage,' her mother went on. 'This is all for your future.'

'Sure,' said Phoebe, who had no intention of obeying this command. Some promises simply had to be broken. Without her contribution to the McLoughlin household, things would be very tight. She'd be sending home as much money as she could.

Ethan was hopeless on the phone. 'Yeah, school's crap as usual,' he muttered, which Phoebe knew was his way of saying he missed her but was bad at actually saying so. He only came to life when he insisted she speak to the dog.

Obligingly, Phoebe said: 'Hello Prince, baba, how are you, honey?' in her doggy voice.

'Prince licked the phone!' said Ethan, thrilled and suddenly sounding like himself again. 'He misses you.'

Phoebe could barely speak. Ethan was easier to talk to when he was monosyllabic. 'Miss him too,' she said gruffly. 'Even miss you, crazy boy.'

'Miss you, Phoebs.'

'Donna is perfectly fine,' Mary-Kate informed her when it was her go. 'I've been minding her. Please take photos, will you? We want to see everything. And film your bedsit – I want to see the seasick-green colour. Oh, and Mrs Costello too.'

'She's a lovely woman,' said Phoebe, mindful of the fact that her landlady might indeed be outside the door with a glass pressed to it, listening to every word. 'Truly a lady.'

'Did she just walk in?' demanded Mary-Kate.

'Always a possibility,' agreed her sister.

'A madser, I knew it!' laughed Mary-Kate. 'Get a picture!'

The phone call had been intended to give Phoebe a boost, but instead it had made her feel very lonely. What was she doing, away in the city trying to become something she wasn't?

She watched the people going into the college, people who looked as if they belonged, unlike her.

She finished the last delicious dregs of macchiato and, out of the corner of her eye, she spotted someone who didn't look like any of the fashionable birds of paradise. He was young but strong, wearing skinny jeans that emphasised large legs, a longish hand-painted T-shirt, and with an artfully draped pigeon-grey leather jacket covering him up but not entirely disguising him. Phoebe, used to being the tallest in any gathering and knowing she could arm-wrestle any man, recognised the covering-up pathology. The jacket was beautiful but too big. She was doing the exact same thing with her parka: hiding the fact that she was nearly six foot and could only fit in a sample size if two of them were sewn together.

Some instinct made her shout out: 'Hello there. You late too?'

The boy had the most beautiful eyes, she noticed as he came close: a stunning grey like the sky on a misty night lit by moonlight. His hair was fair and straight, full of hair product to keep it tamed, she reckoned, and it was clearly a wonderful cut.

'I'm Phoebe.' She stuck out a hand. 'Fashion?'

'Yeah,' he said, looking at her and rudely not taking her hand. He took in her unfashionable outfit. 'You? Really?'

Phoebe gave him the stare she'd long used on hardened drinkers in The Anvil who were giving her backchat.

'You don't shake hands?' she asked icily.

For an instant, she glimpsed anxiety in those

stunning grey eyes and she knew the rudeness was a cover.

'I'm being Howard Hughes this week,' he said, recovering. 'No touching for fear of germs.'

Phoebe grinned and kept her hand out. 'I'm being Jane Russell, whom you famously had a fling with, so pleased to meet you,' she said.

'I'm Ian. I thought you might be a fashion bitch,' he said. 'I know two on this course for sure. I met them on my portfolio course.'

'I'm Phoebe and I didn't even do a portfolio course,' said Phoebe, 'so I'm fashion bitch meat for sure.'

'No you're not, hon-ey,' said Ian, making the last word two syllables.

'I was joking,' Phoebe said. 'I'm strong enough to take on any bitches.'

Ian squeezed her bicep. 'That's for sure.'

'We're the last two, I think. I had to get my coffee first,' she lied, as if she had expensive coffee every day. 'Can we walk in together?' Phoebe asked, then fibbed again as she added: 'I'm a bit nervous.' She wasn't sure why she said it because she was sure none of the other fashionistas would say such a thing. But this boy needed her: she sensed it. He was like one of her beloved animals feeling unloved and out of place. And Phoebe needed someone to take care of.

'Yeah, I'd love that,' he said, and smiled. It was as if an angel had smiled. When Ian smiled, those grey atmospheric eyes lit up his whole face and he looked like someone Michelangelo might have painted. His skin was a luminous olive, which was a glorious combination with that fair hair, and his mouth lifted in a broad smile.

'Come on.' She linked her arm though his. 'Let's face the team.'

Registration was taking place in a large room to the right of the main entrance hall.

As Phoebe had thought, many of the most fashionable types were there: twenty-three in all. There were twenty-five to a year and she and Ian were the last ones. A very tall woman, all dressed in modern black layers, with a shock of grey hair, dark red lipstick, and an armful of turquoise bracelets snaking up one arm, was talking.

'. . . afterwards we'll bring you on a tour and you can settle down into tutor groups. Today will be about schedules and telling you what this year will involve. Each of you is assigned someone from second year as a mentor – this is a new innovation to help you become grounded within the college. In first year, we believe in letting students try a range of design work to see where they feel most at home. We don't pigeonhole here. You may come in with one idea of where your future is and then find yourself in love with an entirely different discipline . . .'

Phoebe almost tuned out. She didn't want to miss out on any new experiences but her heart was set on women's fashion design. Nothing more, nothing less. She wasn't interested in menswear, sportswear, or anything else.

She and Ian were together in their first group, a pattern-cutting class where a man with a heavy accent sat at the end of a large room and gazed at the table in front of him. His voice was so quiet that Phoebe had to strain to hear, and she turned to Ian to see if it was the same for him.

'. . . pattern is more important than illustration,' the man was saying.

Middle Eastern? Phoebe couldn't make it out but she loved his words. Of course pattern cutting and understanding fabric were the most important thing. The drape of the fabric around the body was the way some people designed. They were true geniuses. But she lived by the pattern.

'Drape or pattern?' she whispered to Ian.

He shot her a grin and reached back to stroke his coat, which hung on the back of his chair. 'Draped, babes.'

The class took an hour, during which Phoebe took notes frantically in her big notepad, watching other people typing on to cool, metallic laptops she'd never be able to afford in a million years. She had a laptop, an ancient thing that was almost an archaeological artefact. She'd need a proper laptop, she knew.

She definitely needed a job. She had to get walking around the area close to her place to see what she could get. She'd spent too much of yesterday frantically readying herself for today, going over designers online in a coffee shop with free Wi-Fi, then sketching and endlessly rearranging her possessions to make the bedsit look vaguely more welcoming.

'Er . . . the class is over.'

Ian was prodding her reluctantly with a finger, as if she might bite his hand off. 'We have to go: another lot are coming in now.'

Phoebe glanced up. 'Gosh, sorry, got thinking . . .' Hastily she grabbed her stuff and her rucksack and followed Ian out into the hallway. 'Where next?' she said, entirely thrown.

They ate lunch together in the small canteen, Phoebe ravenous for the sandwich she'd made that morning: salami, salad, cucumber and mustard in a big roll.

Ian, who'd ordered a lot of green things and had bought a banana too, looked enviously at her lunch.

'Can't afford to eat here,' Phoebe said, using a canteen knife to slice one of her sandwiches in half. 'Do you want some? What you've got is all a bit rabbity. Unless you have an actual rabbit stashed in your bag?'

Ian didn't laugh at the joke.

'Is it some health kick?' said Phoebe as artlessly as she could.

'No,' said Ian, glaring at her, but Phoebe could see anxiety and fear in his voice.

Phoebe knew this was very, very important. She stopped eating, eyed him up and down, and then had some of her bottled tap water.

'Thank God for that,' she said, sounding relieved. 'I thought everyone would be a stick insect.'

Ian looked at her warily.

'I want to make clothes for women like me,' she went on. 'I'm a girl who's nearly six foot, I wear a size sixteen and I want to be in fashion: there aren't many of *us* around, now, are there?' Phoebe countered. 'I'm different from what seems to be the norm here. But I want to design for "different". You have to show your clothes on ordinary models for the portfolio, but when I make it—' she beamed at Ian as if this last was in no doubt – 'I'll be making clothes for normal people, not supermodel-sized ones. World domination for the normals!'

'You don't think I'm fat?' asked Ian, who appeared to have heard none of her previous statement. The fear and need for reassurance in his eyes reminded Phoebe of her little brother Ethan. The big sister kicked in even more.

'Who says you're fat?' she asked, as if shocked.

'Well, nobody,' he said, 'but my sister's so skinny. Everyone else here is skinny.'

'Does your sister have incredible eyes and enough talent to get in here?' Phoebe asked, putting the half a sandwich she'd offered on to Ian's plate.

For the first time, Ian really smiled at her. 'No, but she's a good hairdresser, though,' he said.

'Did she cut your hair?'

'Nah. A pal did it. Luigi.'

'I rest my case,' said Phoebe. 'Next, can you set

me up with Luigi?' She put a hand to her hair, which had been ministered to by her hairdresser friend in return for an exquisite jacket, but which was too thick to ever hang in anything other than a crazed way.

'I might,' said Ian archly. 'What's it worth?'

'The promise that if we go out to dinner anytime – assuming I get a job to afford dinner – I pick somewhere that doesn't serve rabbit food.'

CHAPTER 11

Phoebe looked at the double-fronted shop, The Twentieth Century Boutique, and wondered if they'd hire her. Inside, a willowy blonde was leaning over the counter, tapping her nails on it and talking on her mobile phone. Probably had a wardrobe of vintage Missoni and boyfriends coming out her ears. But faint heart never won fair job, Phoebe reminded herself, much in the same way as she made herself clean out the duck shed when she wasn't in the mood for ducky poo.

'Aim high,' Dad had always said. He'd whispered it in the hospital when he was dying after the accident. So much of his body had been crushed by the tractor, it was a miracle he'd survived for three days. His cervical and thoracic spine had been crushed, and his organs were failing; only brute strength was keeping him going.

Sobbing, holding hands, everyone was trying to say everything rather frantically before they ran out of time. And yet the drugs keeping the pain away meant Dad drifted in and out of consciousness.

'Hard not to aim high when you're my height,' Phoebe often joked, and she said it again that last time.

Her father so often had put his hand on hers, but now he couldn't move, so Phoebe placed hers gently on his – a hand that was no longer strong but had grown papery and weak over the past months. The weakness of that hand made it easier for her to let him go. He was in pain, despite the drugs. She wanted him to live so much but he couldn't. Nobody should have to suffer that way.

'That's my girl,' he'd said, his voice croaky.

Dad, you'd like this place, she told him in her head now. *Vintage but not silly vintage – more like out of another time with that old wireless in the window and those posters for the Second World War.*

The *Make Do and Mend* sign in one of the windows had a little red-checked cloth under it, with wooden needles threaded with a delicate half-knitted scarf, and a pin cushion with a selection of old-fashioned cotton reels arranged beside it. Like something from a film of the forties, Phoebe thought, despite the fifties handbags and what looked like a 1990s Betsey Johnson marabou-collared embroidered coat alongside them.

She pushed the door open and a bell tinkled. The beauty leaning against the counter didn't move or even make eye contact. The part of Phoebe's brain that understood customer service, courtesy of her long-time working in the pub, registered this lack of interest. Obviously not the owner, Phoebe decided.

The shop was clearly beloved of someone, even if not the woman behind the counter, because it was treated like a precious treasure. The place sparkled and the round-bellied glass cabinets where the jewellery lay were all glittering mirror and polished glass. Old movie posters and travel posters from the 1930s, 1940s and 1950s were set on the walls, showing Riviera scenes, Alpine holidays with slender, bobbed-hair and beautifully illustrated heroines standing beside wooden skis, while in other pictures, fur-coated girls in jewels and tiny-waisted frocks danced with men with gleaming dark hair. A large mirror had what looked like a stencilled picture of the Gibson Girl to one side. Betty Grable's famous legs were on the other, with Betty looking back over her shoulder with that come-hither yet wholesome smile. The whole place was like a divine little boutique from another era and only the music – something top forty – didn't fit.

If I owned this place, Phoebe thought, *I'd play music from the eras of the clothes I sold.*

She decided to loiter a bit and drifted over to a selection of jackets to see what she could find. The forties and fifties were hard on a woman her size because of the waist-cinching required, but sometimes she found lovely fabrics in 1980s stuff – looser and shoulder-padded – where she could tweak a bit and make a jacket fit. Whoever bought these clothes knew her vintage, Phoebe decided by the time she'd run through the dresses, jackets, skirts and a selection of blouses.

There were clothes for every age group, every size, from every era.

What looked like a woman's riding jacket, in a tweed the colour of autumn heather, caught her eye. The fabric was soft and yet hardwearing, the cut severe. And it was a decent size: not a slinky size ten or twelve, but made for a woman like herself who could be fourteen or sixteen, depending on the brand.

She glanced up at the beauty, who was still ignoring her.

Manners made her ask: 'May I try this on?'

The girl trailed elegant fingers in the air.

Phoebe thought she'd get the same response if she'd said: 'May I steal this?'

She looked around for a changing room and found two in a corner: dusky pink velvet curtains held back with ribbon and a charming French bistro chair painted an eggshell cream in each cubicle.

The jacket was a miracle. A little big on the shoulders, and shoulders were tricky, but Phoebe hadn't spent an entire summer learning the basics with the village seamstress for nothing. Shoulders were her speciality. In her portfolio collection, she'd made a jacket with tiny shoulders, each sleeve topped with pin tucks measured centimetre by centimetre. Lizzy from the hairdressers had wanted to buy it but Phoebe had had to say no. She'd made up another one quickly for Lizzy, as payment for the modelling.

'Wish you could make all my clothes,' Lizzy had said. 'Nobody in work has anything like this, made for me and all.'

'One day, Lizzy, one day, I shall have clothes in shops and you can buy them all, at a discount!' Phoebe laughed and held up crossed fingers.

'No luck required for you, Phoebs,' Lizzy said. 'You're a genius with clothes. Just make something for yourself, will you, girl? Not trying to be a tough cow but nobody would believe you were a genius with fashion. I know you've no time what with the job and the farm, but come on . . . My granny's better dressed and she thinks a new apron is the last word in style.'

This jacket would be perfect for herself. Phoebe did a bit of primping in the Betty Grable mirror, with still not a word from the shop assistant.

Another customer, older and carrying the sort of expensive handbag that Phoebe recognised from *Vogue* and knew was worth the price of a small car, came in and, after a listless rustle around, moved to the old handbags.

Definitely a handbag addict: new, old, whatever. If Phoebe was waiting on this woman, she'd produce one of the crocodile handbags on the top shelf. None of them dusty, some a gleaming black, one elegantly tortoiseshell. This woman could afford the modern equivalent but Phoebe understood the fashion mind: vintage held a powerful sway.

Instead Phoebe said nothing, and rifled some more herself. It wasn't her fault if the beauty was missing sales by not paying attention.

Phoebe paused by a rack of tea dresses stitched with exquisite details like pin tucks and many inserts in the skirts.

A dress, she thought. *Something old and trailing, perhaps.* She'd never been much for dresses back home, but then who wore long dresses on a farm when you were in and out of your wellington boots all day? Looking through the vintage tea dresses, she wondered would the modern jacket in muted grey she was currently designing look good with a bias-cut tea dress underneath? She made such modern clothes but perhaps this was what she needed to boost herself on to the next level – old *and* new. She'd spent so long studying art, finding new influences for colour and design, but her fashion inspiration so often came from the modern. She loved the fit and cut of old clothes, but she used that to create modern designs. The notion of mixing the old hadn't really hit her properly until now . . .

The other customer left and the tinkling of the shop bell coincided with the end of the very important phone call.

'You buying that?' asked the beauty, and Phoebe looked up to find the blonde didn't look so beautiful anymore. She looked as if she'd been interrupted from something very serious and this work lark was a bore.

Politeness is a virtue, Phoebe's mother's voice echoed in her head.

Instead of glaring, she smiled. 'I'd love to,' she said. 'Tell me, are you the owner?'

She knew the answer but she couldn't help herself.

'No,' said the blonde, her nose in the air. 'I'm the manageress.'

In your mind, honey, Phoebe thought.

She put her choices on the counter, having added them up and worked out that if she brought sandwiches to college forever, she could do this. A woman in a fashion college needed clothes.

As the blonde badly folded both garments up, Phoebe's fingers itched to do it differently. There was tissue paper on the counter: Phoebe could see it but the girl wasn't using it.

'Do you need staff?' Phoebe asked bluntly.

The girl stopped with her inexpert folding. 'No,' she said sharply. 'It's me and Coco. She's going through a family emergency right now, but I can cope with it all.'

Phoebe could remember Gillian, the owner of The Anvil back home, stuck with the pub financially and no longer able to afford to hire a manager to take the hardest parts out of the job.

'You're too young,' she'd told Phoebe when she'd asked for a job.

'Give me two weekends,' Phoebe had said. 'Pay

me half what you normally pay. If you think I can do it, then we'll renegotiate.'

As soon as the words were out of her mouth, she wondered where this clever, sassy Phoebe had come from. But she knew, really: she'd been born out of necessity. The family would find it hard to survive on the farm money and the widow's pension her mother was now getting. Phoebe, as the eldest, had to think clever.

Gillian nodded slowly. 'Fine, start tonight. But it's no picnic, I can tell you.'

Phoebe had grinned. 'Neither is cleaning out the duck shed,' she said, 'but I can do that too!'

Gillian laughed.

Within two weeks, Gillian looked calmer and more rested. Phoebe was on proper wages and made decent money from tips too.

'You've a gift with the difficult customers,' Gillian said admiringly.

'It's the farming background,' Phoebe explained. 'They like someone who can talk the talk with them but they know I won't stand any messing about at closing time.'

She got used to being a waitress too at the weekends when the pub served food, swinging in and out of the kitchen with plates of fat fries, chicken in a basket, brown bread and chowder, or a giant slice of apple tart. You needed to be able to swoop and slide among tables like a dancer. You also needed good flat shoes, a pocket on your bar apron for tips, the order pad, your phone, and a sense

219

of humour for the customers who wouldn't have been satisfied if a winning lottery ticket had been served to them with a free meal and a bottle of fine wine.

The beauty handed Phoebe her change.

'See ya again,' she said, and Phoebe nodded.

There was a space for her, she was sure of it. The same way she'd been sure that Gillian needed her. Whatever family emergency was keeping the owner out of the shop, one day she'd be here and Phoebe would come in.

Meanwhile, she had to find another source of income. Package in hand, she left the shop with a regretful glance and headed up the road to see where the pubs were. She'd prefer Twentieth Century to a pub, but beggars couldn't be choosers.

Yesterday evening she'd gone into Doherty's pub to leave her CV in there. She'd a great letter of reference from the pub at home and she had to admit that she loved the look of Doherty's. It was what people might call unusual. Barking mad, maybe. It was as if whoever owned the pub had been given a job lot of Pepto-Bismol-coloured pink paint and had decided: *What the heck, let's make this place bright.*

Phoebe thought there was a good possibility the pub could be seen from space. There were a few premises like that back home, too. It was the bar owner's version of: *If you build it, they will come.*

The man in Doherty's, who said he was the owner, had looked her up and down admiringly.

'A fine hoult of a girl, you are,' he said, looking at her with pleasure. 'You're just the sort of young wan we want in here but I've plenty of staff at the moment. Still, leave me your number and if anything comes up, trust me, I'll give you a ring.'

This last part of the sentence he said with what was either a friendly smile, or a leer – Phoebe couldn't be entirely sure which. But either way, she knew she'd be able to handle him. She hadn't worked a full year in The Anvil and dealt with all manner of men without being able to handle a frisky bar owner who saw himself as a bit of a Lothario.

Today, she was going to hit the last side of the road and just drop her CVs in the small shops she didn't think would have room for another member of staff. She'd also been into the supermarket the day before, where the manageress had looked at her as if she was stark raving mad.

'I have three hundred names on file,' she said scathingly, looking Phoebe up and down. 'People who are prepared to work for next to nothing,' the woman added.

'Oh well,' Phoebe said cheerfully, 'prostitution it is, then,' before she headed off with a wave, leaving the woman behind her with her mouth agape.

I know I shouldn't have said that, Mam, Phoebe said to herself, *but I couldn't help it. That woman was delighted to have three hundred poor eejits all applying to get one badly paid job in her scabby supermarket. I bet she's mean to the people who do work there.*

221

Today she dropped her CV in politely to the little newsagent's that, on weekdays, had a tiny post office at the back. She went into the garage on the main road and dropped it in. And finally – and longingly – she went into the pet store, which was clearly a family-run business because there were loads of staff in red *Dunnes Pet Shop* sweatshirts in there and they all looked exactly the same. Phoebe would have killed to have worked with the animals. After she'd dropped off her CV, she wandered around the cages poking her fingers in to stroke rabbits' heads and talk to canaries.

'You like animals then?' said a teenage girl, watching Phoebe.

'Oh, I love them,' Phoebe said simply. 'I was reared on a farm and I miss the animals so much. But I'm up here for college and I need a job and—'

'And you thought this would be the right place for you.' The girl smiled. 'Sorry, Dad has enough trouble keeping the place going and that's paying all of us buttons, to be honest. But we'll keep your name on file. Phoebe, wasn't it?'

Phoebe nodded. 'Thanks a million,' she said, as she headed for the door.

CHAPTER 12

Red O'Neill walked through the airport, ignoring the stares of a few of the savvy business people who'd been on his flight.

What's he *doing on a commercial flight?* he imagined them thinking.

'You don't make money by flying private,' he wanted to tell the rubberneckers. He'd hated all that 'wheels up' and 'I have the Gulfstream this weekend and was thinking of flying to Hawaii' rubbish. It annoyed the hell out of him. If it was easier to fly commercial, he did it.

Anything else was all ego; nothing to do with business at all. Red had never bought into such vanity, which was one of the reasons why his venture capital business had done so well in the past few years. So well, in fact, that the *Financial Times* had featured an interview with him three weeks ago. An interview that would have once had him clapping his hands with glee. The *Financial Times* was *the* paper for men in his line of work. Them wanting to interview you was like saying: *You've arrived. You're an international businessman of note, not just some young fella from Dublin.*

Less of the young, he thought ruefully. He was nearly forty and there had only been one question with the *FT* interviewer that had left him slightly stumped.

'What's next?' the reporter had asked. 'What does Red O'Neill really want now?'

Red had a great reputation in the business for thinking on his feet: it was how he got out of the San Diego deal just in time, just before everyone else had lost their shirts. But he couldn't think on his feet for this question.

It would have sounded completely ridiculous to say that after working his butt off for so long, he now wanted to actually have a life – and to somehow get over a woman he'd broken up with four years previously. That would have made him sound gauche and foolish, things Red never wanted to appear.

So he'd smiled his enigmatic smile, which normally worked very well – on women.

Sadly, this was a male journalist, so the enigmatic smile on the large, well-sculpted face with the brooding eyes – a smile that turned women's heads, and not just because he was wealthy – didn't have quite the same effect.

'To be even more successful next year,' he'd said lightly, hoping he appeared neither bigheaded nor stupid.

It was so difficult figuring out the right thing to say without sounding like a moron. He hated reading interviews with himself in newspapers because no matter how he meant to sound, it so often came out differently.

There was only one person who'd ever told him the truth about stuff like that, told him how he appeared in interviews, and she was the one who'd left him. It was why he almost never did business in Ireland. He didn't want to bump into her; he didn't want to even be in the same city as her.

It wasn't that the great Red O'Neill hated failure and that Dublin had been the scene of that great failure. It was that he still felt the hurt.

He hadn't told his mother he was coming today. Myra O'Neill would have rolled out the red carpet, delighted to see the return of the prodigal son, but Red always felt that big family reunions were for his brothers, the two O'Neill brothers who'd done it all properly. Who'd got married, who'd had children and reared them within a few streets of where they'd all been brought up in Silver Bay – not far from Delaney Gardens, but the less he thought about that, the better.

Red was high on every 'most eligible bachelor' list in Ireland since the year dot, and now, since the *FT* piece, possibly wait-listed for some other eligible bachelor lists around the world. Yet he wanted what his brothers had.

He'd sound like some 1950s housewife if he said it, but he genuinely wanted the whole enchilada: wife, kids, weekends where he didn't think about the office but just enjoyed the sheer pleasure of being with his wife and children. The same way his brothers did with their families. The way he'd been brought up.

He didn't want seven houses in different places; he wanted a beautiful house in his home city where he was close to his family, because Google and Facebook had shown that you could run any multinational from Ireland.

He wanted it all. Both his parents' marriage and his brothers' marriages had shown him how family life could be, and he wanted that. But big, successful businessmen weren't supposed to think in such a way. They were supposed to be super-glued to their four phones, screaming at harried assistants, and wearing headsets to murmur their secret deals as they marched around galleries with their art collectors picking out investment/kudos-gaining paintings for their kudos-gaining big houses in the right spots in the right countries around the world. They were supposed to want super-thin, Pilates-honed wives who had Birkin handbags in every colour and every animal skin to hang off skinny arms, with an array of shoes that needed their own closet. These men wanted entrée to Davos, not tickets to kid movies with their small children.

But Red – who'd met plenty of Birkin wives, eyes anxiously swivelling as they watched their mega-rich husbands in case someone younger or prettier came along – didn't want that life. He wanted the cinema tickets to *Despicable Me* 3. He wanted a short, curvy woman who'd never tried

Pilates in her life and who would probably only see a Birkin bag if such an unlikely gem passed through her vintage shop.

Nobody knew this of course. They all thought Red was the ultimate alpha male, when in fact he was an alpha-beta, which was a new type of man, apparently, explained to him by an old pal's wife.

Michael and Barbara Doorly had been friends of his forever, and Barbara, who was a journalist, said the metrosexual was old hat and the alpha-beta – 'still macho but also caring and wants a family' – was where it was at.

'This is the sort of man who wants to understand his woman, wants to be with her, wants to nurture her and take care of her and take care of their children,' explained Barbara, who was writing a feature about it.

Michael, who'd got a better fix on Red than any journalist ever would, had looked his friend in the eye and said: 'I think you're right, Babs. Our boy is an alpha-beta. That's where all those high-flying girlfriends have been going wrong.'

Red had pretend-punched Michael, who'd pretend-punched him back.

'The furniture, guys,' said Barbara, who was used to this sort of male bonding and had a broken vase to prove it.

'Mr O'Neill?' A driver stood in front of him now, wearing a dark suit, dangling keys in his hand.

'Hello,' said Red politely. He was always polite.

227

Maybe he wasn't so alpha-beta after all. 'You know where I'm staying?'

The driver said: 'Of course, sir.'

'We'll drop by my mother's first. Twenty-one Longford Terrace, Silver Bay.'

'Whatever you want, sir.'

The driver tried to take Red's carry-on bag but Red refused. 'I'll take it myself,' he said.

No point going to the gym and doing a 90 kilo push press if you couldn't carry your own damn case to the car. They climbed into the car, which was parked in the special VIP drivers' parking area close to the airport. No more parking miles away like the plebs did, the way he and Coco had done for that amazing holiday in Greece once. He sat in the back seat and closed his eyes. Just because he was in the same country as her, he would not think about her. She was the past.

He'd gone out with plenty of women after Coco: fabulous, amazing women. City women, fit, gym-going, smart, clever girls that any man would have been delighted to be seen with. But there was always something wrong, something that ended the relationship abruptly.

'You're just not with me – mentally, I mean. You're here but your head is a thousand miles away,' complained Lara, a brunette lawyer who had a fleet of men after her.

'I don't think you're a player but are you ever going to settle down?' demanded Karen, a no-nonsense girl from New Zealand who didn't believe in hanging around waiting for the man to ask the serious questions.

If Karen was going to be with a man, she wanted to know if there was a future in it. And Red had had to admit that there was no future in it. He didn't know *why*. He wished he did.

'I'm sorry,' he'd said, and it had been very hard not to say, 'It's not you, it's me' – a statement which might have got him a knee somewhere painful.

Michael, who appeared to know everything about women thanks to Barbara, said that the 'it's not you, it's me' thing had come to be a handy way for guys to dump women by pretending they were saying sorry, when in fact, it really meant: 'It *is* you but I can't handle the argument if I say so.'

'How do you know all this stuff?' Red asked Michael, bewildered.

'Barbara. She writes an article a week on men and how weird we are. She knows more about us than we do.'

'Isn't that hard to live with?' said Red.

'Nah. I love her so I just roll with it. It's the secret to marital happiness,' Michael added with a grin. 'Do you want to be right or do you want to be happy?' The grin widened. 'I like being happy.'

In Red's darker moments, he wondered if happiness simply eluded some people. Perhaps he simply wasn't meant to be happily married like his two younger brothers, Mike and Dan, who had loving wives, small children and their mother's adoration. The way to Myra O'Neill's heart was not to be a successful businessman who got write-ups in the *Financial Times,* but to get married and present her with grandchildren to boast about endlessly at bingo and book club.

Or maybe he was just picky, as a couple of his friends had said.

'Are you waiting for a supermodel? Someone from the Victoria's Secret line-up? Is that it?' Sandy, an old pal from the US college where he'd done his MBA, had asked this question when they were having a night out in London, eating the special blackened fish at Nobu before heading on to a few clubs, whereupon they decided they were far too old for this type of carry-on and went back to Red's apartment with its giant windows over-looking the Thames to drink a few beers and talk.

'Of course I'm not waiting for a Victoria's Secret model,' said Red irritably.

A vision of an entirely different sort of woman had come into his head – a woman who was very much the opposite of a leggy Victoria's Secret angel. A woman who was short, curved and would never walk any runway with wings attached to her. Coco Keneally.

'I saw her, that Coco, at the supermarket and, do you know what, I nearly went over and gave her a piece of my mind,' his mother had told him on the phone only the previous month.

Although his mother gave him a hard time about not being married yet, she was his most fearless defender. Far more fearless than Edwards, O'Brien and Edelstein, his lawyers – so tough that the mere arrival of a missive bearing their stationery caused even the most ruthless business people to blanch.

If Red had allowed it, his mother would have gone round to Coco's house and thrown eggs at the windows or paraded outside her vintage shop with placards saying: *This woman ruined my son's life.*

It was a mistake to mess with any of Myra O'Neill's sons. They might be grown men but they were still her babies and she would never, ever forgive Coco Keneally.

Red himself hadn't seen Coco since that horrible day four years ago and he sincerely hoped he wouldn't see her now. That was the problem with coming back to Dublin: there was always the fear that he'd bump into her somewhere.

Yes, the big, strong Red O'Neill was scared of the thought of seeing his former fiancée. He still had the ring he'd bought her, although he'd never told anyone that. He'd picked it up from the street where Coco had thrown it. He kept it in the safe in the London apartment and sometimes, when he was feeling lonely, he took it out and thought that even then he could have afforded something more expensive, but that Coco, being Coco, had wanted something delicate, old and not ridiculously pricey.

He'd never meet her in Dublin, he told himself as the car flew through the Dublin streets. Nowadays, unless he was in the pub with his brothers and his father, he went to such different sorts of places from the sorts of places they'd frequented when they were a couple, before he'd made it really big. Cheap places, interesting places – no troupe of waiters standing behind all the chairs and lifting silver domes from their dinner plates in a choreographed manoeuver, that was for sure.

And yet sometimes, when he was sitting sleepily on a red-eye somewhere, a bit low, the way flying around the world often made him feel, he thought it might be nice to bump into Coco just one more time. As a sort of test, to see if she still held the same power over him. Because if she didn't, then he'd be free.

The big black Mercedes looked faintly ridiculous outside Longford Terrace, so Red sent it away.

'Thanks, sir,' said the driver gratefully. Both he and Red knew that large, expensive, brand-new Mercedes were not normally seen outside Longford Terrace, and there was a definite possibility that, despite the presence of the driver sitting in the car, the hubcaps might mysteriously vanish.

'I'll call you later,' Red had said.

He'd offered to buy his parents a big house in a posher area of the city when he first made money, but they'd refused.

'This is our home, son,' his father had said, and Red understood that. Still, he had to ask.

He went into the house, where his mother was busy cooking up a storm after his phone call on the way from the airport.

'I wish you'd phoned and said you were coming over before you actually arrived in the country,' said Myra O'Neill, with a faint hint of irritability in her voice.

Red grinned. He knew she wasn't in the slightest bit irritable, knew she was overjoyed he was there at all. As soon as he'd rung to say he was in Dublin, he was pretty sure she was on the phone straight after to tell his two brothers, setting up a family dinner to beat all family dinners because there was nothing Myra liked more than a big O'Neill get-together.

'Great to see you, son,' his father said with a thump on the back.

It was how the O'Neill men greeted each other. Myra was an entirely different story. She grabbed her tall son, taller than her since he was about twelve, and held on to him as though she though her heart might break. But despite the hug, her words were sharp: 'It's a long time since we've seen you, Mr Red,' she said, with her back to him now, working away at the oven. 'I hope you don't think you've forgotten about us over there in London. You have to always remember where you come from, Red—'

'I think he knows where he comes from, love,' interrupted his father bravely.

Myra rounded on her husband. 'He knows well enough where he comes from, and we both know that, but—' she cast a fond glance over at her eldest son – 'it's a mother's job to remind her kids sometimes.'

Myra was outraged that Red was staying in a hotel.

'What would you want to be staying in a hotel when we've still got your bedroom here?' she demanded.

Red didn't want to mention that hotels had beautiful en suites, room service, a mini-bar where he could get himself a whiskey and soda, and sit down in front of a widescreen television to watch a match. Hotels didn't have people who enquired about his every move, asked after his social life and whether he'd met any nice girls, and did he hear about the death/marriage of XYZ, people he could no longer remember, but whom, according to his mother, he 'knew as well as you know me'.

The flood of both questions and information was always somewhat dizzying when he came home. He'd forgotten the pace with which the O'Neill family lived. It was his mother, really. Myra O'Neill was a force of nature, a woman who was a stalwart of every charity going, had been on the school board when her kids went to St Fintan's, and who'd been involved in every part of their life. She was the one who'd kept them on the straight and narrow in the years when it was very easy for young fellas with little job prospects to go off the rails. She was the one who'd marched round to friends' houses when there were too many bottles of beer being shared among underage drinkers.

Red could remember one incident when he was seventeen, going on eighteen, and felt perfectly entitled to have a beer if he felt like it, when his mother had turned up at a friend's house and caught him by the ear – yes, the ear – and hauled him out of the room as if he were a fifteenth-century serving boy. She'd belted him on the head all the way home.

At the time he'd been outraged, but now he could understand it. She'd seen plenty of kids from Longford Terrace turn out entirely differently from the way the O'Neill boys had turned out, and she wanted to make sure that her sons had the best chance in life.

He sat at the kitchen table, a mug of tea in front of him and some of her home-made scones, even though he said he wasn't hungry, and weren't they going to be having dinner soon anyway?

'Nonsense,' his mother said. 'Look at you! Not an ounce of fat on you. Too much time in that gym, I imagine, and not enough time eating proper food. Sushi, I suppose, and all that type of mad uncooked stuff. I don't hold with that sort of food. Good, proper Irish cooking is what you'll get here.'

Red and his father exchanged glances and smiled at each other. It was great coming home. Nothing changed here, which was what made it so beautiful.

Red and his father talked a bit about work, football, the local team his father had supported all his life, the government and the grandkids. Little Timmy, Dan's oldest, was walking now.

'He's a total pet, he is,' said Red's father proudly.

How long would it take? Red wondered. He took a quick glance at his watch. Five minutes?

'I see that Coco around sometimes,' his mother said long before the five-minute limit was up, and even though he was turned away from her, Red could practically sense the way her back had stiffened.

Coco, whom his mother had adored, had become '*that* Coco' as soon as she'd hurt Myra's son.

'She's not married, engaged or anything like that. No. Hmm. I keep an eye on her. Not that I let anyone know I'm keeping an eye on her, Lord, no. I see Pearl sometimes in the church or in the supermarket. Decent woman, Pearl is, always has a word for me, but we don't talk about . . . you know. Better not to talk about those sort of things. But still, if I got my hands on that girl—'

'Ma,' said Red. 'That's all in the past. Forget it, will you?'

He heard keys in the door, noises of his brothers and their wives, shrieking of a baby, scampering toddler footsteps, and he knew he was saved. Because the more he thought about it, it wasn't over with Coco, was it? Still, his mother didn't need to know that.

*   *   *

Coco sat in the chair beside Jo's bed in the six-bed St Teresa's ward and wished, not for the first time, that magic existed and she could magic away both Jo and Fiona's pain. Her friend's progress was still painfully slow, despite all the neurologist had said about brain plasticity – or was it elasticity? She still got that wrong. But he was confident about her recovery.

'You may still have some speech issues, but with rehab, I'd like to think we could get you nearly back to possibly ninety per cent original mobility,' he said cheerfully the morning before when he'd come in. 'You've had a mild stroke, Jo, so, although it may not feel like it right now, you're one of the lucky ones, definitely.'

'Don't feel thlucky,' said Jo. 'Ninety per thent. Not a hundred. A hundred's what I want.'

Her speech had come back remarkably well, but she still spoke as if the words had to form much more slowly in her brain. Certain words eluded her and she continually mispronounced others. This was a mild form of aphasia, Coco had learned. Jo had had a certain amount of spontaneous recovery but would still need speech therapy.

Hearing that made her shriek to Coco: 'I don't want it! I teach people; I don't get taught!'

Coco had spent hours searching the internet about strokes and had read miracle stories about recovery, but Coco no longer told these to her friend. Jo seemed so angry all the time. It was as if this injury had changed her from a happy person into someone who saw doom and personal disaster around every corner. Not just random disaster, but disaster deliberately for her.

'Why me?' she said to Coco often. 'What did I do wrong?' Because of her speech problems, this came out slowly as: 'What thid I tho wrong?' with Jo wincing as the words came out of her mouth.

There were no answers for a question like that, and Coco would just rub Jo's good hand whenever she said it.

'You're getting better,' she'd say ineffectually.

Jo had nearly full use of her left hand and arm again, although she still had huge problems with leg control.

'I can't walk,' Jo said loudly. 'I can't talk to my daughter. I can barely concentrate. I can't always control when I pee! I'm wearing old person nappies because there aren't enough people here to get me to the loo and I am not having a bloody catheter. How can I look after her? Someone will take her off me!' Jo said in anguish.

'They won't,' Coco said firmly, but soon after she made an excuse to go out to get coffee for them both and walked wearily to the nurse's station halfway down the corridor.

'Don't you have psychiatric help for people who have strokes?' Jo asked, only to have an older nurse look at her with pitying and sympathetic eyes. 'My friend's not coping well . . .'

'There are help groups and the rehab helps too – seeing other people in the same position seems to take away the "why me" thing,' the nurse said, hands flying as she organised files as she was speaking. 'It's not easy for a young woman to be living an ordinary life and to suddenly end up in a hospital bed, incapacitated, scared, with no way of knowing how it will all turn out. Plus there's the lady opposite her who's also had a stroke and her prognosis isn't as good, as you can see.'

Mrs Leonard was very elderly, she was bed-bound, her speech was entirely gone and she moaned non-stop, which was upsetting to both her family and Jo, who'd hissed: 'Is that going to be me soon?'

'No matter how often Mr Carter—' the nurse said the consultant's name with reverence – 'says Jo is on medication now to stop her having another stroke, I know she keeps looking at Mrs Leonard in the bed across from her and she's scared.'

They both considered this basic fact. Jo had been luckier than Mrs Leonard, who'd been seriously damaged by her stroke, but there were no guar-antees for the future.

'What about Jo's family? I haven't seen any sign of a dad for the little girl?'

'Long gone,' said Coco grimly.

'Parents?'

'You must have missed them. It was quite a show. They brought along some tame preacher guy to say that Jo had sinned but had paid the price now.'

The nurse shuddered. 'That helped no end, I'm sure.'

'Oh, it was a great help,' Coco agreed. 'On the plus side, it was the first time I saw Jo attempt to get out of the bed on her own, though.'

'Frustration makes people do that. Then they risk falling . . . It's a long process. You're a good friend. You're taking care of her daughter, aren't you? Pet of a thing. Never says anything, though, does she?'

Coco nodded and found her eyes filling with tears. 'She doesn't speak as much anymore. Before, you couldn't shut her up, but now . . . Now she just looks at her mother as if she's terrified she'll go away. Or . . .' Coco could barely say it. 'Die.'

'Children react to these things differently,' said the nurse, ignoring the whole dying part of the conversation.

Probably part of the training, Coco thought: ignore any madness from patients' families. 'How she will cope depends on how you and her mother cope,' the nurse went on. 'I've seen it before. If you pretend nothing's happening, kids internalise it. Years later, then they're traumatised by what they never coped with. You've got to keep talking about what's happened to her mother. Face it all head-on. You might say that to Jo. Tell her she needs to cope for her daughter's sake. That might help.'

Coco needed to work up the courage to impart this information, but today she sat and talked quietly with Jo as if they were in a café having a chat, with Fiona amusing herself in the background. The way they used to *before*.

Jo's face was much better but she still didn't look quite like herself. Strange how you could have the same eyes, same mouth, but add in the faintest tilt to one side – which Mr Carter said could be gone soon, given her general progression – and eyes angry with emotional pain, and the person could look entirely different.

She'd never been much for dolling herself up with make-up, but now Jo refused to wear so much as lipstick. It was her personal rage against the world that had made her into what she saw as a helpless woman in hospital.

Apart from the slowing of her speech, Jo's main disability was lack of movement in her left leg. It had improved considerably but wasn't perfect and, for Jo, perfection was what she was aiming for.

The hospital was planning on discharging her soon, pending improvement, and the next question was whether she'd need an actual rehab facility or whether she'd go home and have outpatient rehab for both her physical injuries and her speech problem – assuming, Coco thought, that Jo agreed to have speech therapy.

'The lack of control is so very frightening,' the kind nurse had also told Coco. 'We must try to remember that when a patient is being bad-tempered.'

Fiona sat on the edge of the bed, holding her mother's good hand, while staring up at the television set mounted high on the wall at the end of the ward. Coco had switched on a children's cartoon show on the small TV, the way she did every afternoon she brought Fiona into the hospital.

'What am I going to do?' said Jo, with anguished eyes.

Locked in TV cartoon world, Fiona appeared not to have heard her, but Coco knew she had. She could tell. Funny how spending so much time with Fiona had opened her eyes in so many ways. All Fiona's little mannerisms were obvious to her now. That faint slumping of the shoulders told her that Fiona's heart was breaking but that she was pretending to watch the TV, where three fabulously skinny Hollywood tweens were discussing boys.

'You will survive; we all will,' said Coco fiercely. 'We will get through this and life will be fabulous. And then . . .' Coco cast around for something wonderful. 'Then the three of us are going to Disneyland Paris for a holiday!'

Jo looked at her blankly.

Disney? Like I care about Disney, were the unspoken words.

It was the first time Coco realised that she'd spoken entirely for Fiona's benefit. Jo was in emotional pain but she was an adult and she needed to help herself too. But Fiona was nine. Fiona needed all of Coco's energy to help her. That's what mothers did. And for now, Coco was all the mother Fiona had.

She reached out to touch her goddaughter's small shoulder. Fiona half-turned and, for the first time in a long while, she saw the glimmer of a smile in Fiona's eyes.

She wasn't going to let Fiona internalise this pain and think that it was her fault, or suffer with the whole thing later in life – the way she had, Coco realised. Not being able to deal with her mother's disappearance as a child had made it all the harder when she was older. Cassie had acted out; Coco had assumed that everyone was going to dump her – so she got ready to dump them first.

Like Red.

This would not happen to her darling Fiona.

At home in her apartment, Coco made Fiona's lunch for the next day at school, put water on to boil for the pasta, ran a speedy bubble bath for Fiona, and then, once Fiona was happily nestled up to her neck in bubbles, Coco rang her sister.

'Can you talk?' she asked.

'Course, for you, anytime,' said Cassie, tidying up in the kitchen after dinner. Loud music emanated from Beth's bedroom – a sure sign that quality homework was being done. Lily was at the kitchen table making a model of the solar system in a shoebox, using round things that she was supposed to paint vaguely like the planets. Saturn, with its darned rings, had caused both Cassie and Lily a lot of trouble. During the making of it, Cassie had wondered if a kitchen-table business could be set up by creating a mail-order company for strange school projects that defied even the most diligent cutting up of cereal packets and use of double-sided sticky tape.

'It's about Fiona,' whispered Coco. 'She's in the bath.'

Cassie said, 'Keep going, darling,' to Lily and went into the hall to talk. 'Tell me what's wrong,' she said, the way she'd been saying it for almost thirty years, since almost before her little sister could talk.

'She's so quiet these days . . .'

'She does perk up when she's here, though,' Cassie pointed out. 'She loves Beth and Lily, and even the cat will sit on her lap.'

'He's a healing cat, I told you. No, it's a combination of two things. In the hospital after school this afternoon, she was very quiet – which she usually is – and a nurse said something interesting to me. She said how Fiona copes with all this depends on how the adults around her cope. If we pretend it's not happening and don't deal with it, *she* won't have the skills to deal with it. She'll bury it inside and it will be like a grenade waiting to go off when she's older.'

Cassie took a swift, shallow breath in.

'But if we talk about it,' went on Coco, 'and deal with it, then she can too. Does that make sense to you? I've been scared of talking too much because she's only nine and I don't know how Jo would want to do it, but Jo's not acting like herself right now. I wanted to know what you thought?'

Because of our mother? Because nobody ever spoke about her and we were too little to understand?

Cassie was afraid she'd spoken these words out loud, but then Coco said, 'You know, from a mother's point of view. Does that make sense? Is Fiona old enough to hear all this stuff?'

'It makes perfect sense,' said Cassie, thinking how she still had the grenade sitting inside her. But she was an expert at being like a second mother to Coco, which meant being expert at pushing her own worries aside. 'She and Jo were especially close. They were a unit on their own and it must be terrifying for both of them to have this happen. Jo is scared out of her mind, Coco – you can see that. I saw that when I went into the hospital to visit her last.

'Anger is all she's got right now. So you've got to be Fiona's mother for a while. Tell Fiona what's going on, in a gentle way: explain that her mum is upset, that it's going to take time, but that she is loved and cared for. That her mum will get better, and she might not be as quick at running or things like that, but she'll still be the same mum. And tell her she's got you with her.'

Coco smiled at her end of the phone.

'I want to tell her what you told me when I was small, Cass: "I will never let you down".'

Cassie had been holding it all together very well until that moment. But then her anxieties over Shay, over rejection, over keeping her beloved family together and happy, flowed over.

245

She couldn't let Coco know.

'I meant it, Coco,' she said, her voice thick with emotion.

'Oh sis, I didn't mean to upset you,' cried Coco. 'I loved that saying; still do. I think of how you took care of me, have always taken care of me, and I love you so much. I will never let you down either, you know.'

'I know,' sniffed Cassie. 'Don't mind me, I'm pre-menstrual,' she lied.

'You need a hot bath,' said Coco. 'And I'm going to tell Fiona about how you and I loved each other so much and about what you used to say to me all the time: "I will never let you down". It's the loveliest thing anyone's ever said to me, Cass, and it helped me so much. I don't know why I didn't think of it before. It's just the right way to explain how much I love Fiona. Love you, Cassie.'

When her sister had hung up, Cassie sat down on the staircase in the hall for a few moments before she felt able to go back into the kitchen.

'Look, Mum,' said Lily triumphantly, holding up a finally finished Saturn. 'I used cocktail sticks to keep the rings on!'

Without saying anything, Cassie hugged her younger daughter.

'You're brilliant, Lily, you know that?'

Lily grinned. 'I know,' she said, still admiring her creation. 'So are you, Mum.'

★   ★   ★

Red's friend, Michael, had rung him up and invited him to a dinner party on Friday night.

'You know I hate dinner parties,' grumbled Red.

'When did you turn into such an old curmudgeon?' demanded Michael. 'Come on, it'll be fun. You're never in this country long enough for us to see you. It'll just be some of the gang and a few new people.'

'I hate meeting new people,' said Red. 'I meet enough new people as it is and I can never remember their names.'

His mother was torturing him, dragging him around to the house, where she'd conveniently have a few of her friends sitting having coffee so they could gaze in wonder at her fabulously successful son.

'Ma, stop doing that, please,' Red had begged.

'Well, I have to show off something,' Myra pointed out. 'It's either grandchildren or how successful you are – one or the other, you choose.'

'OK, OK.'

'And there's some big charity event going on with the school to raise money for kids in Africa. You could give a few bob to that too?'

'So I'm a bank to be ogled at, is that it?' said Red.

His mother ruffled his hair, which took some doing given he was a foot taller than her. 'Ah, go way outta that,' she said, smiling. 'You love it really. And you know you'll be off again soon, forgetting about us all. We might as well make the most of this bit of your time.'

'Come on,' said Michael now. 'It'll be fun. Our house, Friday night, half seven, bring a bottle.'

Michael was one of Red's oldest friends from college and he'd been a high-flying executive for many years, married to his childhood sweetheart, Barbara, before one day he'd surprised everyone and given it all up to become a sculptor. At the time, Red had thought that Michael had lost his mind, but when he'd gone around to the beautiful house on the seafront in Silver Bay and had seen the world that Michael and Barbara had built with their daughter, Yvette, he changed his mind.

Thanks to Michael's previous career, they owned their beautiful home. Barbara was a freelance journalist, and with his contacts, Michael had a pretty good career going, making huge sculptures for big businesses. Their daughter, Yvette, was a joy – a little fair-haired moppet the last time Red had seen her.

He was actually looking forward to the dinner party, and when he rolled up at the Doorlys', he was delighted to see more of his old pals there. Unfortunately they were all there with their significant others, except for Ray, another inveterate bachelor.

Ray slapped him on the back. 'It's just you and me in it together, Redser,' he said. 'Here, have a beer. They've invited a few women for us.'

'Oh please, no,' joked Red. 'Unless they're stunningly beautiful blondes with legs up to their armpits.'

'No,' said an amused voice, and a slender brunette appeared beside him. 'The name's Shona,' she said, and held out a hand. He looked down at the hand and noticed that she didn't have the sculpted, manicured nails of so many women he knew. 'I'm in the same line of business as Michael,' she said, following his gaze. 'So no French manicure.'

'She's a fabulous sculptor,' said Michael, coming in from the kitchen with a few nibbles. 'The starters have gone a bit wrong so you'll have to stuff yourselves with crisps and nuts,' he said. 'I thought I'd got the hang of this bruschetta business, but it's still tricky.'

'It's only tricky when you don't start making it on time,' came the voice of Barbara.

Red, Shona and Ray all laughed. It felt good to be here, Red thought, and he liked the look of this woman they'd lined up for him. Michael and Barbara couldn't help matchmaking.

'Hey,' whispered Ray into his ear, 'hands off, she's mine.'

'If she's yours, which one is mine?' Red joked back.

'I'm not here for anyone,' said Shona with a twinkle in her eye. 'Barbara had a couple of crazy single girls lined up for the pair of you but they bailed at the last moment. To be honest, I understand because I'd heard that you were an awful player, Ray: a girl in every port.'

Ray did his best to look hurt but failed.

She took a searing look at Red. 'And they heard that you were too married to your business to ever think about going out with a woman for any length of time.' She grinned at Red. He grinned back at her. There was something about this woman that he liked.

Dinner turned out to be fun, full of chat about old friends, films they'd seen, who they'd have to their fantasy dinner party, what they'd all been up to, and discussions about the pieces Shona and Michael were working on at the moment.

'Isn't it great for you creative types?' said Ray after he'd had a few beers in him. 'You can get up any time you want, whereas I have to be on the job at half eight in the morning.' Ray was a painter/decorator.

'I'm up at six every morning, if you don't mind,' said Barbara, swatting him on the head. 'I'm a working mother with a small child, and if I don't get a bit of work done before Yvette wakes up, there's the day gone.'

There followed a discussion with the other women about children and childcare, while the men moved on to talking about football.

'Do you have children?' Red asked Shona. She shook her head and he noticed a hint of sorrow in her face. *Uh oh*, he thought to himself, *time to get out of this one.* He did not want to be stuck with a woman whose biological clock was set to explode.

It was all going swimmingly until eventually

Michael asked him the question he hoped no one would ask. 'Have you seen Coco since you've come back?'

Of course someone was going to ask him that, Red thought grimly. Back in the day, they'd gone out together as a foursome, and both Michael and Barbara had loved Coco.

'No,' said Red, a little more stiffly than he had intended.

Michael looked at him. 'I sometimes drop into her shop to say hello. She's doing well now. She's somehow involved in this lovely charity thing down on the seafront early next year to raise funds for Africa.'

'Ah,' said Red. 'My mother was on about that.'

'Well, you know Coco: total soft touch. She's involved and her grandmother too. They're decent people, Red. You should talk to her. Might make it a bit easier.'

'I don't want it to be easier,' said Red testily. 'It's over. I don't want to see her anymore.'

Michael, who'd known him for a long time, said, 'Yeah, right. She's not with anyone.'

'How do you know?' asked Red, much too quickly.

Where was the cool, calm and collected business-man now?

'She was the best thing that ever happened to you.'

'Yes,' put in Barbara.

'So I don't know why you don't go round there.'

'It's over,' said Red forcefully. 'She dumped me, remember?'

'You know,' said Michael, 'when I worked in business I'd never have been this frank, but now that I do what I love, I wonder why I didn't do it years ago, and I think that's what's wrong with you too, Red. You're not doing what makes you happy. Oh, you might be in business, that's great, but you're not happy personally. You never come home to see us all. Your mother hates it that you stay away, as if this island is Kryptonite and you're Superman. Every time I see her she's all over me trying to find out if I have any information about you. You're avoiding a whole country because of one woman, so don't tell me it's all over.'

On Saturday morning, Phoebe got up early. Today she was leaving the last of her CVs into all the remaining places in the area and then taking the bus back home. It had been a crazy two weeks. There was so much to tell them all at home. College was amazing; meeting Ian there even better. She had a friend: a quirky, emotionally stressed friend who could be spectacularly rude but who needed her. Someone who needed looking after, and that, of course, was Phoebe's speciality. She could imagine her mum laughing when she told her. 'You like to have something to take care of, don't you, Phoebe?'

After dropping off the last of her CVs, Phoebe walked back to Delaney Gardens, thinking that it might not be so bad to work in the pub because she could work nights and get tips. Dealing with a man who'd called her a 'fine hoult of a girl' might be less fun, but Phoebe wouldn't let that stop her.

Phoebe often stopped the rude, drunk fellas in their tracks when they tried to pinch her bum by slapping them heartily on the back, which made them spill their drinks, and loudly saying: 'Keep rubbing the cream on it, Joe, and I'm sure the itch will go away' – a statement which made even the drunkest, rowdiest men shut up.

She rounded the corner into the square and saw that several people were taking advantage of the lovely late September weather in the small park. There was a woman with two small children who were playing at being airplanes, running around with their arms out and making droning noises. The woman was sitting back in a bench as if she might not be able to drag herself up again and was praying for the airplane game to go on for longer.

The elderly man with his little terrier was in there again, doing stately promenades of the park. They both seemed to have stiff hips from the way they were walking. The old man held a pink nappy bag in one hand, and Phoebe grinned at the sight, thinking of the amount of bird poo she'd undoubtedly have to shift that weekend with the bird sheds. She didn't care. Stinky sheds or no stinky sheds, she couldn't wait to get back home. She wondered if she should invite Ian home one weekend. It might be fun.

As she passed the house she'd come to think of as the square's sunshine house, with its gleaming white walls, azure blue shutters and fabulously verdant garden, she realised that someone was in the garden.

A clearly quite old lady, who was dressed in very un-old-lady clothes – a modern, pale blue A-line dress and trendy sandals with her toenails painted a vibrant coral – was standing with some string in one hand and a cup of tea in the other. Her hair was silky silver and was tied up into a loose knot at the base of her neck. At her feet, perched almost on her feet, was a small soft dog with glossy beige fur and the biggest eyes Phoebe had ever seen.

The dog spotted Phoebe first and leapt to its sturdy legs, doing a little yappy bark. The lady looked up and smiled, and Phoebe, who had felt lost for friendship here in Dublin except for Ian, found herself sinking into the warmth of that smile.

Perhaps it was because she was about to get the bus home and she'd had just about enough of being on her own, but she felt a most un-Phoebe-like surge of self-pity. She was so lonely. She couldn't do this, she couldn't. Why was she even trying to learn to be a fashion designer in Larkin College. She could work at home and do it there, couldn't she? Plenty of people who worked in fashion were self-taught.

'Daisy seems to like you,' said the lady, and Phoebe looked down to see the dog's soft black nose pushed through the gate, desperately trying to reach Phoebe's jeans for a sniff.

'Oh, you are cute.' Bending down, she crooned to the small dog, who shook her entire body in greeting. 'Hello, darling,' Phoebe whispered. She missed her family and she missed the animals. It was so lonely here . . .

'Come in and say hello,' the lady said. 'It's impossible to give Daisy the adoration she wants through the gate bars.'

Faced with such a welcome, and a beautiful animal who was clearly in need of loving, the dog-deprived Phoebe was in like a shot. She got to her knees and petted Daisy. 'She makes the most adorable noises,' she said delightedly. 'It's like she's purring.'

'I know,' said the old lady. 'She's half pug, half cat, I think. I've noticed that a lot with the pugs I've had over the years. They all make different sounds of happiness. I had a beautiful boy pug called Basil, and he used to make little growls of pleasure. But Daisy here, she just sounds like a kitten who's being adored.'

'Oh gosh,' said Phoebe, getting to her feet quickly. 'I'm so rude. My name is Phoebe and I live across the road in—'

'In Rita Costello's. Yes, I know. My name is Pearl Keneally. It's lovely to meet you, Phoebe. I can tell you're an animal lover.'

Phoebe sank to her knees again. 'Yes,' she said. 'I live on a farm in Dromolach in Wicklow and I have to say I'm missing all the animals so much. I'm missing my family. It's sort of all connected, family and animals.'

'That's the way it should be,' Pearl said. 'When I was bringing my girls up, the animals were a huge part of it.' It seemed as if she was about to say more but then she stopped herself. 'So Phoebe, what has you out and about so bright and early this morning? Would you like a quick cup of tea or some lemonade? I have a lovely nine-year-old little poppet coming over later today and I've got home-made lemonade ready for her.'

'That sounds fabulous,' said Phoebe. 'My mother used to make that years ago but she doesn't really have time now.'

'Come on in,' said Pearl decisively.

The three of them went inside and Phoebe looked around in delight, marvelling that a house, which was basically the same in structure as Mrs Costello's, could have such a different atmosphere. This place was alight with beautiful blues and whites, with pretty coloured pictures, scenes of lovely places on the walls, sculptures and artwork, plump couches and lovely crocheted throws – one all white with periwinkle and turquoise accents.

'Come on into the kitchen,' said Pearl. 'Let's not stand on ceremony here. Besides, I've some biscuits just out of the oven and Daisy can smell them. She will abandon you, I'm afraid, for the biscuits. Cupboard love rules Daisy's heart.'

Phoebe giggled. 'Our dog Prince is a bit like that,' she said. 'He is a sweetie. Not terribly clever but very kind and entirely ruled by his belly.'

'It's the same here,' said Pearl. 'I have to be very careful with Daisy, though, because inside every normal-sized pug is a really fat pug dying to get out, and they have breathing issues because they've such flat faces and small noses that it's doubly wrong to let them get fat.'

The kitchen was just the same as the rest of the downstairs: bright, airy and looking out on to a verandah and the most glorious garden Phoebe had ever seen.

'How beautiful,' she said.

'It's my hobby,' Pearl explained. 'I spend a lot of time out here now. I love gardening but it has to be said, digging up weeds is great for stopping you worrying.'

'I understand,' said Phoebe. 'We have ducks and hens at home, and cleaning out their sheds is not the most glorious job in the world, but it does take your mind off other things.'

'Now,' said Pearl, 'given my advanced age, I am allowed to be a nosy neighbour and ask you what has you in Dublin and, more importantly, what has you living with Rita Costello? I was always afraid that she boiled and ate her lodgers.'

Phoebe, who had just taken a sip of some glorious homemade lemonade, almost spat it out. 'Don't say that,' she said, giggling. 'I think it might be true. I'm slightly convinced that she stands outside my door and presses a glass up against it to hear what I'm doing. She warned me against parties with such intent, I think she's either had dreadful experiences with students or else I think she doesn't like us very much.'

'Rita doesn't like anyone very much,' Pearl said drily. 'I think there should be some sort of bad-tempered landlady register because she would certainly be on it. Why on earth did you move in with her?'

'I was desperate, her son showed me around the place, and I thought I could change the paint a little bit to make it nicer,' Phoebe admitted. 'My room is at the front, which is nice, but it's a dreadful green. And I definitely wouldn't have moved in if I'd met her because she's a bit scary. But I'm stuck now. She has my deposit and woe betide me if I break so much as a cup.'

'Darling,' said Pearl, 'no matter what you do, even if you leave that place spotless afterwards and get an entirely accurate version of the Sistine Chapel painted on the ceiling, you will not be getting your deposit back. Rita is renowned for it. There are lots of nice people around here who'd like to take in a lodger, would take much better care of you, and probably wouldn't charge as much.' Suddenly Pearl's eyes gleamed. 'I have the most perfect idea,' she said. 'My friend Gloria lives four houses down from here. You've probably seen it, the house with the white roses – she loves her white roses, Gloria. Her husband has been in a home for some time and she's terribly lonely. You could live with her. What a wonderful idea!'

'But,' said Phoebe, feeling anxious and excited simultaneously, 'does she *want* a lodger?'

Everything was happening very quickly and she wasn't sure if she'd fallen in with an incredibly kind lady or with somebody who was maybe a few marbles short of a set.

'She doesn't know she wants a lodger yet,' said Pearl beadily, 'but trust me, she does. It's a four-bedroomed house with two bathrooms and a garden of white flowers in the back. Gloria's an amazing cook, too. What are you studying in college?'

'Fashion,' said Phoebe, looking around to see if there were any other signs of madness. She had such a good feeling about Pearl but one had to be careful because who knew, after all?

'Fashion,' said Pearl thoughtfully. 'Are you looking for part-time work, by any chance?'

'Actually, that's what I was doing this morning,' said Phoebe, 'dropping my details into the last few places. I've seen almost every shop, café and pub in Silver Bay and nobody has any space for part-timers except perhaps the pub, and I've done a lot of pub work before. I'm not overly keen on doing that anymore but it does pay the bills and you get tips.'

Daisy had settled herself in a comfy dog bed

and was looking longingly up at Phoebe and the shortbread biscuits with beseeching eyes that implied she hadn't been fed in at least a month.

'My granddaughter has a lovely shop around here and she's been very busy lately because there's been a sort of family illness, which means she's not in the shop much. She has someone but . . .' Pearl's sniff implied what she thought about her granddaughter's 'someone'. 'I wonder . . .' Pearl seemed lost in thought. 'I wonder,' she said again. 'Just let me work on it, all right? I'll have a little chat with Gloria too. You need to meet her. How about this afternoon?'

'I'm getting the bus home to Wicklow,' said Phoebe apologetically.

'Right,' said Pearl, 'when you get back we'll set it up. No darling, I'm not deranged, I'm just . . . well . . .' Pearl put her head to one side and smiled, and Phoebe could see how nobody could ever refuse Pearl anything. 'I am either an organiser in the parish or a bit of a meddler, whichever way you want to look at it. But I see you, a lovely girl, who is living with terrible Rita – who never got over her husband leaving and who views the world through charcoal-tinted glasses – when you could be living with lovely Gloria who needs the company and would be so grateful. It'd be far more fun and you could, if I manage it, have a new part-time job into the bargain.' Pearl beamed at Phoebe. 'Leave it with me,' she said.

★　★　★

Cassie never stayed in bed at the weekend. She was an early bird, but this weekend she felt as if she could never get enough sleep. The anxiety she felt over the tragedy in Jo's life had made her sleep badly all week.

The other anxiety – the one she'd been trying to blot out – was the influx of feelings about her mother; feelings she was sure she'd sorted out years ago. Coco's talk about the grenade of undealt-with issues had been slowly ticking in her mind all week.

'So, my mother's gone. So what?' she'd told an old boyfriend who wondered about the unusual family set-up at the house in Delaney Gardens. It had been during her leather mini-skirt and dangerous years when she'd gone out in spite of all curfews set by her father: clubbing, drinking, pushing everything to the limit to see how else she could be punished. Because someone had punished her by taking away her mother – that had to be the only answer.

Anyone who'd asked about her lack of a mother had been told: 'She dumped us, preferred drinking and drugging to us,' in brutal tones, as if Cassie didn't really care either way.

But she had and she still did. How, she thought now, with two beautiful daughters growing up with her, could any mother abandon their children and simply never come back?

She'd felt those feelings most intensely when Beth had been born. As she held her baby, squalling with rage at having been taken from her cosy cocoon inside her mother's womb, Cassie had felt love like no other and found that she now hated her own mother for abandoning her and Coco. A mother abandoning her children was the most unnatural act in the world. The most heinous.

Being loved by that special person who took care of you from the start was the key to the most important development in humans. For that person to behave badly, to not love or to abuse the child, or to suddenly leave, could destroy the child left behind.

Her mother had done that.

As her daughters grew, Cassie had learned to bury her feelings about her real mother. She was too busy trying to do everything right to worry about herself, but now, partly because of how little Fiona was coping with her ill mother, and definitely due to Shay endlessly choosing his mother over her, it had all come rushing back.

The fear of abandonment was irrational, she knew, but it was there all the same: fear of abandonment and of the grenade going off.

Come that Saturday morning, her body had responded by being overcome with aches. Even her head ached, and she wasn't a woman for headaches. She had a million household chores to do after she'd taken the girls to their netball matches, but still she wanted nothing more than to lie in bed and try to doze.

Shay, seeing how tired she looked, said he'd take over. Would she like tea or to try to sleep again?

'You never have a rest,' he added kindly, and Cassie wanted to cry with relief at the gesture.

Kindness, she thought gratefully: *that* was the secret to marriage, the one they never mentioned in magazines – having someone say they'd bring you tea and let you stay in bed when you thought your whole body might collapse if you had to haul it out of bed again.

There was much bad-humoured moaning in the house. Nobody liked Saturday morning sports fixtures.

'It's torture,' said Lily, her oft-repeated theme.

'Hush, your mother's trying to have a rest,' hissed Shay.

There was silence for a beat.

'Mum's not taking us?' said Beth, shocked.

'No. Now brush your teeth, and not ten seconds of vaguely rubbing the brush near them – the whole two minutes,' their father went on.

Cassie burrowed under the covers to block out the noise. This was the reason why she didn't stay in bed often. Shay turned into an army general when he was in charge in the mornings and a row was inevitable. His favoured military approach at leaving the house antagonised the girls used to Cassie's more laid-back and fun morning routine.

She tickled them in the morning sometimes, put on loud music, dropped long-forgotten fluffy teddies on top of them – anything to make them laugh at the notion of getting up. One laugh in the morning was strangely worth two more at any other time of the day.

Even under her duvet, she could hear the row brewing.

'I *do* wash my teeth!'

She burrowed deeper.

'Mum! Dad's been mean to me. He said I don't brush my teeth properly and I do!' wailed Lily, arriving at the bedroom door.

Cassie knew this to be recently true because Lily was beginning to find boys attractive and knew that stinky breath was not desirable in girl-friends because Beth had told her. Not that Cassie had mentioned this information to Shay, who would have trouble learning that his thirteen-year-old daughter had even the slightest interest in boys, never mind knowing that fresh breath was an important part of this dating ritual. He'd probably have a seizure at the notion that Beth knew this too. It appeared that all the books were right: fathers *did* have huge problems adjusting to their daughters growing up and becoming interested in the opposite sex.

'Honey, tell him I know you brush them properly,' Cassie murmured. She reached a hand out from under the covers for a hug.

Lily sat heavily on the bed. 'I wish you were taking us. He won't take us for hot chocolate afterwards. Can you make him take us to the café?'

Was this what it was like being a judge – always having to be the higher authority?

There was no getting away from it – she'd have to get up and referee. Cassie hauled herself from her duvet nest. On the landing, another argument was going on about how Beth's netball skirt and shorts combination – a garment known as a 'skort' – had grown scandalously short when compared to Beth's ever-growing long legs.

'She *can't* go out like that!' Shay said, glaring at Cassie as if their elder daughter's growth spurt was entirely her fault.

'I know it's short but I haven't had a chance to get back to the uniform shop yet to get the next size up,' Cassie said tiredly. She'd done all the back-to-school uniform shopping, not Shay. She wanted to add that they were lucky there was food in the fridge, that anyone had homework done any night, or that without her, nobody would have had cooked dinner for the whole week. She wanted to add that Shay still hadn't managed to speak to Coco *once* about the whole Jo tragedy and ask how she was coping, but she held her breath.

Don't sweat the small stuff. Keep the big stuff firmly at the back of your mind.

'It's not acceptable, Cassie,' said Shay fiercely, unable to move off what he clearly viewed as a scandalous outfit for their daughter to be wearing to a sporting event. 'People will be able to see . . . well, her underwear! It's indecent! You can't let her out like that, Cassie.' It was the 'you' that did it, as if only Cassie had any responsibility for things in their house, while Shay was only responsible for things relating to his beloved mother's home.

Cassie lost her battle with not sweating the small stuff.

'*You* go to the uniform shop then,' she said, surprising them all with her roar. '*You* can do the grocery shopping and make the dinner. And every Saturday we have hot chocolate in the Coffee Bean, which you wouldn't know as you almost never take the girls to sports, but this week you can take them in there!'

With that, she turned on her heel, marched back into their bedroom and slammed the door.

Outside, there was silence.

Beth went into her room, bent over beside the mirror and twisted around to see if she could catch a glimpse of her knickers. Not a sign of them and she was wearing the pink cotton ones with the lace at the top, the ones she liked best because she thought they were really pretty and not at all kid-like, because Mum was obsessed with them wearing age-appropriate clothes.

'You can't see my knickers, Dad!' she roared triumphantly.

On Saturday morning, Antoinette thought she might phone Shay and get him to come round for a few hours in the afternoon. It was a sunny day, still warm for September. The branches of most of the shrubs in the garden needed to be cut back for winter and he was great with the secateurs. Her old hands weren't up to it anymore.

'I cut all my garden stuff up,' her friend Dilys liked to say. 'This gizmo I got in the garden shop can cut anything, whether you're strong or not. The fella that sold it to me said it was the perfect thing for the more mature lady. I think he was flirting with me . . .'

Josette rolled her eyes. 'You think everyone is flirting with you, hussy,' she said.

'Keeps me happy!' said Dilys, winking bawdily. 'There's many a fine tune played on an old fiddle.'

'My hands aren't up to it,' Antoinette pointed out, with a look at the fingers she manicured herself every week. 'The last time I did it, I had pains for ages.'

'I have pains for an hour after I get out of bed,' said Dilys, 'but I still do it. Lord, Antoinette, don't get old before your time.'

'It's nothing to do with age,' Antoinette said, wondering why she'd bothered even mentioning the pains in her hands.

Dilys was very annoying these days, pushing Antoinette all the time and implying that she was relying on Shay too much. Dilys was really taking the whole 'anything a man can do, I can do better' thing too far. Dilys would hurt herself one day with her determination to do it all herself, despite the two new hips. It wasn't as if she didn't have adult children to help. But then not everyone had a son like Shay.

The row over short uniforms and teeth-brushing meant Cassie had as much chance of launching herself up to the International Space Station as she had of going back to sleep, so she made herself some tea and toast, then went back to bed and flicked through a magazine. Her concentration wasn't even up to a book, which was a good indicator of her tiredness. Work was exhausting. Loren, her boss, had taken on four huge jobs and hadn't added any temporary staff to help them all out.

'Conference tourism is good for all of us!' Loren had said in a rallying speech the day before as she'd hurried out the door in head-to-toe designer gear to go to a posh lunch in the Merrion Hotel – an activity she described as 'networking' and on which she claimed oodles of tax back as a business expense.

'Better for some of us than for others,' sighed Belinda, clutching her office laptop she was taking home to work on all weekend.

Cassie had decided to ask Coco and Fiona if they wanted to come to an early Saturday dinner.

'Stay over, perhaps?'

'I'd love to but Attracta's flying in from Sydney on Saturday and she's staying with us. Xavier's coming on Sunday. He's very laid-back about the whole thing, saying it's just a quick trip. They're a weird family . . .'

Cassie thought about it. 'They had a weird upbringing, Coco,' she said.

'Ours wasn't cookie cutter either, Cass,' said Coco lightly. 'No mother, Dad permanently sad about her leaving . . . Only Pearl was normal. Well, and us . . .'

'You've never been normal!' teased Cassie, not wanting to talk about their own lives. The conversation during the week had been hard enough. That was the trick: if she didn't think about the past, it didn't exist. 'And we had love, don't forget that.'

'Yeah, love,' said Coco gratefully.

'That's what you've got for Fiona, and don't forget it. You're not her mum but you love her. That can work, even if it's just till Jo gets better.'

'I guess. I'm just so terrified of doing it all wrong,' said Coco.

Her sister laughed loudly. 'That's the main theme of motherhood,' she said. 'Welcome to the club!'

'We had the big talk,' Coco went on. 'I told her I would never let her down and she hugged me all evening, sitting on me like a baby monkey. She's never done that before.'

'She was scared,' Cassie said, 'and you helped her with that. You're doing amazingly, darling.'

Cassie had finally dragged herself out of bed and was about to start on vacuuming the house when the phone rang. It was just about the time the netball matches should be over, so Cassie thought it might be one of the girls with news of netball matches lost dismally or won triumphantly. Or even an update on the current row with their father.

Instead, it was her mother-in-law.

'Oh Cassie, how are you, pet?' said Antoinette. Then, without waiting for an answer, she sailed on. 'I was looking for Shay. Is he around? I need him to do something for me.'

Shay had been at his mother's twice this week and the previous week. He'd been there the night Jo had been rushed to hospital – the night when she'd needed him.

Cassie felt a surge of anger rise from somewhere inside her. That night she'd really needed her husband and he hadn't been there – it still rankled.

The words *abandonment* and *choice* rippled through her head. Antoinette was making Shay choose.

'He's taking the girls to netball, Antoinette,' she said coolly.

'Oh, right. I thought that was your thing, the netball and all that,' said her mother-in-law.

Cassie realised that her plan for not sweating the small stuff wasn't going too well that morning.

'He loves to do things with the family,' she said, knowing there was a hint of bitchiness in her voice but unable to contain it. 'The girls love having hot chocolate with him after a game,' she

270

added, thinking that a great divine foot might come out of the sky and stomp on her for such a barefaced lie.

'Isn't that lovely?' said Antoinette in such nice tones that Cassie felt guilty immediately.

Poor Antoinette lived on her own and she was just phoning up for a chat, that was all . . .

'Can you get Shay to phone me, then, pet?'

'Of course.'

'You see, I need my garden sorted out. I know he's a dab hand with the old shrubs, even if he doesn't have a clue what's a shrub and what's a weed, but if he comes soon, he could tidy it all up for me today,' Antoinette went on.

Cassie thought of the wilderness of their own back garden, which was an unattractive combination of semi-wild and semi-barren due to places where plants had either gone feral or died altogether. Only the patio, with pots delivered from Pearl, was decent. Shay hadn't been near it all summer, too busy at his mother's beck and call, and Cassie hadn't inherited her grandmother's gardening gene.

'I don't know if you know how lucky you are with Shay, you know.' Antoinette was still talking. 'Not many husbands are so good around the place, but Shay, Lord, that man can fix anything. He takes after his father, of course. Our garden was the pride of the road once. Not anymore, sadly, but Shay will fix it all up—'

'Have you thought of getting a gardener in to

do some work in it?' Cassie interrupted suddenly, unable to take any more.

Her mother-in-law wasn't poor and despite the state of their own finances, Cassie would have contributed something to the gardener from her own pay packet if she thought it would get Shay away from Antoinette's clutches. Better still, Miriam and Ruth could cough up to help their mother.

'Pay good money for a gardener when I have Shay?' said Antoinette, shocked. 'You must think we all have money to throw away, Cassie.'

No, Cassie reflected sourly, *only marriages*.

'I'll get him to phone you,' she said shortly. 'I think the girls are back. Bye.' And she hung up.

If Shay so much as set foot in his mother's house this weekend, Cassie would find her own long-lost, rarely-used garden implements and stab him with them. And then she'd pack his bags for him, she thought grimly.

The sports' club party arrived home at one, hungry and grumpy.

'We didn't go to the Coffee Bean,' grumbled Lily.

'There was no parking,' said Shay defensively.

There never was parking, Cassie knew. It was the best coffee shop for miles, so you had to park a long way around the corner and schlep. But nobody minded. The Coffee Bean had cranberry and orange muffins and hot chocolate to die for . . .

'We went to Freddie's crappy coffee shop,' said Beth scathingly.

Freddie's made the hot chocolate with water instead of milk and had rock-hard scones that people joked were sponsored by the local dentist, so good were they at dislodging fillings.

'Dad met some of his friends and they talked for ages about *football* . . .'

The litany went on. He'd missed Lily scoring a goal because he'd been talking to another father and hadn't run between the two girls' matches the way Cassie did, determined to give of her time fairly to both daughters.

Under normal circumstances, Cassie would have told the girls not to be so hard on their poor dad, to apologise and remember who'd taken them to netball. Diffusing family rows was her speciality. She'd have privately told Shay that hormones were ruling the house and not to mind, that the girls did exactly the same thing to her all the time.

But not today. Today she felt unhinged, attacked by memories and problems from every side.

'Freddie's is a dreadful coffee shop, Shay, and you know it,' she snapped. The words were out of her mouth before her brain had fully kicked in. 'Oh yes, and your mother rang. Her garden needs doing. I should point out that *our* garden needs doing too but I feel we're rather low on the list. *Again.*'

And with that, she swept into the kitchen,

slammed the door and headed for the coffee maker. The calming herbal tea thing could go hang; she needed proper caffeine.

Shay looked at the kitchen door and idly wondered if the wood was still vibrating from the slamming. Cassie had been saying the girls' hormones had been a problem lately, not that he'd really noticed, but he wondered if his wife's hormones were really the worrying ones. What was wrong with her? So they hadn't gone to the coffee shop the kids wanted. What the hell? Nobody had taken him to coffee shops when he was a kid.

And since when did Cassie worry about the garden? She was as hopeless at it as he was. They had grass, a deck and few scrubby shrubs along the garden walls. It wasn't a bower like Pearl's, but then Pearl lived with her secateurs in hand for deadheading and a bit of twine in her pocket to tie up trailing things. You were either born like that or you weren't.

Flowers and wine, Shay decided. That would sort things out. He'd phone his mother, get out of the house for the day, sort out Ma's garden, let Cassie's mood improve, and bring home gifts. That always worked. She had a bee in her bonnet about him going round to his mother's but what else was he to do? He had a duty to his mother; surely Cassie understood? But then, he supposed, she hadn't had a mother and Pearl was the most competent person on the planet, so beside her, his poor mother came up badly in the taking-care-of-herself stakes. Still, Cassie would get it. She never lost her temper for very long. It was one of the things he loved about her.

Except she might lose her temper over the house-selling thing. Shay felt a twinge of discomfort. He still hadn't broached that with her.

He'd seen a place in the property pages that looked good – far too expensive, but the sort of thing they were theoretically looking for. If they couldn't find a house that suited with the sort of flat in the garden, this property in the paper made him think they could sell his mother's house, she could move into theirs, and they could buy some-where and build on it with a bridging loan . . . It was a good plan.

'Hope you approve, Dad,' Shay said to his father, who he hoped was up above playing cards with his pals and watching the footie on some celestial big-screen telly.

Thinking of his dad made him think of his sisters. He'd need to talk to them about the whole moving thing with their mother and how it would all work out. He'd talk to Cassie when she calmed down. Next week, for definite. When she wasn't so hormonal.

Ruth answered the phone on the second ring.

'Waiting for someone?' Shay teased his sister.

'No, just beside it, working,' said Ruth. 'How are you?'

'Fine. Just off to Ma's to sort out the garden for her.'

'Fabulous,' said Ruth, sounding pleased. 'She was onto me the other day saying it was a mess and what was she going to do. I said not to ask me. Hardly my strong point.'

'I don't know a weed from a flower,' Shay said, 'but she'll just tell me what to do.'

'How's Cass and the kids?' said Ruth, sounding as if she was still working, despite talking to her brother.

'Fine.'

Not that fine, said the tiny little voice in Shay's head. He knew he ought to get his sisters to share the burden, as Cassie so often said, but Ma rang and asked *him*, and he felt such guilt that she was lonely.

'Listen, Ruth, can you spend more time with Ma these days? She's going through a lonely patch right now and—'

'She's been going through a lonely patch since Dad died and that's over four years ago,' Ruth interrupted. 'I have taken her to places, to exhibitions, to comedy shows, to the concert hall, to a fashion show once . . . She's not interested. She wants everything the way it was before when she was belle of the ball, when we were kids and she was young, when Dad was alive, and that's not happening anymore. I'm forty-one: *I'm* hardly the belle of any ball,' Ruth said with a hint of bitterness. 'So she can forget it at her age. She needs to make a new life for herself, do charity work, do something, and stop moping about the past—'

'Ruth!' interrupted Shay, but there was no stopping his sister now.

'Shay, we can't all have what we want. I wanted a husband but I didn't get one, so I have to live with that. Ma doesn't think normal rules apply to her. She thinks that if she wants it, she can have it because that's what life was like when Dad was around. He indulged her and you know it.'

'Yeah, but they had a good marriage—'

'Fine, they did, but sadly Dad is gone now and while that's horrible for *all* of us, especially her, death is part of life. She has to understand that and stop pretending you're him. So you run after her all you want, but I won't.'

'You're hard, Ruth,' said Shay in dismay.

'I live in the real world,' said his sister grimly. 'Ma wants what she wants and she doesn't care who or what she goes through to get it, so watch out.'

Shay didn't feel up to phoning his younger sister after that, although Miriam would have a welcome for him because she was a million miles away from Ruth, who'd always been the toughest of the three Reynolds children. It was being the eldest, Ruth said when they teased her: being the one responsible for making sure the other two had their teeth brushed in the morning and had their shoelaces tied before school.

Ma had looked lovely in the mornings, Shay could remember. She had a flowery dressing gown with pale pink ruffles around the neck, she'd have tied her hair up prettily and put on lipstick, and

277

she'd stand at the door and wave at them as they walked down the street under Ruth's strict guidance.

Ruth had only been two years older than he had, he realised now with a start. It was like relying on Beth to take care of Lily, but times were different then. There weren't predators like there were now – no stranger danger. Kids walked to school with their brothers and sisters even though loads of mothers didn't work; they cleaned and baked and took care of things. His mum had been brilliant at that. He owed it to her to take care of her.

Cassie would get it. He knew she would.

CHAPTER 13

Phoebe had phoned Tommy Joe about picking her up from the bus station.

'No bother,' he'd said, 'seeing as it's you. Have you got citified, Phoebe? Will you be looking at us like we're all muck savages from now on?'

Phoebe had laughed.

'I shall always think of you as the debonair Tommy Joe who brings my luggage right up to the bus,' she said cheerfully.

'Go away out of that, Phoebe,' he'd said, obviously pleased.

As the bus neared the village, Phoebe felt the excitement heighten. She was going home and she could hardly wait.

But once she'd hauled her stuff off the bus, there was no sign of Tommy Joe's bright red head of hair above the crowd. He was so reliable, he'd never forget. Something must have happened to him . . .

'Surprise!' roared Mary-Kate and Ethan, jumping out from behind a sign. Their mother followed, beaming.

'We couldn't resist,' said Mum, as all three of them tried to hug Phoebe at the same time.

'I squared it with Tommy Joe; he knows he's getting his fare to bring you back.'

'You have no idea how good it is to see you all,' said Phoebe, breathing in the scent of her beloved family: the deodorant Ethan was using by the bucketload, Mary-Kate's modern floral Body Shop scent, and the lavender smell that seemed to emanate from her mother's very pores from evenings spent sewing it into embroidered little bags for sale in the craft shops in Wicklow town.

They all chattered nineteen to the dozen as Mum drove Doris, the family's big old jeep, up the village and into the hills where the McLoughlin farm lay.

'Sabrina from his class fancies Ethan,' said Mary-Kate, earning herself a thump from her younger brother. 'Well, she does!'

'Mary-Kate wants to get her belly button pierced . . .' began Ethan, before getting an even harder thump.

'You *promised!* He overheard me and Jen talking, and it was only an idea anyway,' said Mary-Kate mutinously.

'Everyone's fine,' said their mother serenely, concentrating on the road, which got quite potholed up their way as they were high in the Wicklow Hills. When there was a dusting of frost in Dublin, Wicklow got snowfalls that slowly and inescapably ripped its way through the roads and made potholes from hell.

Phoebe listened to talk of school, friends and how well the hens and ducks were, and gazed out of the jeep's grimy windows at the fifty-five acres her father's family had farmed for at least a century. It was rocky, hilly land and nothing but hardy Wicklow Cheviot sheep could be reared there.

The family owned sixty ewes with two breeding rams, and the work was endless. When the sheep were grazing out on the common ground in the good weather, farmers needed to get their hay ready, fertilise the grass for when the sheep were back on it, repair fences, gates and walls, get ready for the sheep dipping and, later, the sheep shearing. There were vet bills from scanning the sheep when they were pregnant and constantly taking care of sick animals. The shearers needed to be paid, as did the men with the heavy machinery for cutting and baling the hay for winter feed. When the sheep gave birth after Easter, the farmer would be up morning, noon and night in the shed for lambing, hand-rearing any whose mothers had died. In October, those same adorable lambs were big enough to go off to market to be sold – something Kate McLoughlin had always found hard, despite the fact that she was a farmer's wife and that was where the family income came from.

Other local farmers, a kind and tight-knit bunch, had helped so much when her husband had his accident, but at the end, coming in and out of the consciousness of the drugs, he'd been aware enough to know that Kate wouldn't be able to manage the farm on her own.

'Get your mother to sell up, Phoebs,' he'd told Phoebe, his big strong voice gone to a whisper.

'Dad, you'll be back in no time,' began Phoebe, holding back the tears.

'I won't, my darling girl. I won't. Please make her sell.'

'But you love the land, Dad,' Phoebe had said, tears coming now.

'I love the land but the land isn't what's important, my darling: people are. You mother will kill herself farming it out of loyalty to me. She's not made for this life. None of you are. It's backbreaking and we could do it when I was there, but not now I'm going. You must sell.'

'You're not going,' sobbed Phoebe, and her father had looked at her with great sadness, too worn out after his speech to say more, but telling her that he was going.

He'd died that night. When the funeral was over, and the McLoughlins, white-faced with grief, had gone back home, Phoebe finally repeated this conversation to her mother, who'd instantly lost her temper – an unusual occurrence.

'I'm not selling the land your father loved so much!' she'd said furiously, then burst into tears. 'It's all we've got left of him.'

Today, looking at the land and the sheep spread out on it, Phoebe – recently used to the pretty gardens of Silver Bay – realised how harsh a landscape it was up here. You got used to the land when you came home to it everyday, but now she could see it.

The Wicklow Hills weren't plump with grass like some parts of Ireland, where lush fields reared fat livestock. Here it was untamed and beautiful, but the height above sea level and the wildness of the countryside meant vicious winds, lashing rain, and a landscape that fought with you even as you battled to save fences, mend walls and breed sheep.

When Phoebe had been there to help, her mother had been worn down with it all. Now Phoebe wasn't there and the job somehow seemed impossible.

At night, to makes ends meet, Mum managed – if she wasn't too tired – to indulge in her first love – sewing – yet even that was to make money. She harvested lavender from her kitchen garden and sewed the dried lavender heads into little linen bags that she'd dyed pale pink with beetroot dye, tied with heliotrope velvet ribbons and sold to some local shops. It was all natural, all handmade, and it was what Kate McLoughlin had really wanted to do when her children were old enough. She'd had a business plan in place, enough ideas in her creative head for ten people, and a light in her eyes at being able to make money for them all. But that was before her husband had died and all their lives had changed.

Every animal in the place appeared when they drove up to the old homestead. Phoebe got out, picking up her beloved chicken, Donna, and crooning nonsense to her. A troupe of wildly clacking ducks emerged too.

'Giorgio,' said Phoebe, delighted with her welcome, and ran into the shed to get some feed to give the ducks as reward.

Prince danced around her, muddy paws up to her ribs, barking until he was hoarse.

'See how much we've all missed you,' said Ethan, holding on to his sister in a way he'd never have admitted to in school, because hugging family members was so uncool.

After the time spent this morning in Pearl Keneally's beautifully painted little house, Phoebe was startled at how run-down the homestead actually was. Nobody on Delaney Gardens had much money. Pearl was an old lady with a verandah, she'd proudly told Phoebe, which had been made of old packing cases by her husband many years ago. Nothing in her house was new and yet it was all beautifully maintained and painted well. By contrast, the old McLoughlin place that Phoebe adored was shabby and hadn't seen a lick of paint in years. There were cobwebs in the corners, because who had time to get up there with a duster and clear them away?

Phoebe was both ashamed of herself for noticing this and angry that circumstances meant her family had to live in a home that could have been beautiful if only for time or money.

Mum was making tea, Ethan was telling some

convoluted story about a hurling match in school, and Mary-Kate was showing how she'd been transforming some of her clothes with the skills Phoebe had shown her.

'I took apart a necklace and sewed it on the collar of this sweater, see?' said Mary-Kate proudly.

'It's wonderful,' said Phoebe, but she was only half-listening to any of it. Instead she was seeing the peeling wallpaper her mother had tried to glue down, and how the tiles on the floor were chipped and cracked because they'd been ancient before Dad had died, and after that nothing got done anymore.

She had time, too, to really look at her darling mother and see, with the fresh eyes of someone who'd been away a few weeks, that her mother was no longer the beautiful, fresh-faced woman she had in her mind's eye but was thin, far too thin, and her hair was limp from no time to wash it.

But when would her mother have a moment to herself anymore? Never, was the answer.

Kate McLoughlin's clothes were threadbare, her jeans had been patched many times, and they were now held up on the tightest notch of her belt. There were lines on her face etched in as though Rembrandt had wanted to paint a servant woman with exhaustion written all over her.

Keeping this farm alive was killing her mother, and it had taken Phoebe going to Dublin to college to realise it.

Phoebe did all she could on Saturday: cleaned

out every bird shed until it gleamed, walked the land with her mother, and helped repair fences and clear ditches.

'You're down here to relax,' said her mother as Phoebe threw herself into the work like a woman possessed, but Phoebe could see she was grateful for the help.

Ethan and Mary-Kate, despite having homework to do, trailed them, eager to spend time with their big sister. Finally Phoebe suggested they go in and get started on dinner. She'd brought cream cakes for dessert, she said, from money eked out of her college savings, and that had them racing in to have a look at the cakes, with Prince racing after them, always eager for a game when he'd rounded the poor sheep up to his satisfaction.

'How's it going?' asked her mother when they were alone, fixing a gate where a second person was needed to hoist the iron gate off the ground in the first place. Phoebe knew that if she weren't here, that gate might never be fixed, because neither Mary-Kate nor Ethan had the strength to lift it.

'It's going fine, I'm making friends,' said Phoebe, and told her mother some more about Ian, her new best friend, about college, and about how she might be moving out of the bedsit from hell and into somewhere nicer.

'I'm so glad you're happy,' said her mother.

'I miss you all.'

Phoebe watched as a tear dripped down her mother's face.

'Yes, but that's to be expected,' said Kate, wiping the tear away with the sleeve of her ancient fleece, as if tears had no place on this windswept hill. 'This is your dream, Phoebe.'

'Mum,' said Phoebe cautiously. 'Please don't take this the wrong way, but coming back makes me think we should sell up, the way Dad wanted us to.'

Her mother stopped what she was doing and was uncharacteristically still.

'Sell? How can we sell? This land has been in your father's family for years. We can't. It was his birthright; it's yours too. Mary-Kate's and Ethan's . . .'

'It's killing you, Mum. Look at how shattered you are. I didn't really see it when I was here because I could help, but when I'm not here . . . Mum, you can't go on doing this. You'll keel over and have a heart attack or something. Please . . .'

'Oh Phoebe,' said her mother, white-faced. '*Don't*, OK, just don't. I know you mean well but I've got to keep going. You can't understand what it means to me.'

Phoebe backed off. For now.

'I love you, Mum,' she said simply. 'I want what's best for all of us, and that means you too. I don't want to see you run yourself into the ground.'

'I'm not,' said Kate staunchly, standing there as thin as a wraith in her old clothes. 'I want you to have every chance you'd have had if your father was still alive. That's what he'd have wanted too.'

Phoebe nodded. She didn't trust herself to say anything else.

Normally Cassie hated arguments, but tonight she felt as if she wanted an argument with just about everyone who lived on the street. Bring it on!

Shay came back from his mother's at six on the nail, filthy dirty and with a Tupperware container full of scones.

'Ma made them,' he said, putting them down on the counter, where Cassie was angrily dishing up the Thai green curry the girls loved. With one move, Cassie shoved the container to one side and went on dishing up silently.

'She made them for all of us,' Shay said, determined not to have any arguments.

'She made them for you,' hissed Cassie. 'And don't think you're going to sit and eat with us when you're covered in muck from her garden.'

At this, Shay put the small bouquet of flowers and the bottle of Spanish red wine down on the table too. Cassie looked at them and then glared at her husband.

'You're gone all day, after everything I've said to you about your mother trying to drag you back into her life, and to make up for that, *this* is what I get?' Cassie said with fury.

At the table, Lily and Beth traded silent, stunned gazes. This was a side of their mother they'd never seen before. Mum never got really angry or shouted, or if she did, it was for something rare, like that time they were late for school because they'd overslept and she'd had an important meeting that morning, which she was now going to miss because everyone was dawdling. Beth had yelled: 'Chillax, Mum!' and Cassie had laughed and instantly said sorry.

Mum had yelled at Lily the time she'd nearly been hit by a car because she let go of Mum's hand and ran across the road. That had been yelling, but it was different.

'She asked me nicely,' said their father, sounding as if he was losing his temper too, which never happened.

'Why can't she ask Ruth or Miriam nicely? Better still, why can't she pay for someone to do it or get up off her precious backside and do it herself, like Pearl does? Pearl is fifteen years older and she does her own garden!' Cassie was roaring now. 'I told you before, Shay: I am fed up with your mother! She needs her own life! She needs to let you go!'

'Maybe you're the one who needs to let go,' said Shay quietly. 'It's not a battle between you and my mother. Why are you making it into one? I'm going to shower,' he added, and left the room.

Both girls held their breath. The shouting had been terrible. Dad was easy-going, everyone said so, but what if he went mental like Mum too? Mum had been really scary.

Their plates were slammed down on the table in time with the sound of the kitchen door slamming.

'Thanks, Mum,' said Lily, then whispered, 'Why are you so angry with Dad?'

Beth kicked her under the table. 'It's Gran,' she whispered. 'Say nothing.'

'Parents fight,' said their mother icily.

She didn't bother putting her own plate on the table. Instead she went to the cupboard, where she kept bottles of wine or gin for visitors, and picked up a fresh bottle of white. The fridge wine box was empty. This wine wasn't cooled but, to be frank, she couldn't care less. Perfect temperature wasn't the point. Uncorking it, she poured a huge glass into one of Shay's special red wine glasses. Lots of rubbish spoken about glasses, she thought grimly, taking a huge slug. She wouldn't, on principle, drink his wine gift. Bought in the convenience store on the way home, she knew. She recognised that type of bouquet too. Not cheap, no, because of the ludicrous mark-up in the local shop, but not proper flowershop flowers. An emergency present to try to smooth things over. Well, there would be no smoothing over with dreadful flowers and cheap wine. He had gone off to his mother's house for the whole of Saturday, not lifted a finger at home, and hadn't even thought that this might be a problem, even after what she'd said.

Although it was a family rule that they never had the TV on while they ate dinner, Cassie angrily flicked it on and found something innocuous about animals on the Discovery Channel. Then she sat at the table, picked at her meal, finished her glass and poured another. A tiny voice inside her head told her that this type of rage-induced drinking was not good. She was relying on alcohol to calm her, to soothe her. That was a mistake. And she was certainly going beyond the weekly allowance of fourteen units of alcohol in the past couple of weeks. Unhealthy too.

But, she reminded herself, as she filled up her glass: people with drinking problems had to race out and slam vodka into themselves first thing in the mornings. Their hands shook, they went out and got drunk at night, they messed up at work. She was nothing like that, so a few glasses of wine could hardly hurt. After all, wasn't *wine o'clock* practically in the dictionary now?

By the time they heard Shay come downstairs, they were putting their dishes into the dishwasher, the girls helping silently, without their mother even having to ask. They could all hear the front door loudly slam shut.

'Dad's gone out?' said Lily, sounding scared. This never happened. Dad always came into the kitchen for dinner, tousled her hair, tickled Beth, although she said she hated it, grabbed Mum and hugged her.

He never just went out – and without saying anything, either.

'Must have forgotten something at your grandmother's,' said her mother, and slammed the dishwasher shut so fiercely that all the glasses rattled perilously.

The girls fled and Cassie retreated to the old kitchen couch with her bottle of wine and the TV remote. From a distance, Fluffikins stared at her.

'I don't think you can heal me tonight, honey, even if you are a healing cat, as Coco believes,' Cassie told him grimly. 'It'll take more than a cat to sort this one out.'

She stared at the television and brooded.

Beth sat on her bed texting her best friend, Mel.

Wsh I woz at urs. Boring here. Mm n mood. Rlly bad md. Sumtin VV wrng. Plz fone n say uve emergncy???!!! Nthin on tv. Wish we'd Ntflix. ☹

After that, she had nothing else to do. Well, she could do her nails but her glue pen was in Mel's house and she hated just painting her nails. Sticking art on: that was the fun bit.

What other fifteen-year-olds were in alone on Saturday nights? None, that's who.

Dad was a useless cretin and Mum was being weird. She was drinking the wine again. Beth hated that. When she had wine, Mum changed. She never used to drink, but these days there was often a half-open bottle in the fridge and it was always gone next day. Always.

Mum used to lecture her on alcohol and how bad it was. It was all something to do with her and Coco's mum drinking. Beth knew this because

Coco had told her once, explained that Mum was too sad about it all to ever tell them, but that Coco and Mum's mother had left them and she'd been some sort of addict.

Now Mum was drinking wine when she used to drink herbal tea, Dad had gone off without telling anyone, and it all felt horrible and scary.

Beth's eyes were spiky with tears. Stupid tears. She didn't know why she was crying. She wanted everything to be the way it was before, and it wasn't. Were Mum and Dad going to get a divorce? It felt like that.

And Gran, stupid Gran, was somehow involved. Why couldn't Gran be more like Pearl?

Pearl.

She might talk to Pearl about it all. She'd understand even if nobody else did. Coco would be better but Coco was so busy with poor little Fi these days. Beth shuddered and snuggled closer into her bed and her soft pillows. It was scary how things could change in an instant. She'd always admired Jo: she was tough and cool even though she was old and everything. But now Mum said she couldn't talk properly and couldn't walk. How horrible was that?

Beth rubbed at a bit of something wet in one eye and tried to concentrate on how to do proper smoky eye. There were brilliant demos on YouTube but Mum had this thing about nobody using computers at night. Still, Mum was stuck into her wine, so she mightn't notice. And Beth needed some comfort. She hauled the laptop from under her bed and fired it up. She'd go on to Facebook first, then YouTube, whatever she felt like.

She was breaking the rules. So what? Everyone else in the family was.

Saturday was one of the busiest days at the shop, and Coco wouldn't get her head in the door that day what with Jo's family coming to visit, so she had to content herself with phoning in.

'You're sure things are doing OK at the shop? And you're keeping up with the Facebook page? That's so important.'

Coco had a list of things in her head to talk to Adriana about Twentieth Century, but now that she'd grabbed a moment to make the phone call, it had all run out of her brain. Like what was the stock situation like? Had a delivery come from that auction in Belfast? Would Adriana drop any mail off at Coco's?

Before she got a chance to ask these questions, Adriana assured her employer that the shop was a haven of customers, that it was clean and tidy, and did Coco want her to drop any mail off?

'Yes,' said Coco in blessed relief, and hung up feeling pleased at how hard Adriana was working.

It was so nice to have someone offer to do something for her like drop off the post, something practical. Friends of hers and Jo had phoned, all saying they were thinking of Jo, Coco and Fiona, and if there was anything they could do, to just ask. But Coco was so frantic with worry that thinking of what she needed most made her head ache.

Ludicrously, she knew, she wanted help without having to conjure up visions of what that help might entail. She really wanted someone with kids who might bring them over to play with Fiona, who didn't want to go out at all. Now that would be a help.

She'd like a round-robin system so that someone else would phone all Jo's teacher friends to pass on information about Jo's progress instead of everyone phoning all the time, meaning Coco had to spend ages on the phone repeating herself when she got in at night.

'No, she's not in good form. Yes, do go in, but prepare yourself for her to be very tearful. No, there's no miracle cure, I'm afraid. Time, hope for spontaneous recovery and rehabilitation are what it's going to take. Fiona is here beside me,' she'd add brightly when they asked, in low, sad voices, how Jo's daughter was.

Some people didn't take the hint and would keep saying how awful it was for a child, and Coco would have to say, even more loudly: 'Fiona, who is *right beside me,* and I are having fun. We're doing baking tonight! Purple and pink cakes, right, Fi?'

What would be especially lovely would be if someone else would cook dinner for her and Fi one night. They'd been to Cassie's three times last week after being in the hospital, but Fiona needed some normality, and right now that was Coco's flat.

And besides, there was something going on with Shay and Cassie, which was subtle, just under the surface, but there all the same. Normally Coco would insist on knowing what was wrong and would help out in some way. But now, burdened with a friend in hospital and a child to look after, she didn't have any part of her left over for coping with anyone else's problems; even her sister's. Cassie would sort it out – Cassie could sort anything out.

Fiona had been due to go into school for the first time in a week since her mother had been rushed to hospital.

The school had been very helpful about Fiona having some time off to be with her mother in hospital under these difficult circumstances.

'I'd like her to have some routine, and school is a great routine,' the principal had said, 'but if she really wants to go into the hospital first thing, you should do that. She could come in for a few hours in the afternoon, if possible, to see her friends, to get some normality into her life, and then start her back full-time on Friday,' said the principal. 'Then she'll have the weekend to adjust.'

Fiona had got up quietly, put on her school uniform and even sat at the table with Coco, poking at her Pop-Tarts (desperation food as she wasn't eating much), as if she might possibly have some, and then she'd whispered: 'I can't go to school without seeing Mum, Coco. I can't.'

She'd cried then. Not loud, noisy tears like the ones Coco had seen many times before when Jo was well. *'I need Chunky Monkey ice cream or I will explode!' 'Can we go to the cinema, pleeeeease . . .?' 'Can you write a note saying I don't have to do my homework, Muuum . . .?'*

These tears were different, silent grief pouring out, and Coco couldn't bear them.

She shoved her chair away, threw her arms around Fiona and held her tightly.

'You don't have to,' said Coco wildly, knowing she was saying the wrong thing, but desperate to say anything to help. 'Mum is going to be OK, darling. It may take time, but she will, and you have me with you. I'll never let you down. I am here for you always. I'll keep you safe, Fi, darling.'

Somehow they ended up on the floor in a sodden heap, with Coco rocking Fiona like she was a baby, and Fiona making little mouse-like noises that Coco somehow knew weren't bad noises. It was like she was finally letting go of the fear and pain she'd been holding inside her small body. The pain of seeing her beloved mum in hospital, the pain of Jo not being able to walk or even hold her properly or talk. The pain of loss, and the fear that that loss might come again, bigger or worse.

Coco, who'd never known her mother, understood those fears. One loss made you frightened that there would be many more. It made you wear a cloak of armour in case you got hurt again, and that never worked, not in the real world.

'It's all right, darling, I'm here now Fi. Mum will get better, I promise you, and I am going to be here for both of you.'

CHAPTER 14

'I can't believe you're off again.' Myra O'Neill's current expression was what her loving husband might have described as 'a face that would stop a clock'.

'Business,' said Red blandly, sitting in his parents' kitchen for a quick cup of tea before heading to the airport.

Saying 'business' covered a multitude of excuses. Nobody could argue with a man like himself when he said he had to leave because of business.

'But you only just got here,' wailed his mother.

'Ah, leave the man alone,' said his father. 'If he needs to be in New York, he needs to be in New York.'

Red didn't need to be in New York. He just knew that he didn't want to be in Dublin anymore. The dinner party the night before had unsettled him so much. Michael and Barbara had said the sort of things he didn't want to hear, reminding him about Coco and telling him he should see her.

Why would he want to do that? Why put himself through the pain?

The driver dropped him off at terminal two departures.

'Thanks,' said Red, getting out of the car.

Just ahead of him was a woman with long black hair curling down her back. She was muttering to herself.

'I always get these floors mixed up,' she said, even though she was alone and there was nobody else to hear her.

Red recognised that voice; he'd have recognised it anywhere, under any conditions.

'Impossible to know if you're in arrivals or departures,' the woman muttered.

Dressed in a long pink circle-skirted dress with a nipped-in waist that showed off her Venus curves and slender ankles was Coco Keneally. She used to worry they were fat – they weren't.

'You forget something, sir?' the driver asked, looking at him curiously before he got back in his car.

'No,' said Red, and began following her.

Coco headed off towards the escalators up to arrivals and Red couldn't help himself following her. She glanced at an old-fashioned watch on her slender wrist and sighed with impatience. She was running late, he thought. Late for whom? She was beautifully dressed, with a small elegant black handbag – the sort of thing she'd longed to sell in the shop but had never been able to afford in the early days.

Some instinct made her turn as she got off the escalator, and he turned too, bending his head as if he was looking back for someone on the ground floor.

Please let her not see me stalking her.

She didn't. He got off after her and watched her walk, hips swaying in that utterly unconscious way of hers, over to the arrivals area.

Red, who had a boarding pass on his phone and no checked luggage, took the next escalator up and looked down at her. She was biting her full lower lip, the way she did when she was nervous and trying to find the right place to wait. Who was she waiting for that was making her nervous? A lover? A new fiancée?

Red was shocked by how jealous he felt of this unknown man.

Then she was out of sight and Red was joining the fast-track queue for the flight to New York. Maybe it was the previous late night, and the conversation he'd had with his friends, but Red had an overwhelming desire to turn around, race downstairs to where Coco stood, pick her up and never let her go.

Instead, he took off his belt and his shoes, laid his phone and laptop in the security trays and moved through. She didn't want him in her life. She'd made that perfectly plain four years ago.

Thank heavens for Pearl, Coco thought as she hurried through the airport car park to reach arrivals, where Jo's sister's flight was due to land soon.

She arrived at the car park in front of the airport

entrance proper to realise that, yet again, she'd mixed up the areas. She was at departures check-in, not arrivals. Muttering to herself, she took the escalator up to the right floor and she had the weirdest sensation of being watched. But when she looked around, there was nobody looking at her.

It was nerves, she thought. She'd felt nervous since she'd dropped Fiona off at Pearl's, and was feeling incredibly anxious about meeting Attracta – the aunt that Fiona didn't remember at all.

It was the emails that made her feel this. First, Attracta had sent emails to her sister, which was insane because Jo wasn't able to type answers into her laptop, and this made her doubly frustrated. It was as if Attracta didn't grasp the severity of the fact that her younger sister had had a stroke, or how huge an uphill battle her rehab could be if there wasn't the much hoped-for spontaneous recovery.

Then Attracta had sent emails to Coco, too: *update me* emails where she wrote as if she was coolly enquiring if a pair of shoes had arrived in the shop.

Actually, Coco thought, she'd had far warmer and more interested emails from buyers contacting Twentieth Century about items of clothing. Ones where people wrote with emotion and feeling. Nothing Attracta wrote had an iota of emotion in it: *My plane from London lands at half ten on Saturday morning. I will have slept: I use melatonin on long flights. I suppose we should go straight to the hospital?*

'*I suppose we should go straight to the hospital,*' raged Coco to herself. *How cold is that? If it was Cassie, I'd move heaven and earth to see her.*

'I don't really remember her that well,' Coco had confided in Pearl when she'd phoned to ask if her grandmother would take care of Fiona on Saturday morning when she went to the airport. 'She was so much older than us. She was tough, she taught Jo to be tough—'

'Which is good,' Pearl reminded her, 'because Jo needs to be tough now to get through this catastrophe.'

'That's it!' said Coco. 'I know it's a catastrophe, you do, darling Fi knows it, and she's only nine, but Attracta and Xavier – it's like they don't realise this, or if they do, they've distanced themselves from it. Xavier's flying in tomorrow for *one* night. At least Attracta's made a big effort to come from Australia, but he's in Paris – it's not half way around the world. I don't understand them!'

Pearl wished she could use the obvious example to explain this to her granddaughter, but she'd spent thirty years not discussing Coco's mother with her, so she said instead: 'Sometimes people with traumatic or dysfunctional families move away in every sense of the word. The Kinsellas are not normal, no doubt about it. They've driven their children away and it's hard for Xavier and

Attracta to come home. Home is linked with pain, hurt and never being good enough.'

Again, Pearl thought of Marguerite. Had she stayed away from her daughters because of that hurt and pain, of having been told she wasn't a good enough mother? If so, Pearl had had a hand in it. It was a heavy burden to carry. But she'd been so scared for them, thinking what could go wrong because Marguerite's behaviour had made it abundantly clear that she wasn't able to take care of two children.

Pearl had changed her mind about telling her granddaughters the truth so many times. She would; she wouldn't.

Not now, though. Not now.

'I suppose that makes sense,' reflected Coco. 'If it were Cassie and I was on the moon, I'd come home as fast as I could.'

On the other end of the phone, Pearl smiled. Something she'd done right; those sisters adored each other.

Coco found a spot in arrivals where she could see the doors opening, disgorging passengers, and waited. The London flights processed people quickly. Twenty-five minutes after the arrivals board said the plane had arrived, a woman in her early forties arrived, pushing a trolley carrying one small suitcase and a carryon. She was the right age and she had a look of Jo about her eyes, with the same dark eyebrows, but the resemblance ended there. Jo was tall, slim and loved colour, even ones like lemon yellows that Coco had to steer her away from. This woman was nowhere near as tall, didn't have Jo's enviable shape, and wore head-to-toe black, from her long, loose cardigan to her flat shoes, as if she was dressed for a funeral.

Was that her? Coco stared. The woman stared back and then pushed the trolley in Coco's direction.

'I've got photos on my wall of you with Josephine and Fiona,' said Attracta, holding out a formal hand. 'That's how I recognised you. Hello Coco, it's good of you to collect me.'

'Oh, it's nothing, the least I could do,' babbled Coco, thinking that she'd barely recognised Attracta because it was years since she'd been home. Jo had only very old photos of her sister on her wall.

'Attracta hates the camera,' she'd said once.

It all came back to Coco now. Attracta had been told that being interested in your appearance was not thinking of God.

'I told you my parents were nuts,' Jo had said years ago when she'd explained this to Coco.

Nuts didn't entirely explain it, Coco thought.

'Welcome home, Attracta,' she said now, trying to pull herself together. 'I'm sorry it's not under happier circumstances.'

'I'm Tracey now,' said Attracta briskly. 'I hate Attracta.'

Coco missed a beat. The emails had been to a T. Kinsella but she hadn't thought anything of it. People's email addresses often bore no resemblance to their actual names. And yet, Attracta had never mentioned the name change in her emails . . . Weird.

'Right. Tracey,' she said evenly. She simply wasn't going to even question this. 'I'm on level two. Shall we walk?'

'Sure. Are we going to the hospital then?'

'Er, yes,' said Coco, just stopping herself from saying: 'No, we'll take in a movie first.'

She must remember what Pearl had told her: this journey might be a very hard one for Attracta in so many ways.

On the drive, Coco learned that Tracey – how hard was *that* going to be to remember and why hadn't she mentioned it before? – lived in Sydney, worked in administration in insurance, lived alone in an apartment in Manley, and had slept for the leg of the flight from Hong Kong.

She didn't ask about her sister and or say any of the expected things like how was her niece coping, or wasn't Coco good to be there taking care of her.

Was it nerves or medication? Coco wondered, entirely on edge.

Tracey stared out of the car window at Dublin city and remarked occasionally how different it all looked now. It was only in the hospital that Coco finally realised that Attracta – sorry, Tracey – was wound up like a spring.

They walked into the ward together, where Jo was feeding herself lunch. Because of her inability to use her left arm properly, she wasn't able to cut up her chicken, so was hacking away at it with a blunt knife and had clearly splashed food on to her pyjamas. The enormous fatigue she'd suffered since the stroke meant each forkful was an effort, and before Coco could smile and say that Jo had improved so much in the past two weeks, Tracey gasped and slapped a hand over her mouth. She took one look at her formerly vibrant sister reduced to someone feeble, unable to feed herself properly, and a torrent of tears emerged.

'Josephine, oh no, Josephine,' she wailed, and threw herself at Jo, who glared at Coco over her sister's head as if this outburst of emotion was all Coco's fault.

Coco shrugged. She had learned that this was the best way to deal with Jo when she got stroppy. Reasoning didn't work.

Your sister, she mouthed, and left the ward to wait outside.

After ten minutes, she grabbed one of the nurses she'd grown to know well.

'Lesley, Jo's sister's just arrived from Australia to see her. Would you mind peering in to see how it's going? I'm worried her sister might upset her. I don't think she's coping very well with Jo's condition. I know you're wildly busy but it'll only take a few seconds.'

'Sure,' said Lesley, and walked into the ward.

She was back in a minute with Tracey in tow. Tracey was still crying; her face was swollen with tears and was blotchily red.

'The café?' suggested Lesley, with a meaningful look at Coco.

'You are truly an angel,' whispered Coco to Lesley as she escorted Tracey towards the lifts.

They'd just ordered coffees, and Tracey was brokenly muttering about how she never expected it to be this bad, when Coco realised that she'd just committed the cardinal sin with someone immobile in a hospital bed: leaving without telling them what was happening.

She paid, whisked their coffees off to a table, grabbed a few sugars, left them beside Tracey, and said: 'I'm just popping up to see Jo. You sit here for a while. I'll come back for you, right?'

Holding her coffee, she raced off.

Jo hated coffee now. She couldn't drink anything very well except through a straw, and her love of strong Columbian coffee was gone. Coco never, simply never, brought a takeaway coffee cup into the ward in case it reminded Jo of her inability to drink properly, but right now she thought it was time to stop treating Jo like she was anyone different from the person she'd been before.

There would be no 'does she take sugar?' in their relationship.

Jo was still Jo, would need rehab and might never physically be quite the same again. But mentally she was the woman Coco had been friends with for twenty-six years, even if she'd gone through an emotional earthquake. Getting Jo back on her feet would take more than physical exercises.

'What did you bring her in for?' demanded Jo instantly. 'You saw what she was like. That helps me *how* exactly?'

'First, she flew thousands of miles to see you, and secondly, I am not a psychic,' protested Coco. 'I didn't know she'd burst into floods on seeing you. She barely spoke about you in the car—'

'Then she went on and on about our bloody parents and how we're the most screwed-up family on the planet, and how she hates her life, and now this,' interrupted Jo angrily. 'Oh yes, and the clincher is, do I think my stroke is a judgement from God because none of us are religious—?'

'Fiona's doing well today, thank you for asking,' said Coco acidly, doing some interrupting of her own.

Jo was silent.

'I left her with Pearl. They're going to bake something covered in sprinkles to bring into you later this afternoon. I was going to come with Tracey . . .'

'I can't believe she changed her name,' said Jo, sounding totally like herself for a brief moment. 'She's always hated it, but changing it . . .'

'You did OK. Josephine's fine. Attracta's such an Irish name, it might not travel as well as Jo,' agreed Coco.

'I wish my mother had been channelling something weird like yours and Cassie's mother,' Jo added. 'Coraline and Cassiopeia – now *they're* amazing names.'

'Which she gave to us and then left,' Coco emphasised. 'What was that about saying you have the most screwed-up family ever?'

At that moment, Jo laughed – a sound Coco hadn't heard since before her stroke.

'You win that one. But nobody in your family ever tried to immerse you in the bath to wash away your sins. I win!'

'Sounds lovely,' said Coco, grinning. 'A family spa day. You never told me that before.'

'It's not the sort of thing you can discuss when you're eleven, but it was a very fundamental phase they were going through . . .' And Jo laughed again.

What a lovely sound, thought Coco.

'What am I going to do with Attracta?' Coco asked Pearl in a manic whisper when she went to pick up Fiona.

Attracta/Tracey had said she'd wait in the car as she didn't like meeting new people.

Coco wanted to say she didn't like new, wildly unsociable, slightly unhinged people staying in her flat, but controlled herself.

'She completely freaked out when she saw Jo. I was going to bring Fiona in this afternoon but I certainly don't think I can bring Attracta – sorry, Tracey – in. It'll make Jo crazy and upset Fiona.'

'Fiona's the one you have to think about,' said her grandmother wisely. 'Not Tracey. And not Jo. Jo is an adult and you can only do so much for her. She has to learn to cope with this on her own, but you're taking care of her daughter. Her nine-year-old daughter. That's your job now.'

Coco thought about it. Pearl was right. Taking care of Fiona was the main thing, and the longer that they spent together, the more she realised how much went into mothering. It was more than the fun things she, Jo and Fiona had done over the years, like going out to restaurants or to the cinema or to the park. Even holidays they'd taken together. No, this was totally different. Being a parent meant – and she supposed she was Fiona's parent for the moment – so much more. It meant being responsible for the fears that went on in Fiona's little head.

'You're right,' Coco said decisively, agreeing with her grandmother. 'Fiona is my main priority. I'll tell Tracy to stay at home or to go out for a walk, or to do whatever the bloody hell she wants, and I'll bring Fiona in to see her mum. Then maybe we'll go somewhere out for dinner?'

'Only do what's right for you and your family,' said Pearl. 'That's what you have to do when you're taking care of children.'

It all sounded very sensible to Coco.

When her granddaughter had left, Pearl was thinking of exactly how true her advice really was. She thought of the earth-shattering decisions she'd made when she was trying to protect Coco and Cassie all those years ago. *Protect your family no matter what else.* But she hadn't protected everyone.

311

She hadn't protected Marguerite, and that was one of the things she regretted most. Marguerite had had nobody to take care of her, and Pearl had been thinking only of the children.

Tracey didn't want to go out to dinner and was being so moody and miserable that Fiona went silent and sat in her room among her teddies. So Coco ordered in Chinese takeaway, but even that didn't lift the gloom. After eating most of the prawn crackers, a vast quantity of the fried rice and at least half of Fiona's leftover sweet and sour chicken, Tracey sat down in the best armchair after dinner.

Ignoring the fact that the television was on with a DVD of *Frozen*, because it was Fiona's favourite movie and Coco was trying to take her mind off her deeply stressed aunt, Tracey then proceeded to talk loudly in a sad monologue about how stressful things had been and how strange she felt being back in Ireland, how confined and suffocated.

'Well, that's great,' said Coco sharply in a tone she barely recognised as her own. She never normally spoke like that, but somehow taking care of Fiona had turned her into an alpha mum with a hint of lioness added in for fun. 'Let's talk about something else,' she'd growled, giving Tracey a very meaningful glare and then staring at Fiona. 'Something less upsetting.'

It was a command and, finally, Tracey copped on. 'Er, of course,' she said.

Luckily, jetlag, despite the melatonin, hit Tracey like a lead balloon and she had to go to bed early. So Coco and Fiona left her to the couch and snuggled up on Coco's bed, watching the rest of the film on the TV in her bedroom. Coco wished they had her grandmother's pug, Daisy, sprawled on top of them.

She should get a dog, she thought. A dog would be fabulous for Fiona. Children told things to dogs, told them their deepest, darkest secrets.

She had.

She'd sat in Basil and Sybil's bed when she found out her mother had left, and she'd whispered the secrets that she couldn't speak to anyone else, and the dogs had understood. They'd consoled her with loving pug licks that made Coco feel *somebody* understood how upset she was.

'Your mother left because you were a crybaby,' were the hateful words that had haunted her for years.

The more Coco thought about it, the more she realised that *she* was going to be Fiona's mother for quite a while to come.

'I'll be in rehab for fucking months and I might never be back to normal,' Jo had hissed at her a couple of days before.

That thought had been rattling around in Coco's brain ever since. She'd been avoiding it, not because the idea of taking care of Fiona was so onerous, but because she didn't think she could be a stand-in mother.

She had never, ever planned to have children. How could she? She'd probably make a very good granny, because Pearl had been the most fabulous granny. A granny-cum-mother and a wonderful role model but still, not a mum.

Dad had been there too, but Coco could remember Pearl and Cassie doing most of the raising. Her mother leaving had broken something inside her father.

The Keneallys had never been an ordinary family. Coco didn't know how to do ordinary, and she'd decided a long time ago that children weren't in her future. But now she was forced into being a mother. The incredible thing was that she was enjoying it. Loving it, actually.

'Should we get a dog?' she asked Fiona.

'Yes!' Fiona snuggled in tighter. 'I'd love that. I've been asking Mum for a dog for ages but she always says . . .' She stopped, as if talking about Jo was somehow out of bounds.

Fiona did this a lot. Talked about the past and her mother, and then suddenly reality hit and she knew what was happening. She knew that her mother was in a hospital bed, angry and upset, injured.

In that instant, Coco felt she understood all of this almost like she could see all the cogs whirring in her goddaughter's head.

'Your mum will get better, darling,' she said. 'I promise you she will get better. One of the hardest things for her right now is not to be able to take care of you because she loves you so much.'

314

'But she's so angry!' whispered Fiona. 'She's so angry when I go in, and she's angry with you and everyone. Mum isn't like that.'

'She's like that because she's scared, I told you that, darling. She's scared because she doesn't know what's going to happen and doesn't realise that you, me and your mum are a team.' Coco smiled. 'We're a family, Fiona. *A family.* I'm here for your mum and, most importantly, I'm here for you. Do you believe me?' She looked at Fiona gravely, willing her to say *yes*.

Fiona's little face broke into a smile. 'Course I believe you, silly billy. You are a silly billy sometimes, Coco. You're my other mummy.' She curled up closer to Coco, who thought her heart might explode with love.

'Let's get a dog,' she said decisively. 'What sort of dog would you like, Fiona?'

For the first time in a very long while, possibly since the night of Jo's stroke, when Lily and Beth had been in Coco's house and they'd all been dressing up with such childish glee, Coco saw a gleam of sheer joy in Fiona's beautiful blue eyes.

'A pug,' she said, like she was saying *a fairy princess castle filled with Barbies.* 'Like Pearl's.'

'OK,' said Coco, her heart aching to see Fiona's joy in this simple move. 'A pug it is.'

'Can I get it clothes and dress it up?' said Fiona.

'Well, we'll see,' said Coco. 'The puglet might not like clothes . . .'

'She will,' said Fiona happily.

Bribery, Coco thought, as they hugged tightly and went back to watching *Frozen.* But she didn't care. If the thought of a dog brought a smile to Fiona's face, then bribery it would be.

The next day Coco felt glad she hadn't offered to pick Xavier up from the airport. Look at what had happened when she'd picked Tracey up – that had gone *so* well. As a morning guest, Tracey was stressed until she got her coffee, and then seemed stressed even when she had it. Simply being in Silver Bay, close to her home, had ignited some anxiety in her.

At least Xavier had sounded laid-back on the phone; so laid-back, in fact, that it didn't even sound as if he was flying over to see his sister, who'd had a hideous, premature stroke.

'I'm getting quite an early flight, but I'll drop in and see some pals,' he'd said casually to Coco on the phone. 'Then I'll head out to the hospital and possibly come around to yours later.'

He wasn't staying with Coco, a fact for which she was very grateful. With Fiona in her spare bedroom and Tracey on the couch, space was at a premium. Space, not to mention sanity.

But Sunday afternoon came with no word from Xavier since the night before when they were discussing his flight arrangements.

'Did he come in to see you?' Coco asked Jo in the hospital that afternoon.

'Yes, he was in this morning. He flew in early,'

said Jo, and she looked animated for the first time in ages. 'It was amazing to see him. I'd forgotten how much fun he is. He made me laugh. He even fed me lunch and told me I was a gimpy old eejit, and the sooner I got into rehab, the better, so I wouldn't embarrass him when Fiona and I next came to Paris. He said he's moving apartments, somewhere in the sixth arrondissement. Very cool, I'm betting. And there'll be a spare room for us.'

Coco grinned. Jo hadn't talked about the future in anything except negative terms for the last few weeks. Was it a gradual acceptance, a strength, a courage? Or just Jo's natural optimism finally reasserting itself?

Xavier turned up at Coco's flat that evening with a bottle of wine, a tiny box of handmade French chocolates, and clearly no intention of staying any longer than about half an hour, which made Coco very happy because she had no more beds and only one nerve left.

He greeted his sister warily. 'Tracey,' he said, and gave her a little peck on the cheek.

Very Parisian, but only one, so only half-French, Coco wondered? Or was this some subtle Parisian way of saying: 'You're bonkers, so you only merit one kiss'?

'And Fiona.'

He picked his niece up in a big bear hug and swung her around and around the room, so that Coco began to fear for her table lamps. It wasn't a big apartment and she had a lot of stuff in it. She kept thinking about what she was going to do when Jo got out of hospital and how the three of them were going to manage. Jo couldn't live on her own as she was still relearning to use her left hand and she walked with a limp, which meant stairs might be out of the question. So Coco's apartment – one flight of stairs – would be tricky, particularly as it had only two bedrooms. But then Jo's own place was smaller and was up three flights of stairs, with a temperamental lift, so how would she manage that?

Of course, Jo might not want Coco taking care of her and Fiona, but it seemed like the most obvious choice, and after all, *nobody* was going to be able to take care of Fiona like she could.

'You've grown, honey,' said Xavier when he finally put a now dizzy Fiona back on her feet.

Fiona gave him a pitying look. 'I'm nine. Course I've grown. We're getting a dog,' she then announced, as if there was one waiting to be delivered instantly. 'A pug.'

'Oh, I love pugs,' said Xavier. 'They're *très délicieux*.'

'You do?' said Fiona. 'My granny, Pearl, has one.'

Coco grinned. Pearl wasn't Fiona's granny and yet she was. Pearl had been Coco's mum. It was all a little mixed up and yet that was OK, she thought, looking with adoration at the child she loved like a daughter. *Daughter*.

Suddenly her beloved rose velvet couch was behind her knees and she sank down on to it with a shock.

She was the woman who was *never, ever* having

children, and now here she was looking after Fiona with more love than she'd thought possible. She'd adored Fiona before, but now that love seemed to have increased tenfold. And yet Fiona would eventually go and Coco's heart would break because she loved having her goddaughter with her all the time and—

She wanted a baby of her own. A real baby. Her own child. A child she'd never, ever leave.

'You OK, Coco?' asked Xavier politely. 'You've gone a bit white.'

'Have a chocolate, Coco,' said Fiona, cosying up to her and ripping open the chocolates with expert ease. She picked out the richest-looking one – white chocolate with pistachio pieces and caramel sugar trailing into little shapes on top of it – and handed it to Coco. 'This,' she said gravely, 'will make you feel better.'

'*You* make me feel better,' said Coco, gazing at Fiona earnestly.

'I know,' said Fiona. 'Bite it. Is it nice?'

She picked an equally rich-looking one for herself and stuck the whole thing in her mouth.

'Uncle Xavier,' she said, mouth full, 'these are yummificacious. When we have a pug, we can't give him chocolate. Pearl told me that. It's bad for dogs' hearts. It's not bad for my heart,' she added, just to make that clear. 'I can eat lots of chocolate and it never makes me sick.' She took another one and ate it quickly, just to prove this fact. 'See?'

★   ★   ★

When Xavier was gone, Tracey was settled into a jetlagged sleep on the couch, and Fiona was curled up in her bed with her teddies and dreams of the holiday in Paris her uncle had promised her, Coco went into her own bedroom and sat on the windowsill looking out at the night sky. It was a cloudless night and she could see so many stars.

Her father had loved the heavens. One of her fondest memories of their time together was when the teenage Cassie was out and Coco and her dad would sit outside on Pearl's verandah and try to identify various constellations.

'Dad, I hope you're happy wherever you are,' Coco whispered up at the sky. 'I told you once I never wanted children and I knew it made you sad,' she said. 'But I've changed my mind. I do want children. Babies and toddlers and little girls like Fiona running around, or little boys – whatever I am lucky enough to have. I was wrong before, but I know what I want now. There are no men on the horizon, not even the safe ones you tried to get me interested in. None. But I'll work it out. I'll be a good mum, I promise.'

CHAPTER 15

On Monday morning, Cassie wished her head wasn't throbbing quite so much. It was all her own fault. 'Entertainment tax' they used to call it in college, when you had to pay the day after for too many drinks in the bar the night before. Cassie used to look down on the wild ones who were clearly paying entertainment tax most mornings. They were stupid, she'd thought in those far-off college days. Where did drinking too much get you? Nowhere. And now look at her, a married mother-of-two with a throbbing headache and the sense that her stomach was so acidic she might throw up at any moment.

She'd shouted at the girls that morning too; shouted more when she realised Shay had got up early and had left the house before anyone was up, not so much as a cup of tea left by her side of the bed as a peace offering. He'd been out all day Sunday, barely speaking to Cassie as if it was all her fault.

So she'd ignored him and he'd ignored her right back. Cassie had got stuck into the wine after buying another wine box from the supermarket.

Fabulous things, they were: nobody could look at them and see how much was gone, she found herself thinking – and then was horrified at such secretive behaviour. Wasn't that how addicts always said they behaved? Drinking or taking drugs secretly, hiding what they did?

She couldn't even phone Coco to talk about it because Coco had Jo's family with her at the weekend and, according to Pearl, it had been stress city over there with Jo's sister having a mini nervous breakdown now that she was on Irish soil, and therefore close to her Bible-thumping parents.

Pearl had also been full of chat about this lovely girl she'd met and how Pearl thought the girl could come and stay with Gloria from Delaney Gardens, whose darling husband was in a home, for the college year, and wasn't that a nice idea?

'Gloria needs someone in the house. She's so lonely and that lovely girl would cheer her up. Phoebe is the girl's name, and she's in a bedsit in Rita Costello's house, which is penal servitude, if you ask me. The last time Rita cracked a smile, Nixon was in the White House. Plus that house hasn't been painted in donkey's years. Are you all right, Cass? You sound a little stressed?'

'Me, stressed? No. Just tired,' said Cassie.

The modern lie when you didn't want to answer something. Everyone was tired all the time. There was even an acronym for it: TATT. Nobody ever questioned you about it.

Cassie phoned Coco.

'Can't talk. I'm here in the hospital and Jo's sister is in with her.'

'I'll be quick. How's it going?'

'Attracta, who is now called Tracey, by the way—'

'Tracey?'

'Yeah. Guess she wanted to change everything her parents ever gave her. Anyway, Tracey came home after seeing Jo in hospital on Saturday and went into a decline. Then Fiona got really upset. I almost sent Tracey off to a hotel but it was her first night back in Ireland and I felt so guilty. Still, I have to think of Fiona. It's not fair on her,' Coco went on. 'Heck, Tracey's coming out again. She's only been in for ten minutes. Same as yesterday. Have to go,' she whispered into the phone and hung up.

Cassie had opened Shay's apology bottle of red wine then. She liked red wine but it gave her a headache if she drank more than two glasses. That's all she'd have then, because she'd already had some of the wine box stuff.

But somehow she'd got more maudlin, drank the whole bottle, and that was why her head was killing her now.

Blasted Shay. Blasted Antoinette.

The anger rose in her again, quickly followed by the anxiety: what was happening to her and her marriage? She should have smoothed things over.

What if Shay had had enough and left her? He could: she'd pushed him enough. She spent plenty of time with Pearl, after all, but then Pearl wanted the whole family there and Cassie was in no doubt that when Antoinette wanted her son, she wanted him alone.

She slipped into her seat at the Larousse conference table, aware that she reeked of perfume because she was sure the fumes of an entire bottle of wine *and* two glasses of white box wine were seeping out of her pores. An ozone-killing blast of deodorant followed by four massive squirts of her current Jo Malone perfume was adding to her headache, but better that than to be outed as a woman who'd sunk so much wine by herself.

What sort of role model was she for Beth and Lily? And it wasn't as if she, of all people, didn't know how alcohol could affect a family. Not that Pearl had ever said too much about her and Coco's mother, but the only crystal-clear fact was that addiction had been at the heart of her leaving.

'She was a troubled soul,' Pearl had said on those few times they'd actually talked about Marguerite.

Pearl seemed to think that the less she talked about the girls' mother, the more they'd forget about her. Which was sort of unlike Pearl, really. Pearl was surprisingly modern in her parenting and always talked about stuff: boys, periods, breasts, all the stuff younger parents needed to discuss.

So the three monkeys approach to Marguerite was unusual.

Still, who cared what had made their mother

leave. Stupid cow had still gone and never bothered coming back, right? That was all that mattered.

Cassie thought of her sister's discussion about Fiona and how unanswered issues in childhood turned into exploding hand grenades later, but then pushed it out of her mind.

Belinda was at the top of the room outlining plans for the pharmaceutical conference Lorenhad won by undercutting their nearest rival.

'The highlight is the bonding day on day two,' she was saying. 'I've got footage of the wall-climbing guy explaining it. In-house, we're calling it the Bear Grylls' Effect – everyone wants to do something dangerous. Out of house, obviously, it's called the Action Adventure part of the week, as nobody wants to pay fees for the use of Bear's name.'

Loren smiled. She liked Belinda, admired her no-bullshit work ethic and the fact that Belinda had raised a son on her own.

'If she had the slightest clue how much deranged behind-the-scenes stuff went on to manage a career and a child, she mightn't be so admiring,' Belinda liked to say. 'Loren hasn't any concept about any world apart from her own.'

'Must be nice to be so emotionally isolated,' Cassie agreed, who at any one time had a group of people looking for her help, advice on husbands, boyfriends, children, how to approach Loren for time off.

'Not that I'm advocating Loren, the Ice Queen,

as a role model, but perhaps you should try it sometime,' Belinda advised. 'You're too nice to people. You never get a moment's peace.'

Today, sitting at the conference table with a raging hangover and no headache tablets inside her because she didn't think she'd be able to keep them down, Cassie fervently wished nobody came near her for help today.

I know nothing! That was what she'd have to say to them.

My husband is ignoring me. He's destroying our marriage.

No, his mother *is destroying our marriage and I'm not smoothing it all over. I screamed at my kids this morning for no good reason other than having a hangover – ME! A hangover! – and my head aches. Go find someone who actually has all the answers.*

When Belinda's presentation was finished, she took her place beside Cassie. 'Sauvignon Blanc or Chablis?' she whispered.

'That bad?' said Cassie, appalled.

'No, you don't smell of wine, I just recognise the look. Been there, done that, got the T-shirt, darling. You got time for lunch today?'

Cassie thought of her desk, the email inbox from hell and the phone message slips.

'Sure,' she said. Carbohydrates might help. Plus she needed to spill out her bruised feelings to someone.

They sat in the barrel-shaped cavern of a bustling restaurant near the office and, as a waitress cruised past with a martini and several glasses of wine on a tray, Cassie suddenly thought she knew what would fix her.

'A martini, vodka,' she said confidently to their waitress when she arrived.

Belinda's eyebrows raised the fraction they were capable of thanks to her three-monthly applications of Botox but she said nothing as she ordered tap water.

'Hair of the dog,' Cassie said when her drink arrived.

''Fess up – what's wrong?' said Belinda, studiously ignoring the bread. 'I don't think I've ever seen you drink alcohol at lunchtime. Now you're hungover and ordering martinis. I was half expecting you to demand it shaken and not stirred . . . Is everything OK?'

Cassie avoided answering the question by taking a deep drink of her martini: sharp, kick-ass and instantly hitting the spot. She'd hardly ever had one before. They were pre-marriage and pre-kids drinks, fun and frivolous, along with cosmopolitans and mojitos – silly expensive things for fun nights out with single girlfriends.

'Of course, we don't have to talk about it but I will have to use my mind-bending techniques on you,' Belinda went on. 'And the thing with the thumbscrews gets pretty messy . . .'

'That's not mind-bending.' Cassie laughed for what felt like the first time that day.

'Yes! A smile! Spill.'

Cassie grabbed a fat bread roll, spread it liberally with butter – because what was the point of staying slim? – and explained.

'And do not,' she said at the end of her tale of Antoinette's hostile takeover attempt, 'take Shay's side and say you can see how tough it is for him.'

'As if.'

A salad appeared in front of Belinda, and fish and chips in front of Cassie.

'Never having been married, I have never had a serious mother-in-law problem,' Belinda said thoughtfully, removing all the croutons from her salad. 'Jake – remember him? Many years ago, casualty of a dreadful divorce and with a mother who thought he was a prophet in disguise? Now *she* was a nightmare. Straight out of a Stephen King novel. He was living with her and she felt it was her job to protect him from making any other relationship mistakes again. Any girl – royal descent, movie star, charity worker who gave all her money away to lame dog foundations, you name it – they weren't good enough for her Jake. I'd say she had a hand in dismantling the previous marriage. We were together one Christmas and she bought me this perfume for a fiver; smelled like air freshener but not as nice. Plus she wore Guerlain perfume herself, so it wasn't as if she didn't understand how to buy nice perfume. I don't mind if you can't afford a present, but just buy a nice card instead. But she had money for sure and she was simply taunting me.'

'Antoinette's not like that,' sighed Cassie. 'She's lovely to me, kind, all that stuff, but—'

'But she wants her son to take over where her husband left off.'

'Yes, that's it in a nutshell.'

'So Shay's torn. He's being the hero to his mother, while you, being Mrs Capable, are supposed to be able to keep the home fires burning. You should have been the fainting, useless type from the start.' Belinda grinned. 'You know, the women who can't change light bulbs, take out the bins or phone the gas people to argue about the bill. Tough Scarlett O'Hara versus delicate Melanie Wilkes.'

They both smiled at this, as they were both *Gone With the Wind* fans.

'I was sensible from when I was seven,' said Cassie.

Belinda knew her mother had walked out, knew that Cassie had felt responsible for Coco as a child.

'Even when I went through my "wild period" in my teenage years, I was still sensible. My Great-Aunt Edie thought I was out smoking pot and having sex with college kids, but I wasn't. I was too sensible to do anything but fake being wild.'

They both laughed at this and Cassie slurped some more of her martini.

'What about Shay's sisters?' Belinda asked. 'Can't they help out with their mother?'

'Miriam and Ruth?' Cassie considered this while she looked at her cocktail glass and wondered if she could possibly have another martini because all the stress had gone with the drinking of this one, and she felt another one might make her perfectly calm, which would be lovely. 'Now *that* does annoy me,' she confessed. 'Antoinette never asks them to do anything, and they don't offer either.'

The more she thought about this, the more annoyed she got. Ruth didn't have a family to care for and she lived near her mother. Why didn't Antoinette phone *her* as if she were the fire brigade?

'There's your answer,' said Belinda with the firmness of one who liked straightforward solutions. 'Talk to them. Say they need to pull their weight and help their mother through her grief. It means you don't have to go into battle with Shay, and yes, I do feel sorry for him, poor love. He's one of the good guys, Cassie, and you know it.'

Cassie nodded and felt tears well up. She never cried in public. Never. She'd learned that lesson years ago when she was seven. This was ridiculous. What was happening to her?

Suddenly she decided that she didn't care what Belinda said or how shocked she looked: she was having another martini instead of dessert.

Yes, Shay was a good man, she knew that, but it seemed as if Shay had made his choice – and he'd chosen his mother. Doing this had broken Cassie's heart.

He wasn't the first person who'd chosen to leave her: her mother had too.

A martini might not be the answer but, for today at least, when she felt in such emotional pain, it might help anaesthetise the hurt.

Coco's visitor was gone. She'd put Tracey into a cab for the airport just before twelve on Monday and had even hugged her goodbye, which was like hugging a board, as Tracey clearly didn't do physical stuff.

'I'm sorry I'm going home early but I can't cope with any of it, being here or seeing poor Josephine,' said Tracey, trying not to cry as she sat, all dressed in black, with her long-distance neck pillow – also black – sitting on the cab seat beside her.

'I understand,' said Coco, who didn't but who was deeply relieved that her guest was leaving. She had no idea how Tracey had reorganised her flight details and, to be frank, didn't care.

Once Tracey was gone, Coco decided she had time to drop in unannounced to the shop and do some work, because she hadn't been in for nearly a week and no matter how well Adriana said things were going, there would always be things only Coco could do.

She swung into the coffee shop en route and picked up a take-away for herself and one for Adriana. They could have a chat, look over the website and Facebook page, and then discuss plans. Coco was thinking about all of this as she walked down the road. When she reached Twentieth

Century and found it shut with the shutters down, she did a double take.

What?

She looked at her watch. Half twelve. The shop was supposed to open at ten but there was no 'back in five minutes' sign hanging anywhere, no lights on, shutters still down. Adriana hadn't opened up yet.

Gritting her teeth, Coco put both coffees on the step, opened up the shutters and, standing back, cast a cold, hard eye over the front of the premises. The windows, which she often cleaned herself after bad weather despite the window cleaner coming once a week, were grimy. The shop displays were exactly the same as she'd left them, although Adriana had sworn blind that she'd redone them with one funky 1960s window and the other a window of models in pre-war suits. She'd emailed every single detail to Adriana, who'd replied perkily and said: *No problem, consider it done.*

Consider it not done, thought Coco furiously.

She opened up and went inside. The place smelled musty and of old sweat – a constant problem when you sold vintage clothes. If clothes weren't treated carefully when they came in, they would remain musty and sweaty, but Coco went to such effort to revitalise everything she sold. She kept the whole place freshly smelling at all times because nothing put customers off vintage more than to enter into a dusty, smelly place – like this, she realised, seeing nothing but dusty counters, dirty glass on the cabinets and cobwebs dangling from corners. It was like a grimy veil had been thrown over her beautiful jewel of a shop. She wanted to scream with fury at Adriana.

Sipping her coffee, she threw the other one down the sink and found her cleaning clothes, where she kept them in a cupboard upstairs along with the mops, window-cleaning stuff, alcohol sprays for clothes, and essential oils for use on the floor in truly desperate times.

She'd just changed when she thought of the girl Pearl had mentioned to her: someone who was studying fashion in Larkin College and was looking for part-time work.

Texting Pearl, she asked for the girl's details, and Pearl, who was a whizz with her phone because her poker friend Peter was a fan of technology and had shown her how to use it, texted Phoebe's details straight back.

I've just got Gloria on board and she says she'd love to meet her and, if all goes well, she could move in on Friday,

Pearl added.

Lovely girl. They'll get on a like a house on fire and it will do Gloria the power of good.

Hopefully she could do the shop the power of good too, Coco thought grimly.

She printed up a sign:

Shop closed for renovations
Open Wednesday
30% discounts!

And then she stuck it on the front door, which she then locked.

She sent a quick text to the girl, Phoebe, asking her if she still wanted part-time work and if so, could she do a trial in the shop as soon as college was over today. Then Coco began to clean up.

Phoebe and Ian were sharing a coffee in the college canteen. Phoebe was wearing her newly renovated jacket from the vintage shop along with a skirt Ian had made for her: a draped grey jersey masterpiece he insisted he'd run up from some fabric he had lying around. It clung and pulled her in in all the right places, going wonderfully well with the fitted jacket and her biker boots.

'Thank you, thank you,' she'd said with passionate gratefulness when he'd given it to her.

'Wanted to drag you out of the misery pit,' said Ian, pleased and then taken aback when Phoebe had hugged him fiercely in front of everyone.

'Stop. People will think I'm straight,' he'd hissed.

By 'people' he meant a second-year graphic

design student he fancied, who still had barely noticed that Ian existed.

'There are so many gay guys around here, Mr Graphic Design hasn't even spotted me yet,' grumbled Ian, who was thinking of having a pink streak put in his hair so he could rise above the competition.

Ian refused to hang out with the fashion fag hags who just wanted someone to go shopping with. 'They have this TV show vision of gay men,' he said mournfully. 'They think it's all squealing over Instagram and what Kim Kardashian is doing. None of them are into design at all or understand that I'm a serious artist with more ambition than hanging out in clubs and pretending to be a designer. There.' He tweaked the skirt a bit on Phoebe. 'Those are not the ideal boots, I should add. You need something flat and sedate with perhaps a hint of zebra, just a hint. But shoes are beyond me right now. Give me time. And cheer up, babes.'

She'd been so miserable since coming back from Wicklow, and realising how impossible a task her mother was living with every day, that Ian had been racking his brains trying to cheer her up.

It was proving difficult.

'I'll have to leave college,' Phoebe said tearfully. 'I can't leave Mum to run the farm all by herself. It will kill her. She needs someone to look after Ethan and Mary-Kate too. Ethan will fall behind with his homework if he isn't overseen, Mary-Kate is fragile since Dad died, and they need my money from the pub coming in or they'll never survive.'

'Please don't say that,' Ian begged. 'You're a brilliant designer – you have to stay.'

'Not according to that bitch over there,' said Phoebe, all the hurt coming up now.

One of the fashion bitches had been particularly horrible about Phoebe's latest design in pattern cutting, and had made subtle cow noises whenever Phoebe came near, to imply that Phoebe had better return to her farm.

Ian, valiant in defending his friend, had sauntered over and said to the girl: 'Tell me, how you do your hair to hide the horns, sweetie?' in such a saccharine voice that the whole place had erupted into laughter and Ms Bitch had been the one to turn puce with embarrassment.

'Ignore her,' Ian said now. 'She's just jealous. Couldn't design her way out of a paper bag. You, Ms McLoughlin, have talent, and don't let anyone scare you away. There's got to be a way to sort things out for your mum. We simply need to figure it out.'

Pearl's friend, Gloria, still hadn't rung about meeting her, and Mrs Costello had been particularly poisonous when Phoebe had been leaving her bedsit this morning.

'Are you sure you aren't having men staying over?' Mrs Costello had said, accosting Phoebe at the front door, eyes beadily looking Phoebe up and down as if she had 'harlot' painted on her somewhere.

Ian had slept over one night, but he was like her brother. Still, no point saying that to Mrs Costello, who was probably homophobic to add to her other flaws.

'There's no room for men in my bedsit,' she'd replied tartly. 'No room for anyone.'

'Don't get snappy with me, missy,' snapped back Mrs Costello. 'I can have you out in a flash, believe me.'

So when two texts pinged in – one from Pearl asking her to meet her friend, Gloria, and one from Pearl's granddaughter, Coco, asking her if she could come for a trial in the shop – Phoebe could barely believe it.

'Look!' she squealed, showing Ian. 'A job and hopefully somewhere to stay!'

'Well, paint me pink and mail me to Ballydehob,' said Ian. 'Guess you're not going home after all, Dorothy!'

Such was her desperation for the job that Phoebe texted Coco saying she'd be there by two, which meant cutting the colour appreciation class.

'You know more about colour than old Murcheson,' said Ian, naming the lecturer giving the class. 'Go. I'll get the notes for you. Just remember: blue and green should never be seen – unless you're a designer, when the rules don't apply and the wilder the better. Just ask Roberto Cavalli. Have fun.'

★   ★   ★

Coco had moved at least a quarter of the stock upstairs – an exhausting job – and was about to start on the other side of the shop when the door opened.

'Helloo!' said a voice.

Adriana.

Coco looked at her watch, which said ten to two – almost four hours after Adriana was being paid to open up. Coco had gone online and found that keeping the shop clean and tidy, and redoing the window displays, weren't the only areas where Adriana was failing in her duty. There had been no Facebook listings of new stock for at least five days, both Facebook and the shop's email inbox was full of queries, and someone had emailed five times, increasingly angry emails at that, as she asked for the whereabouts of a skirt that she'd paid for in full ten days ago.

Coco emerged from the office wearing her old white boiler suit and with her hair tied up in a scarf. She knew she had an uncharacteristically grim look on her face because Adriana's pretty smile instantly disappeared.

'Oh gosh, you caught me on the hop,' said Adriana. 'You see, I had this thing, and obviously I didn't want to bother you—'

'Stop right there,' said Coco, hoping her face looked as glacial as she felt. 'You've been telling me you've done all these wonderful things, like changing the window displays, and you haven't done any of them. Why on earth would you lie, Adriana? If you couldn't cope, why not tell me?'

'You see,' began Adriana, 'I've had so many things go wrong . . .'

Once, a few weeks ago, in fact, Coco would have listened to this litany of woes and, even if she hadn't quite believed it all, she'd have caved totally once Adriana's huge blue eyes filled with tears.

But that was the old Coco. The new Coco, the one who was being a de facto mother, who was coping with a best friend suffering in hospital, who could see her sister being entirely miserable and simply couldn't help – *that* Coco was a different employer altogether.

'How many days have we been closed because of these issues?' she asked coolly.

'Well, I closed early on Saturday,' said Adriana slowly.

'How early?'

Adriana winced. 'Three p.m.'

Coco kept staring.

'OK, half one. I had something to go to and there's nobody to help me. If I need to run to the loo, I have to lock up, and I can't get nice coffee or anything,' she added sulkily.

'Your tyre wasn't flat that morning ages ago, was it?' Coco asked. She had to know.

Adriana looked sulkier than ever but said nothing.

'The thing is, you want to be paid for working but you don't want to actually work, Adriana.

Worse, you lie to me about it. You lied to me on the phone the other day, telling me what you thought I wanted to hear. "Yes, I've redone the window displays; yes, the place is clean." All lies. I can't trust you, and if I can't trust you, I can't employ you.'

'What?'

'Sorry,' said Coco, shrugging. 'I need someone I can rely on. You'll have to go.'

Adriana burst into tears. 'But Coco, we've been through so much together and I need this job, and—'

'Keys,' said Coco, holding out her hand.

'You don't mean this,' sobbed Adriana.

'I do,' said Coco patiently, her hand still held out.

Shocked that her tears hadn't worked, Adriana handed over the keys, still sobbing. 'But you need me!' she said.

'I need someone who doesn't lie to me . . .'

'I only closed early a few times, and I was going to change the window displays . . .'

Phoebe pushed the door open and took stock of the situation. 'I'm Phoebe McLoughlin,' she said to Coco. 'Should I come back later?'

Coco drew herself up to her full five foot one. 'No,' she said pleasantly. 'Welcome, Phoebe. Come on in. Adriana, I'll send your wages on, and I'll be examining the till carefully and the stock for any discrepancies.'

Adriana snorted. 'I would never steal.'

Coco held the front door open. 'By taking wages and not working, you already have,' she said sweetly. 'But more fool me for not getting rid of you ages ago. I guess I'll have to chalk this one down to experience.'

Adriana marched past, Coco shut and locked the door, and then leaned against it.

'I've never done that before,' she said, thinking she might cry herself.

Phoebe grinned. 'First time for everything,' she said. 'Now, I'm not dressed for cleaning but I guess that's what we're doing today. I like your overalls. Any in my size?'

Pearl was changing her duvet and struggling with it when the doorbell rang. *Goody,* she thought. It might be someone who could help. Daisy, who kept having to be stopped rolling in the bits of the duvet on the floor and escaping into the cavern of snowy white cover to play hide and seek, was of no assistance at all.

'Coming,' yelled Pearl as she went carefully down the stairs.

She was beginning to see the allure of those stairlift yokes. It was so easy to slip, and while she wasn't like Edie – terrified to put a foot under her in case she fell when she was on stairs – Pearl was getting more anxious about the thought of a fall. Falls were the bogeymen of old age, she knew. Hips and pelvises shattered like glass when you got older, and hospital stays merged into nursing home stays, and before people knew it, they were stuck there forever. She wanted to remain in her own lovely home with her things, and with darling Daisy to snuggle into her bed at night, and darling Peter around the corner. She wasn't ready to let go of all that.

Mind you, she reminded herself, *look at poor Josephine and what she was going through, and her only thirty-one, the same age as Coco. Tragedy can strike at any age.*

And that dear Fiona, such a glorious little imp with the most gorgeous smile, and Coco said she'd been so upset when Josephine's sister had been over from Australia.

Pearl was thinking sadly on the unfairness of life as she opened her door, and was surprised and delighted to see her older great-granddaughter standing there in her school uniform, rucksack slung across one shoulder.

'Beth, my love, come in!'

'You sure I'm not interrupting?' said Beth in a tremulous voice that wasn't like hers at all.

Pearl could recognise those signs as well as she could read the day's weather from the morning sky. She'd raised three teenagers after all: her son and, later, his daughters too.

'Come in, lovie,' she said, and put an arm around Beth's slender shoulders.

She rarely saw Beth in her school uniform and it made her look younger than she normally tried to look. As per the school's strict instructions, there was only a little make-up on those blue and amber eyes – eyes that looked suspiciously red today. Beth was tall like Shay and had the lean build Coco would have killed for at the same age. She was nearly sixteen now and her figure was womanly: slender hips but with the rise of her breasts visible under the deeply unflattering green school jumper. Her hair was tied up into a knot: now *that* was like her mother's. Raven's-wing dark and curly, suited to a Renaissance beauty in a corseted gown. Cassie's hair was glorious but Cassie insisted in scraping it back and dressing in very businessy, androgynous clothes, and Pearl had never quite been able to understand that.

Now with Beth, Pearl kept up the chatter, knowing that nothing was more off-putting to a teenager than bluntly being asked: 'What's wrong?'

'Shall I make us tea? Down, Daisy,' she added as Daisy bounced in her puggish fashion, desperate for love and attention. 'How's school, lovie? Still haunting you with that dreadful A-line skirt?'

Beth finally laughed and her tense face softened. 'Horrible, isn't it? Who wears green, red *and* purple in a kilt?'

'There's probably an outraged Scottish clan somewhere who want their tartan back and don't want irate schoolgirls turning the hems up so they look like belts when they get into sixth year,' Pearl said, her cheerful tone hiding her worry.

Coco hadn't tried the skirt-as-belt look for all her ability with clothes: too self-conscious about her figure. But Cassie had turned her kilt up to mini-skirt proportions when she was in her Doc Marten's phase, much to Edie's chagrin.

'I don't know where to look!' Edie had said the first time she'd seen this apparition.

'Close your eyes and breathe deeply then,' Pearl had advised. Pearl decided she wouldn't mention all of this right now and pretended to be deeply interested in taking out the contents of the biscuit cupboard. 'I have shortbread, but they are a couple of days old—'

'Oh Pearl . . .' And then the tears came, as Pearl had known they would.

Pearl wrapped Beth up in her arms. She wished she could hug the pain away but she couldn't, never could. Life had pain in it and people had to go through the pain. She could only listen and offer support.

'Sit down with me and Daisy,' she said, steering them all to the couch.

At first Beth couldn't talk; she simply held on to Pearl and sobbed into her white cotton cardigan.

'Let it all out, my love,' crooned Pearl, stroking Beth's hair.

On the other side of Beth, Daisy sat on the couch in a state of agitation: one of her people was upset and she wasn't able to do her face-licking to fix it. Daisy was a prodigious face-licker and she knew it helped when there was crying. Upset herself, she began to make anxious little whimpers until Beth stopped and pulled the dog on to her lap and held her close, as if Daisy was a cuddly toy and Beth was a small child.

The magical healing power of animals, thought Pearl.

When Marguerite had left, Pearl's two black pugs, Basil and Sybil, had understood better than any of the humans that heartbroken little Cassie needed small, warm, furry bodies to cuddle at night. Cassie had cried herself to sleep every night until the dogs were left to sleep in her room.

No dog could replace a mother, but they'd given her the unconditional love she needed.

'It's Mum and Dad,' Beth finally blurted out. 'They barely spoke to each other all weekend and it's been like that for ages now. Dad's always out, Mum's upset . . . Oh Pearl, I think they're going to get a divorce.'

CHAPTER 16

Antoinette found the house in the newspaper property section in the library. A person couldn't possibly buy all of the papers, so she'd taken to going into the library to peruse the various supplements and use the internet, which a nice young man had shown her how to do, and today, *bingo!* There it was: an old red-brick not far from where Shay and Cassie lived now, with a modern glass extension at the back and a beautiful guest cottage tucked away behind it.

The garden looked pretty, although there was lots of gravel and low plants, which Antoinette hated. She'd have to get rid of that. There was a separate entrance for the cottage too, which meant she'd have her privacy, and two bedrooms – imagine that, *two!* – plus a small kitchen and a spacious living room. Obviously lot of the pieces of furniture from Oakleigh Avenue wouldn't fit in such a neat little house, but she could sell them. Buy new things. She could have a foldaway table and set it up for dinner parties. Shay could help her source the perfect one. With that old Lismore lace tablecloth she and Arthur had been given on their wedding day, she could prettify it with her Belleek china and have the girls around for dinners. Best of all, Shay would be on her doorstep, there for when she felt low or needed to see a friendly face. Cassie and the girls too.

Cassie sounded glum these days on the phone. Possibly the change of life, Antoinette thought, although she was a bit young for it. Still, who knew? It hit different people at the oddest times. And so many women lost their looks at that point. All the hormones abandoned them and they lost interest in men, sex and even themselves.

Not that this had ever happened to Antoinette.

'Look after yourself,' her closest family friend, an aunt, had said meaningfully when Antoinette had reached that age. And Antoinette had. But looking after herself hadn't been enough. She'd entered a third age: an age where she felt her wisdom should be valued and it wasn't, not at all.

It hurt her the way people didn't notice her as much as they used to. Nobody said, 'Antoinette, lovely hair, such a pretty smile.' Those sort of compliments had boosted her all her life but then, with Arthur gone, she didn't see his old friends anymore and there were no more compliments around the golf club, no more men saying nice things and making her smile.

Not that Antoinette had ever any intention of so much as putting a foot wrong with Arthur's friends. She was a lady, not that sort of girl at all. But compliments cheered one up so. She missed all that desperately. The company of women just wasn't the same.

She slid her gaze back to the newspaper photo of the red-bricked house with the guest cottage. There was an ensuite in the master bedroom but an ugly family bathroom. Obviously the house revamp had got as far as the extension downstairs and perhaps the money had run out. The cottage might have been a separate rented-out property because it looked different from the main house. Still, Beth and Lily could live with an ugly bathroom.

Antoinette gathered up her handbag and jacket, and then left the library. She had phone calls to make. If she couldn't get Shay at work, she'd leave a message for him at home.

Belinda and Cassie met at the lifts that evening.

'Remind me never to drink at lunchtime again,' whispered Cassie. 'I nearly fell asleep this afternoon.'

'I ignored those two martinis,' Belinda whispered back, 'but that's it, honey. We're not in an episode of *Mad Men*. Drinking on the job is the number-one firing offence with Loren, and you know it.'

'I won't, I won't, I promise. Stress-cubed, that's all.'

When she heard her phone ringing with Beth's personal ringtone, she answered quickly.

'Hello Beth, all OK?' It was her constant answer to her daughters, as if all calls had to be emergencies.

Beth teased her about it, so did Lily now that she, too, had a phone.

'Mum, we're fine!' they'd say, laughing at her. 'The phone is not an instrument of doom!'

But then their mother had never left when they were seven. They didn't understand that bad things could happen.

This time, however, Beth's voice was so frantic on the phone that at first Cassie thought there *had* been an accident.

Be calm for Beth's sake, she thought, every mothering instinct she had kicking in, even though she wanted to screech 'What's happened?!' at the top of her voice.

'You never told me you and Dad were splitting up! Granny's found a house for her and Dad, they have it all organised, but what about us, Mum? When were you going to tell us? Pearl said it would be OK when I was imagining you getting a divorce, because I was with her earlier and she said all married people fight. But then I got home and heard the message, and now I know it all. When were you going to tell Lily and me? Tell me that?'

Stepping into the silent boardroom for privacy, it took Cassie five minutes to get the whole story out of Beth.

First, Beth had gone to Pearl's instead of staying in the after-school programme to do her homework, and Pearl had calmed her down about the possibility of Cassie and Shay getting divorced.

'How could you think that?' asked Cassie with a lump in her throat, feeling entirely to blame because she knew full well how Beth could think such a thing.

'Mum, I'm not seven, so stop treating me like I am. It's been Screamsville all weekend with you two either shouting or ignoring each other, so I knew there was something wrong but I didn't know what!'

The next part of the mystery was simple: when Beth got home from Pearl's, there was a message on the answerphone from Granny Reynolds.

'She says she's got a house for her and Dad to move into together, and nobody told me or Lily, and I don't know why you think you can do that,' shrieked Beth down the phone. 'How could you not tell us you're breaking up?'

'You sure you've got that right, honey?' said Cassie, confused.

'Listen,' said Beth, and pressed *play* on the answering machine.

Once she'd heard it, everything made sense to Cassie.

Yeah, thought Cassie grimly. *How could you not tell us, Shay?*

'Nobody's going anywhere,' she assured her daughter. 'There are no plans to move, no plans for Antoinette to move in with Dad. It's a mix-up.'

She was damned if she was going to call Antoinette 'Granny' anymore. Antoinette had long since crossed the barriers from 'granny' to 'meddling cow'. How dare she leave such a message on their answering machine? How dare she ring up and talk to Shay as if none of the rest of them were there, as if none of the rest of them mattered? No, Antoinette had gone too far this time and, if he was in on it, so had Shay.

Cassie had rapidly worked out what Antoinette was thinking. It made sense. She had said something about a 'granny flat' on the message and Cassie quickly figured out that Antoinette saw herself installed in a cosy apartment in Cassie and Shay's back garden. A new back garden with a new house – one Antoinette was happily picking out from the property supplements.

It would be the ideal solution to all her problems: she'd have Shay on tap all the time. They could all be one big happy family . . .

Somewhere in the back of Cassie's mind, the sensible part of it, she knew she should think about all of this before acting. But she felt a little unhinged, whether from the stress of the past few weeks or from the martinis she'd had at lunch, and the sensible part of her was not operating.

She was going to sort this out once and for all.

Cassie knew it was unreasonable to phone her mother-in-law first – like a cheated-upon wife phoning her husband's girlfriend before confronting him – but she wanted to get the story straight from Antoinette before she talked to Shay.

It took a few rings before Antoinette answered.

She was probably looking through the property pages, working out how much she could get for her own house, Cassie thought angrily.

When her mother-in-law finally answered, it was with her normal, slightly wavery tones. 'Hello?'

'Antoinette, it's Cassie here,' she said, surprised at how fierce she sounded. She hadn't planned to sound like an avenging warrior queen, but she couldn't help it. She was so angry. Lunchtime martinis and hurt were a very potent mix.

'You left a message on our answering machine at home, something for Shay about a property you think we'd all like. Of course, that's the *family* answering machine, Antoinette, so Beth heard it and she's very upset. What's more,' Cassie emphasised, '*I'm* very angry. I know absolutely nothing about any plan to sell our house or for you to move in with us. Now, if this is some notion you've come up with yourself, I think it would be nice to share this notion with Shay. Or,' she added, this time her voice dangerously low, 'if this is something you have cooked up with Shay, then I am so angry, I can't begin to tell you.'

For a moment there was silence at the other end of the phone.

'Well . . .' began Antoinette, clearly taken aback by this type of anger from her daughter-in-law. Cassie had never been anything but polite to her. And Antoinette didn't like angry people. It was upsetting.

'It seemed like such a good idea,' she muttered, 'and we'd all have more space. I mean, well, *you* would. You and Shay could buy a house nearer Pearl and, and . . .' Her voice tailed off.

'And you'd have Shay at your beck and call all the time,' said Cassie silkily.

'I'm getting older,' said Antoinette, playing what she considered her trump card.

'I don't think age has anything to do with this, Antoinette.' Cassie paused. She hated having had to admit to her mother-in-law that she'd known nothing about this plan, but she needed to know who had come up with it. 'Tell me, whose idea was this? Was it your idea, or did you and Shay cook it up together?'

'Shay's so thoughtful and he thinks about me all the time,' said Antoinette defensively. After all, Shay had been her son before he was Cassie's husband. 'He knows I'm lonely here and that I need someone around to do things.'

'What's wrong with your two daughters?' demanded Cassie. 'Ruth and Miriam live much nearer to you than us, and you never, ever ask them to help.'

'Oh, they're busy with their own lives,' Antoinette went on, as if this was all perfectly obvious.

'And we're not busy with our own lives?' Cassie sounded dangerous now, and anyone who knew her really well would probably hang up. But Antoinette didn't seem to realise that the danger point had been reached and an explosion was imminent.

'Cassie, I know we should have talked it over with you. I thought perhaps Shay had, but it doesn't sound as if he has. But don't panic. I think

353

it's such a good idea and it would make things easier for me and—'

Cassie interrupted her. 'Easier for *you*? Why should I do something that's easier for you, Antoinette? You have your life and I have mine. You do not impinge on my life without it being something that myself and my husband discuss. And you seem to forget that he is my husband.'

Cassie wished she were beside her mother-in-law now because she wanted Antoinette to see how angry she was.

'I'll be talking to him in a moment, but I can tell you one thing, Antoinette: there will be no shared house, no little granny flat where you can drop in and out any time you want, and keep Shay over there morning, noon and night. If you were ill, if you needed care, it would be a different story. I've always been nothing but kind to you. I don't have a mother of my own so I know how important a mother is, and if you were sick I would have done anything to take care of you. *But—*' she wanted to emphasise the words carefully – '*you're not sick, Antoinette*. You're in perfect health. You simply want your son back. Well, you can't have him,' she hissed, and with that she hung up.

Before Cassie dialled Shay's number, she looked through the glass walls of the boardroom at the few people still sitting at their desks in the office, all seemingly happy and content – well, as content as a person could be working for Loren.

Loren liked to keep her foot jammed to the pedal at all times, which meant that her staff were generally overworked and underpaid. But no matter how stressed they all were, was there anyone else here in the office who was about to phone her husband and tell him what a bastard he was and that she'd had enough? Probably not.

Cassie mentally rehearsed what she was going to say to Shay. She forced herself to calm down after her conversation with Antoinette and she was ready. Ready to tell him how dare he make such an important decision about their family without her knowledge. She really wanted to scream, but she wouldn't scream. No screaming. Screaming was a sign of a deranged woman, and she would not be a deranged woman on the phone.

She would be calm and businesslike, and sound like the one sane person in this hideous triangle of people. No wonder triangles never worked in love affairs. Somebody always wanted more and in this case, that somebody was Antoinette.

Was it different when you had sons? Did having a boy mean you longed for him and his companionship much more than you longed for the companionship of your daughter? Cassie didn't know.

Antoinette had one son and two daughters, yet she wasn't going to Miriam and Ruth for friendship, consolation and help: she was going to Shay, and Shay alone. It was as if she wanted him to replace his father, and that wasn't a viable option.

The more she thought about it, the angrier Cassie got. She was angry with Antoinette for trying to break up the natural order of things, and she was angry at Shay for the same reason.

'Same old, same old,' she muttered to herself.

She'd been a small child, just seven, too small to fight and scream and yell when Marguerite had walked out all those years ago. But she'd fight and scream now. She would not let her husband run away on her and their children. Shay would not know what had hit him.

She was going to keep her voice down, keep calm, and keep the high moral ground, because she was entitled to it after all.

'Hi, Cass,' he said when he answered, as if all was right with the world.

At his cheery greeting, all her good intentions fled. She thought of Lily and Beth, and how they deserved a proper family and a father who was there – not a father who was running over to his mother's because his mother had just clicked her fingers.

'I've just had the most unbelievable conversation with Beth,' said Cassie icily.

'What?' said Shay, sounding bewildered. 'Is she OK?'

'No, she's not OK. She went home and heard a really odd message on our answering machine, a message from your mother where she explains how she's found a wonderful place that you two will love living in. Apparently she's selling her house and you're going to live with her, happily ever after. No mention of us.'

There was complete silence on the other end of the phone, but Cassie could hear her husband breathing heavily.

'There are so many problems with this ludicrous idea that I almost don't know where to start, Shay, but I'll explain the one that's made me most annoyed—'

'Cass,' began Shay. 'You don't understand . . .'

She ignored him. 'We're married, have two amazing daughters, own a house and a cat, and suddenly you come up with an incredible, life-changing plan for us all, and you don't even mention it to me! You've told me nothing! Please tell me Antoinette was somehow given hallucinogens instead of her normal vitamins in the pharmacy so that I know she was and still is talking complete and utter rubbish. Otherwise, Shay, it seems you have made a huge decision and kept me out of the loop completely. Oh yes, and before she heard this message, Beth thought we were going to get divorced, which, to be honest, sounds like a damn good idea right now.'

'Listen,' sighed Shay, 'I meant to talk to you about it. It's this plan Mum has and the whole thing got out of hand. If you think about it, Cass, it's not a bad plan really. Mum's not getting any younger, she's lonely, she's never got over Dad dying and—'

'I never got over my mother leaving but I didn't

run out and steal somebody else's mother, did I?' screamed Cassie, and then the gloves were entirely off. She couldn't have stopped herself screaming if she'd been paid to. 'She's sixty-four and is perfectly healthy. Don't you see what this is? She wants you back. Not us, just you. And you're letting her. How dare you do this to us? How dare you do this to me, to our children, to our marriage? It'd be easier if you were having an affair because . . . well, men have affairs. It's quite normal. Not nice, but normal. But to betray me with your mother like this? How can I ever trust you from now on?'

'Oh honey, don't be like that, it was just an idea,' butted in Shay.

'A pretty crap idea at that,' said Cassie. 'How about you decide where you want to live, Shay: with us – me, Lily and Beth – or with your mother. Because right now, that's a choice you've got to make.'

Then she hung up.

The weird thing was she didn't feel any better after getting all this off her chest. She didn't feel the joy of vindication or the power of having stood up to someone who was hurting her.

Instead she felt like crying. Shay hadn't shouted back at her or said he'd do what he damn well pleased. That wasn't Shay's style. He'd sounded worn out and hemmed in on all sides.

Cassie stuffed her phone into a pocket and made for the ladies. She found an empty cubicle, pushed the lid down, sat on the toilet and allowed herself to cry. You couldn't cry in public in Loren's office. But here, even for a short while, it was safe.

Loren caught Cassie as she was storming out of the ladies'. 'Cassie, I need to see you in my office immediately,' she said in the tone she used to imply that she was the most important person on the planet and everyone else could go hang. Normally, when Loren spoke like that, Cassie and pretty much everyone else in the building kowtowed and said, 'Yes of course, Loren, how soon do you want me there? How high do you want me to jump?'

But today Cassie looked at her blankly and said, 'I don't have time.'

'What?'

Under other circumstances, Cassie might have noticed that speaking to Loren like this actually worked. For once Loren took an actual physical step backwards – taken aback in every sense of the word.

'Well, I need you,' she said, almost stammering.

'I have an emergency at home,' Cassie said, and it was true.

What bigger emergency could there be than going home to pack your husband's suitcases and throw him out? Yup, that all registered pretty high on the emergency-ometer.

'We've things to discuss,' said Loren, flustered.

Briefly, Cassie actually noticed what was going

on around her. It seemed as if Loren, when threatened or confronted in any way, retreated.

'I'll talk to you in the morning,' Cassie said abruptly, making it clear that the conversation was now over.

She made her way out of the building, not really caring about Loren or her company. She didn't care about anything. Most specifically, she didn't care about her damn mother-in-law and the interfering that had brought Cassie's marriage to this point.

Forty minutes later, Cassie parked the car on her drive. She couldn't have said precisely how she drove home or what route she'd taken. All she knew was that somehow she'd gone through traffic lights and up lanes and down roads, not banging into pedestrians or cyclists, operating on an automatic pilot that had kept her safe.

She slammed the door of the car and marched into the house. There was very loud music coming from upstairs. That was almost her undoing.

Beth was home.

She was the one who'd heard the message on the answering machine, the message that made her think her parents had deliberately kept her out of a vitally important piece of family news. She was the one who was scared her parents were going to split up because of the tension between Cassie and Shay.

Cassie would never forgive Shay or Antoinette for that. In fact, as far as she was concerned, the blame lay equally between them.

Once, she might have said that Antoinette was the one who was creating all the trouble, always wanting Shay, always needing more than he was willing to give. But now it was plain that he was going along with it to the point that they had actually discussed and planned selling Cassie and Shay's family home – and the last people to know were going to be Cassie and her children.

Cassie ran upstairs and knocked on Beth's door. 'Let me in,' she said.

There was no reply. Given the loudness of the music, it was no surprise that Beth couldn't hear her.

'Please, let me in, Beth,' she shouted.

The door opened a grudging inch or two and Beth, red-eyed, peered out. 'What?' she said.

'Honey, I would never do anything so enormous without telling you. You know that. This is something that . . .' Cassie thought about it carefully before she continued. 'This is something that Gran dreamed up.'

She had to give Shay the benefit of the doubt in front of their daughters. She would not use them as ammunition.

'It's your gran. Some silly idea she's taken all the way without telling anyone – well, without telling me, you and Lily.'

'How could she, Mum?' said Beth tearfully, and she began to cry loudly.

'Your gran just wasn't thinking straight. It's all going to be OK,' her mother said.

Somehow she managed to get into the room, turn off the music and sit down on the bed. She held Beth tight to her until the sobbing subsided.

'It's OK, it's OK,' she kept saying, the way you'd quiet a crying baby, and all the time, in the back of her mind, she kept thinking: *I will kill you both for this.*

When Beth had finally calmed down and Cassie had told her it was all a storm in a teacup, and really Granny sometimes lost the run of herself, Beth agreed to come downstairs and watch some TV in the kitchen while Cassie made dinner. She made Beth hot, sweet tea and gave her a chocolate bar.

'Now,' said Cassie, taking the TV remote, 'what delicious telly rubbish can we watch?'

Soon Beth was engrossed in another episode of a fashion reality show she loved.

Cassie knew Lily would be home soon, dropped back by her friend Karly's mum after their karate class. Shay was sure to be home very soon too.

And Cassie would be ready for him. She would give him the ultimatum that would finish Antoinette's stupid interfering forever. He simply needed to see what he'd be losing, that was all. And she knew just how to make that fact plain to him.

Talking hadn't worked, but this next step would.

She didn't have much time. She went to their room, opened his wardrobe and started pulling clothes out. It was amazing how satisfying it was to rip things off hangers, not caring how they fell.

She ran downstairs, grabbed a few bin bags, ran back upstairs and started stuffing the suits, shirts, underwear and everything she could find into the bin bags. It took four bin bags. Amazing, really. He had a lot of clothes.

Cassie didn't think she had that many clothes, which said a lot about her, she thought, wonderingly. Her husband owned more clothes than she did.

Maybe she needed Coco to take her in hand and dress her.

She'd tied up all the bin bags, hauled them downstairs and put them carefully on one side of the utility room where the girls wouldn't see them, when she heard Shay drive up.

Whether she gave him the bags or not entirely depended on how he behaved, she decided.

She opened the front door and waited for him. There was no sign of Lily or Karly and her mother yet, but they'd be there in about fifteen minutes. Fifteen minutes to let her husband know just how angry she was. Fifteen minutes to repair their marriage.

They could weather this. She'd promised Beth it would be fine but . . . but Cassie had to be sure, really sure, that Shay loved them.

Because some primal instinct told her that she could not be rejected again. *She* would do the rejecting this time.

Shay had left the office at high speed. He didn't bother telling anyone where he was going. He thought, ruefully, that they might be used to that: he spent a lot of time going to his mother's to do things for her lately. Probably too much. Cass was right about that.

But how could Cassie even begin to think that caring for his mother was abandoning his family? It wasn't. He loved his mother and he had a duty to her. Duty was important and didn't just end to your mother on the day you got married.

This hiccup was just Cassie and her fear of being abandoned.

He was fed up with that. It had been present all their married life and when he'd talked to Pearl about it, she'd been cagey, as if this was a subject she could barely touch upon.

'Cassie was so young when her mother left, Shay,' was all she'd say. 'That has a long-term effect on a person, particularly when the person who leaves is their mother.'

'Yeah, but she had you,' said Shay, exasperated.

Pearl had looked at him sadly. 'It's not the same.'

The traffic was hell. Rush hour no matter what time you left at, he thought with irritation. Cassie would have gone into boil mode by now.

Sure, he had been stupid to even think of listening to his mother's plan about them all moving in together, but hell, it hadn't been the worst plan in the world. Who knew what sort of help Pearl would need in the future, and no matter what plan Cassie came up with, he'd go along with it. He wasn't threatened by his wife's relations, so why was she so threatened by his?

Shay walked in and slammed the front door behind him.

Slam the door, did you? thought Cassie, alert to the slightest thing.

They met in the hall. Conscious of the fact that their voices might carry into the living room where Beth was watching TV, Cassie said: 'Let's have this out in the kitchen. Beth's home, as you know, and she's already devastated enough. I don't want her to hear this.'

'I want to go see her,' Shay said, 'and tell her it's not what she thinks.'

Cassie glared at him. 'You sorting out your messes will have to wait, because you and I need to talk' she said. 'You betrayed me.'

Shay had been expecting a row but not this.

'Betrayed?' he said. 'C'mon, Cassie, don't be overdramatic. It's hardly betrayal when you talk about something with your mother,' Shay shot back.

Cassie stared at him as if all her suspicions had been correct. 'You're defending this,' she said in astonishment, 'this cack-handed idea to sell our home and move somewhere with your bloody mother.'

It was hearing Cassie say 'your bloody mother' that finally sent Shay over the edge.

'Do you know what,' said Shay, his blood beginning to boil, 'it was a stupid idea, a very stupid idea, and certainly very stupid to consider any of it without talking to you, but do you know what, Cassie, for most people this would not be that big a deal. It's only a big deal because of you. Because of your issues.' He pointed his finger at her. 'You're so afraid that everyone's going to leave you, that all it takes is one notion that somebody could be planning something behind your back and you're convinced that's it, they're going, they're off. You're crazy, just like your crazy mother, and I'm sick of it.' He enunciated each word slowly. 'I love you. I made a commitment to you when we got married, and has that changed? No, that hasn't changed at all. You just keep thinking it's changed, you keep being determined to think it's always going to change, that I'm going to leave, that I'm going to dump you like your mother did.'

'How dare you?' whispered Cassie.

'I dare because it's the truth. You've been acting weird ever since Jo went into hospital. I don't know what that meant to you, whether it brought up all the stuff about your mother leaving when you were a child or not. Maybe you identify with Fiona, poor kid.'

Cassie could say nothing, only stare at him. Everything he was saying was true but it was all being said so coldly, without comfort. How could he speak to her like that?

'But you're not a kid anymore, Cassie; you're a grown-up. A grown-up with a grown-up husband who did a really dumb thing, yes, and my mother

366

didn't help with her stupid phone message, and I should have told you. I am sorry for not discussing it with you, Cass, so let's have an adult conversation about this and you can tell me, "This is a dumb idea and I don't want to live with your mother, end of story". But let's discuss it like grown-ups and not kids.' Shay paused. 'I suppose you rang my mother?'

'Yes, because I knew this was all her idea—'

'She's lonely, Cass, that's all.'

'And *I* don't get lonely without you?'

It sounded so stupid once the words were out of her mouth, but she did feel lonely. The girls were growing up so quickly, they needed her in different ways, and she needed the stability of her relationship with Shay. Except that felt as if it was gone too. She came last with him and she couldn't bear that.

'Why didn't you say that then?' he roared in exasperation. 'Why didn't you tell me? I'm not a bloody mind reader.'

'I tried to talk to you,' said Cassie coldly. 'How many times did I say to you please stop running to your mother like a lapdog every time she clicked her fingers? How many times have we had this conversation over the last four years? I know she misses your father but she's trying to replace him with you. That's not how it works. When the girls are older, if they're married and something happens to me, will you expect them to run back to you just because I'm not here anymore?'

Shay looked at her as if he didn't even understand this convoluted line of female thought.

'No,' she said, 'neither of us would, because that wouldn't be fair, because that's not what parenting is about – something your mother has conveniently forgotten. I'm fed up of your mother and I'm fed up of you.'

The words 'crazy mother' kept running through her brain. She was *nothing* like her mother. She'd worked so hard to create the perfect family, to be everything to everyone. She was nothing like the woman who'd walked out on her. *He* was that person. He was the one who was doing the leaving all the time.

Finally, all this in her mind, Cassie went over the edge. 'If you really want to be with her, I've gathered all your stuff in bin bags. You can walk out this door right now.'

As soon as she'd said it, she knew she'd gone too far.

'What?' For the first time, Shay was well and truly jolted. 'You've packed my stuff?' he said, his voice dangerously quiet.

'Yes! If you want to live with Mummy dearest, far be it from me to stop you. I've packed it all up, it's in the utility room ready to go, so you can move in with her tonight. Don't let us keep you away from where you really want to be.'

'I can't believe you're doing this.'

'Believe it,' said Cassie shakily. 'I got left before and yes, maybe I do have some issues with abandonment and maybe I did have a "crazy mother", as you so eloquently put it, but I'm nothing like her. I'd never leave Beth and Lily. This time *I'm* not going to be the one being abandoned. I'm going to be the one saying "go". Now get out of this house.'

'You can't mean that,' he said. 'Over something so stupid. I know I should have told you, Cassie, but—'

'I mean it,' she hissed. There was no coming back from this. 'Now get out and tomorrow morning I'll be seeing my lawyer.'

'Our lawyer,' said Shay absently.

'Our lawyer can be your lawyer,' she said with grim determination. 'I'll be going to find my own lawyer, some absolute killer, and who knows, in the divorce I'll get to keep this house and then you and your mummy can live together happily,' Cassie said, knowing she sounded vicious but unable to stop it.

The combination of fear and rage had taken over. Shay had chosen someone else over her and their children, he'd said she was like her mother, and she'd never forgive him for any of those things.

Shay looked at her coldly. 'If that's what you want,' he said.

'That's what I want,' said Cassie.

She ran upstairs and found Fluffikins on their bed, on Shay's side. That cat was spooky, she thought, before she lay down on the bed and began to cry.

369

CHAPTER 17

LONDON

Elsa knew she must look tired when a young guy wearing headphones on the Tube got up and let her have his seat.

'Thank you,' she said, feeling as if this little bit of unexpected kindness might break her. She had so many friends, so many do-*anything*-for-her friends, and yet, occasionally, she felt the loneliness of a lack of family with a bone-deep pain.

'No hassle, man,' said the guy, and then stuttered, 'er, missus.'

Despite her exhaustion, Elsa smiled. 'Missus' was in the same location as 'ma'am', a vaguely regal name for any woman who could no longer fit into the middle-aged category and was now shuffling along in the 'old lady' box in the mind of anyone under thirty.

But elegant ma'am types didn't take the Tube first thing in the morning and face the massed humanity pushing along, determined to get into work on time. And ma'am types wore low, sensible heels, but in honour of her meeting in the TV studios, Elsa was wearing her high but comfortable Vivier heels and a midnight-blue trouser suit that Mari – her oldest friend in London – insisted looked like Dior but was a fraction of the price.

'It's Zara, just fabulous. Looks expensive with that silk blouse,' Mari had said when they'd bought it. She'd accessorised the whole thing with a second-hand Hermes scarf that Mari had given her as a gift, with some exquisite embroidery stitches hiding the jagged tear along one edge.

After the production company meeting, Elsa and Mari had a date for lunch.

They'd climbed the same difficult path together and had a friendship that would endure anything. Elsa knew that whatever she faced in her life, Mari would be there, holding her hand.

Production meetings at Smart TV were a buffet with phone calls, in Tanya's mind, as she talked incessantly on her smartphone as if to prove that she was wildly important and her time was more precious than gold. She always nibbled up the nicest snacks and left half-filled skinny cappuccinos all over the place because she was permanently putting them down and forgetting she'd had them in the first place. Then some poor runner would be sent off to get another one.

When Elsa walked in, she could hear nothing above the husky growl of Tanya telling someone that: 'Yes, of course it sounds like a good opportunity, but is it worth my time?'

Stanley, producer of the show and a man who'd had to gently coax reasonable behaviour out of

Tanya for ten years, grinned hello at Elsa from one side of the long boardroom table.

Tanya was determined to move her career along. Ten years of what she sometimes called 'daytime hell!' meant she felt she'd served her time and was due a starry TV break.

'*Strictly Come Dancing* or *Dancing With the Stars*, I'd shine on those,' she'd said a few times to Elsa and Malik, the child psychologist, who were both well-trained enough to hide their shock. 'I honestly don't know why they haven't asked me yet. Or the ice dancing one.'

It wasn't so much that Tanya couldn't dance. This factor was not the one in question. The issue was that without the façade of caringness of *The Casebook* and Elsa and Malik to hide behind, Tanya's basic competitiveness was going to burst out like the alien from John Hurt's chest. People were going to see that her attempts at sweetness were about as real as her eyelash extensions.

Elsa hated to see anyone hurt publicly and it would only be a matter of time before Tanya's social veneer shattered, and what would follow would be the inevitable ripping apart by media like so many hyenas. Tanya would behave behind scenes in the same way as she behaved behind the scenes in their show: screeching at lower-level staff, talking to wardrobe as if they were serfs, demanding coffee, complaining if it was too cold or too bitter. This would infuriate the show's team and the news would inevitably get out.

No matter how bitchy Tanya could be on a daily basis, Elsa was therapist enough to see it was all born out of pain and fear, and she wouldn't wish the inevitable public humiliation on anyone.

'Are you sure about this?' she asked slowly, wishing she could be honest and tell Tanya that this plan was filled with danger.

But Tanya wasn't listening, eyes trained on some distant spot as she imagined herself suddenly transformed from daytime queen to general TV queen – Oprah without the TV station.

'*Big Brother*, even.' She was on a roll now. 'I could be the normal one in the house, the kind one who helps everyone.'

Malik and Elsa exchanged sympathetic glances. *The normal one?*

'With that much filming and very little time onscreen, they absolutely cut the show's footage to suit what they want, you know,' Malik offered tentatively. 'You don't always come out the way you really are in these reality TV shows. I mean, we cut things to suit our audience too, Tanya.'

Briefly, Tanya came back to earth. 'I know that,' she said scathingly. 'Having toiled away within the system for years, it's not as if I don't know how to work it.'

Stanley, the producer, and Luigi, the director, and the top researchers all arrived, and everyone chatted about the forthcoming shows for an hour until eventually, when Tanya got bored, she said that if this was all they had to talk about, she had places to go, people to see.

'Bye,' she said, grabbing her phones, her big leather handbag and her jacket.

Tanya was always eager to be out of the room, any room. Probably keen to meet her agent and discuss great new plans she had for her burgeoning new TV career, Elsa thought without rancour.

She was slightly fascinated by Tanya. It was interesting to watch someone who was so dedicated to their personal growth curve that they noticed absolutely nothing else around them. For example, Tanya never noticed when anything was wrong with any of the crew or any of her co-workers. Or if Stanley, who had an autistic son, was looking particularly down or weary. No, Tanya was oblivious to it all. Today she hadn't even noticed that there was a faint air of tension in the room, something that could often be put down to Tanya herself and whatever mood she was in.

As soon as she left, the tension evaporated. Stanley pushed his chair back, rested his hands behind his bald head and stretched. He looked relaxed for the first time, as did Luigi, the director. They exchanged glances and Elsa watched them, thinking that they were gearing up for another conversation and she needed to be out of there soon. She'd arranged to meet Mari but she'd wait a few minutes, ask Stanley how his small son was, how his wife was coping, how was the new school working out.

They talked for a little while but Elsa could see Stanley had something else on his mind, so she bent down under the table and was picking up her handbag when Stanley said: 'Elsa, could Luigi and I have a chat with you in my office?'

She looked up at him in surprise. The show meetings were always held in the conference room. Tanya was the person who got offices for confabs with her agent, where sometimes the walls shook from shouting.

'Sure,' said Elsa.

She wondered if she was about to be fired. If Tanya's jealousy had finally won the day and Elsa was to be shown the door.

Stanley's office was large and full of pictures of his small family. He offered her tea or coffee again. Sustenance for the condemned woman?

'No, I'm fine,' said Elsa, thinking of Mari, who'd be at the restaurant soon. She'd picked a Greek place not too far away: cheap and cheerful, the sort of place they liked to meet.

Whatever happened, she'd weather the storm. Losing a job was hardly the worst thing to have happened to her in her life, she thought with a sad smile.

'The thing is,' began Stanley, 'we've been thinking about, well, broadening the series.'

'OK,' said Elsa, nodding. Broadening, she could go along with that. It sounded better than being fired.

'Actually, broadening's perhaps not the right

word,' said Luigi, looking at his producer. 'Changing is what we're talking about. You see, we'd like to do something else. Do you remember that long-lost family segment we did?'

Elsa could remember it very clearly. Sisters, reunited after twenty years apart. A stupid family row, she remembered. The sisters' show had nearly broken her. It was the first time the past had ever threatened to shake her working life. She'd managed the right responses and when Stanley said he could see it was upsetting her, she'd cobbled together a reply about how this was so hard to deal with even for a professional, seeing all the time that could never be recovered. She'd pretended that she felt uplifted at the end when the sisters were reunited, when their families met, cousins who'd never even seen each other since they were tiny babies. Instead, she'd felt empty.

'We were thinking,' Stanley went on now, 'that we could do another show, slightly more in-depth, along those lines. Not just reuniting families but bringing more to it. Doing several episodes on the same family, bringing them together, seeing that magic moment, and then following through, seeing them later. Helping them come to terms with finding their family after many years apart.

'It would be quite a project, possibly filmed over a period of a year, and we could perhaps do eight or nine families, and we could get eighteen to twenty episodes out of it. We could do a couple of families per show and then follow them.'

'OK.' Elsa's mind was whirling as she took it all in. She kept her breathing as steady as she could, tried to keep calm, thinking of the past and how she could possibly cope with an entire series of reuniting families parted for so long.

She couldn't; she knew she couldn't.

'The thing is,' Stanley went on, 'we've had some focus groups working on our show lately and the feeling from the groups is that Tanya's too abrasive.'

Luigi snorted. 'We don't need focus groups to tell us that!'

'The ratings have been dropping too. Of course, television is cyclical and this particular series has been running for quite a while, so it is time to change it, but I think we need to change it and leave her behind. We want to broaden it and we've researchers working on it all already. We're getting a lot of hits, ones from Ireland too. We also thought we might do a few Australian shows, you know, move the idea out around the world. It could be fabulous.' He paused. 'The focus groups like you, Elsa. They think you're real, authentic, that you actually care. That you're not faking it.'

Elsa stared at him and kept her rueful grin to herself. She'd had to fake it for the sisters reunited show because her real responses wouldn't have been appropriate.

Instead, she said: 'I'm not faking it. Sometimes I want to go home with them and help fix it, which is not what a psychoanalyst is supposed to say, because—' she held her fingers up in quotes – '"There is no fixing it, there's only understanding."'

Luigi clapped his hands. 'That's what we love,' he said jubilantly. 'That's what we love about you: that reality. Those brilliant phrases, things that people will remember and quote. We could call it *The Dr Elsa de Marco Show*. We can go upmarket with this. What do you think?'

Elsa felt hollow. She would never be able to do these shows. It would break her heart. And she could imagine the press around it. Even though she looked so different and had a different name, people might finally link her with the woman who'd abandoned her own two little girls all those years ago. She could not do this to them, not after all this time, not knowing how they felt about her.

'I'll have a think,' she said, managing a smile. 'But now I have a lunch date, guys. I'll be in touch and we can talk.'

She left the room gracefully, knowing she would have to get her agent to phone them and say no. She had her private clients and she loved that. This TV career had been a glorious piece of joy in her life, but that was over now. Life moved on.

Mari was tall with long blonde hair, cut so that it fell in blades around her perfect face.

Once a catwalk model, at fifty-eight she still had the poise that turned heads, but had none of the clothes that she'd been given by the suitcase-load. They were all gone – lost in hotel rooms, forgotten in seedy motels and bars, left in airports around the world – because addiction had stopped Mari from looking after herself, never mind her things.

'I do regret the clothes,' she sometimes said, and would then instantly laugh. 'I know, don't regret the past or wish to shut the door on it,' she paraphrased. 'But Elsa, the stuff I *owned*! If I sold it now, I'd make a fortune. I could open my own blooming vintage shop.'

Mari was already in the small Greek restaurant when Elsa walked in, and as usual, people were studying her. Even now, with no money for the cushioning effects of a few injectables here and there, Mari was stunning. Elsa watched people surreptitiously watching her friend. Today, Mari was channelling the seventies, with a cream jacket and a long suede skirt that nobody would ever guess had come from the Cancer Research charity shop.

It was Mari who dressed Elsa for her TV shows, Mari who'd shown her how to look both authoritative and nothing like that naïve, lost and broken woman from many years ago. Given free rein, Mari would have made Elsa grow her hair long so it curled down to her shoulders, but Elsa said no. Long hair was from her past; her present was this very short, chic, brushed-back style. It framed her face with its dark eyes, strong brows and wide mouth. There was plenty of grey in her hair now, and one pure white stripe that swept back from her forehead in a striking manner.

She knew some people in the restaurant might recognise her from television. The elegant suits she wore for the show had that effect. Once she wasn't working, she slipped back into simple jeans and soft floral blouses, wearing the necklaces she'd collected on her travels over the years. Nobody ever seemed to recognise her then. It was as if the woman with the turquoise knot necklace she'd bought in Santa Fe, with the scarf wound casually around her neck, was a different woman from the starkly dressed therapist from the television. When nobody recognised you, you could melt into the crowd and nobody knew your secrets.

Mari sniffed the air appreciatively as Elsa slipped into her seat after hugging her friend. 'Guerlain's Jicky,' she said. 'I do love that scent. Suits nobody as well as it suits you.'

'The one thing I haven't changed,' Elsa said softly. The scent both cheered her and made her sad. It traced the lifeline of her womanhood, from the heady days of the 1970s when she first smelled its glorious scent and could barely afford it, to now, when it reminded her of the good times as well as the bad. It was spicy and woody, with lemon and lavender notes plus a hint of vanilla: scents she couldn't live without.

'Nothing wrong with a few changes,' Mari said, smiling back.

Waiters materialised the way they always had for Mari, and after a certain amount of one waiter telling Mari she was the most beautiful woman he'd ever seen – 'Please, tell me I have the chance, my beauty' – they got to order.

'I can't help it!' Mari protested when they were all gone and she could see Elsa grinning at her. 'I don't do anything.'

'I know. Bees, honeypot.'

'It's torture. The effort I have to put in with some of the fathers. They see me alone in this tiny house, figure out it's just me, because really only one person could fit, and they carry on as if I must be lonely, and suddenly it's all "Shall we have wine, while Tinkerbell/Charles is practising?" And that's with a child – *their child* – sitting at the piano, watching the whole thing!'

Mari was a piano teacher and taught long hours in her tiny Putney mews. She rented the house rather than owned, and bought clothes from charity shops so she could put money into the pension she'd neglected during her wild modelling years. Both she and Elsa agreed with the legendary Bette Davis that old age was not for sissies, and they were trying to catch up financially now.

'For lessons with troublesome fathers, you could wear all black and pretend to be a grieving widow,' suggested Elsa. 'Or – and this is what I prefer – you could stare at them grimly, tell them how inappropriate they are being to suggest alcohol in such an environment, and ignore them for the rest of the lesson.'

Mari signed. 'I know, but I need the work. I can't alienate the clients, even if I want to tell them that women who live on their own are not dying for attention from any idiot who comes calling. I've had enough men to last me several lifetimes.'

Once their soft drinks had arrived, the two old friends talked in what was almost a verbal shorthand.

'Danny?' asked Mari.

'Great form. He's ready to do an Iron Man; has two per cent body fat, apparently. That's what comes from being thirty-one.'

Both women grinned ruefully.

'Clare?' Elsa asked.

'Still in denial,' said Mari. 'She thinks if she keeps begging, he'll come back.'

'I must phone her,' Elsa said.

'I went round yesterday. Made her have a shower and I cleaned the kitchen. She's stuck in that place of where if *he's* not coming to see her, then there's no point in taking out the bins or even washing up. I hate to see her that way. Plus she's not coming to meetings.' Mari shook her beautiful head sadly and reached down to her handbag. 'Blast,' she said, sitting upright again. 'I have to give up smoking. I don't know how you did it.'

'I wasn't really an addicted smoker,' Elsa said, shrugging. 'I know, staggering given my history. Just didn't have the smoking addict gene, clearly. Ten years on and off and I never got hooked. Who knew?'

'Could there be a TV show in that?' Mari asked mischievously. 'Wildly addicted to some things and not to others?'

'Brat,' replied Elsa. 'If we do, I'll drag you in and get them to put you on nicotine patches as a test subject.'

Mari laughed. 'Good luck with that.'

Their food arrived and they talked about the man Mari was tentatively seeing.

'I told him straight out, when he asked me on the date,' Mari said. 'He took it very well. Said his sister's been in Narcotics Anonymous for ten years, so there's hope for us.'

For the first time that day, the beautiful face showed the real fragility behind Mari's bright smile.

Elsa reached out and stroked her friend's hand. 'When do I get to meet him?' she asked.

'Soon. He picked me up after Sunday,' Mari said. 'By the way, you missed Sunday. You never miss the Sunday meeting. What's up?'

Suddenly, Elsa's vegetarian dolmades didn't look so tempting.

'I have a lump under my arm,' she said flatly, looking down at her food. 'I wasn't sure at first. It could be anything. A cyst, you know. Not hormonal since the hysterectomy. Having the ovaries out puts paid to any hormonal action.'

'But you went to the doctor?'

Elsa hesitated. 'No,' she admitted. 'I know, it's ludicrous. I tell people to face things and I'm not facing this, but I think it's nothing.'

'If you think it's nothing, why did you miss Sunday?' demanded Mari.

'I was tired,' fibbed Elsa. 'Besides, nine out of ten . . .'

'Yes, nine out of ten lumps are harmless,' repeated Mari, 'but you have to get it seen to. And with your history . . .'

They were both silent, thinking back. Mari gave up all pretence of eating and made Elsa sit beside her on the banquette.

'You want a drink?' asked the owner, appearing and seeing that comfort was called for.

Both women managed a wry laugh. 'No,' they said in unison.

'Actually, perhaps English breakfast tea,' amended Mari, 'with milk and sugar. She's Irish; she needs it.'

'Irish need whiskey!' said the owner cheerfully. 'I have no whiskey but I get you best brandy, free on the house—'

'No, thank you.' Mari was firm. She had finished her cranberry juice and couldn't face another, no matter how good it was for her urinary tract. 'Tea would be lovely.'

She turned to her friend. 'You haven't even been to the doctor yet. I have the oddest feeling you've already diagnosed yourself as being ill. Elsa, remember: we're in this just for today. Tomorrow hasn't happened yet.'

'I know. I know it all. It's been over twenty years, Mari.'

Elsa held up her wrist with the tiny tattoo of the circle with a slightly unusual triangle in it. Tattooed in a type of sepia ink, the tattoo was barely noticeable, and on television Elsa covered it with make-up. She could cover it with bracelets too, but with her special friends, those who understood, she kept it on show.

It was the sign of Alcoholics Anonymous, where she and Mari had met many years before, and where they'd done their best to beat the damn disease by going to meetings, staying in touch with their friends, and trying to forgive themselves for the past. Drugs had been a harder problem for Mari, but the age range of so many of the people in NA was so young that she stayed with the AA set. She had nineteen years of being clean and sober – a little less than her dear friend.

'I know what's wrong with you,' said Mari decisively. 'You've got this lump, hypochondria has set in, and you keep thinking of the past and that you're being punished, which is rubbish, Elsa. Why don't you do something about it? By that, I mean contact them again.'

Elsa shook her head. 'No, not now. I can't wreck their lives just because I'm feeling fragile. They've chosen not to be in my life. Just as I chose to drink.'

Mari hugged her close. 'I don't know if any of us ever chose alcoholism, love,' she said. 'Who – if they knew what it meant, what they'd have to sacrifice – would choose it? I like to think it chose us, and somehow we got away. Scarred but still free.'

That evening, Elsa couldn't settle in her home, no matter that a lovely breeze blew from Wimbledon Common into her tiny garden, where she had a little Zen oasis set at the very end with a tiny water feature and an exquisite Bonsai tree she cared for diligently. She liked to sit and pray here in the early morning; not the prayers of her youth but different, spiritual prayers where she thought of all the people she loved and prayed for them to have strength and courage that day.

As a longtime member of AA, Elsa sponsored several newer members, which meant they phoned her for advice and help, and talked to her when they felt they couldn't possibly cope with not picking up a glass at that exact moment because the pull was too hard, the pain too bad not to want to numb it.

Not everyone made it. Many people went back off into the world of drinking and there was nothing she could do about it. She had no magic trick to make them stay. It had to be their own choice. Nobody could stop the addict from picking up the glass.

Elsa loved her little house, bought with the proceeds of her TV career. It was painted in buttercup yellows and soft ochres, lit with gentle golden lamps, a haven of calm, full of books, photos of places she and Mari had been, artefacts brought back from her travels around the world. Missing on the walls were photos of her darling girls, but she kept them hidden in her study and could only bear to look at them sometimes.

If only she had been allowed to see them again, she'd have told them how much she loved them, explained that she'd been in the grip of addiction, and begged them for another chance. But Cassie and Coco hadn't wanted to give her another chance and she had to respect that.

She knew so many women who'd raised children as they battled alcoholism and had relationships damaged beyond repair. How often had she sat with women who would never have relationships with their children because their drinking had destroyed their whole family.

'You're lucky – they don't hate you!' one recently sober mother had shrieked at Elsa once, when her family had thrown her out of the family home and her grown-up daughter refused to let her even see her grandson.

Elsa had said nothing. Her daughters must have hated her to have never wanted her in their lives again, even when she'd turned her life around and apologised for the pain she'd put them through.

Maybe her daughters and her husband had been right, and their lives were better without her after all. Perhaps that was her punishment. Perhaps this worrying lump under her arm was more punishment, and it was right that she take it without complaint.

She wrapped a mohair throw around her shoulders, took her Earl Grey into the garden and listened to the sounds of the city around her. She loved London: loved the buzz of the city and the fact that it was here she'd finally found peace.

She'd been drunk here too – drunker and wilder than she'd ever been at home in Silver Bay, when she'd still been Marguerite with two beloved daughters to take care of.

Having them taken away had sent her on a spiral of destruction from which she didn't think she'd ever have recovered had it not been for the outreach programme that had found her living in a squat, malnourished and yet facially bloated, her broken nose and many bruises on her body the living document to her life in the darkness of addiction.

The people who looked up to her as a television guru would never have recognised that Marguerite Keneally, née Donnelly, in the calm, elegant Dr Elsa they knew now. The mental health charities Elsa had tried to help, raising funds for people with schizophrenia and bi-polar disease to bring these illnesses out of the cold and into the understanding of more people, would never know that she understood all too well what they meant.

CHAPTER 18

THE PAST

Marguerite Donnelly's best friend, Eithne, felt that music had power. Jim Morrison, from The Doors, was her absolute hero. 'He makes me want to scream and cry, and rip off my clothes, and . . .' Eithne ran out of words for Jim Morrison. She had a poster of him inside her wardrobe door.

Her mother, Betty, who had two sisters – both nuns – would have needed to be resuscitated if she'd seen Jim's brazen bare chest with his nipples showing. Eithne did all her own ironing now in case her mother ever put anything away in the wardrobe, her precious Jim poster got ripped down, and she was never allowed out of the house and into the record shop ever again.

'I'd die if I couldn't buy albums,' Eithne said, and everyone believed her. 'Vinyl is my life.'

Marguerite loved music. She loved the way it could take you away somewhere lovely where you were adored, intoxicating, clever, special. But music's power was limited. Music couldn't take away the most powerful thing of all: fear.

Fear had the most power of all.

Fear wasn't the strange men on drugs they were all warned to beware of these days.

'Drugs are the evil stalking the land!' the headmistress often thundered during assembly. Sister Phillip read the papers and heard about strange cigarettes and how they were leading young girls astray. Astray meant sin and pregnancy.

Marguerite had no fear of funny cigarettes. Fear wasn't walking near the graveyard on the way down to Marguerite's house, a graveyard where young fellas sometimes hid and leapt out at night just for the lark of it. Fear was in her home, in her heart. And fear had such power.

From the outside, the Donnellys were more or less a normal family. Two kids, Rafe and Marguerite, the inevitable sheepdog lying at the gate chasing after cars, at the lower scale of the Newcastle Bridge community – not poor but without a ha'penny to spare either.

Tony Donnelly had a job driving trucks for the quarry, and if he spent a bit of time in the pub, well, nobody begrudged a man a few pints when his work was done. He was the silent type even with a drink on him.

Veronica Donnelly was an odd woman, no doubt about it. Kept herself to herself. Didn't go to Tupperware parties or join in the keep-fit classes in the parish hall.

Eithne's mother Betty did her best, when the two girls became friends in the convent, to make friends with Veronica. The best way to keep an eye on girls was to know the other family, make sure that when one said they were off to the library, that they were really off to the library.

But Veronica wouldn't go along with it.

'"They can look after themselves," that's what she said,' Betty recounted to her husband. 'They're fifteen now. Eithne needs to have an eye kept on her and I've barely set foot in that house of the Donnellys' over all the years the girls have been friends. Kept me standing on the step again this time. Wouldn't let me past the door. What is she hiding in there?'

Fear was what Veronica Donnelly was hiding.

Marguerite could have told people that, but by the time she realised that her family wasn't normal – that her mother wasn't normal – who could she tell?

'She takes out the strangest books,' commented one librarian to the other as Marguerite walked out.

'Who?'

'That Donnelly girl. Ones about war, death and the Holocaust. She has Emily Dickinson out permanently, and she now has one about the Second World War ghetto in Warsaw, *Mila 18*, by that Uris fellow. I said, "I don't know why you don't read nice books instead of all those sad, depressing ones," but she looked at me like I was gone in the head.'

'They should be eighteen to read the adult

books,' said the other librarian, sniffing. 'I've said so but does anyone listen to me? No.'

Marguerite loved her sad books. They made her feel less alone knowing that crazy, bad and horrific things could happen to ordinary people living ordinary lives. That she might not be imagining it. That she could be living in a small town in the middle of Ireland with a woman who walked a tightrope between sanity and insanity. That she could live in constant fear, fear that made her startle if she heard a loud noise. Fear that made Rafe determined to get out of there as soon as he had his final exams.

Not that they could tell anyone. Mental illness was something you could never speak about. People being 'not right in the head' was almost the worst thing you could say about a person. Mother's *not-rightness* was controlled by drugs, but she didn't like them because they made her tired and sleepy, and then she might not take them, and then . . . Chaos would reign. She'd scream, want to fight, go after Rafe and Marguerite with kitchen implements, accuse them of trying to poison her.

'Your mother will be fine,' Da would say when Mother had gone to bed after a bad incident. He'd clean up the broken glass – they barely had any glasses left in the house, and if it hadn't been for the marmalade coming in glass pots you could then use as glasses, they'd have had none at all

– and sweep up the shattered plates. Some might have blood on them. Mother had cut her hands on the shards and shrieked: 'Look at this, look at me! I'm bleeding to death.'

It might take an hour, but eventually she'd allow Da to clean the cut and bandage her up. Da went to Clonmel to buy bandages and antiseptic. He couldn't buy as much as they needed in Byrne's Chemist & Animal Foodstuffs in their tiny village. Mr Byrne would start to wonder. The doctor might be told. The doctor who'd been told that all was well, that Veronica Donnelly was happy on her drugs and she was taking them. No, that could never happen.

'They'd put your mother in a hospital if they knew,' Da would say.

The hospital was what they were all supposed to be scared of. Mother had been there twice before, and she'd been tied in a chair, drugs pumped into her, God knew what else, Da said. Inhumane was what it was. She needed love and care, that was all.

Marguerite wasn't scared of the hospital. She wanted her mother taken away. But it wasn't her choice. It would be inhumane, she tried to tell herself.

So instead Marguerite slept with her door locked, the old plastic suitcase up against it and the kitchen paring knife under her pillow. She leapt a foot if she heard a loud bang, and her body was set permanently to alert, adrenaline racing through her like the horses her father had once followed on the racetrack, only he never got to go there anymore.

'Your mother needs me,' he'd say.

But what about us? Marguerite wanted to say. *We need you too.*

Schizophrenia, a word almost never uttered in their house, had taken both parents away from her, and harder still was the fact that they must be secret about it all. Nobody must ever know.

Why, wondered Marguerite? *Why can we speak about a person with a heart attack and not talk about a person with the attack going on endlessly in their head?*

The crowd of teenagers all watched their class-mate behind the bar. He'd be murdered if his father found out, they knew. Murdered for letting a gang of sixteen-year-olds into the family pub after hours; murdered for having a lock-in when it was illegal to open after closing time.

But this was an adventure, this was Paudie's sixteenth birthday, this was special.

Paudie had worked in the bar unofficially since he'd been small and could fill a glass with spirits from the optics as fast as any adult barman.

'Paddy and coke,' ordered someone.

'Pint of Guinness,' said another.

One by one they ordered until it came to Marguerite. Marguerite was shy and had never fitted in.

'Wouldn't say boo to a goose,' Paudie's pal said of her.

But she didn't look shy. She could smile at people, and she'd smiled at Paudie before because he was kind, didn't treat her like a weirdo because she didn't go to discos or parties like everyone else in their class. Her only pal was Eithne, who was wild over The Doors and had gone into mourning over Jim Morrison's death.

'Summer was over, life was over,' according to Eithne, a view not shared by The Lake Cottage B&B where Eithne had a summer job chambermaiding and where she constantly stopped work to look moodily out of the window and think of poor Jim in his cold bed in Père Lachaise.

Marguerite kept herself to herself, but tonight she'd come with them to Paudie's birthday. He'd asked her when he met her down the town.

'Yeah, I'll come out, why not?' she'd said, with a broad smile he so rarely saw in school.

Now she looked at him and he felt as if he might drown in those brown eyes. They were the colour of beech trees, of the rich dark furniture in the church, polished and mysterious, gleaming with some hidden mystery. The summer sun had given her skin a light colour and she had freckles all over her nose. Her hair was long and rippling, and he wondered what it would feel like to touch it.

'I don't know, Paudie, what would I like?' she asked now, replying to his question about what drink she wanted.

Paudie knew that with Marguerite, it wasn't a

clever answer aimed at sounding smart or cool; it was unsure, like her.

'Gin and orange,' said Paudie decisively. 'It's sweet and hides the taste of the gin.'

He was sweet on Marguerite, so a sweet drink made sense. He poured her a triple shot in a big glass. Lord knew how long they'd have in the bar before they'd have to get out. Might as well treat her well now that she'd come out. All these years he'd been admiring her and finally she was with the gang. His girl for the night, he hoped.

Marguerite took a sip and, apart from the underlying bitterness, thought it wasn't too bad. Plus all the rest of them were happy to be in the bar drinking illegally. She found she liked that wave of good-humouredness; being around happiness was infectious. She sipped some more. It was strong, she thought, but it was warming. She felt happy too.

Peanuts were produced and she had some. A joke was told and Marguerite giggled. This morning she'd been in bed reading about people dying and understanding that pain; tonight she was laughing at a joke, eating peanuts, feeling a pleasurable warm feeling in her belly.

Someone had found the radio the bar staff used to listen to big football and hurling matches and was trying to tune in Radio Caroline.

'Turn it down!' said Paudie, anxious. 'It's two in the morning. If my da hears, he'll skin us all alive.'

He was banking on his parents being so exhausted that they wouldn't hear eleven teenagers sneaking around the bar, serving themselves shots. If it weren't for the beer in his system, he might regret all of this, but he'd had two pints now and was feeling mellow.

On a stool in front of him sat Marguerite, smiling now, those amazing eyes a little blurry. She mustn't be used to drinking, he thought, but then how come she wasn't? Her father liked the pub, but he wasn't a heavy drinker.

Paudie's mother had an opinion about Marguerite's mother; his mother had an opinion about everyone.

'Strange, that's what she is. I can see it in her eyes. There's something wild there. Probably in the kids, too. Paudie, you stay away from that girl. There's trouble there, I can see it.'

That girl was staring up at the bottles behind the bar. She'd rarely been in a bar, and had never had a drink before. There was no alcohol in their house ever, except when Mother bought it and things went downhill.

'Did you not take it off her?' Da would yell when he came home. 'She won't take her medication if she drinks.'

Sitting in Paudie's father's pub, a thought came to Marguerite: she wasn't her mother's keeper. It wasn't up to her to keep drink away from her mother or to make her mother take the pills. None of that was her job.

She felt a strange confidence with the warmth of the alcohol inside her. She didn't feel shy the way she felt so much of the time, no need to keep her head down and hide her face behind the curtain of her hair. Suddenly she belonged.

'Paudie,' she said in a louder voice, 'I'd like another of those orange yokes.'

Paudie grinned.

Marguerite found magic in a bottle. Any bottle. She learned to drink quickly, running to blackout every time she drank and ending up in the most crazy of situations.

'What's wrong with you?' Eithne had yelled at her one night at a dance when she discovered Marguerite in a corner with two men entwined around her. 'You're disgusting!'

'Yes, I'm disgusting,' Marguerite agreed sadly, and leaned her head on one of the men, who was kissing her neck.

She left school with her final exams and got out of her home town at speed.

'I won't go back there,' she told Rafe, who'd already gone to Dublin with a view to heading further afield.

'Me neither,' he said, taking a deep drag of his cigarette. He hugged her, which was unusual in itself because their family was not given to shows of affection. 'Take care of yourself, sis. Watch the demons.'

'What demons?' she asked playfully, head to one

side. She'd already had several gins before meeting him, knowing this was a goodbye, wanting to numb the pain.

'The ones that make you want to block it all out,' he said slowly. 'We come from the same wound, Marguerite, and that makes us dangerous. To ourselves, and to other people. Take care.'

The city was the perfect place to hide. Nobody knew who she was or that she'd once been an A-grade student in her home town school. Nobody knew she had a firm moral code or that she only meant to have one glass of wine. Nobody knew that once she started, she couldn't stop.

She met Jim at a party for college students, one she'd crashed with her friend, Niamh. Niamh had the hardness that Marguerite tried to adopt. With Marguerite, it was a veneer, sliver-thin.

When she met Jim that night – tall, with those striking Spanish-Irish good looks and a gentle charm – Marguerite felt as if she had found the man who could save her.

That night she'd drunk very little, enchanted by this lovely young man who talked to her about his hopes and dreams, and somehow extracted Marguerite's long-forgotten hopes and dreams from her.

They'd sat on the top step of the stairs while the party raged around them, talking about places they'd like to see, what they'd like to be.

'I wanted to be a teacher when I was young,' Marguerite said hesitantly, feeling Jim's arm around her soft cotton blouse.

'Why haven't you?' Jim asked.

It was very simple, the way he saw it. He'd told her about his mother, Pearl, and father, Bernie, and somehow their home life sounded idyllic: as if a person could emerge from such a home to be anything they ever wanted to be.

'You could be, if you wanted to,' he went on.

In the face of such belief in her, interest in her – something Marguerite hadn't felt in many, many years – she felt herself fall in love with not just Jim, but with his family, his life, his hopes and dreams. With him, she could be a different woman: the woman she wanted to be and not this girl who became crazy as soon as she picked up the glass.

Pearl had seen lots of girls come and go in her son Jim's life. There had been the lovely nurse, a sweet girl from County Donegal with a beautiful accent and a kindness about her that made Pearl wish Jim would choose her.

Of course, mothers had nothing to do with it when it came to sons choosing their brides, or even their girlfriends, come to that.

The kind Donegal nurse had gone and Jim had moved on to a less suitable girl called Yvonne, who liked going out to discos, dancing and generally partying until the sun came up. She had permed blonde hair that kept getting stuck to her lip gloss, and appeared to wear nothing but hot pants or very tight jeans.

'Life is for living,' she told Pearl one evening when Pearl had invited her around for dinner.

Bernie had been very quiet that evening, although it was hard to be anything but because Yvonne could talk enough for four people.

'I didn't know what to say,' he'd confessed to Pearl later that night. 'Lovely girl and all that, but . . . but sort of lively, almost too lively. Hard to get a word in edgeways.'

Pearl had been very glad when Jim had moved on from Yvonne. He was seeing sense at last.

After that, there was the student from college who was studying business, like Jim. Lavinia played tennis, her father was a solicitor who played golf, and they all lived in a mansion in Foxrock.

Edie, who happened to be there when this paragon came to visit, was wildly impressed.

'Lovely sort of gel,' said Edie, whose accent reached pre-war British Empire standards in certain company.

'Yes,' said Pearl truthfully, because she thought Lavinia was a sweet girl, but it was clear that Lavinia was merely having fun dating the sort of people her parents would find unsuitable. Delaney Gardens, with its hodgepodge of one-time council houses and citizens who considered third-level education a thrilling notion, was wildly unsuitable for the likes of Lavinia.

'She'll marry a boy from her father's firm who plays in the same golf club,' Pearl said to Bernie, and indeed it wasn't long before Lavinia dropped Jim and moved on to a Hugo, who was nearly a scratch golfer, 'Whatever that is'.

'What sort of girl do you think he'll bring home next?' asked Bernie, who thought it was all great gas.

He didn't mind what sort of woman their son turned up with as long as Jim was happy, and Pearl said she didn't mind either – in theory. But in practice she found she worried greatly about the women who came through the door. At least that was one good thing: Jim brought his girlfriends home. He was tall and dark-haired like his father. 'Black Irish', as they used to say: descendants of the Spaniards from the Armada hundreds of years ago. He had the pale skin, the blue eyes, the raven hair and eyebrows of the Spaniards, and women seemed to find him irresistible.

Then came Marguerite. She'd slipped into their lives quietly, without the fanfare the other girlfriends had merited. Jim was sort of vague about where he'd met her.

'At a college party,' he'd said, and Pearl had wanted to ask was Marguerite at college too or was she just at the party. There was a difference. Pearl was very proud of her son having gone to college. He was the first member of the family to have gone on to third level and it made her so happy.

'Imagine, our son in university,' she'd say to Bernie in the evenings when they'd sit out on the veranda he'd made from the old wooden packing boxes.

Bernie would be out there, hammering in a nail that had come up or putting up a hanging basket for Pearl. He always wanted to be busy. Never sat down. The only time he really sat was late at night when he'd sit down for a few minutes with his pipe and smoke it. Sitting on the front step and looking out over Delaney Gardens, where the kids played in the gardens or raced up and down on their bicycles, was when he was happiest.

'I know,' he'd say to her. 'Imagine that, our lad going to college. My mam would have been very proud to know that.'

The first time Marguerite had come to their house for dinner, Pearl had sensed something in the young girl; it was something Pearl couldn't quite put her finger on. There wasn't a thing out of place in Marguerite's behaviour. In fact, she behaved so perfectly, it was like she thought she was meeting the queen. She was full of pleases and thank yous, hopped up from the table every third minute to see if she could do something, never seemed to sit still, but not in the active way Bernie was always on the move. He liked to be doing things, while Marguerite moved because she seemed afraid that if she sat, someone might yell at her.

That was it, thought Pearl, shocked when she

realised what had been troubling her about Jim's new girlfriend. Marguerite was anxious, like the Maguires' dog across the road, who'd run away, and when she'd returned a week later, she'd been terrified of her own shadow. People had mistreated the dog while she'd been away, everyone decided, watching her quivering with fear.

Though Marguerite had poise and politeness, she reminded Pearl of that poor, scared dog.

She didn't think Jim would stick with Marguerite, for all that she was so very beautiful: that oval face, those shaped eyebrows, the big brown eyes with the lustrous lashes, and the wild dark hair curling down her back, with paler brown tinges in it, sort of like a lioness's mane, but darker. She was too exotic for Jim, anyway. She wore unusual clothes, the sort of stuff you might get in a second-hand shop or Dublin's Dandelion Market. She was just too different for their family; too different for Jim and for Delaney Gardens.

When there hadn't been any mention of Marguerite for quite a while, Pearl decided that her son must have split with the girl and she felt sorry for her. Marguerite wasn't at college, as it turned out. She'd a job as a waitress in a café in town and she worked long, hard hours. Home was some place in the country and she'd never been forthcoming about it, even though Pearl had politely asked about Marguerite's people at the meet-and-greet dinner.

'She doesn't talk about her family.' Jim had

shrugged. 'Not everyone wants to talk about where they've come from, Ma.'

Yes, Pearl had felt sorry for Marguerite, left out of the lovely charmed world they lived in in Delaney Gardens. They might not have much but they had happiness and love and good neighbours who'd look after them.

Jim was still going out to parties and seeing friends and seeing films. But there was no mention of Marguerite. Pearl decided she'd be the sort of mother who wouldn't pry. One of those modern ones.

'You're mad,' said her sister Edie, who liked poking her nose in where it didn't belong. 'I'd want to know everything he was getting up to. Young people today, you don't know what they're doing. The world is full of young pups and they need an eye kept on them. I'm not saying your Jim is a pup, because he's not, but you don't know who he's hanging around with every night. I'd want to know all the details. I'd want to know every night where he was, who he was with—'

'You can't do that,' said Pearl.

Edie annoyed the heck out of her sometimes. For a woman with no children, Edie had very firm opinions on how to raise them.

'He'll tell me about who he's going out with soon. It's not that Marguerite one, anyway.'

'Good,' said Edie. 'Didn't like the sound of her.'

'She was nice,' Pearl said. 'Just anxious. Like she was scared.'

So they were all surprised when Jim came home his face alight, and told them he was going to marry Marguerite.

'Get married?' said Pearl, having to sit down on the couch in shock. 'But why, love?'

'She's going to have a baby, Ma – my baby.'

Marguerite knew that without the pregnancy hormones surging through her blood, she'd have been scared stiff of the wedding. But she wasn't. She had Jim beside her and his mother, Pearl. Marguerite was almost as in love with Pearl as she was with Jim. She'd moved into Pearl and Bernie's house in Delaney Gardens and she loved it there.

'It's just for the moment, Mum,' Jim had said, 'until we get settled with a place ourselves.'

'No, it's fine,' said Bernie firmly. 'We want you, Marguerite and the baby to be safe and happy.'

Marguerite knew that Bernie and Pearl weren't delirious that their only child was getting married because his girlfriend was pregnant, but she was determined to do the right thing, to be the most wonderful mother, the best wife and the most incredible daughter-in-law.

She knew what happy families were like. She'd seen them before, from a distance. She'd seen her school friend Eithne's family, so she knew how it was done. She could be a part of that, and her darling child could be a part of that too. This was a new start.

Her parents arrived for the wedding. Pearl had

thought it a little strange that Marguerite didn't want the wedding in her home town, but Marguerite, who'd found she was remarkably good at lying over the years, because she'd had to do it so much when she was a kid, said her mother was a bit of an invalid and had never got involved in the local community. Marguerite had implied that Veronica Donnelly's invalidity was more along the lines of the physical rather than the mental. God forbid that Marguerite hinted at the reality.

Marguerite didn't have Eithne there. It was almost the first thing her mother said when she turned up at the church.

'Where's Eithne? I want to see Eithne,' she'd said plaintively. 'She's a lovely girl; I don't know why you're not more like her.'

Marguerite, dressed in the long, flowing white dress that she'd loved picking, felt her heart sink. Da said he'd made sure Mum had had her meds, but Marguerite wondered if he hadn't gone a touch too far. There was such a fine line between making sure Veronica wasn't manic and keeping her calm, because there was an anxiety in her that even drugs couldn't quench, and sometimes she became fixated on certain things. Today it was Eithne.

Pearl came up at that moment and threw her arms around Veronica. 'Veronica, you look lovely. So nice to see you again. Wasn't the dinner last night just fabulous?'

Marguerite blessed Pearl from the bottom of her heart. The dinner hadn't been fabulous because her mother had sat there, tense and anxious, drinking slowly even though Marguerite's father had tried to stop her. After a certain point she'd become what she'd described as 'the life and soul of the party', which everyone else thought was charming, but which Marguerite and Tony knew was very dangerous.

'Why didn't your brother come?' said Jim, sitting beside his wife-to-be, nuzzling into her long, dark hair.

'America's a long way away and who knows, if he leaves he mightn't get back in. You know the way things are getting with the immigration,' Marguerite had said.

It was funny how all the lies as a child meant she had an answer for everything.

Mam is a bit high-spirited; she gets sad sometimes; she likes being by herself.

All those lies to cover up. If only Mam could be a bit normal today.

Marguerite had had no bridesmaid. Pearl had helped her to put the flowers in her hair and Pearl's friends, Gloria and Annette, had assisted with crocheting a tiny little handbag and making a beautiful posy of ribbons and flowers for her wedding bouquet.

'You're like a queen,' Annette had said, and Marguerite had beamed. If only she'd had a mum like these women.

As Da walked her down the aisle, she told herself to stop looking at where her mother sat, to stop worrying, to focus instead on the new life in her belly and on Jim standing, tall and strong, at the top of the aisle. It was all going to be perfect. She'd got away from home. She hadn't had a single drink since she found out she was pregnant. She could keep away from alcohol for her baby, even if it was impossible to keep away from it for herself alone. She was fine. Everything was going to be fine.

In the small church hall, decorated to look festive and weddingy by Pearl and her friends, the DJ, Annette's son, played all the songs of the time. With her long hair flying as she twirled, Marguerite danced with Jim. The DJ was playing 'Dreams' by Fleetwood Mac. Dreams could come true, Marguerite thought, held in her husband's arms. She knew her mother had gone back to the B&B where her parents were staying, so there was no need to see her again. That part of the wedding was over. That part of her life was over. It could only get better.

Cassie was such a sweet child. Even as a baby she was just happy and sunny. There were no problems with colic and not too many sleepless nights. She slept through the night once she was past two months old, which was incredible, according to the women in the mother and baby group in the church hall. Pearl had urged her to go.

'It would be good for you to get out of the house,' Pearl had said kindly. 'You might get bored sitting here with just your mother-in-law looking at you.'

They still hadn't got a place of their own. It would take time, Jim said. Time before they found the perfect spot.

Marguerite was impatient to have her own home. For all that she loved Pearl, it was difficult living with her because she could feel Pearl's eyes on her all the time. Not judging exactly, just watching with a sort of pity, and Marguerite hated that.

She hated that she'd begun drinking again. She hadn't meant to; it had just happened. A sherry one day when she was no longer breastfeeding, and suddenly the hunger for alcohol was upon her again. She'd managed to escape the next day on the pretence of going for a walk on her own, leaving the baby with Pearl, while she bought some cheap gin.

Oh, the relief when she drank it, like finding that safe haven again. She could handle this, she thought, watching Cassie asleep in her baby basket. It was just a little drink to tide her over.

But one little drink quickly became more. Marguerite began to worry that Pearl would notice. She needed it, she felt. Taking care of a baby was hard work. Sometimes at night, when she couldn't sleep and all the shameful memories were rolling around in her head of the crazy life she'd had before she met Jim, a drink or two helped calm her.

Living with her mother-in-law meant it was

difficult getting rid of the bottles, but Marguerite managed it. She smuggled them out in Cassie's pram, and if sometimes Pearl looked up when she heard a rattle, she never said anything.

Marguerite would have hated Pearl to find out. She desperately wanted Pearl and Bernie to approve of her. To think she was a good mother. And she *was* a good mother. She did everything for Cassie. She loved her and adored her.

The mother and baby group didn't really work out. Marguerite didn't fit in. It was strange hanging around with a group of women who seemed to have come from ordinary, happy families. All smiling and talking about mothers coming round to help and sisters babysitting.

'And what about you, Marguerite?' they'd say.

'Well, I've got Pearl and Bernie,' she'd say, 'and they're so good to me.'

'But your own family?'

'They live down the country. They can't get up: a farm, you know.'

'Oh,' everyone said, as if that explained everything.

Life went on. She and Jim got their own home. Marguerite adored her daughter and tried so hard not to drink. She could go months without touching a drop, but then she'd give in and buy a bottle of gin, sink into its depths and forget who she was all over again. There would be rows with Jim, screaming, recriminations, and then her promises never to do it again.

And then she fell pregnant again.

'Please, darling,' Jim said, holding her quivering body when she told him the news. 'Let's try again. Let's make this work.'

'I won't hurt her, you know I won't,' vowed Marguerite.

Coco was nearly a year old and Marguerite hadn't had a single drink since she'd become pregnant. Everything in life was perfect: Cassie, baby Coco, her husband, everything. It had been so long since she'd had a drink, Marguerite had told herself she didn't have a problem: that was in the past, she was better now. And then Niamh had phoned.

Niamh, who'd been her closest friend in Dublin when they'd shared a flat on Capel Street, when Marguerite worked in a café. Niamh now worked in a club in town where the glamorous society people went to let their hair down.

'Come on out,' Niamh begged. 'It's boring without you, Marguerite. We need a bit of fun.'

Tentatively, Marguerite went to Jim.

'I don't have to go,' she said. 'I won't stay out long. I'll be back to give Coco her last bottle.'

She and her husband gazed into each other's eyes. She was telling the truth and he believed her.

She dressed up and brought her make-up in her handbag so she could apply it on the bus. Jim had never been one for make-up, even though he'd fallen for her when she'd been wearing plenty of it. But it was as if now that she was a mother, she was to be somehow different.

They went to one of the clubs where some of Niamh's friends worked.

'We'll get in here for nothing,' she'd said, bringing them down dodgy steps into a place that was only just opening up. 'We could eat here,' she said thoughtfully, then she and Marguerite had looked at each other and laughed.

'You're right,' agreed Niamh. 'Why waste our money on food. The wine is brutal here but we'll get it very cheap: I know the barman.'

'I should be careful,' said Marguerite. She had so much to lose, after all. She was different now. Mother to two beautiful girls. She would not risk it all on too much alcohol. She would control what she drank.

And then had come that ripple of cool on her tongue, sliding inside her, the first taste of wine. All rational thought went out the window.

The wine came, and then gin.

Gin was the thing that brought Marguerite to that special place where she stopped caring, where the fear wasn't there anymore. She looked hazily at the bar and the bottles ranged up behind the barman, and wondered what she'd have next. She wanted to be totally numb.

'Come on up and dance,' said Niamh as night turned to the wee small hours of the morning.

'No, I have to go home now, it's late, the baby and everything,' mumbled Marguerite, who was very drunk. She hadn't meant to have that much.

How had this happened? She felt so dizzy, and where was her handbag?

'You're allowed one night out. You're not glued to that house,' said Niamh, and pulled her up to dance, so they danced. Danced and partied and drank with all sorts of men, and somehow Marguerite had ended up in a hotel room, waking up at six in the morning with no clothes on and a man she didn't recognise naked and snoring beside her.

The room looked like it had been trashed. There were drink bottles everywhere, Niamh lay on a couch half in and half out of her clothes, her skin a mottled colour in the grey dawn.

Marguerite felt a shudder go through her, a shudder of shame and self-loathing. What had happened here? Oh God, Jim would be so worried. She had ruined everything. She moved, but the pain in her head was monstrous.

She ran to the bathroom and threw up violently. It wasn't the first time she'd thrown up in there, she realised, as she looked at the vomit all around the loo. Somehow she gathered herself together, pulled on her clothes and went out into the world, looking ridiculous in her night-time black tights and dress with a flimsy little cardigan and the make-up sliding down her eyes.

She had only just stopped Jim throwing her out.

She'd stayed at Niamh's, she told him. The wine had made her sick. It was only that.

Somehow he believed her, but the fear made her

go back to the off-licence and buy gin the way she used to. The gin would help her cope with the fear of Jim finding out about that dreadful night where she'd blacked out with alcohol.

No longer living with Pearl, she had nobody to hide her drinking from during the day. She'd worked her way through that bottle, and then another. And then came that last day, that terrible day when she'd crashed the car with both her beloved children in it.

She'd picked Cassie up from school and little Coco was firmly in her carrycot, seat belt tightly around it. It was sheer fluke that Cassie was in the back of the car with her sister. If she'd been in the front, she could easily have been flung out through the windscreen on to the street. Marguerite was white with shock thinking of Cassie's tiny body lying bloodless on the street, instead of sitting in the back seat, crying with fear and shock.

The man in the other car was angry because it was all Marguerite's fault. He was angrier when he got closer to her and could smell the booze on her breath.

'I'm calling the guards,' he'd roared, so Marguerite clambered back into the car and drove off.

They were waiting for her when she got home: Pearl and Jim. Some neighbour had seen it all, seen Marguerite careening down the hill near Mill House Road, had waited for the accident.

'She knew you were drunk, knew you were going to crash, and she couldn't wait to tell us,' Jim had hissed. 'You had the kids in the car, Marguerite. What were you thinking?'

It was like an inquisition, then; her lovely, gentle Jim suddenly the grand inquisitor. She thought she'd concealed it from him these past months. But they had found the bottles and half-bottles of gin she thought she'd hidden cleverly around the house, and worse, Pearl took Coco from Marguerite's arms and wouldn't let her hold her.

'You're not able to take care of these babies,' said Pearl with an anxiety Marguerite had never heard before. 'You have to get help now. There are places you can go, Marguerite. We can help you.'

'I'm not helping her,' shouted Jim. 'She's not coming near my kids any more. She's a drunk, and who knows what else.'

He didn't sound like the Jim she knew: he sounded possessed with rage and disgust. It was all her fault, Marguerite thought, distraught. All hers. The shame rose up like bile in her throat and she knew she could never, ever make up for this.

'Mama!' said Coco, and they all turned to look at her, her little face pale with all the shouting.

Pearl shot a look at both Jim and Marguerite. 'It's all fine, baba,' she said. 'Let's get you your snack.' In a low voice, she whispered to the other adults: 'We'll deal with this tomorrow.'

Marguerite had hugged her small daughter, feeling as if she might break. They'd take her children off her now for sure. And at that moment, she craved a long, cool drink, pure alcohol to take away the fear.

The evening passed in a blur, and though she managed to be up for the children in the morning, she knew Jim was angry at her because he hadn't come into her bed.

It was when Cassie was at school and Coco was down for a nap that Jim struck.

'You've got to get out now, you crazy bitch,' he said, his face harsh with loathing.

'Jim,' reproved Pearl.

'You want her to kill the kids?' Jim hissed.

'No, but we can't treat her like this . . . Marguerite, you need help—'

'Help as far away from us as possible,' Jim said. 'I'll pack your bag, get out now. And don't come back, we don't need you.'

'*No!*' sobbed Marguerite, trying to rush upstairs to grab Coco for a hug, but Jim held her back. 'You touch them and I'll call the police and tell them about yesterday. Your blood alcohol level must have been off the scale. You'll rot in jail and will never see your daughters.'

'Oh, Marguerite, you have to get help,' Pearl said, distraught herself at this confrontation.

'Stay out of this, Mother,' Jim said. 'I won't have this drunk around my kids.'

He shoved Marguerite to the door and left her outside, the door shut.

A few minutes later, he opened it with a suitcase for her.

'Take that. Get sober, don't, whatever. I don't care. The moment you nearly killed my children, you ceased to exist for me.'

Only the sips of gin she'd taken that morning gave her any warmth and allowed her to move down the pathway, out into Delaney Gardens and away.

CHAPTER 19

DUBLIN

Cassie had never known that a house could feel so lonely, even though there were still three human beings in it; four living creatures, if you counted Fluffikins, which she couldn't because Fluffikins was currently hiding on top of the wardrobe, as he did most of the time now, and refused to come down at all.

Clearly he'd loved Shay after all and was suffering from withdrawal symptoms.

We all are, thought Cassie miserably.

Without Shay, the house felt so incredibly strange. The balance had shifted. They weren't a family anymore; they were something fractured and broken.

When she was feeling angry and self-righteous, she told herself things like: *It's his fault. He chose his mother over me, so what did he expect? Me to welcome him with open arms and say: 'Yes, darling, of course we can move house to accommodate your mother. Pick your mother over me any time. I don't mind.'*

When she was feeling sad, which was far more often, she thought of what a huge mistake she'd made. This throwing Shay out had brought nothing but pain.

She must have been mad, she thought, which was exactly what Coco had said to her.

'You did what?' Coco had said the next day when Cassie had phoned her with the news. 'You just threw Shay out? Cassie, haven't we gone through enough mad behaviour in our lives without adding to it!'

'I know,' Cassie said tearfully.

'Antoinette can't help herself,' went on Coco. 'She's one of those women who needs a man around, and since there's nothing there for her romantically, she wanted Shay back. You should have handled her much more diplomatically and organised some family things so she saw you all as a family unit. Letting Shay go off to hers all the time made her think you didn't want him. Shay was only trying to do the right thing . . .'

'When did you get so wise, oh Great One?' demanded Cassie bitterly.

'Since I've had to cope with Jo's stroke, taking care of Fiona, sorting out Jo's benefits for her rehab, investigating grants for fixing up her place, and firing staff members,' said Coco. 'What does Pearl say?'

'That's the totally weird thing,' Cassie said. 'I rang her before I rang you and she kept saying she was so sorry, like it's all her fault.'

'Odd,' remarked Coco. 'Have you spoken to Shay today?'

'No,' said Cassie. 'It's up to him to talk to me first.'

'What, are we in school now?'

'You are no help,' said Cassie.

'On the contrary, I want you to see sense, Cass. You love Shay and he loves you. Don't let Antoinette's crisis get in the middle of that.'

Cassie and Shay's bed, which she always thought was too small before because there wasn't enough room for either of them to sprawl out and they always ended up spooned next to each other at night, had actually turned out to be too big to sleep in on her own.

Not that she slept. When she got into bed, Shay's pillows seemed to look at her reproachfully, if pillows could look. Everything in the room seemed to be reproaching her for her behaviour, from the book Shay had been reading, left spine cracked open on his bedside table, to his aftershave in the bathroom. She'd remembered to fling his toothbrush into the carry-on bag but not his aftershave, and now she couldn't touch it to shove it into a drawer, out of sight.

Weirdly, she thought she could smell it, which was ludicrous because she hadn't sprayed it anywhere, and yet that scent, so evocative of her husband, seemed to linger in the air.

Like her mother's old scent had been evocative and held sway over her.

Her blasted mother, Cassie thought bitterly. It

all came back to that, to her leaving all those years ago.

Cassie wondered if she was going entirely mad. Was it genetic? Who knew? She had no mother to compare herself with. Maybe that *was* what had happened with her mother and her dad, and Pearl just hadn't wanted to explain when Cassie and Coco had been old enough to understand.

How could you say to a seven-year-old child: 'Your mum has gone crazy and she's leaving because it's safer that way'?

Cassie wondered what it would be like to go mad, to feel yourself lose your grip on reality, because that's what she felt like so much of the time now. She tried really hard at home to be normal, but what was normal anyway?

The girls were devastated. Lily was quiet and tearful, casting sad glances at her mother, glances that said she blamed Cassie for everything. Not that she said as much. She barely said anything. *Yes, no, thank you.* She wasn't eating much either, her little Lily who used to be able to consume the whole fridge and then come back and ask was there any Chunky Monkey ice cream in the freezer.

Cassie was trying to watch Lily carefully to see if she was getting thinner, but winter was coming and Lily was responding to the increasing cold by wrapping herself in big jumpers. She had one of her father's that she wore non-stop: a big, cream, soft Aran thing that Pearl had knitted for him once and which Shay had only worn when it was incredibly cold because it was so warm. It was far too big for slender Lily.

'Why are you wearing that, darling?' Cassie had asked once, and then wished she could take back the question because how stupid was that?

'It's Dad's. I like wearing things of Dad's,' said Lily, and she'd run from the room, her sobs audible as she ran up the stairs.

Beth had taken an entirely different approach: she was stroppy and angry.

'I don't know what's going on but I know you could have sorted it out like normal people. That's what you're always telling me, isn't it? To be a grown-up, to be responsible, and to think before you do anything. Well, did you think before you threw Dad out? Not bloody likely. You didn't think at all.'

'Don't curse,' said Cassie, hypocritically because she cursed the whole time in her head now; cursed Shay and Antoinette and her own bloody-mindedness.

'I'll curse if I want to. If you can act stupidly then so can I. Fuck, fuck, fuck,' said Beth, glaring at her mother, daring her to reprimand her.

'I said please don't curse.'

Once Cassie would have jumped on her elder daughter for using such language, but she'd long ago lost the high moral ground. Then she noticed Beth was wearing a leather jacket that Cassie had never seen before, and she was carrying her little rucksack, the cool Superdry one she used when she went out.

'Where are you going?' Cassie asked shrilly. 'It's eight o'clock at night. You should be finishing your homework and having a shower.'

'I'm going out,' said Beth, and her voice was antagonistic.

'What do you mean "out"?' demanded her mother.

'*Out* out,' said Beth. 'If you can do mad things, then so can I. I'm going out, OK? I might go and see my father, wherever he is, or I might go out and drink too much and take drugs and do something crazy.'

'Beth Reynolds, you will do no such thing,' said her mother grimly.

'Oh yeah, watch me,' hissed Beth, and she was gone, another door slammed.

Cassie ran after her but Beth had been faster. Cassie ran down the path and looked each way up the street but there was no sign of her daughter. Where had she gone? Into the lane where Cassie and Shay told Beth never to walk at night? She was only fifteen, after all.

Oh Lord, who knew what she was going to do now. *Think, Cassie, think.*

She ran inside, fumbled for her phone and rang Beth's mobile. It went straight to voicemail, with a cheery Beth from what seemed like a long time ago happily saying: 'Leave a message!' *Think,* where else would she go?

She dialled Mel, Beth's closest friend, and that

too went straight to voicemail. Beth liked to joke that Mel was on her phone so much that she hardly ever answered an actual call, she just had to return them.

Cassie left a message. 'Mel, please ring me back, it's Cassie. I'm worried about Beth. She's left the house and she won't tell me where she's going. Please ring me if she gets in, OK? It's a school night. Just . . . please, thank you.' She hung up.

Next she rang Mel's mother, who answered the phone on the third ring. In the background was the sound of television and the rattling of dishes being loaded into the dishwasher.

'Deirdre, it's Cassie. I'm just wondering, could you tell me if Beth turns up there?' said Cassie, knowing how pathetic she sounded. 'We had a row and she ran out.' There was no time for false pride here.

'Hi Cassie,' said Deirdre. 'I know things are tough round your place at the moment. I'll ask Mel. Hold on.'

Cassie waited on the phone, feeling the pain and anxiety of a woman forced to wait on the phone for a perfect mother to check if an imperfect woman's daughter was there.

Finally Deirdre returned. 'Mel says Beth's on her way over. I'll get Ivan and Mel to go and meet her at the bottom of the road. Don't worry, as soon as she comes in I'll call you. If I can do anything . . .?' Deirdre's voice trailed off and Cassie felt the tears spring to her eyes.

'There's nothing anyone can do, but thank you.

As long as you tell me when she comes in so I know she's OK.'

'If she wants to sleep over tonight will that be all right?' said Deirdre.

'Sleepover on a school night?' said Cassie.

'They've been planning it and I told both of them that they needed to run it by you. I figured with all the hassle you were having at the moment you'd be fine with it. I'm sorry, I should have thought to ring you. I . . . I just didn't want to bother you in case you thought I was phoning looking for gossip.'

'I wouldn't think that of you,' Cassie said honestly, although she knew plenty of other women at the girls' school would be turning the handle of the gossip mill with the juicy news about the Reynolds' break-up. Deirdre wasn't one of them. 'That's fine, she can stay over. Thank you, Deirdre.'

Ten minutes later, her phone rang and Cassie leapt to it.

'She's here. She looks a bit miserable but I've put some pizza on and we've got the blow-up bed in Mel's room. They'll be fine. I'll keep an eye on them. There'll be no sneaking out, don't worry. I run a tight ship here,' Deirdre said with a hint of pride in her voice.

'Thank you, thank you so much,' said Cassie gratefully before she hung up.

She used to run a tight ship herself, but not anymore. Now she ran a sinking ship.

'Mum?'

Cassie looked up.

Lily stood in her mother's bedroom door carrying her pillow and a teddy she normally slept with in bed, but which rarely came out from under her bedclothes anymore. With her sad eyes, her hair fluffed up around her face and her downturned lips, she looked about ten instead of the self-confident teen she seemed to be most of the time now.

'Can I sleep with you?'

Coco and Fiona had got into a routine, the sort of routine that Coco remembered her sister talking about. She'd never really experienced it before. Even on those times when she'd babysat Lily and Beth when Shay and Cassie had gone away for a weekend, there'd been an air of fun about the whole thing, a sense of unreality about getting everyone up for school, putting out cereal and driving them to school. It had been exciting, play-acting. But there was nothing of the play-acting about her relationship with Fiona now, and yet it was still fun. Somehow Fiona had fitted perfectly into Coco's apartment, despite her vast selection of cuddly toys, dolls, books and comic books, shoes, and clothes

The morning routine was simple: Coco would wake early and would get up, make herself coffee and put on the radio to the bright sparkly music channel that Fiona liked. There was no more news and doom and gloom on the radio in the mornings. Fiona had enough doom and gloom in her life, and Coco was now operating to an entirely different set of standards. She'd go in and wake her goddaughter, normally by climbing into bed with her and tickling her and having Fiona moan, 'No, stop, stop,' until finally she woke up and could really get into tickling back, trying to wriggle down the bed so she could get to Coco's feet, which were her tickliest bit ever.

'OK, pax, pax,' Coco would shriek, and they'd hug and get up, laughing.

Fiona was a morning person. Full of energy and conversations and questions.

'If you added up all the people in the world and put them in Ireland, would they fit?' she might ask. 'Or do dogs go to heaven when they die? Do rabbits go? Is there a different heaven for rabbits and dogs? Because dogs and rabbits don't like each other and would the dogs chase the rabbits?'

In the beginning, Coco had had no idea how to answer these questions.

'I don't really know,' she'd say to Fiona, floundering. 'I mean, I've never really thought about that.' But now she made a stab at the questions. 'All the people in the world on the island of Ireland – so that's, let's see, seven billion. Ah no,' she said, 'I don't see that working at all; we'd all be terribly squashed. You'd have to have people getting piggybacks on top of other people, and what about all the babies? They'd have to be held up really high so they weren't squished. And think of the lakes and rivers: people might get wet feet. No, that's not going to work at all. Why?'

Fiona would look at her with those deep, little girl eyes and say: 'Dunno, just wondering.'

The dog and the rabbit heaven one was a serious one because of the conversation about getting a dog. A conversation that Fiona had certainly not forgotten. Coco knew that once you made a promise to a child, you did not break it, so they were investigating pug puppies belonging to a friend of Pearl's one evening that week.

'I don't know what colour I'd like,' said Fiona, 'but I s'pose it wouldn't matter what colour we get because we'll love it anyway. Mum's talked about when you and Cassie were small and you had black pugs, and I thought they sounded so cute. I've seen pictures of black pugs but I'd be OK if it wasn't a black pug because Daisy's a lovely silvery, pearly colour and I love her, so it doesn't really matter because it's about how much you love them, isn't it?'

'Yes,' said Coco, gravely trying to clear up the table because, despite her best efforts, the chocolate cereal would somehow have been spilled everywhere.

It was a full-time job this cleaning up after a child and trying to make sure said child got enough vitamins and minerals in her food. She wondered if she should go into the chemist and get some sort of a child vitamin to be sure? Chocolate cereal was all well and good but was it the best thing? She wasn't sure. Plus Jo really had been telling the truth when she said that Fiona was not a good person at eating her vegetables.

Why didn't they make cereal full of green, healthy things and disguise them with chocolate? Now that was a food innovation if ever there was one.

Once breakfast was over, they both dressed, teeth were brushed and checked – Fiona was a great one for saying, 'Of course I've brushed my teeth, Coco,' when in fact she'd done nothing of the sort – and then out of the house, handbag and schoolbag in hands, ready to face the day.

'It's amazing what you've done with her,' said Ms Ryan, the principal of the school where Fiona went. 'Was it the counselling, do you think?' she said. 'They do wonderful things, counsellors. I've seen children who are just devastated and after a few sessions they come out and they're miraculously able to be with us again. Children bury their feelings so deeply, don't they?'

'She hasn't actually had any counselling at all,' said Coco apologetically. 'I had been planning it but somehow we seemed to get by without it, and her mother is improving a lot, which has helped hugely. Fiona and I are having a lot of fun in the middle of all this pain. I don't know, I think love has fixed her. Does that sound awfully silly?'

The principal smiled. 'Love is a fabulous thing to have,' she said. 'Fiona is lucky to have you, and Jo is certainly lucky to have such a real friend. I've been in to see her and she seems in quite good form.'

'You should have seen her ten days ago,' said Coco, and immediately regretted it. 'Of course, she's very strong and courageous, you know. It's been very difficult for her,' she backtracked.

'It's OK, Coco, you're not letting her down, don't worry,' said the principal kindly. 'When serious illness strikes, it hits us all in different ways, but the Jo I saw was full of energy and determined to get back to normal. She's made a remarkable recovery. She's certainly one of the lucky ones.'

'That she is,' said Coco fervently. 'I'm on my way into my shop now and then, after a couple of hours, I'll be going into the hospital. Jo's going to be getting out and going into a nursing home for a week tomorrow, so after that she should be coming home.'

Coco paused. Where home was going to be exactly was the knotty question and she still had to work that one out. But she and Jo would work it out together; they were now working as a team.

The shop was doing marvellously. Phoebe had it running like clockwork. She'd drafted in Alice, who used to work in her father's pet shop up the road, to do extra hours.

Alice was overjoyed to wear pretty clothes and get actual money for work.

'Dad does his best but he can't really employ us

all,' she said, 'and I have been bitten by too many hamsters for my own good.'

Phoebe loved the way Coco merchandised the clothes and used the internet to sell her goods far and wide, and she'd quickly taken over updating the Facebook page and keeping in touch with people who were on the lookout for something special.

Phoebe had added a new feature: getting beautiful pieces and tweaking them with her seamstress skills to make them more modern and up to date. 'You don't mind?' she'd said when she'd suggested this to Coco. 'It's just an idea I had after I tweaked a beautiful jacket I bought here from Adriana.'

'Oh, don't mention Adriana,' said Coco, who still felt terribly guilty. 'I worry about her, you know.'

'Oh no, you mustn't worry about her,' said Phoebe sweetly. 'Adriana will get on wonderfully well wherever she is. She's an absolute survivor, couldn't you tell? She's working in a luxury boutique in town. I met her on my way to college one day.'

'Is she?' said Coco, in shock.

'Yes,' said Phoebe, 'so worry not. She's perfectly happy. It's more of a full-time job and she has to turn up on time or she'll get fired. It was good for her you letting her go. You did the right thing. Sometimes we have to be firm.'

'Oh, thank you,' said Coco, dizzy with relief at

the thought that Adriana wasn't out on the streets. 'I'm no good at being firm.'

'Yes, you are. Now, as I was saying . . . Because of that jacket I tweaked with darts to modernise it, I suddenly thought there were a few other pieces we had that I could tweak, so I've put them up online and it's brought in a whole new community: the sewers who are interested in new projects and love the idea of being able to work on vintage clothes.'

'That's wonderful,' said Coco, thrilled, 'I knew it was a good idea to hire you.'

Phoebe laughed. 'I knew it was a good idea to come in here,' she countered.

'It's all down to Pearl.'

Thanks to Pearl, Phoebe was now living in a pretty turquoise and white bedroom overlooking the square in Gloria's house, and even though she hadn't got a penny of her deposit back from a pea-green Rita Costello, Phoebe and Gloria were getting on like a house on fire. Phoebe, who was a good cook, was making sure that Gloria ate properly, while Gloria made sure Phoebe had a wonderfully warm welcome home each night.

The cloud in Phoebe's life was worrying about her beloved mother, and even though she was now able to send money home, the downside of her new job meant she hadn't actually been able to go home since the trip where she'd realised how exhausted her mother was.

She'd told Coco a little bit about it, because

she'd already told Ian and Gloria so much that she was terrified of boring them.

'I love my mother so much and I know the farm means a lot to her, but here, when I'm not up there in the hills, I can see it's all too much for her.'

'You're not boring me, you daft cow,' Ian had said crossly. 'You're my friend. Let me put my brain in gear, all right?'

Gloria had wondered how easy it would be to sell a farm in the hills, and Phoebe had explained that while many farmers would like a bit of extra land, part of the importance of the farm was the fact that the family could build houses on it for themselves if they ever had enough money.

'That's another thing that makes the land important for Mum,' Phoebe explained. 'The planning laws mean if the land is in your family, you can build on it, but not if you just buy it, so it's not valuable as development land.'

'Ah, right,' said Gloria. 'Goodness, it all sounds like an awful lot of work for your poor mother.'

Being Coco, she never forgot another person's problems, and checked in with Phoebe about how things were for Kate McLoughlin, Ethan and Mary-Kate.

'Fine,' fibbed Phoebe, seeing how stressed her boss was under all the relief about the shop. 'Myself and Alice will keep the home fires burning here.'

★　★　★

When Coco finally headed off from the shop, she planned to go straight into the hospital to see Jo. But instead she drove around to Delaney Gardens, hoping that Pearl was in. She parked the car, ran up to the front door and knocked, but there was no reply. Worrying slightly because, after all, Pearl wasn't a young lady anymore, she took out her key and let herself in, greeted by delighted barks from Daisy, who did her impersonation of an abandoned dog.

'We might have a puppy friend for you to play with soon, Daisy,' said Coco, getting down on the floor to snuggle with the pug.

Daisy looked thoroughly thrilled at this, but then Daisy looked thrilled at everything: food, cuddles, butterflies, rain, sun, whatever. She was easily pleased. There was no sign, however, of her mistress, so Coco left a note to say she'd dropped in and perhaps might phone her grandmother later. She signed the note with a flourish of kisses and she left thinking of all the things she really wanted to write:

I need to talk to you, Grammy. I'm so worried about Cassie. It's like she's heading for a total breakdown and I don't know what to do. I'm so tied up with trying to take care of Fiona that I can't really be properly there for Cassie, but I'm worried about her and I'm worried about Lily and Beth. We need to figure out what to do. It's like she fell apart that night

when I came home from the hospital and we
started talking about Mum. I don't know how
to help her anymore.

If you want to know me, come live with me went
the proverb, and Shay could see the sense in that.
Since moving in, reluctantly, with his mother
after Cassie had turfed him out on to the street,
he'd begun to find that there was a big difference
between dropping in now and then and being the
golden boy who fixed light bulbs, plugs and
washing machines, and actually *living* with
Antoinette after a gap of some twenty years.

That first night, it had been a relief to drive up
to his mother's house and feel her hug him. He'd
felt the comfort of being told it was all right, not
to worry, and he hadn't done a thing wrong, which
was precisely what he wanted to hear after having
Cassie shrieking at him.

'Cassie's being totally unreasonable and I don't
understand it at all,' Antoinette had said, going
around the kitchen and getting out the good china
dishes.

'You poor boy. I suppose you haven't had a
thing to eat either? I'll make you a good, decent
dinner, none of that frozen stuff or ready meals
from the supermarket,' she said dismissively, as if
ready meals from the supermarket were all that
was wrong with the world.

'Thanks, Mum,' said Shay, and although he

knew that Cassie didn't feed their family from the frozen aisle, he didn't say so.

He'd gone into the living room, where he'd spent so many years growing up as a kid, and sat down in the big comfortable armchair that used to be his father's.

'Now, pet, here are the TV zappers,' said his mother cosily. 'I'm afraid I don't have the sports channels, but I could get them for you if you want. I know you like your bit of football; your father was the same.'

Shay found himself ensconced in an armchair with the fire on, something about renovating cars on the TV, and a gin and tonic on a small table beside him. His mother had even conjured up nuts in a little bowl as an appetiser.

'Nuts, Mum!' he roared out to the kitchen. 'Am I in the right house?' he joked. 'We never had nuts when I was growing up, did we?'

'Oh, on the odd special occasion when we had people over,' his mother said skittishly, 'but you deserve a treat, pet, while you're waiting for your dinner.'

An hour later, he had a tray on his lap, he was in control of the television remote – something that never happened in his house – and he had now a glass of wine in place of the gin and tonic. It was like being in a hotel.

'Isn't this lovely?' said his mother, picking at a salad as she sat on the couch.

'Mum, why aren't you eating this?' he said, gesturing at the stew she'd conjured up out of nowhere.

'Oh pet.' His mother smiled. 'You know I have to watch my figure, darling.'

Shay looked at her and realised that this was the moment where he was supposed to say: 'Oh no, Mum, you don't, you look fabulous.' So he did, and Antoinette beamed, patted her flat stomach and smoothed her skirt over her still slim hips.

'I always say you've got to look after yourself and dress like a lady.'

She touched the pearls that her husband had bought for their twenty-fifth wedding anniversary. They weren't real pearls, of course. There hadn't been money for real pearls in their household any more than there'd been much in the line of gin and tonics in front of the television, but somewhere along the way his mother had gentrified the Reynolds family, and Shay – now that he was exposed to the full blast of it – wasn't sure he liked it. When his father used to sit in this seat and watch the footie, he might have a pint of beer, just the one, and roar at the TV, telling the ref he was blind and muttering about goalies with butter fingers.

'Now, tell me exactly what did she say?'

His mother wanted to do a complete post-mortem on his throwing out and Shay did not want to talk about it at all. It felt like being disloyal to Cassie to even discuss this marital row. Keeping secrets from her with his mother was what had got them into trouble in the first place, and the more he thought about it, the more he realised that selling up and moving in together *had* been a pretty big secret. The pangs of remorse hit him hard.

'Mum, I don't want to talk about it, can we give it a rest?' Shay said.

'Of course, pet,' said his mother, looking slightly peeved. 'I only wanted to help you get it off your chest. I think Cassie is being completely ridiculous that she doesn't realise how important family is to you. I mean, just because she doesn't have a mother . . .'

'Mum, I just want to watch the TV and forget about it,' begged Shay.

'Fine.'

His mother's expression was one Shay hadn't seen for quite a while, but he recognised it from his childhood, much more so than the little bowl of nuts or the gin and tonics. It was her *I'm annoyed but I'm pretending not to be annoyed* face.

She used to do that a lot, and Shay could remember himself and his father, Arthur, staring at each other, realising that when Antoinette's face bore that particular expression, it was better to get out of the house.

Cassie never played that sort of game, Shay thought suddenly. It was one of things he loved about his wife. There were no sides to Cassie. She was straightforward. If she was annoyed, she told you. She didn't sulk or play at being a martyr. What you saw was what you got, with one exception, and that was the tricky issue surrounding her, Coco and their mother. That was the part of Cassie that nobody got to see because she never talked about it, brushed off conversations if they so much as veered in that direction.

Fear of abandonment, Shay had long since diagnosed it as, and with another pang, he realised that his secret with his mother would be the ideal way to make his wife think she was being abandoned all over again.

So she'd abandoned him first.

He picked up his mobile phone and turned it back on. There were several messages from Lily and Beth, and he felt a surge of guilt. He put the tray down on the floor and said, 'Mum, I'm just going out to make a few calls.'

His mother looked even more piqued. 'If you don't want to finish your dinner . . .' she said in the tones of one who'd spent hours slaving in a Michelin-starred kitchen to produce the stew.

'It's all right, Mum, I'll eat it in a minute.'

He got Beth first.

'Dad,' she said, and he could tell from the thickness of her voice that she'd been crying. 'Dad, what happened? I didn't mean to start it all. I only told Mum that Granny had left a message on the answering machine, and I was so upset because I thought you were going to get a divorce and then

I heard that. I phoned Mum but . . . I'm sorry, it's all my fault.' She burst into tears.

Blast his mother for leaving that message, Shay thought with irritation.

'Beth, we're not getting a divorce. It's my fault. I talked to Granny about something, it was just an idea, and I never discussed it with your mum, so of course she's annoyed with me. She's every right to be annoyed with me. Don't worry. We'll sort this out in the next couple of days. I'll make everything OK, I promise. Mum is just angry with me. Now, is Lily with you?'

'Yes, she's in my bed,' said Beth, snuffling. 'You know she's not supposed to get into my bed with her stinky feet,' she added, and Shay grinned at this sound of normality returning to his daughter's voice.

'Daddy,' said Lily tearfully, 'why did you leave tonight? When are you coming home?'

'Soon,' he said. 'It's going to be fine, Lily. I love you both and I love your mum. Please be good to her. She's just upset right now, but we're going to sort all of this out, right? Now ring me and text me any time. I'll have my phone on morning, noon and night.'

'You say we're not supposed to have our phones on at night,' Lily pointed out.

'You can keep them on now,' Shay said, his heart bleeding for the sorrow he heard in his younger daughter's voice. 'I love you. I'll be home soon, sweetie.'

He hung up and wondered if he should ring Cassie. But no, it was probably better to let her cool off. He needed to make this better. He sent a text instead.

Sorry, Cassie. It was all a terrible mistake.
I love you.

From the sitting room, a plaintive voice called: 'Shay, your dinner's getting cold.'
'Coming,' he said resignedly.

CHAPTER 20

Coco looked at the tiny apricot-coloured pug puppy and decided that puppies in general, and pug puppies in particular, were God's way of reminding people that He existed. There could be no *reason* for such utter beauty and pure squishiness, as Fiona called it.

'Coco! They're so squishy and velvety,' she'd cried when she'd first seen the three puppies in the breeder's house.

Coco had been reminded of adorable Agnes from *Despicable Me* – which they watched on a loop – and how happy she'd been when she'd won her beloved unicorn at the funfair.

'Squishy, squishy, squishy,' Fiona cooed again as she got to her knees and tried to hug all the puppies at once.

The breeder, a very down-to-earth woman who lived in a house covered in dog fur, watched benignly.

'I love watching the kiddies with dogs,' she said. 'Our four grew up with dogs all around them, not just pugs. We actually started with Shih Tzus but then we took in a rescue pug.' Seeing Coco's horrified face, she said, 'I know, who could dump any animal, but this beautiful little creature was abandoned by the side of the road and we took her in and that was it. Once you've seen a pug, you're hooked. Blossom here has a lovely temperament,' she added, referring to the three puppies' mother. 'Very calm and gentle. My three grandchildren play with her all the time and she's never so much as nipped any of them. They really are beautiful family pets. Now the puppies, they *do* try and bite everything, and those teeth are very sharp, let me tell you. So try not to let your daughter—'

'Fiona!' interrupted Fiona, but she didn't add that she wasn't Coco's daughter, Coco noticed with a pang.

'Fiona,' agreed the woman, 'don't put your fingers in their mouths, because those teeth are like sharp needles and they'll reach a point when they really need to chew furniture and shoes when they're teething. They're just like babies.'

'Babies don't chew furniture,' Fiona pointed out.

And then she sighed, and somehow she was sitting cross-legged on the floor with just one pug puppy nestled in her arms. It was, inevitably, the smallest of the puppies, the apricot-coloured creature with eyes that seemed too big for the pup's face.

'She is an unusual colour, given her parentage, no doubt about it,' said the woman. 'Blossom's a pearl and the father's also a pearl, but somehow this darling has come out apricot. It's so long since we showed dogs – we only showed the Shih Tzus and not the pugs – and I have this notion in my head that apricots are rarer if you want to show her.'

'We don't want to show her,' said Coco quickly. 'She's a pet. We don't care about pedigrees or anything like that. We only talked to my grand-mother's pal at the kennel club because we wanted to make sure we weren't getting a dog from a puppy farm.'

She and the woman, Anna, both shuddered.

'Horrible places, using bitches like breeding machines and treating the puppies like money. This little one is able to go with you now but you have to be sure you want her, and of course they're purebred so they're not cheap. Her father is Sir Wilberforce Pumpkin the Third.'

Coco and Fiona both giggled at this.

'It is a bit of a serious moniker,' agreed Anna, 'but then Blossom's own kennel club name is quite long. She's Blossom Princess of the South Seas. Adorable, isn't it? We did think of showing her but it's a very intense industry and you really have to be into it.'

'I think I'm going to call her Banana,' announced Fiona in the car on the way home as she sat with a box on her lap and an overexcited puppy trying to clamber out of it.

'Banana, right,' said Coco thoughtfully. 'That's an interesting name. It's, well . . . She doesn't look much like a banana.'

'OK, Minion,' said Fiona.

The Minions from the *Despicable Me* films were her favourite creatures of all time. She had a Minion pencil case, a Minion rubber and her own cuddly Kevin Minion dressed in a French maid outfit.

They stopped at traffic lights and both gazed into the box again.

'I'm not really seeing her as a Minion either,' Coco pointed out.

'Onion,' suggested Fiona.

They giggled all the way home while Banana/Minion/Onion clambered and climbed and licked and nibbled and panted her way happily through the journey. She really was a happy puppy. She was twelve weeks old, because Anna said she believed in letting the pups stay with their mother as long as possible.

'Works better in the long run,' she'd said. 'They're more able to adjust to the separation, which I think is very important. Makes for a happier dog and that's what we want, after all.

At Coco's, the puppy instantly peed on the carpet in front of the couch and then ran around investigating, with Fiona beside her, explaining everything.

'This is the bathroom. You are too small to wee in the toilet,' she said gravely. 'This is my room where you can sleep. On my bed.'

Coco peeped in to see the pup being hoisted on to the bed, already full of teddies. Onion instantly began chewing a precious pink rabbit's ear. Coco waited to see how Fiona would react.

'Isn't she adorable?' she said, looking at her new pet with love.

'How about Miracle as a name?' said Coco.

'Ugh.' Fiona shot her most disgusted look at Coco. 'You are so bad at names, Coco. Miracle is really bad. I think she's Apricot, because she's that colour and she's small and roundy.'

'Apricot is fabulous,' said Coco reverently. But she thought: *She'll always be a miracle to me.*

Daisy and Apricot both made otherworldly squeaks of pleasure when they first set eyes on each other.

'I tried quite a few names, Grammy,' said Fiona earnestly, 'but I thought Apricot suited her because she looks like an apricot, except she's sort of a different shape.'

'She's beautiful,' gasped Pearl, snuggling the puppy in her arms and petting her.

On the ground, Daisy was jumping up and down insanely, trying to get near the puppy, and once she did, it was love at first sight. Daisy kept trying to lick the smaller animal's belly and eyes, and Apricot responded by climbing all over Daisy and nibbling her ears.

'It hurts when she nibbles,' said Fiona conversationally. 'She's eaten my fingers and several of my dolls, but it's OK because I love her. She's very beautiful.'

Pearl agreed. 'And I love that you're calling me Grammy now. Can I always be your grammy?'

'Oh yes,' said Fiona, and threw her arms eagerly around Pearl.

Over Fiona's head, Pearl and Coco exchanged glances. It was wonderful what a few small pounds of velvety dog could do for a child. The downside of Apricot was that she did want to chew everything and she had the most incredibly sharp teeth, like baby shark teeth. She was going around nibbling table legs, chair legs, anything she could get her tiny teeth on.

'I'm always leaving cupboards and wardrobe doors open,' Coco said, 'and trust me, I don't anymore, ever since she completely destroyed the heels on my Cuban heels. They were so beautiful: patent leather, a tiny button at the front. I'll never wear them again.'

'She didn't mean to, did you, Apricot?' said Fiona.

Pearl laughed. 'They never mean to, darling, they just can't control themselves. Why don't you take the two girls out into the garden and have a play, and myself and . . .' She stopped, astonished, because she'd been about to say: 'your mother'.

She corrected herself quickly: 'While Coco and I have a chat.'

Fiona cajoled the two dogs outside, and Coco sat down at the kitchen table in her grandmother's gloriously coloured kitchen and stared unseeing at the azure blue wall with its family photographs.

'Things are going so well with Jo,' she said. 'Her speech has returned nearly one hundred per cent. The consultant says it's incredible, although some people, if they have very mild strokes, can recover their speech like that. There are just a few words she stumbles over but she may never get that back. And she's nearly got total control over her left arm, it's just her leg that's the problem – it still drags and she's going to need rehab for a while. But she's happy, she's looking forward to the future, she's looking forward to getting out and having a normal life again. And yet . . . I'm just so worried.' She paused. 'About Cassie. I can't believe she and Shay haven't sorted it out yet. It's just so unlike her.'

'I know,' said Pearl as she sat down.

She didn't want to make the inevitable cup of tea to try and make everything better. She was fed up of making tea as a distraction from real life.

'What do you think pushed her over the edge?' Pearl asked anxiously. 'I've talked to her on the phone but I think she's avoiding me. She cries all the time when I phone, or else she's angry and says: "It's Shay's bloody fault". As for Antoinette . . . Oh Coco, I don't know what to do. I mean, Antoinette was behaving in a silly manner, but for Cassie to throw Shay out . . .'

Coco played with the sugar bowl on the table, twisting the silver spoon around and around in the grains of sugar.

'Should we go round together?' Pearl said. 'Do

you think that would help? Tell her it's crazy to break up her family for this?'

Coco thought about it. 'I honestly don't think that's going to work. It's like . . .' She felt that she was betraying Cassie by even saying this, but Pearl might know what to do. 'It's like she's become a little crazy ever since the night Jo had her stroke.'

'And you think that's it?' said Pearl, confused. 'Jo having a stroke?'

'No,' said Coco. 'That's not it precisely. It was the conversation we had afterwards when I came home from the hospital. We started talking about our mother and what it had been like. I was talking about how I didn't remember her, and Cassie said she did and how she'd always tried to protect me because she didn't want me to be scared, but that she was always afraid that people left . . .'

Pearl breathed in heavily. 'Oh, poor Cassie,' she said, her hands beginning to shake. 'That's . . . that's so sad. I had no idea. I thought it was just something with her and Shay and Antoinette. She tries so hard to make everything perfect . . .'

'I think she tries to make everything perfect because she still wants the perfect family,' Coco said. 'That doesn't mean that you and Dad didn't give us the perfect family, but there's some part of Cassie that wants the mum and the dad thing, and she's determined to give the girls that. Antoinette messed it up and made Cassie think that Shay could leave. That's what she's afraid of: that people leave. And I don't know what to say to her about that because, well . . .' Coco shrugged. 'Look at us. Our mother *did* leave so there's no happy answer to that.'

'Cooeee,' said a voice from around the side of the house.

'Oh heavens, no,' said Pearl, closing her eyes wearily. 'Not now.'

'Anybody home?' came the voice again.

There was a barrage of small puppy and larger puppy barking, and suddenly Edie was at the back door, resplendent in a beige suit with a little fur collar and a hat more suited to Ascot than a cool autumn day.

'I just popped round for a minute and when nobody answered the front door, I thought I'd come round the back. Hello Coco, you're looking very well, I must say. Red suits you, you should wear it more often, but I do think something modern, maybe.'

Edie's basilisk gaze took in Coco's bombshell dress: a glamorous creation that wasn't vintage but looked somehow exquisitely forties and showed off her bosom and tiny waist to great effect.

'Nothing short or ugly like young girls are wearing these days, but perhaps not anything as tight as that either, because I did love the style of the clothes from the forties and fifties, Coco, but they *are* gone, after all.'

Despite everything, Coco giggled. Edie had that effect on her.

Pearl got to her feet and laid a hand on Coco's.

'We'll talk about this later,' she said in a low voice. 'You and Fiona might as well get out of here because we won't be able to talk with Edie here.'

Once Fiona, Coco and Apricot had gone, Edie sat down at the table like a duchess and watched her older sister make tea. It had always been the same: Edie had somehow managed to behave as if she was the aristocracy while everyone else in the family was there to serve her.

Sometimes Pearl knew exactly why Harry had cheated. It was very hard to live up to her sister's exacting standards, and one always felt that one was somehow not matching up.

'Coco looked very well,' said Edie, rubbing a bit of fluff off her beige skirt.

Daisy did not sit at her feet. Daisy was a clever dog and knew that Edie had no time for small, velvety animals with big eyes. Instead, Daisy sat, slightly scared, behind her mistress's chair, her eyes bigger than ever.

'I still wish you'd tell her to wear ordinary clothes, Pearl,' Edie went on. 'She'll never catch and keep the right sort of man in anything that shows off her chest. Well, she'll catch a man, but . . .' Edie paused for effect. 'I suppose I did tell you that Red O'Neill was back in town recently? He's quite a catch, you know. Plenty of money, apparently. I'm not sure what it is he does but he's been in the social columns—'

'You mean in the gossip pages?' interrupted Pearl acidly.

'You say tomayto, I say tomaato,' said Edie. 'Anyway, he's back, he's still not married, and I don't see why she shouldn't make a play for him again.'

'Oh Edie,' said Pearl in exasperation. 'Coco split up with Red over four years ago, and she's hardly likely to *make a play for him* now, as you so indelicately put it. She's getting on with her life.'

'No she's not,' Edie insisted. 'She's looking after someone else's child and her life is on hold. I never hear of her going out on dates, and even if she did, who is going to look at a woman who wears outfits from the forties and fifties? For good-ness' sake, she's a beautiful girl. She should be wearing elegant, modern clothes. Maybe some-thing long and flowing with little court shoes and—'

'Edie,' interrupted Pearl sweetly, 'I hate to tell you, but those aren't modern clothes. Those are old-fashioned clothes, but they're simply the old-fashioned clothes that *you* approve of. Coco likes wearing old-fashioned clothes that *she* approves of: the sort of things she sells in her shop.'

Seeing as she was getting nowhere, Edie changed the subject. 'How's Cassie?' she said. 'I hear she threw the husband out. Girls today – they haven't a notion how to handle men.'

Pearl's lips tightened as she poured the tea. 'Shay and Cassie are having some problems. I wouldn't say she threw her husband out; I'd say that they are living separately while they work it out.' She closed her eyes momentarily and said a prayer that she wouldn't burn in hell for such a blatant lie.

Cassie had indeed thrown Shay out, and even though Pearl had been around twice and had phoned most days to talk to her about it, Cassie refused to talk about the idea of Shay coming home, beyond saying: 'There's no coming back from what he did, Pearl. No coming back at all.' All of which was followed by bursting into tears.

Pearl would then hang up and feel like bursting into tears herself.

'I hope you aren't spreading stories about our family business, Edie,' Pearl said, slightly cross now.

'Don't be ridiculous, of course I'm not. It's just people ask and I need to have some story made up to tell them. I could say he's gone off somewhere for work. His mother lives on the other side of the city, after all, so I'd get away with that. Stupid woman, always trying to look younger than she is. I don't know why people don't give in to growing old gracefully.'

'So says the woman who dyes her hair,' Pearl added with a hint of rancour.

Edie got to her feet in a stately manner. 'There's no pleasing you today, is there, madam? I don't know what upset you but I'm going to go,' she said. 'I know when I'm not wanted.' And she sailed out to the front door, closing it with an almighty slam.

Pearl reached down, picked Daisy up and put her on her lap. 'For a woman who says she's quite frail, Edie can certainly slam a door,' she told her dog. 'Come on – let's go to Peter's. I need to talk to someone who'll listen to me.'

'So what am I going to do?' said Pearl.

She was sitting in a deep, comfortable armchair in Peter's house and as she looked around, she wondered why they hadn't held the Thursday night poker club in other people's houses over the years. Somehow they'd all got into the habit of having it in hers, and yet Peter's house was so beautiful, the walls full of paintings done by his late wife, Loretta, who was a talented botanic artist, and everywhere else decorated with things from his travels over the years when he and Loretta used to go on cruises to exotic lands.

Loretta had loved Egyptian pictures on papyrus, and they vied for space with her exquisite water-colours and funny prints of New Orleans chefs in patisseries making beignets and other delicacies. Pearl had never spent a lot of time in Peter's house. It was as if there was some old-fashioned idea in her head that a lady never went to a gentleman's house, and there'd be less talk if a gentleman visited a lady.

What poppycock that had all been, she thought now. Who really cared if they saw her crossing the garden to visit Peter in his house?

Peter hadn't offered to make tea. Instead, recognising the stress on Pearl's face, he'd opened a bottle of good French white wine, and put it on the table in front of them.

'Tell me,' he said.

It was one of the many things she liked about him, the way he wanted all the information before he made any pronouncements on any subject; entirely different from her sister, who decided her opinion long before she had any of the facts.

Pearl explained how Coco had come to visit and how she'd put down Cassie's total misery and anxiety to the night they'd talked about their mother leaving.

'I knew that's what it was but I kept hoping I was wrong, so when Coco made it obvious that Cassie's abandonment issues are at the heart of it, I wanted to cry,' Pearl said to Peter. 'I wanted to say: "It's all my fault, Coco. All my fault." I thought I was doing the right thing and, over the years, I've realised I didn't do the right thing at all; it just seemed like the right thing at the time. But when you don't tell the truth at the start, when do you tell it later?'

Peter knew the story: she'd told him before and she trusted his judgement.

'I think at the time it didn't look as if you had any other option,' he said gently. 'You were trying to protect those two girls, Pearl, and you did. You raised them, looked after them, loved them. You gave them everything you could—'

'Except a mother,' Pearl interrupted. 'I helped take their mother away from them and she never came back.'

'Jim was involved too,' said Peter. 'And he was the girls' father, after all. He knew what could happen. He'd seen what had happened with Marguerite and the car crash. He knew it was just a matter of time before there was a really serious accident. You did what you thought was right at the time, Pearl. Marguerite needed rehab and you had to use tough love to make her get it.'

'But I don't know if she ever did get to rehab – she just disappeared. I can't get that thought out of my head, Peter. She was a lovely woman and she was damaged, I see that now. I should have tried harder to keep her here and help her.' Pearl buried her face in her hands. 'I wish I could turn the clock back and make things different. We thought we were doing the right thing but we were so harsh, so tough, and now look: two wonderful women both terrified of being abandoned. That's why Coco and Red split up, you know. She was sure he was leaving her for someone else, so she pushed him away, and that's what Cassie's doing now. She's pushing Shay away before he can leave her, before he can choose his mother over her. Now where do you think they learned that lesson?'

CHAPTER 21

Having children as a single mother: it was the sort of huge subject she once would have talked about with Jo or Cassie, Coco thought as she went around tidying up the apartment. Fiona was asleep in bed, snuggled up happily with the nightlight on in her room and all her precious teddies clustered around her. Apricot was asleep in a furry dog bed on the floor, also surrounded by teddies. Coco had explained that if Apricot fell out of the bed in the night, she could seriously hurt herself, so she lay in her bed on the floor beside Fiona's, snoring gently.

The spare room was totally Fiona's now. Coco couldn't see it any other way but with a child in it. It was amazing how difficult it was looking after a child on your own, and yet how incredibly rewarding. She went around picking up pencils, dolls' clothes, bits of paper, all the stuff that seemed to fall and drop on to the floor. There were tiny Barbie shoes in the fluffy rug under the coffee table, half-chewed by Apricot, a couple of kids' CD cases open with their discs missing, stuff everywhere – stuff that was a sign that this apartment was fully lived in. Coco loved it. She loved taking care of Fiona and the sense of sheer joy it gave her.

Fiona had stayed over before, a couple of times but not often, except then Coco had felt that they were both on their best behaviour, because even though she was Fiona's godmother, Coco wasn't a mum; she didn't understand how things were done, but now she did. Now she realised that you had arguments over cereal in the morning and teeth-brushing, and were able to say things like: 'Oh, stop complaining, you little monkey,' or tickle Fiona to ease things along when she tried to brush Fiona's hair with a special brush to remove tangles.

Before, she wouldn't have known how to do those things, would have been afraid to say the wrong thing in case she upset Fiona, but now their relationship was so much stronger, pliable, able to withstand the give and take of two human beings living together – even if one of them was nine years old going on for twenty-three.

All of which had brought Coco to her current state: of thinking about how she could have her own baby – and with neither her closest confidants around with whom to discuss it.

Cassie was living in a devastated wasteland of misery over Shay having gone.

'You told him to go,' Coco had reminded her, because it was her job as her sister to make Cassie see the truth. She'd even told Shay he needed to come and see his wife, but he hadn't done that either. Idiot.

And there was no point in talking to Jo. Jo was coming out of the black hole that was her stroke and was still emotionally fragile. She wasn't able to cope with other people's problems, so Coco was researching seriously on the internet herself how single women could have babies. There were so many choices: sperm banks, friends, or – more controversially – friends who didn't know what she wanted them for.

She hated the idea of her baby's father being a man she'd used purely as a donor and not told. But there was no point waiting anymore for Prince Charming to come along either. She'd had that before and he'd betrayed her.

The little niggle in her heart that said: *maybe you didn't give him a proper chance?* was pushed firmly to the side.

If he'd really been the one, he'd have come back, wouldn't he?

Dan O'Neill met his brother for a pint in the bar in the Merrion and started the conversation by saying: 'What's up, bro?'

'Does anything have to be up?' said Red testily.

'It does if you clandestinely slip into the country, ask to meet me and Mike, and tell us to say nothing to the parents. Ma will disembowel you, by the way, if she discovers you have been in Dublin and haven't called in. I don't care how many millions you have in the bank – you're toast.'

'I told him that,' said Mike, coming back from the lavish bathrooms. 'I love this place,' he said. 'There's art everywhere – even on your way to the loo.'

'You know, money has changed me – I can't go unless I've passed an expensive, highly insured painting on the way,' deadpanned Red.

'You won't be able to stop going once Ma has ripped out your intestines,' Dan laughed.

The two Dublin-based brothers roared until they thought they might throw up.

'I'll drop in, all right?' said Red.

'And you never met us,' Mike warned. 'Or we'll be killed too.'

'So, what is up?' Dan asked.

Red cradled the pint he didn't really want and looked at the two men he was closest to in the world: men who'd fallen in love and had managed to stay in love, get married, and even have children. It all seemed like a miracle to Red now.

'I want your honest opinion here: did I screw things up with Coco? Should I have stayed around, tried harder?'

Mike and Dan sat back in their chairs.

'*Now* he asks us,' said Dan. 'Four years later.'

'I told you at the time: women can be tricky,' Mike pointed out. 'But would you listen? No. You knew it all.'

'Cut the sermon,' begged Red. 'Just tell me if I

screwed up because I'm going crazy here. I don't think I'm over her—'

'Knew it!' said the brothers in unison, high-fiving each other.

'If it's any help,' said Mike, 'Dolly's cousin, Trixie, is a stylist and she's in and out of Coco's shop all the time, and apparently Coco is never with anyone. No man in her life. Trixie tried to set her up with some bloke last year but Coco said there was no point, she was hopeless with men.'

'Really?' breathed Red.

'Yeah, really,' said Mike. 'So Dolly comes home and tells me, and I wanted to tell you but you were seeing that Latvian model at the time.'

'We weren't going out, I just met her at a fund-raising dinner!' said Red, irate. 'Why didn't you tell me?'

'Because Dolly said after the way you'd treated Coco, you didn't deserve her. And I said what had she heard about the whole thing, and she said you'd two-timed Coco—'

'Which is why both our wives glared at you for the first year after you broke up with Coco. Alix said you broke her heart,' said Dan.

'Dolly said the same,' agreed Mike. 'Now you told us that Coco dumped you, and everyone else thinks you two-timed her, so what did happen?'

Red sighed. 'I was asked to do a favour for a friend . . .' he began.

*   *   *

'She's a brilliant accountant, Red,' said Teddy Mitchell. 'She just needs a start and she's having trouble getting off the starting blocks.'

'Why?' said Red.

'The country's falling down with kids with good degrees, and there are no jobs right now. The other problem is that she's drop-dead gorgeous, got a Cameron Diaz thing going, and everyone thinks she's going to walk out of the job one day and straight on to the set of *Britain & Ireland's Next Top Model*, so why would they bother hiring her.'

'You're kidding, right?' said Red wryly.

'I'm not. Her father told me one HR person actually said that to her. They told her to tone down her looks, but to be honest, and I've known her since she was a baby, she can't. Unless she goes in like a plain-clothed nun, she hasn't a hope.'

'I don't buy that. Rightly or wrongly, good-looking people do better in business,' said Red matter-of-factly. 'She needs to try harder. Has she tried getting female mentorship?'

'Look, Red, just talk to her, give her a job for a few months,' begged Teddy. 'You must have a space somewhere for her, just to get her started. All she needs is some job on her CV. Her father's my oldest pal and she needs a start someplace.'

'Fine, Teddy. Send me her CV, but I'll need to meet her too. Lots of places to hide on a CV, but none in person. I can't believe that being good-looking is a disability in getting a job. Now I've got to rush, Coco and I are off out to dinner.'

'You've set the date, I hear?'

Red smiled. 'Yup,' he said. 'I can't wait.'

The brilliant accountant's name was Kirsten Marker, and her CV sounded pretty brilliant too. She'd aced her way through college, so there had to be a good reason why she wasn't employed yet. Red didn't buy all this stuff about being too beautiful and scaring people off – there had to be more to it than that. So he phoned her up and she sounded shocked to hear from him.

'I'm off on a trip on Friday but I could see you Thursday night,' he said. 'I've a business dinner in the city at six thirty, so I could meet you briefly afterwards. L'Ecrivain at nine. Coffee for half an hour and then I'm gone.'

Kirsten searched her wardrobe for something to wear: something as unsexy as possible. She had clear glasses and tied her naturally blonde hair back into a knot to try to dampen her natural sex appeal, but then guys kept saying she looked like a really hot ice-maiden type. She'd had four years of that in college and she was sick of it.

'Dye your hair, why don't you?' her sister had said, who didn't have Kirsten's looks and was fed up with being told how being good-looking was a problem when it came to getting a job.

There was just no winning.

If tonight didn't work out, she might well go for the hair dye, she thought grimly. Tonight she was going to look like Ms Corporate when she met Red O'Neill. Her grey trouser suit, which kept her long legs hidden, with the button-up white shirt underneath, was perfect. As well as tying her hair back, she wore almost no make-up.

'Don't I know you from TV?' asked the guy on the bus as Kirsten paid her fare.

'No,' she sighed. Brown hair might be nice. Or should she go the whole hog and go for coal black, which really wouldn't suit her and therefore might be the answer?

Red had asked Kirsten to wait downstairs for him in L'Ecrivain until he phoned and asked her to join him upstairs.

Didn't want the guys he was with to see him with her, Kirsten reasoned, which made her like the sound of him even more. According to the gossip columns, Red was engaged to a girl named Coco, who ran a fabulous vintage shop and looked like a petite and gloriously dark-haired showgirl in all the photos. Red looked pretty good in the photos too – the tall, brooding type. *Lucky Coco*, thought Kirsten.

Finally, at five past nine, she got a text on her phone.

Come on up, Ms Marker.

This is it, Kirsten thought nervously. This man had the power to give her a job and finally get her started on her career. People would stop thinking

465

she was nothing but a good-looking girl and appreciate her brain.

Red O'Neill was better-looking in the flesh than in photos, but he looked sternly forbidding as he showed her where to sit, which was as far away from him as a four-person table with two empty spaces could allow.

'Tell me about yourself, Ms Marker,' he said, 'and how you could help my company if you came to work for me, as Teddy thinks you can.'

Definitely not a cheesy flirt merchant, Kirsten thought with relief, and found herself relaxing a little.

Coco loved late-night city shopping on Thursdays. Red was still hinting about their honeymoon, and even though Coco knew for a fact that they were going island-hopping in Greece via a luxury yacht, he was still pretending she might need a few sweaters.

'You can't penguin-watch without a few sweaters,' he kept saying. 'A few fleeces too. Take that old navy one with the paint on it: I love that.'

Messer, she thought fondly.

Tonight she'd bought two bikinis and a colourful chiffon coverup, along with a sun hat and a pair of sandals far more expensive than the sort of footwear she'd normally buy.

Red was always going on about how it was their money, but Coco was sort of old-fashioned that way and liked buying her own stuff.

She bundled everything into her car and thought about Red's business dinner. It was in L'Ecrivain, he'd told her, which was only a few minutes' drive away. He said he hoped to be finished and home by ten, so she thought she might meet him there for a drink. Normally she didn't crash his business meetings, but he was always so precise about times, so if she got there at twenty-five past nine, he was sure to be nearly on his way out the door.

Red liked Kirsten. She was smart, savvy and was clearly trying very hard not to look even vaguely attractive with that ugly grey suit and a shirt buttoned up to her neck.

'Are those real glasses?' he asked, gesturing to the heavy black frames that took up so much of her face but still couldn't hide her natural beauty.

She blushed. 'No, but I hope they're off-putting.'

When he laughed, she blurted out: 'It's not funny! Guys say why do I want to work in accountancy when I could be a model or an actress. I don't want to be either of those things. I'd like to run my own consultancy eventually, but I'll never get my foot in the door when people keep thinking I'm nothing more than the sum of my looks.'

'Sorry,' Red apologised, and rubbed his eyes. 'It's been a long day. Hey, do you want a glass of wine? I am not hitting on you, by the way,' he added, holding his hands up, but grinning at the same time. 'I've only had water myself because I wanted a clear head, and a nice glass of wine would be lovely. By the way, I'm getting married in a month and I adore my fiancée, right? So I'm not falling for what Teddy calls your drop-dead gorgeous looks,' he said with heavy irony.

Kirsten blushed.

Lucky, lucky Coco.

'You've a first-class degree,' he said, flicking through her CV. 'Teddy Mitchell says the problem is you've got the face to be a model, and in this day and age, people assume that if you look like one, why the heck would you not want to be one.'

'And I don't,' said Kirsten earnestly. 'Nothing against models, but I want to use my degree, and I need a start. Please, Mr O'Neill, that's all I'm looking for.'

Red was tired and his eyes felt gritty. Thank heavens that dinner meeting was over; he just needed to sort out this thing for Teddy Mitchell and he could go home to Coco. He liked this girl, though – she had determination and he liked that in an employee. He opened his top button and loosened his tie, while Kirsten signalled a waiter and they ordered two glasses of wine.

Red had Kirsten's CV open on the table but wasn't looking at it by the time Coco made it up the stairs and looked around the room for her fiancé. They'd gone through her college highlights and Kirsten, in an attempt to make herself sound like a rounded person, because that's what you were supposed to do in interviews, was telling him the story of how she'd done a sky-diving jump, even though she was terrified of heights, and how she'd screamed the poor tandem guy's ears off all the way down.

'Hilarious,' said Red.

It was ludicrous that nobody could see beyond her looks. Sure, she was stunning if you liked that sort of thing, but she wasn't as stunning, in his opinion, as his darling Coco.

'Hello Red,' said a cool voice behind him, and he turned to see Coco staring at him, doing her best to look fierce, but instead just looking grief-stricken. 'I was late-night shopping and I thought I'd crash your business meeting,' she said, looking now to Kirsten, who had taken off her horrible black glasses because it was clear that she didn't need to wear them anymore.

To Coco's eyes, it was all very simple: Red was with an exquisite-looking blonde woman when he'd told Coco he was meeting three guys for a business dinner. Game over.

'Coco!' Red jumped to his feet. He felt cold all over. He knew exactly how this looked, and so did Kirsten.

'I'm related to a friend of Red's, Teddy Mitchell,' Kirsten said frantically. 'Mr O'Neill was kind enough to say he'd meet me about the possibility of working at his company.'

Coco could only stare at this vision, the sort of five-foot-eight beauty she'd always longed to look like: Grace Kelly mixed with Cameron Diaz mixed with the magic of a fairy-tale princess. Utterly beautiful. What tosh about wanting a job with Red. She was clearly a model. And what job interview took place over a glass of wine in one of the city's top restaurants?

She didn't waste her time looking at the Cameron Diaz girl but stared at Red instead, who was watching her horrified face. 'Please, Coco, this is so not what it looks like. It's honestly a job interview. I'm doing someone a favour.'

'Is that what they're calling it now? I think I'll go,' said Coco, and she ran down the stairs.

In the moments it took for Red to quickly pay the bill and for Kirsten to apologise endlessly to him, Coco was gone.

He drove to her flat but she wasn't there; she wasn't at Cassie's either, or at Pearl's.

It was like she'd disappeared off the face of the earth.

'Some gossip columnist was in the restaurant and wrote a piece in the paper about it,' he told his brothers. 'Remember?'

'Yeah: *What up-and-coming businessman had his tête-à-tête with a lady friend interrupted by his fiancée?*' recited Dan.

'Teddy Mitchell rang and said Kirsten had gone to London. I don't know where she got a job but he said she was very, very sorry and if only she could talk to Coco, she could explain it,' Red said. 'What was the point of that? If Coco didn't believe me, what sort of relationship did we really have? Coco closed the shop, wouldn't return my calls, although I begged her. She wouldn't speak to me. She left me one message: "I know what I saw". And wouldn't let me explain.'

'But you met her?' Mike said.

'I did,' said Red sadly, 'in town on the street, as if she didn't trust me enough to sit down anywhere with me. I tried to explain, but she said she'd seen what she'd seen – she'd even seen the piece in the newspaper – and I said that if she couldn't trust me, then we couldn't get married, and that was it.'

'Well played, big bro,' congratulated Dan in fake tones. 'Don't you know *anything*? Women need to make you suffer. You needed to keep apologising, you needed to explain it a hundred times. She loved you.'

'If she had, she'd have listened,' said Red testily.

'Bull! She needed you to keep apologising. But no, you have to fly off and not come back to the country for a whole year.'

'Ma will never forgive you for that, by the way,' Dan added. 'Never.'

'I tried to talk to her,' protested Red.

'You didn't try hard enough,' said his brothers in unison.

'You been practising this?' Red asked sourly.

'Yeah,' said Dan. 'We can do it a cappella too.'

'So what are you going to do now?' asked Mike.

'I saw her in the airport the other day,' Red

replied. 'I wanted to go over to say hello but I didn't, and since then I can't stop thinking about her.'

'We're here because you can't decide what next,' finished Dan.

'Exactly.'

His brothers looked at each other.

'At the risk of repeating myself, you really know nothing about women, do you, bro?' said Dan. 'You needed to apologise till you were dizzy saying it, and then she'd have forgiven you. That's what works with Alix.'

'And with Dolly.'

'Coco's different. You know how sensitive she is about her mother not ever having been around. She thinks I dumped her the same way.'

'Yeah but the mother was a dope head, wasn't she? Coco can't compare you. Go on: see her. What have you got to lose?' Mike said. 'Self-respect doesn't keep you warm at night, man.'

Red woke early the morning after meeting his brothers. It was so early, he had time to go to the hotel gym, pounding away with weights, running – doing anything to get the excess energy out of his body. Coco used to laugh at him in the kindest possible way.

'Can you do ten minutes for me at the gym?' she'd say when he'd leave her in bed in the morning on Saturdays for his workout. Leaving her was always difficult: rosy from lovemaking, smiling with tendrils of her crazy dark hair all over the pillows. Sometimes Red wouldn't go to the gym at all: he'd get straight back into bed.

'We could do some exercise now,' he'd growl, and Coco would giggle.

Saturday morning would fly by with them getting the papers and coffee, lounging around her apartment, discussing plans for the future, what they'd do, all the places they'd go to . . .

Today he got a taxi to her shop. He was pretty sure it was still in the same place because he checked it on Facebook occasionally. Read those cheery missives from Coco where she chatted to her customers.

Red got the taxi driver to drop him a street away from The Twentieth Century Boutique. He needed to build up the courage to walk in there. Imagine – him, Red O'Neill, having to build up the courage to do anything. This was what she'd reduced him to, he thought wryly.

When he reached the shop, he paused for a minute, and then thought, *You've got to do this*, so he pushed the door inwards. Instantly he could see there was no sign of Coco, but a tall, attractive young woman stood behind the counter and beamed at him.

'Hello,' she said. 'Sorry, the door shouldn't have been open – I forgot to lock it. We don't open till ten. You can come back then – or do you need a special gift?'

Phoebe couldn't help herself – a sale was a sale,

even if she was just meeting Coco first thing for a chat about a plan for the shop.

Red couldn't help grinning. The tall girl had him sussed out immediately: it must have been the slightly anxious look on his face.

'Er, no,' he said. If Coco wasn't there, there was no point hanging around. He turned to leave but then he heard her voice.

'. . . you could stay with Phoebe in the shop this afternoon after school. I have to go to the accountant.'

'I want to stay with Phoebs,' said a child's voice firmly.

Red turned slowly and saw Coco emerging from down the stairs, a little girl glued to her side. The girl looked like Coco, which was crazy because of how old she was; it had only been four years and this child was, what – seven, eight, nine? Red was bad on children's ages.

The girl threw her arms around Coco. 'I'll miss you, though,' she said.

He watched longingly as Coco buried her face in the child's neck. 'I'll miss you, too, honey bunny,' she said. 'But when I come to collect you after the accountants, we'll do something exciting. Maybe drop into Grammy Pearl's and take Daisy and Apricot for a walk, OK?'

'Do you think Apricot's all right on her own at home?'

'She'll be fine, honey,' said Coco. 'Now that

she's stopped eating the kitchen table, she's been very good.'

'Yeah, suppose,' said the child.

Coco turned, and that's when she saw him. Red closed his mouth. Coco's jaw dropped at the exact same moment.

'Red,' she whispered. 'I didn't expect to see you.'

Red had it all worked out in an instant. His mother was wrong – Coco *did* have someone else, someone with a little girl. She'd always loved kids and now she was dating some guy with a ready-made family. This child looked as if she loved Coco like a mother, even if she wasn't her real mother. She talked about Coco's grandmother as Grammy Pearl. Coco had replaced him with someone she liked even more: someone who had a ready-made family.

Some lucky bastard was in Coco's life, someone who'd given her the things Red had always wanted to. Who was he to think he could waltz back into her life and mess all of that up? He'd never seen her look so happy as she did staring into the kid's eyes.

'I'm sorry,' he said. 'I shouldn't have come. I was in the area and I just thought I'd drop in.'

Coco stared at him mutely because she couldn't speak, she could only stare. 'I . . . I . . .' she kept trying to say.

'Bye,' he said, and he wrenched the door open, letting it slam behind him.

Both Phoebe and Fiona turned to look at Coco, who was clearly holding back tears.

Phoebe knew she wouldn't want Fiona to notice, so she began blandly chatting to Coco about the latest batch of stuff they'd got in from an auction.

'There are these amazing Shanghai-labelled silk blouses with the most beautiful silk painting on them. You are a genius, Coco. I don't know how you get this stuff.'

Fiona, in her school uniform, had begun rifling through the jewellery as she always did when she came into the shop, picking up bracelets and sticking them on her arm and rattling them all together, going: 'Lovely, I'm going to a dinner party,' in a posh put-on voice, then giggling at herself when she spotted herself in the mirror.

Coco stood as if rooted to the spot. She was looking at the door, as if she could still see the man.

Phoebe steered Coco into the office, still chattering about silk blouses so Fiona wouldn't notice.

'Coco, what's wrong?' whispered Phoebe urgently.

Coco turned to her and, for the first time since Phoebe had known her, which admittedly wasn't very long, she saw true anguish in her employer's eyes. Even when Coco spoke about Jo and the stroke, there was courage and determination there. Coco was going to help Jo get over this and do everything she could to make Jo and Fiona's lives better, despite the stroke. But that fire and determination were missing now. Instead, Coco's beautiful face looked as if she'd received the worse news ever. Tears brimmed from her dark eyes and Phoebe could tell that she was holding back great sobs because she didn't want to upset Fiona.

'Just look at the computer for me for a minute,' Phoebe said loudly, the sort of words that wouldn't particularly interest Fiona, who was still playing dress-up with bangles and necklaces.

Phoebe got Coco seated in the office chair and then rushed out, turned the sign on the door to closed and locked it, which she wished she'd done earlier. She ran back into the office, where Coco still sat, gazing into space.

'What's wrong?' asked Phoebe. 'Please tell me. Maybe I can help.'

Coco looked at her with those anguished eyes and Phoebe wanted to hug her tightly and make her better, the way she tried to make things better for Ethan and Mary-Kate.

'Please tell me, is there anything I can do?' asked Phoebe.

'No,' said Coco brokenly. 'There's nothing anyone can do.'

'That man, who was he? Is he a stalker or something?' Phoebe asked.

If he had been frightening Coco, she'd run out and hunt him down and hit him for upsetting Coco. She had a punishing right hook, developed at school when there'd been a brief period where they'd had a PE teacher who was keen on taekwondo.

'It's nothing like that,' whispered Coco. 'He was someone I was in love with. We . . . we were engaged.'

'Oh,' said Phoebe.

'And I haven't seen him since . . . it ended. That's the first time, and I thought I was over him.' Coco clamped a hand over her mouth. 'I'm sorry. I'm talking too much. You don't want to know this.'

'Course I do.'

'Can you . . . can you mind Fiona for a moment? I just have to talk to Cassie.'

'No problem,' said Phoebe, straightening. 'I'll take Fiona for a hot chocolate, say you're working on something on the computer, something boring, and perhaps take her to school?'

Moments later, Coco heard Phoebe telling Fiona that it was so exciting, they were going for a hot chocolate, and because Coco had some boring computer stuff to do, she'd take Fiona on to school. Wouldn't that be fun!

Fiona rushed in for a hug but was gone again in a flash.

Coco followed them to the door and locked it again.

The pain she'd felt that night in the restaurant was as bad as it had ever been. She wasn't over Red O'Neill. She probably never would be.

Cassie was driving to work. She looked at her phone briefly to see who was calling in case it was one of the girls, but it wasn't – it was Coco.

Searching for somewhere to pull the car over, she answered.

'Hi honey, I can't really talk. I'm on the way into work and – oh, there's a garage I can pull into.'

Gratefully, she drove on to a corner of the forecourt.

'Cassie,' said Coco, 'you're not going to believe it, but Red just walked into the shop.'

'Red?'

'Yes,' said Coco, sounding as if she'd been crying for hours. 'I don't know why he came in. He knows it's my business and he looked around, took one look at me, and then glared at me and left.'

'Are you sure?' said Cassie, thinking that this behaviour didn't sound like Red.

She'd always been very fond of him, and had been devastated when he and Coco had broken up. To hear that he'd just marched into Twentieth Century, glared at her sister and then marched out again sounded very odd.

'He did, I'm telling you. Just glared at me.'

'OK,' said Cassie. 'Do you think he wanted to see you on your own? Was anyone else in the shop?'

'Well, he could have rung the shop,' said Coco, 'and there weren't any customers. There was just Fiona and Phoebe and me. We weren't even open.'

Cassie thought about it. 'Just the three of you,' she mused. 'I don't understand.'

'Neither do I,' said Coco tearfully. 'It was horrible, just horrible. I tried so hard to get over him and then he just marches into my life again and then marches out. I just can't do this anymore, Cass.'

'Well, I'm not sure I'm the best person for advice,' sighed Cassie. 'I made a bit of a mess of it myself.'

'But what should I do?' Coco said.

Cassie tried to think logically. She put her big sister head on.

'If Red came in to see you, then he's got something to say to you and perhaps he did want to see you on your own. He doesn't know that Phoebe works there or who Fiona is. She was only small when he left. If I were you, I'd contact him and say you want to see him. Just for a coffee. Just to finish it all because you never did. You simply walked away and you didn't sort it out. Just like I did,' added Cassie with an unhappy laugh. 'I didn't finish it either. Maybe it's another genetic thing.'

Coco grimaced. 'We're not doing too well on the romance front, are we?' she said. 'We're good with business, though.'

'You're brilliant at everything,' Cassie said loyally. 'But I think until you – if you'll pardon the expression – put this to bed, you're never going to be able to forget about Red. He's always going to be *the one*. No one is ever going to match up to him because you're still thinking about him. So see him, tell him you're getting on with your life, and you'd love to see him getting on with his life. Then Aunt Edie can stop telling Pearl about things in the paper she's seen where he's mentioned.'

'She does that?' said Coco.

'Oh, all the time,' said Cassie. 'Drives Pearl nuts. Edie thinks she's being helpful and she thinks if Red's unattached you should run out and grab him right now.'

'As if he wants me,' said Coco.

Ruth Reynolds watched her brother bury his face in his hands as she said: 'Don't say I didn't warn you.'

'Yeah,' Shay said in a sigh that was halfway between exhausted and I-might-hit-someone-in-a-moment. 'You warned me, OK, you warned me.'

'You'd just forgotten what Mum is like,' Ruth went on.

'I'm remembering now,' said Shay.

They were sitting in the serene surroundings of a lovely medieval-themed hotel, close to their mother's Clontarf home.

Miriam and their mother had gone to the bathroom, because they liked going together.

'Us girls just need to touch up our lipstick,' Antoinette had said happily. 'Plus we can have a nosy around.'

The three grown-up children and their mother were in the hotel to see if everything was up to scratch, as Antoinette put it, to host her sixty-fifth birthday party dinner.

Shay thought the hotel was perfect and didn't see the point of this at all, but since he had nowhere to go that evening, he'd got roped into this.

They'd had a meeting with the banquet person. 'Although I don't see why we're meeting the banquet person,' Shay had pointed out to Ruth as soon as their mother was out of earshot. 'It's only going to be a small group of us. You, me, Miriam, Liam and the kids, Dilys and Josette, Aunt Aggie and Uncle Phil. I mean, how many other people are coming? I thought it was a small dinner.'

'You haven't been working on the guest list?' Ruth said, eyebrows raised in mock astonishment.

'Don't be a cow, Ruth. She's driving me nuts,' groaned Shay. 'I think I must have fixed everything in the house. And we can't have dinner at home, no. Every second night we have to go out. It's like she's showing me off in the area. I feel like a dog in Crufts. We go down to the pub, we have something there, then we walk home. You know the weather's starting to get cold and it's damn freezing, but we do the long loop home as if she wants to show me to all the neighbours. *Look at my son: he's living here with me!* No mention of: *His wife threw him out.*'

'Shay, I told you. Ma wants what she wants and she's good at getting it. She doesn't want to be lonely and she wants someone else to fix it. It's called not taking responsibility for yourself,' Ruth said. 'And I'm sorry, but I'm having nothing to do with it. I'm busy. You screwed it up, you sort it out.'

'Yeah, thanks a bunch, sis,' said Shay.

'Have you spoken to Cassie?' Ruth asked more kindly.

'She won't talk to me, although she sends me icy texts telling me what the girls are up to and when I can see them. I've seen them twice in the last ten days. Both times they cried for half the visit, and Mum was no help at all because she kept going on about how fabulous it was having me around and what a wonderful arrangement it was, as if I was never going home. The girls were devastated. I don't know if Mum really doesn't get how upsetting separation is for children, but the girls want their father back and she's carrying on as if that's never going to happen because I'm with her and that makes her really happy. So zip-a-dee-doo-dah, one sixty-four, nearly sixty-five-year-old woman is very happy and two teenagers are crying.'

He could see his mother and Miriam approaching, looking delighted with themselves. Antoinette was dressed as if going to a garden party in a floral dress quite at odds with the season, along with high, pale pink shoes and a little short-sleeved jacket that showed off her delicate wrists. She was wearing her pearls. She always wore her pearls when she was going somewhere where she wanted to impress people, Shay knew.

He wished his mother would stop trying to impress everyone. Cassie never did that. Cassie was just . . . Cassie. She was beautiful, he thought sadly. He remembered what it was like to wake up next to her in the morning and see her staring at him with those sleepy, dark eyes. And her smile: she had such an amazing smile. She'd lie there in bed, her hair all tousled on the pillow. He grinned to himself. She hated that hair, always said she could never do anything with it, but he loved it. Cassie's hair was curly and a little bit wild, like her. For sure, sometimes he wished she'd dress in sexier clothes, more fitted things, and show off those gorgeous legs of hers, but that wasn't what she liked. She wasn't like Coco.

She'd had to be the tough one, the grown-up one, from a very early age. He understood that. That's why she wore those clothes. She'd told him that once, years ago, when she was still Library Girl and he was Jock Boy. When they'd talked. All the talking had gone out of their marriage what with the conversations about groceries, taking out the bins, and paying the bills.

He wished she were here now. She'd know the right thing to say to his mother to make her feel that her day was special, instead of his desire to tell his mother that it was only a damn birthday and what was the big deal?

That was the craziest part of all this – Cassie had always got on wonderfully with his mother. It was like she was surprised he had a mother at all, as if mothers weren't on her radar.

On their wedding day, Cassie had made such an effort to involve Antoinette.

'I think the groom's mother gets totally left out of things,' she'd said before the actual wedding. 'It's like she's an also-ran. And you know Pearl obviously is like my mum, but Pearl isn't slightly precious about her side of things, so I want your mum to be involved, it's important to her.'

She'd consulted his mother about all manner of things and his mother had been thrilled.

He thought of that now as he watched his mother happily working on the long list of people for her allegedly small birthday dinner, and she didn't seem in the slightest bit put out that Cassie was not on the list.

He hadn't said: 'Don't put Cassie on the list because it would be awkward', but she simply hadn't.

He'd seen the list, had watched her working on it, had endured many an evening while she discussed it as if it were some matter of vast national importance. And nowhere was there a mention of his wife or daughters.

Suddenly, Shay had the strangest feeling that Cassie had been right all along: that his mother wanted him and nobody else from his nuclear family.

She had focused on what she wanted and that meant her beloved son, nobody else. It was, he realised, monstrously selfish, and he'd stupidly gone along with it because he felt being a good son was his duty. As if duty was a black and white thing, instead of being many shades of grey.

Shay got to his feet. 'Do you know,' he said,

'I'm getting a killer of a headache, so I'll go home. Girls, you'll drop Mum back?'

Ruth looked up at him with a faint, knowing grin, while Marguerite and Miriam stared at him in astonishment.

'Don't you want to help us sort everything out?' said his mother.

'I've got some paracetamol in my handbag,' offered Miriam, who was always prepared.

'No, really, thanks, I'd just be in the way. This is more your sort of thing.'

And his mother smiled at the notion that there were things women were innately better at than men, lovely things like arranging parties – not dull things like changing light bulbs, the sort of things that Cassie did without blinking.

Cassie had never asked him to fix the washing machine; she'd have a go at it herself and if she couldn't fix it, she'd just call the plumber.

His funny, strong, lovely wife, who had done her best to make their family perfect, even if perfection was entirely impossible. But she'd tried her best.

He missed her so much, but how could he tell her that now?

Shay stood outside the hotel and breathed in heavily.

'What's wrong, sweetie?' said a voice, and he turned to see his mother coming up to him, tottering slightly on the high heels she'd insisted on wearing.

'Nothing,' he said flatly. 'Nothing's wrong, just thought I'd get some air, and you are better at that sort of thing than I am.'

'Are you sure you don't want to come back, Shay? We're trying to decide the menus. It may only be a small, select gathering but I want the food to be perfect.'

At that moment, Shay looked at his mother through different eyes. She wasn't thinking about Cassie, Beth and Lily at all. She was thinking about her own party, her own friends and nothing else.

She wasn't thinking about him either, he realised with a start. He was just another part of her life, like a chess piece to be moved around.

Not that she didn't love him; of course she loved him.

But she loved herself more. She was the centre of her universe and he was a mere satellite.

If he didn't get out now, he'd be with her forever, getting older and more bitter, with her giving him new jobs to do every day, because the jobs would be never-ending.

He could imagine it: *Shay, pet, can you go to the post office for me? Shay, I don't feel like driving today. Will you bring me to meet the girls?*

Things that his mother was well able to do would suddenly become things that he would have to do.

Pearl came into his mind at that moment. Strong, courageous, and still going strong at seventy-nine. Pearl had had to bring up two girls as her own daughters and she'd made a damn good job of it. He thought he'd ring Pearl or maybe Coco again, if Coco was still talking to him, to see how Cassie was.

'Are you sure you won't come in, sweetie?'

'No,' said Shay, and he stalked off away from her, taking out his mobile phone.

Coco sounded wary and strangely tired when she answered the phone.

'Hello Shay,' she said.

'I know you think I'm a complete bastard, but I'm not, Coco,' he said. 'Please help me out here.'

'Help you out, Shay?' said Coco, sounding not at all like the sweet Coco he adored, but like a tougher woman altogether. 'What were you *doing* making some plan with your mother to move everyone into a different house so your mother could move in? I've nothing against your mother, I think she's lovely, but you're not married to her: you're married to Cassie.'

'I know,' muttered Shay.

'I don't think you do, you moron,' snapped Coco, astonishing him. 'Do you have any idea how abandoned Cassie felt when she was growing up? How abandoned I felt? And then you went and did it again, you just walked off, chose your mother over Cassie. No wonder she did what she did. Yes, I think she should have talked it over with you, but still Shay, come on, you were asking for it.'

'I know, I know,' he agreed miserably. 'It was the stupidest thing ever, but Mum had this idea and I thought it was going to suit everyone and—'

'Shay, I love you, but I'm up to my ears in my own ruined life,' Coco cut in. 'I don't have time for meandering conversations. I'm in the shop, Fiona's with Cassie, and I've only got a couple of hours to sort stuff out. I don't have time for chit-chat. What precisely are you phoning me for?'

'I'm trying to find out how Cassie is, how the girls are. I talk to them at night but Cassie refuses to speak to me.'

Coco was silent for a beat. 'Well, refusing to speak to you and refusing to see you are two entirely different things,' she said. 'Why don't you come and see her?'

'If she doesn't answer my phone calls she's hardly likely to want to see me,' said Shay.

'OK then,' said Coco, sounding exasperated. 'I guess nothing is going to change. You're a great guy, Shay, a lovely brother-in-law, but please, cop on.'

She hung up and Shay sighed. Whatever was going on in Coco's life, she didn't sound too happy either.

In the shop, Coco glared at the phone.

Men, she thought with fierce irritation. *Why did they make everything so darn complicated?*

CHAPTER 22

'A medical?' said Elsa to the voice on the phone.

'Yes, a medical,' said the girl from the TV company. 'I know it sounds a bit odd, Dr de Marco, but with the new show and a whole host of new investors, everyone's being really cautious.'

Elsa sat in the lovely wing chair in front of the fire in her pretty home and looked around at all the things she'd collected over the years: the pictures, the books, the treasures from travel abroad. She and Mari had gone to India once on the cheap, and while the memory of poor Mari's appalling stomach problems had receded, Elsa would never forget that amazing trip because of the beautiful Indian ornaments that were dotted around her room.

'Are you still there?' said the voice again.

'Yes, I'm here,' said Elsa.

She hadn't spoken to her agent. Hadn't said, 'No, I can't do that family reunited show because it will break my heart.'

'Give me the details of who I have to talk to,' she said crisply, professional as ever.

No point in breaking the news to this poor girl. She'd make the phone call to her agent tomorrow and be ready to face the onslaught of Stanley and Luigi wondering why she couldn't take this incredible televisual break.

When she finally hung up the phone, she sank against the back of her chair and breathed in and out very deeply. *This too will pass.* She reached under her arm, past the cardigan she wore because it was getting colder, and felt the lump. It hadn't gone away. Still there, obviously not any sort of infection, and given that she'd had a radical hysterectomy ten years before, it certainly couldn't be hormones. Elsa knew she wasn't going to do any TV show medical, but perhaps this was a message from above telling her she needed one anyway. She picked up her phone, dialled her GP and made an appointment.

Elsa knew that Dr Patel was an incredibly busy GP because there was a room full of patients waiting to see her and her partner, but never in all the years Elsa had been going to see her had she felt in any way rushed.

'Come in, doctor,' said Dr Patel, a little wicked smile on her beautiful face.

'Thank you, doctor,' said Elsa, continuing the joke.

They'd had a very good relationship over the years, with Elsa not needing to visit the doctor much in the last ten years after that dreadful two-year period when fibroids had made her life a misery.

'So, what can I do for you?' said Dr Patel, looking up at her patient.

'I'm embarrassed to say it,' Elsa began, 'but I found a lump in my breast a little while ago and I couldn't bring myself to come in and see you.'

'As if it would go away if you left it alone?' Dr Patel said, having changed rapidly from smiling to non-smiling. 'Elsa, how could you do this?'

Elsa shrugged. 'Stupid, I know.'

'How long have you had it exactly?' the doctor said.

'A month,' said Elsa reluctantly. 'I of all people know you can't put your head in the sand but I . . . I somehow did. *Physician heal thyself.*'

'OK,' said Dr Patel, smiling once again, but this time it was her let's-reassure-the-patient smile. 'Let's examine you.'

Stripped to the waist, Elsa lay on the couch, one arm raised, while the GP carefully palpated her breast. She checked the lump very carefully.

Is she spending an awfully long time examining it? Elsa wondered.

Then the doctor examined the other side, checking under her arms too.

'Right, put your clothes back on, thank you,' Dr Patel said in a cool, impersonal voice that Elsa knew spelled trouble.

She dressed as Dr Patel washed her hands, then came out from behind the screen and sat in the chair while the doctor finished typing a note on her computer.

'I can't say for sure,' Dr Patel said, 'but I feel that lump is a little iffy, Elsa.'

Elsa froze.

'I want you to go to the one-stop breast clinic as soon as you can. They should have the results on the same day and they can take it from there.'

'What do you mean, they can take it from there?' asked Elsa.

'Just if there is anything that needs to be taken care of, they can take care of it,' Dr Patel said. 'You can't leave these things too long, Elsa.' And then she stopped, as if she knew she shouldn't say this. 'As we all know, a large percentage of lumps are perfectly benign – cysts, other things – so don't worry, just . . . We'll get you in to see the people at the clinic and we'll see what happens, OK? I'm sorry, Elsa.'

Elsa took the letter and shook her head. 'Hardly your fault, doctor,' she said, a smile nailed to her face.

If Elsa and Mari didn't have work, they often met up on Wednesdays at one with a group for coffee. But when she went to their usual place, Mari found no sign of her friend with their gang. She tried to ring Elsa when everyone was having coffee and got her voicemail. Mari left a message.

'Hi Elsa, hope you're OK. Missed you today. Tell me what you're up to, sweetie. Hope you haven't got that terrible sore throat. There's a dreadful one going around. Half the place is down with it. I've had two cancellations for lessons tonight. Yippee for me! Talk later. Love you. Bye.'

Elsa listened to the message the next day as she sat among the queues in the one-stop breast clinic in the hospital. There were so many women there and it seemed to be a first come, first served scenario, even though she'd been given an actual appointment. She'd brought some work with her: professional magazines she liked getting and the most recent report on new therapies for post traumatic stress disorder. She might not have a TV career anymore, but she had a private practice to keep going. However, Elsa couldn't concentrate on work. Instead she looked around at the women waiting with her: young, old, middle-aged, many of them with partners or daughters or sisters or friends, people looking anxious no matter how hard they were trying to hide it.

Elsa didn't feel nervous because she knew what this was: karma, the great reckoning. She'd never been able to make amends to the people she'd hurt and the end result was now here.

Despite her fear, there was a rightness about it all: we must pay for the pain we put others through.

When she was finally seen, she had a mammogram first and then the nurse brought her in to discuss the results.

'Yes,' the nurse said, 'there's a definite lump

there. We need to do further tests. You had a hysterectomy and your ovaries out at fifty?' she said, rereading the notes.

'You think it's cancer?' blurted out Elsa.

The nurse looked at her seriously. 'There's a possibility,' she said reluctantly, 'but let's not jump to any conclusions. Now, we're going to do a needle biopsy here, so I'll stay with you while that's being done. It's very simple. A small specimen will be taken from the lump. We'll give you a local anaesthetic first, obviously. .'

Seeing Elsa's white face, she added: 'It's early days and the mammogram didn't appear to show anything in your lymph nodes, which is excellent.'

Elsa felt pain when the needle went in for the biopsy. The needle itself looked big enough to tranquilise a horse. All she could think of was cancer. This could be cancer and that was OK. She deserved this. She had brought it upon herself. It was her fault for everything she'd done in the past.

'Are you all right there, pet?' said the nurse, holding her hand comfortingly as the doctor took the biopsy. Elsa refocused her eyes and stared at the woman who was being so kind to her, so helpful and determined to put her at ease and yet let her know what was happening.

'I'm fine,' lied Elsa. 'Fine.'

She was due back in five days to get the results. 'Don't worry too much,' said the nurse. 'You can't do anything until we know the facts, OK? Remember: be positive.'

Elsa walked out of the breast clinic and all she could think of was that she'd known this day would come after all. You had to pay for your mistakes. And she wanted to pay.

Father Alex Wiersbowski turned up at Pearl's house just as she was absentmindedly organising the place for the Thursday night poker club.

'Come in, Father,' she said, and stood back to let him enter.

Father Alex loved Pearl's house. It reminded him of holidays before he'd joined the priesthood, a different time and a different life when his father still had hopes of him getting married and settling down.

'You'll be the last one to carry on the family name,' his father had said.

Alex felt so guilty about that now. He knew that many families were so proud to have a priest in the family, and yet for his small Polish family there had been a sense that he was giving up something by giving his life to God.

'Mrs Keneally, your house is so pretty,' he said, as he always said. He'd come to talk about the charity fair but Pearl seemed to be miles away, which was so unlike her.

Daisy wriggled against him delightedly. She liked this man in his dark clothes. He never seemed to mind if she got fur all over him the way some people did, and if he was given cake, he always gave her a bit. All in all, he was the perfect sort of visitor.

'Could we perhaps have a cup of tea?' said Father Alex, who was used to visiting elderly parishioners who worried they were taking up too much of his time. 'I can make it,' he added, again used to elderly parishioners who were not so steady on their feet.

'Nonsense, I'll do it,' said Pearl, and together they marched into the kitchen.

As Pearl rattled around in the cupboards, Father Alex noticed she seemed to be worryingly distracted. It was as if she couldn't look him in the eye, and normally Pearl was one of those wonderful women who looked a person straight in the face, eyeball to eyeball, smiling, engaging.

Not at all like her sister Edie. He wondered, with a shudder, if Edie was there.

'Your sister is around, no?' he asked, as if Edie might leap out of a cupboard and rail against him for some church crime. Edie complained if the heating hadn't been on long enough for early morning Mass, which made Father Alex, juggling a tiny budget, open and close his mouth like a goldfish. What did you say to a woman like that?

'No,' said Pearl, 'she's not. I'm getting ready for the poker club. Do you disapprove?' she asked. 'It is gambling, after all, and I don't think the church is very keen on gambling.'

Normally Pearl would have said such a thing

with a laugh in her voice, but she sounded so flat that Alex realised something was really wrong.

'Please, Pearl – if I may call you Pearl – sit down. You seem a little upset, perhaps? I can make the tea if you tell me where everything is.'

Astonishingly, she did as he said. Pearl sat and pulled Daisy on to her lap, holding the little dog as if she was a talisman against misery. Father Alex thought he'd love a dog too but there was no way he could have one in the house what with Father McGinty being so erratic. He left all the doors open and would be sure to let any small animal out on to the road, where it would be killed.

Then there was the basic fact that priests got moved on every few years and there were many places where you couldn't have a dog. What would he do then?

'That cupboard over there, the teabags are in a steel canister,' said Pearl.

In a few moments, he'd made a pot of tea for two and sat it down in front of them. He was too shy to wonder where Pearl kept her beautiful, home-baked biscuits.

Sometimes it felt odd to be a young man whose job was to counsel people far older and wiser. But Pearl appeared to be looking for something from him, so Father Alex sat and waited. Waiting was the key. If you waited long enough, people told you what was really on their minds.

'Father, I did something a long time ago and I'm very ashamed of it,' Pearl said.

Alex, who had heard many confessions before, was not surprised. All people had secrets, and sometimes things that people thought were absolutely dreadful were not so dreadful after all once they were taken out of the dark caverns of the mind and held under an open microscope in clear light.

'Would you like to talk to me?' he said. 'I can hear your confession or we may just talk if that suits you better?'

'No, I don't want confession,' said Pearl. 'I don't know if you can get absolution for this.' She looked up at him and he was shocked to see such anguish in her eyes. 'I made a mistake a very long time ago and it's coming back to haunt me now. Not simply to haunt me, either, but to hurt two people I love very, very much. I just don't know what to do.'

Father Alex sat and waited some more. He'd need a little more to work on but it seemed as if Pearl was finished. He began to think of the correct homily, one about how asking for forgiveness was key, when Pearl interrupted him.

'I may come and talk to you one day,' she said, 'but perhaps not now, not when the gang are walking across the gardens, ready to bet everything they've got on a few hands of poker.' And it was as if she'd removed the horrible thoughts from her brain and put back on a mask of calm.

'I could go to the door and tell them to come later?' he suggested.

'No.' Pearl put a warm hand on his. 'You are a sweet young man, but no, that's fine. I need to deal with this. Talking and crying about it won't make it any better, will it?'

Father Alex found himself out in the street, wishing he had more tools to help people who were hurting.

'So, how did it go?' Dan was on the phone.

'How did what go?' said Red irritably to his brother. He was in his London office and was having a bad day. All his days were bad lately. He couldn't think why. Maybe he needed a holiday.

'With Coco,' said Dan, who could do irritable just as well as his big brother.

'She's got a kid,' muttered Red. 'Or, to be more precise, she's obviously seeing some guy who has a kid, so all those "she's not seeing anyone" rumours were entirely wrong. I didn't see any guy but it couldn't have been her child, so what else, right?'

It still hurt. So much. Ridiculous to think he'd been holding a candle for her for so long only to have it snuffed out by a child. *They* could have had children by now: a couple of small ones whose faces would light up when they saw him.

'Newsflash, bozo,' said Dan. 'That's Josephine Kinsella's little girl. Jo's sick, had a stroke, they say, and Coco's taking care of her daughter.'

'Are you sure?'

'Yeah. Horrible story, although I hear Jo's doing OK, but imagine having a stroke at that age . . .'

Red was out of his leather office chair so fast that it fell to the ground, bashing off the window behind him.

'What was that noise?' said Dan curiously.

'The sound of me being very happy,' said Red triumphantly.

Coco was in the shop bright and early after dropping Fiona to school. She'd no plans to visit Jo in rehab today. She couldn't go in every day and, to be honest, she was completely exhausted. She was on her own all day in the shop today, with not even Phoebe dropping in later to give her a hand, and there was so much to do. Phoebe and Alice were brilliant but only Coco could do the accounts and work out how well the business was doing.

Phoebe was trying to catch up with the college work she'd neglected since she'd started working for Coco. Plus she and Ian, a fabulous designer from Phoebe's college who had come in and spent several happy hours examining how beautiful old garments were put together, were hatching some plot to help Phoebe's mother make some money that didn't involve farming.

'Are you sure she'd like that?' said Coco, wary of people interfering in other people's lives.

'My mother's worked herself to the bone trying to run a sheep farm when she's not made for it; not on her own, anyway,' said Phoebe.

'Phoebe's mum is a size two, and not in a good way,' put in Ian, who had been to the McLoughlins' farm for a weekend and, apart from an unfortunate incident where one of the rams had run after him, he'd loved it: loved Phoebe's mother, her brother and sister, the dog, and even Phoebe's beloved chickens and ducks.

'We're trying to work out how she can keep the land, sell the sheep, and do something else,' Phoebe said.

'I have plans,' said Ian mysteriously. 'But I need to investigate small new industry grants, which is more complex than eighteenth-century dress codes. If only I'd stayed friends with that old boyfriend who did business studies.'

'You had a boyfriend in business studies?' demanded Phoebe.

Ian shrugged. 'I was going through my "guys in suits" phase. I am so over it, though.'

Coco could have done with a guy in a suit or any sort of assistant to help her negotiate the labyrinthine system of getting Jo's home fitted out for her return. The upshot was that a top-floor apartment with an unreliable lift was hardly perfect for a person with limited mobility. The shower in Jo's ensuite was in the bathtub, which would have to be replaced with a freestanding shower with special handles, because of Jo's uncooperative leg. The door needed to be replaced to cope with the wheelchair Jo used when she became tired, and the hall in the apartment was too small for the turning circle required for it.

The counters in the kitchen were also too high

if Jo was in the wheelchair, but fine if she wasn't, and all the variables and unknowns in the calculations meant it was impossible to discuss facilities and money with the insurance company, or the fabulous people in rehab, with any degree of certainty.

She fired up the laptop in the office and sat down. It was nine: she had an hour before the shop was due to open. She could get a good lot of work done in that time, but first, she thought, maybe a cup of good coffee . . .

'How's it going, Coco?' said the guys at Coffee Magic when she went in asking for her usual short skinny cappuccino. 'Are you going to be wild today and have chocolate on top?'

'Oh, let's live a little,' said Coco with a grin. 'Chocolate on top it is.'

'How's Jo?' asked Tommy, the better looking of the two guys who ran the café and who was always ultra-friendly to Coco.

Phoebe and Alice insisted he fancied her, but Coco's opinion of her own fanciability was so far in the doldrums that she insisted he was simply a nice man who tried to cheer up the area's lonely old spinsters.

'Ha! Spinsters!' Alice said, giggling. 'He doesn't look at me the way he looks at you.'

'You still have a hope,' Coco would reply sternly. 'Tommy saves that special look for people like me and my Great-Aunt Edie, though it's a waste on Edie as she might slap him for insubordination!'

She chatted to Tommy, telling him how Jo was and that she'd be home soon, which made him cheer, and made Coco grin. He was sweet.

She was still grinning as she walked down the street back to Twentieth Century, thinking she was lucky to live and work in such a beautiful place with such friendly people all around.

And then she saw him.

He was standing outside the shop, leaning against the window, arms folded, staring off into the distance, looking in the opposite direction. She kept walking. What was Red O'Neill doing outside her shop? She'd open with that.

'Hello Red, what are you doing here?' she asked, trying to hide the shake in her voice.

She was glad her coffee was in a takeaway cup with a lid so her shaking hand wouldn't spill it.

'I'm doing what I should have done a long time ago,' he said, and she felt herself melt at the sound of his voice. Oh, she missed that voice.

'Can I come in?'

'What do you want?' she asked, trying to sound like a determined businesswoman and not some pushover. What was he really here for?

'I wanted to talk to you, Coco.'

'OK,' she squeaked. 'Here, hold this.'

She handed him her coffee with shaking hands and fumbled for her keys. Somehow she managed to open the shop door and walk in.

'Put it on the counter there,' she said as she locked the door behind him. 'So, what is it you want?' Swiftly she went behind the counter; she needed something between the two of them.

'To talk. To discuss what really happened four years ago.'

'You know what happened four years ago,' said Coco, brave now behind her counter.

'No, I want to talk about what really happened four years ago and not what you *think* happened.'

Coco's eyes flashed. 'I know exactly what happened,' she said, and took a sip of coffee to steady her nerves.

Up close he was still as disturbing as ever. Everyone was taller than her but he seemed so much taller, a giant of a man, and charisma came off him in waves. That suit was made to measure, she noted, and his aftershave was something she'd never smelled before, something that reminded her of holidays in Italy, and lemons, and juniper and . . . Oh damn him for coming here and upsetting her. She'd been bad enough the last time he'd come.

'If you want to talk, why did you march out of here the other day without saying a word?' she demanded, eyes still flashing.

He loved her when she looked like that, Red thought: all hot-tempered and angry. Everyone thought Coco was sweet and mild-mannered, but he knew another side to her – the wild, passionate side.

'A mistake,' he said and grinned, a grin that could fell lesser women. 'I jumped to conclusions and assumed the little girl with you belonged to whoever you were going out with. You seemed so close; it made sense in some dumb way.'

Coco blinked. 'She's Jo's daughter, Fiona. Jo's ill.'

'I know and I'm sorry, but the way Fiona looked at you . . .'

'I know. I look at her the same way,' Coco said, and for a moment all hostilities were suspended. Her blind fury left her and she looked at Red wearily. 'Say what you need to say and get out, OK? There is so much going on in my life, Red, I don't have time for rehashing the past.'

'I am so sorry about Jo,' he said. 'I had no idea that day when I came in. How's it been?'

'Horrible.' Unbidden, Coco felt the tears well up. She never cried about Jo now. She was beyond all that. Her efforts went into taking care of her beloved Fiona and of figuring out a way for Jo and Fiona to be happy and safe together. She tried not to think about not having Fiona with her all the time, because she would have to return to her mother, and that thought nearly broke her . . .

Red's strong fingers reached out to grab her hand and wouldn't let go. 'You poor darling. I'm here now, if you want me.'

Startled, Coco tried to pull her hand away but he wouldn't let her, and somehow it felt nice to be holding his hand, as if merely touching him meant some of her fear and anxiety were dissipating. He was taking the pain away and giving her comfort and strength back.

He looked her straight in the eye. 'I love you. I think I've never stopped loving you. But I was so angry when you wouldn't believe me that there was nothing between me and that girl. I'd met her fifteen minutes before and it was purely a favour for Teddy Mitchell, who has had the good sense to keep away from me ever since. She was looking for work and she thought nobody took her seriously because of how she looked.'

'That's it?' said Coco grimly, remembering exactly how the girl had looked.

'That's it. I love you and this is our last chance saloon. I am laying my heart out on the table for you, Coco, because I can't think of anyone but you. I don't want anyone but you. I told you the truth then and I'm telling you the truth now. I meet people all the time but I don't love them, and I don't and never wanted to cheat on you with anyone. I need you to understand that. I needed you to believe me, Coco. That's why I left.' Red hitched a hip on the counter, still holding her hand tightly. 'If you don't trust me, we don't have anything.'

Coco's mind whirled.

'Who do you trust absolutely, Coco?'

'Cassie and Pearl. Jo and Fiona,' she added, smiling.

'But not me.'

'I did trust you!' she whispered.

'Except when it counted,' he replied. 'You were ready to believe on absolutely no evidence that I would cheat on you weeks before our wedding. How could you marry me if you thought I'd leave?'

'Because people leave!' Coco shouted now.

Dislodging several displays and an art deco box full of jewellery, Red climbed over the counter and put his arms around Coco.

She almost moaned at the feeling of his holding her again. It felt so familiar and yet so long gone. It felt like . . . like *home*.

He loved the feeling of her in his arms again. She was wearing – what was she wearing? Something silly and furry? No, mohair – a form-fitting mohair sweater that clung to her, and it was dropping little cream hairs all over his suit.

'I love your crazy clothes, Coco Keneally. I love everything about you.' He slid to his knees, still holding on to her hands. 'I swear to you that I never cheated on you, Coco, and I will never leave you again. I am here for you and will always be here for you. I apologise for running away, for not fighting for you. Can you believe that?'

Somehow Coco's head was on Red's shoulder and then he was kissing her, and she felt that heart-soar she hadn't felt for four years.

'Oh Coco, say we can try again, please? I know it's been four years, I know you've changed and I have too but I can't seem to live without you, no matter how I try.'

Coco put both small hands around his large skull

and looked deeply into his eyes. 'I'm sorry,' she said.

'You won't . . .?' Red felt his heart sink. The pain, he couldn't cope with the pain.

'I will,' she replied. 'I'm saying sorry I didn't trust you all those years ago. I . . .' She didn't know how to say it. 'It was hard for me to trust but I trusted you totally, and yet when I saw her, I felt as if you'd have to leave me for her. People leave.'

'They do if you send them away,' Red murmured. 'I should never have gone. I wasted four years when I could have been with you. I will never leave, and you can always trust me, darling.'

Coco ran this idea around in her head. It was the truth. She'd known that, known almost from the moment she'd walked away from him that she'd made a terrible mistake. But she'd been too scared of turning back in case he'd gone, in case it was a one-off offer.

It was like having a burden lifted from inside her heart, and Coco leaned her head on his shoulder.

'I do trust you, Red,' she said, breathing in the smell of him. 'But it's been four years. How can we just start again—'

She didn't get any further.

His hands gently took her face and he kissed her softly, lips just touching, as if she was something precious that might break if he was in any way rough.

'We take it day by day,' he murmured.

'But you've had other girlfriends,' said Coco suddenly.

'And you've had boyfriends . . .?' he asked.

'A few,' she admitted, thinking now was not the time to discuss her appalling dating history.

'So we forget that. We move on.'

Someone knocked on the door of the shop. 'Are you open yet?' said a voice.

'Not today,' shouted Red, and went back to kissing Coco.

'I still have the ring,' he said finally, lips against her forehead, her body soft against his.

'I threw it on the street.'

'I picked it up.'

'You were going to give it to someone else?' she teased, amazed that she could joke about it.

'No, I'm a one-woman sort of man, it seems.'

'It seems?'

'Yeah, it seems. And you're it.'

Coco moved so she could see his face and trace its contours. 'Good,' she said, 'because I'm definitely a one-man woman.'

CHAPTER 23

LONDON

Elsa sealed both the letters and wrote the girls' names on the front.

Cassiopeia and Coraline.

She wondered, as she always did, what they looked like now? If Cassie was still that grave little girl with her mother's hair and how Coco looked because she'd been just a baby when Elsa had left.

She was Elsa now, not Marguerite anymore, because being Marguerite had always brought pain – apart from the sheer joy of her two daughters – and changing her name to Elsa so she could start a new life had signalled the beginning of the first time in her life that she'd known true peace.

Her life as Elsa meant peace from the fear of her mother, and peace from the fear of trying to numb the pain with alcohol. The only sadness was that in giving up the name Marguerite, she was saying goodbye to the woman who'd given birth to two beautiful daughters.

She kissed each letter softly.

Who knew if they'd ever receive them, or even want to receive them, but she wanted to write to them all the same. It was giving her some sort of release, some sort of peace. She hated the word *closure*. It wasn't a word she used as psychoanalyst. Closure implied that everything could be tied up neatly and put away in a box, and she didn't believe life was like that.

Life was about understanding the realities and living with them. Understanding what could be changed and what couldn't. Coping and making peace with who you were and what life had thrown at you.

Had *she* done that? Elsa didn't know. But what she did know was that she'd never been able to make amends to her two daughters and she'd felt the pain of their absence every day since she'd left.

Jim had never wanted her back. No matter how many letters she'd written, he'd either ignored her or sent solicitors letters to her telling her to stay away.

We don't want you. Not just me but my girls either. You destroyed us. You destroyed me.

It had been a long, long time since she'd tried to contact him. She'd given him her new name and address, tried to show him how she'd changed, how many years she was sober, and she'd begged – *begged* – to have the chance to see her daughters.

I will never let you see them because they don't want to see you, he had written, and she'd felt the guilt anew that she was responsible for turning that once-charming man into such a bitter, angry person.

When she'd been in the rehab place, two long and horrible years after she'd left home, there'd been nobody there for her family day, so she'd had to sit there while other people's family members came in and told them how it really was. There'd been so many tears that day, people breaking down and sobbing, people storming out and saying they were never coming back. Addiction destroyed families.

Elsa had never had the chance to make amends to Jim, her daughters, to Pearl, to tell them how incredibly sorry she was for what she'd put them through.

She thought of Cassie's little face the day she'd crashed the car, how Cassie had looked at her, those big dark eyes still full of belief in her mother even though Marguerite had ploughed into another car at the bottom of the hill. That was the day it had all changed, the day when it was no longer possible to hide everything. Elsa had never been able to make it up to her beautiful children, and no matter how hard she tried to work both her own analytical training and her twelve-step programme, that failure had haunted her.

Today, whatever she learned, it would be what she deserved.

The consultant and another nurse met her in the unit. The consultant sat calmly and delivered the news.

'There's good news and bad news,' he said. 'I'm afraid there is cancer present in your breast but the good news is that it's small, it seems to be in the early stages and the prognosis is good. I'm suggesting a lumpectomy so we can remove the cancerous tissue and some healthy tissue as well, and then six months of chemotherapy. First we'd like to do a PET scan to make sure the rest of your body is clear of cancer.'

He said it so matter-of-factly, even though his face was kind. *He must deliver bad news all the time,* Elsa thought blankly.

The nurse squeezed her hand. 'It's all right, pet,' she said gently. 'You don't have to lose your hair, you know. There's so many new treatments where people don't lose their hair and you don't need that awful cold cap anymore.'

'No,' agreed the consultant, who was totally bald, 'no need for hair loss these days with some of the newer drugs.'

She didn't care if she lost her hair. She wanted to lose her hair. She wanted her whole face and body to be ravaged to make up for the crimes she'd committed. To make up for what she'd done to those beautiful children and to her husband.

She kept zoning out as the consultant discussed prognosis for her type of cancer.

'It's not an aggressive cancer even though it is hormone positive,' he was saying. 'Your radical hysterectomy has helped there.'

Elsa barely heard him.

'And of course there is always the chance of recurrence, but we'll take it one step at a time. Now, we'll try and fit you in for the lumpectomy as quickly as we can.'

She wanted to die. She wanted to be punished for everything she'd done. Something was going to go wrong with this surgery. Something was going to finish her off, because what else did she deserve? She was a mother who'd left her children. What worse crime could there be?

Elsa had got sober in Solstice House, a rehab facility for addicts who'd been living on the streets like she had. It was, she thought later, an incredible and magical place where people were taught to look at the past but be able to move on.

'One day,' said one of the counsellors in the unit, 'you'll look back at yourself and you will feel pity for the person you hate so much now.'

'I doubt that very much,' growled Elsa. 'I'll never feel sorry for her. I'll never like her. I hate her. I hate me because of what I did.'

The woman had put her hands on Elsa's and said, 'No, I promise you, you will.'

'How do you know?' said Elsa rudely.

Sometimes she couldn't stop the anger that came out of her, the anger that came from nowhere. It had been the same when she'd been drinking, the fights she'd got into. She reached up and touched her nose, still misshapen after being broken in a bar brawl that she'd started.

How could she ever *like* that person?

'You don't know what you're talking about,' she said dismissively to the woman, who looked so settled and happy and middle-aged in her flowery skirt with her pretty blouse and her comfortable boots. She had a polished leather handbag, no doubt jammed with pictures of children and grandchildren and a perfect life that had never featured drink or drugs in it. How could she understand what Elsa, or any of the other alkies or junkies, were really going through?

'I know because I was like you; I *am* like you,' said the woman.

'How?' sneered Elsa.

'I'm an addict, an addict in recovery. Drink was my weapon of choice, the accelerant I added to the fire. And towards the end, I didn't need very much accelerant.' The woman looked off into the distance. 'It's funny, that,' she said. 'For a very long time you can drink everyone under the table and then you reach a point that you almost can't drink at all. Alcohol makes you want to throw up and yet your system craves it. Every part of you craves it. I craved drugs too, but not in the same way. It was alcohol for me. And I hated myself. My husband had taken the children away from me. I was living on my own in a disgusting bedsit.'

Elsa stared at her in confusion.

She'd been living in a squat surrounded by other alkies and a couple of junkies, who were really quite harmless as long as they got their fixes. She thought she was going to die there and she wouldn't have minded, really, until she'd somehow managed to pull herself out and find Solstice

House after one person had left a flyer for it in the doorway.

'I never thought my life was going to get any better and I never thought I could possibly like myself,' said the woman, 'but one day something happened and I still don't know what it was. I suddenly realised that I didn't have to be like this every day. That I could stop and I could stay stopped. That it wasn't the second or the third or fourth drink that sent me off the rails – it was the first one. It was the first drag of the roll-up. It was the first drink. As long as I didn't take them, I was fine. For that day alone, things would work out.'

Elsa stared at her with astonishment and grudging respect. 'And how did you do that?'

'I promised myself that I wouldn't drink or drug for one day. Just one day. Tomorrow was a different story, but for one day I wouldn't drink or drug, and I'd admit I was powerless over both those substances. You've got to do that. You can't think you can control it, that you can be in charge of taking just one drink or just one drug, because you can't. No drink, no drugs. End of. And I had to face me, which is the hardest bit.' She stared deeply into Elsa's eyes. 'That's why we're here. So you can face all the inner stuff that you've been burying for all these years, smothering it with drink and drugs and self-hate. You'll come out the other side and maybe one day you'll be sitting in my place, helping another woman. You can choose. We're here to help.'

★   ★   ★

Elsa thought of all her years of being clean and sober as she waited for the taxi to take her to the hospital. Twenty years. She'd never collected her twenty-year chip from AA, the symbol of her two decades of sobriety, but she'd gone out to dinner with some of her friends and they'd celebrated – celebrated that, along with someone else's new grandchild, some-one's engagement: all the markers of life.

Celebrating the fact that they had been clean and sober was the thing that held it all together.

But right now Elsa didn't feel like a proper member of her group of sober friends. She felt as if she deserved to suffer still. The people she was friends with, they'd all made amends with the people they'd hurt in the past, they'd made it up to families and friends, to children and husbands.

She'd made it up to nobody.

She thought of all those letters she'd written to Jim that he'd returned with the short sharp terse replies saying: *We do not want you in our lives. The girls do not want you. Don't contact us again.*

She still kept those letters. She sent him more and more letters but he'd stopped even replying or sending hers back.

She sent cards on their birthdays until Coco was fifteen and Cassie was twenty-one, and finally she stopped. They had different lives now, they were grown-up. Cassie might be married with children, and why would they change their minds and suddenly want to see the mother who'd walked out on them when they were so little?

Still, today she'd written the letters to them to be opened if something went wrong, because she felt so deeply that something was going to go wrong this morning.

The doorbell rang. It was the taxi driver. Taking in Elsa's white face and small bag, and the fact that she was going to the hospital, he reached forward and said, 'I'll take that for you, love.'

She sat in the back of the black cab and sent a long text to Mari.

Mari, sorry I didn't tell you. I didn't want anyone coming into the hospital with me. Having a lumpectomy today. It is cancer and I've got to have chemo. I'm texting because I've given them your number as my next of kin. I have such a bad feeling about all of this. Like it's my time. If anything goes wrong, will you take the letters I've written to my daughters and post them? They're on my desk. I've tried to stay out of their lives but it's impossible and I can't do that anymore. I know they don't want me but I needed to tell them I love them and I'm sorry.

I love you too and thank you for all our years of friendship. You, Anastasia and our friends, you have been my family. Thank you.

Love, Elsa

CHAPTER 24

Mari was doing a high-speed, early-morning food shop when she got the text. She'd just dropped into the supermarket for a few things; one needed little when one lived alone. *But,* she thought, *things are looking up with the new man on the scene.*

Mari was wary of men. All those years she'd spent as a model, hanging around with rock stars and getting thrown out of hotel bedrooms, had left her with a sour taste in her mouth, broken teeth, a fractured thigh bone from that motorbike accident in Tahoe, and a few hidden and wildly tasteless tattoos on her body.

It had all seemed so much fun at the time, such a glamorous, exciting lifestyle: being beautiful and wanted, and having men dragging her into their suites and into their Jacuzzis, lacing her with cocaine and Southern Comfort . . . Not that she'd needed any help with taking drugs or drink. No, she'd done that herself. One could never blame other people for what one put in one's mouth or inhaled or injected. An alcoholic and drug addict in recovery knew that.

Mari generally went to AA meetings because the people in NA were often so much younger, and someone like her, who'd been clean for so long, was like an elderly lady.

Her best friends were in AA, like Elsa and Anastasia. Anastasia knew everything. She was so wise, incredible and loving.

And this new man had a sister who was in Narcotics Anonymous: that helped. He wasn't turned off by dating the concept of an addict in recovery. Mari cheered up immensely, thinking how she might ring him and ask him round to dinner as she didn't have any late piano lessons that evening. It had been years since she'd invited a man impromptu round to her house.

Her phone pinged again, reminding her for the second time that she had a text. She found her glasses, put them on and looked at it.

It was from Elsa. Quite a long text . . .

When she read it, she was so shocked she had to put the basket down.

Elsa had cancer and she hadn't said anything about it. Mari was her next of kin – and Elsa felt something bad was going to happen.

Mari abandoned her basket, ran outside and rang Anastasia.

'Anastasia, I've got to talk to you,' she said. 'There's something really bad going on with Elsa and I need your help.'

Anastasia, stately, late sixties, and white-haired from tragedy in her life and a disabled husband she took care of lovingly after a horrible car accident, fretted.

'I'm worried about this, Mari,' she said. 'It's such a huge step to take. We don't meddle in each other's lives. We are there for help but not to push.'

'Anastasia, Elsa doesn't think she deserves the love of her daughters. She thinks she deserves nothing good because she was a bad mother then. That's not sanity talking; that's the inner voice of someone who is still paying for her crimes. That's all I'm proposing: the chance for her to know her daughters and—' Mari shuddered at the thought – 'if they really don't want to know her, then I won't tell her.'

'She's enough to deal with if she's got cancer,' Anastasia said. 'Don't play God, Mari. I've been around long enough to know that doesn't work.'

'I'm not playing God,' insisted Mari. 'I'm giving her a chance, that's all, and if it doesn't work out, she doesn't know about it, but if something happened to Elsa and she never got to say goodbye to those girls . . .' Her voice cracked. 'I wouldn't be much of a friend.'

'Either he never loved me or he's a coward,' Cassie told Coco bitterly.

Coco was trying to play down her great happiness with Red, who'd come round to Cassie's to hug her and the girls, but the couple's joy was infectious and they couldn't contain it.

'I am so glad for you,' Cassie said as they sat

on the old kitchen couch together and watched Fluffikins consider if he wanted to sit on Red or not, while Fiona and Lily fleeced Red at Monopoly and Beth downloaded things on to his cool new ultra-light tablet.

'I made a mistake four years ago, Cassie,' said Coco. 'Maybe you've done the same thing. Maybe we just think people automatically leave and that's the problem.'

'That might have been it with you and Red,' said Cassie bitterly,' but it was more with me and Shay. He chose someone else.'

'Choosing his mother because she's being tricky isn't the same as him choosing another woman, not really,' Coco said.

'I'll pretend I didn't hear that,' said Cassie wearily.

'*His mother,*' repeated Coco. 'You are miserable, Cassie. The girls are miserable. I don't know why you don't go over to Antoinette's and challenge her to a bitch fight.'

Somehow, it worked. Cassie actually laughed.

'You are too insane for words, Coco. Bitch fight indeed. Where do you think of these things?'

'OK then.' Coco's eyes sparkled. 'Go over and tell Antoinette you've had enough of this passive-aggressive stuff, that you married Shay and he gets to live with you.'

'Except he doesn't want to—' began Cassie.

'He did until you threw him out,' Coco pointed out.

'But why didn't he come back, then? Tell me that? Red did.'

'It took him four years,' said Coco quietly. 'Do you want to waste that much time?'

Mari wondered why she hadn't tried being a detective before. It was so easy, thanks to the internet. Plus the girls' names made it so much easier. Cassiopeia and Coraline Keneally were unusual names. Elsa had once said that Coraline was never called Coraline: she had always been Coco.

All it had taken was a few moments searching on Google and she'd come up with several references to Coco. Nothing for Cassiopeia or Cassie, but then perhaps she was married or lived off the grid.

It was hard to disappear totally, but not impossible – Elsa was proof of that. Elsa had changed her name by deed poll a long time ago, gone to college, earned her doctorate, and she looked so different from how she'd looked even when Mari had first met her.

Mari herself had come from a wealthy Gloucestershire family who'd long since disowned her, and the climb to being clean and sober had been a tough one. When it had been reported in the newspapers that she had a conviction for possession with intent to supply class-A drugs, she'd found that the name Barrington-Beaufoy was like a millstone around her neck. Newspapers had loved to write about the posh model who'd fallen from grace. It made great headlines to go with the photos of an exquisite but clearly out-of-it Mari with the rich and famous.

Now Mari had chopped off the Beaufoy – far too grand for a humble piano teacher – and went by Mari Barrington. People often looked at her if she strayed to the upper echelons of Knightsbridge, because with her long blonde hair and the straight aristocratic nose, she was definitely recognisable. But Mari always walked on by previous pals because none of them had stood by her when she'd been sent to prison for eighteen months. When she'd come out, still an addict due to the availability of drugs within the system, the old pals had melted away. The ones who wanted to be her friends when she was dating rock stars and modelling, with access to vast quantities of booze, coke and every drug imaginable had long since vanished.

In the rooms of Narcotics and Alcoholics Anonymous, she'd found friends – real friends. They were the people she could phone up in the middle of the night in those early days and say she craved a hit, craved it like she craved breathing. They were the ones who talked her through the pain, who brought her to meetings because she had no money for even the bus.

They helped her get well. And chief among those friends was Elsa.

Online, Mari looked at The Twentieth Century Boutique website for pictures of its owner, Coco

Keneally. The name was so unusual – it had to be her. When she saw a photo, she'd know.

There were lovely pictures of clothes, lively updates of what had come into the shop and its provenance, plus merry tales of a new dog named Apricot who had to be kept away from vintage shoes and anything with a fluffy collar. And then finally she found it: an old photo of someone who clearly didn't like the camera that much. She was obviously small, with a mass of dark curls, huge dark eyes that sparkled at the camera, and perfectly shaped eyebrows that were hers by genetics. She was curvier than Elsa, who was slimmer and taller, even now, but there was no doubt in Mari's mind: Coco Keneally was Elsa's younger daughter.

Mari bit her lip because she thought she might cry.

She couldn't believe these girls wouldn't want to see their mother, no matter how much their father had poisoned them against her. They deserved one last chance to be reunited. If it went wrong, so be it, but Mari refused to let her friend go through her cancer battle without thinking she had some hope of redemption. Because that was all any of them were looking for: redemption and peace.

Coco was sitting at her kitchen table looking at the finances and trying to work out how she, Fiona and Jo would cope together in Jo's house, but she was being distracted by texts from Red.

Stop,

she texted back, adding a few kisses.

Am working.

Nobody knew how long it would take for Jo's rehabilitation to be complete. The doctors talked about there being possible further improvement over at least eighteen months, so she could improve over that period of time. But how could Coco best take care of her friend and darling Fiona? She could rent out her own apartment, though she hated the idea. But needs must.

Red was insisting that he was there now and could help out, but Coco knew Jo would hate that. The idea of being dependent on Red's money would be anathema to her. Coco had to come up with a solution that pleased everyone. The shop was doing marvellously at the moment, which was another boon. Now with Phoebe there part-time and also Alice, that lovely girl from the family pet shop down the road, things were doing well. With Fiona in school, Coco was able to be there a lot more now, but what would happen when Jo came out of the rehab? Who knew when she'd work again? Her medical insurance could cover only so much.

She was writing figures down on a piece of paper when the phone rang. It was Alice from the shop.

'Hi Alice,' said Coco. 'Anything wrong? I'm going to be in in half an hour anyway.'

'Well,' said Alice, 'something weird happened. It's this woman – she rang from London. Very posh-sounding, actually, and I thought maybe she had something to sell or had seen something on the internet and wanted to buy it, but she was looking for you. She was really adamant about that, said . . .' Alice paused. 'She said she was a friend of your mum's, but I thought your mum was dead?'

Coco dropped the pencil she'd been holding. She looked at it blankly: it was one of Fiona's pencils with a furry purple bird on top where the rubber should have been. The house was full of colouring pencils and little adorable rubbers shaped like strawberries and other fruits, and smelling like them too.

'She said she was a friend of my mother's?'

'Yes,' said Alice, 'and she wanted your number, but I wouldn't give it out, obviously. She wanted to know if you had a sister called Cassie and, I'm really sorry, I know I shouldn't have done this from a security point of view but I'm sorry, I did; I said yes you had a sister called Cassie. I just thought she might be some relative or something. Did I do the wrong thing?'

'No,' said Coco, 'you didn't do the wrong thing. What was her name? Did she leave a number?'

'Her name is Mari, M-A-R-I,' said Alice, 'and she did leave a number. It's her mobile.'

She read the number out twice on Coco's request to make sure she had it down correctly.

'OK, thanks, sweetie,' said Coco, trying to sound a bit normal. 'I'll see you in a little while.'

She hung up and wondered should she ring Cassie first. A friend of their mother's . . .

She almost didn't know what to do, what to think. She was thirty-one years old and she hadn't seen her mother since she was one, just a baby. Truthfully, she could say she hadn't seen her mother at all because whose memory went back to when they were a year old? Cassie, on the other hand, could remember their mother. No, she needed to call Cassie first. It wouldn't be fair to phone Red first and tell him this incredible news.

Cassie was at home. She'd taken the day off, something she'd done a couple of times since Shay had left. It was his mother's birthday – Cassie had it marked on the calendar. Not a word from Shay, either. He picked up the girls every weekend for a few hours but never came near the house, instead sitting in the car outside and phoning them to come out.

'What'll I say is wrong if Loren asks where you are?' said Belinda when Cassie phoned in to say she was taking the day off.

'Say it's stress,' said Cassie, who really didn't care anymore.

'Oh honey,' said Belinda sadly, 'I'm so sorry. I wish there was something I could do. Shall I come over this evening after work and bring a bottle of wine?'

Cassie thought of all the wine she was already getting through on a secret basis. She preferred drinking on her own. You could drink more quickly that way, get into that nice state of forgetting how wrong everything was, how strange the house felt, how upset the girls were and how she was filled with a sense of doom because something very precious was now gone.

'No,' she said. 'Thanks Belinda, but no, I'm fine. Really, I'll be OK tomorrow.'

'Don't worry, I'll handle Loren,' said Belinda.

'Thanks for that,' said Cassie, 'but actually, I'm OK if Loren does ring. I've almost never taken time off before in all the years I've worked for the old cow.'

'Unkind to cows,' Belinda said. The friends laughed.

So Cassie was home when Coco phoned.

She was sitting listlessly on the kitchen couch still dressed in her pyjamas, watching something on TV, a repeat of a comedy show she used to watch twenty years ago, when her mobile rang. She looked at it briefly, determined not to answer unless it was either of the girls or their school, but it was Coco. She could talk to Coco no matter what.

'Cass,' said Coco, and her voice was urgent, excited. 'You won't believe this but there was a phone call to the shop and I wasn't there. Alice took it. A woman rang from London, posh voice apparently, and she says she's a friend of our mother's and she wants to talk to us.'

Cassie almost dropped the phone but somehow she managed to hold on to it. 'What? Our mother?'

'Yes, I wanted to ring her immediately but I wanted to do it with you. We've got to, haven't we?'

'Should we talk to Pearl first?' said Cassie, her head whirling with all the implications of this.

'No,' said her sister, 'let's do it together. I'll come round to you.'

Cassie had barely managed to wash her face, comb her hair and throw on an old tracksuit before her sister came around.

'You must have driven like a maniac,' she said as she opened the door.

'Yes,' said Coco. 'I'm so excited. Aren't you?'

'I don't know,' said Cassie. 'All these years and now she wants to get in touch with us? What did Alice say – this woman wants to get in touch with us or our mother wants to get in touch with us and is using this woman to do it?'

'I don't know, I'm not sure,' said Coco impatiently. 'Let's just ring.' She turned her phone to speaker and dialled the number.

'Hello,' said a voice, and Cassie and Coco looked at each other. It was indeed a posh voice. Elegant, received pronunciation vowel sounds.

'Hello, this is Coco Keneally, and my sister Cassie is here with me,' said Coco hesitantly. 'You rang my shop earlier today looking for me about my mother. I don't know what to say,' she said.

531

'You're both there?' said the woman, sounding just as shocked as they were.

'Yes,' said Cassie, 'we're both here. We've been here for a long time – thirty years, in fact – and this is the first time our mother has seen fit to contact us.'

She couldn't help herself, it was coming out now: the anger, the bitterness, the betrayal.

'I see,' said the woman. 'My name is Mari Barrington and, as it happens, your mother tried to get in touch many times. She's one of my dearest friends and has been for twenty years. She's gone into hospital for surgery for cancer and I'm her next of kin. I've known about you all the time I've known her, and I've known that not being able to see you was one of the most painful things in her life, but your father wouldn't let her. So you see, she has tried to get in touch. If you don't want to see her, that's fine.'

The world seemed to tilt.

'No,' said Cassie weakly. 'No, that's not what we're saying at all. *She* never got in touch with us. Honestly. She . . . she just disappeared.'

Mari doodled on the pad on her desk with the fountain pen she'd used at school. Funny how one held on to old things.

Of course, she thought. Elsa's husband's bitterness had ruled the roost.

'I think your father may have had a hand in stopping you from ever finding out,' she said now.

'Your mother wanted to see you both, she tried to come back to you, tried to be your mother again, but your father wouldn't allow it. He said you were all happy, that you'd said you didn't need her or want her anymore. She wrote letters, lots of them. He sent some back, but not all of them.'

Cassie clutched her stomach as a sharp pain hit her. She didn't know what it was: grief, pain, the sense of so much lost time?

'No,' she said, almost a moan.

'And she's sick now?' said Coco.

'She's gone into hospital this morning,' said Mari, her voice softening slightly. 'She's so private, your mother, she didn't even tell me she was going in for the surgery. She has cancer and she never told any of us.'

'Cancer,' Coco echoed sadly.

'You said she never told "any of you",' said Cassie. 'Did she get married again or have a family?'

She didn't know why but that would have been the most painful of all – to discover that Marguerite had started again with new children, having left them behind. It was ridiculous, childish . . .

'No,' said Mari, 'she only had one family and you were it. But she has another family with her friends who love her dearly, and I couldn't let this time pass without getting in touch with you. She might absolutely murder me for this breach of confidence, but I just thought I'd give it one last try.'

'One last try?' breathed Coco. 'You see, we've honestly never heard from her all our lives,' she said slowly. 'Our father never told us that our mother had got in touch, never said she'd written. He just said she'd gone and had never come back.'

'How very painful that must have been for you,' said the elegant voice on the other end of the phone. 'People do the strangest things when they're angry and in pain. She always said she hurt him so much. I can't tell you how sad all this makes me. You've found her now. If you want to see her . . .'

Coco and Cassie stared at each other.

'Yes,' they said as one.

The skies darkened and it started to rain heavily just as Pearl was taking a load out of her washing machine. Daisy shivered under the kitchen table.

'Yes, it does look like thunder, sweetie,' said Pearl, looking up at the sky.

Daisy hated thunder and took to her doggy bed whenever it arrived.

'It didn't say anything about this on the radio this morning, though,' said Pearl thoughtfully. There was a superstitious part of her that said unexpected bad weather meant something. Her mother used to believe that and had a host of old sayings about everything from weather to dropping cutlery on the floor.

Burning the bread meant visitors; a dropped

knife meant a gentleman caller; and thunder . . . thunder never meant anything good.

When the doorbell rang, it made both Pearl and Daisy jump with the loudness.

'Goodness, who's out in this weather?' said Pearl, slowly making her way to the front door. But it was already being opened.

'Grammy, it's us,' called Coco. 'I just buzzed the bell so you wouldn't get a fright.'

Why would the girls be coming to see her during the day? There was something wrong, Pearl knew: the thunder was never wrong.

She knew for sure when she saw their faces.

Sometimes she felt her age and she felt it now, felt the rush of seventy-nine years overwhelm her. Coco looked excited, while Cassie . . . Cassie looked white and shocked.

Coco blurted it all out.

'Mum isn't dead, Grammy. A woman rang my shop from London, says Mum is alive, sober and is going into hospital for cancer surgery. The woman said Mum wrote many, many times but Dad wouldn't let us see her, told her we had our own lives and to leave us alone. You see? She didn't just abandon us!'

Pearl had to sit down. She felt her heart race and a pain in her chest, and she wondered if this was what it was like to feel your mortality come to greet you.

'Pearl, it's all right,' said Cassie, rushing to kneel at her grandmother's side. 'We don't blame you.'

'No,' said Coco tearfully, 'we don't. We just want to understand, that's all.'

'Can you get me my blood pressure tablets?' Pearl said quietly. 'And I'll tell you everything.'

She began to feel nauseous but she had to tell her girls the truth. Perhaps her heart could give way now and she'd never get to tell them the truth, of how she'd always felt she'd made a mistake by not keeping their poor mother closer.

She took the tablet and sat quietly, holding her mobile phone close in case she had to dial a number. If the ambulance came, she wanted Peter with her.

With Daisy on her lap, she told the whole story: how she'd been so fond of Marguerite but how she'd worried because Marguerite seemed so fragile, and of how the drinking had increased until the accident.

'At the time, I didn't think your father had any other option,' Pearl said sorrowfully, 'but in my heart, I knew there were better ways of helping people like your mother. I felt so guilty that we'd just sent her off without any help or love, and it always broke my heart that we never heard from her again. I couldn't understand that. She loved you both so much. I just—'

She started to cry and they both looked at her in horror. Grammy never cried.

'I just can't believe Jim wouldn't let her come back to see you at least. That was wrong, so wrong. I never knew.' She looked at her beloved granddaughters. 'He was wrong to do that. I couldn't bear to tell you about her because she'd never come back. I thought it would break your heart to know that, but it seems your hearts were broken anyway.'

'Mari said when she tried to come back, Dad said none of us wanted her.'

At this, Pearl crossed herself. 'Bless his poor soul,' she said. 'I knew his heart was broken but that was wrong, so very wrong. Why didn't he tell us? We both knew you needed a mother.'

'We can't blame him, Grammy,' said Cassie. 'His heart was broken too.'

'But the letters – why didn't I ever see them, why didn't I notice?' said Pearl in anguish. 'It's my fault. I swear on my life, girls, I never saw a letter from your mother!'

'Hush, Grammy, it's OK.' Coco shot a worried look at her sister and tried to mouth the word 'doctor', but Cassie seemed lost in thought.

'The other house, Grammy,' Cassie said. 'Marguerite would have sent letters to our old home, her old home.' They'd moved into their grandmother's lock, stock and barrel and their father had rented out their old house to keep the mortgage paid. 'That must have been where she sent the letters.'

The house was long since gone, old and needing much work, it had been sold. Marguerite sending the letters there made total sense.

'You couldn't have seen the letters, Grammy. I know you'd never lie to us like that,' Cassie said.

'I wouldn't,' sobbed Pearl, and a heartbroken Daisy sat beside her mistress and began to howl at all the pain in the room. 'But I should have known, I should have fought for her. I let her down, I let both of you down.'

Shay had been given instructions to polish both his car and his mother's. Both might be required that night for the great party. He'd had to take the day off work because there were so many flowers to be transported – guests needed to see how many bouquets Antoinette had received – and an elderly aunt, whom he knew his mother had absolutely no time for whatsoever, had to be picked up from the train station and delivered to the house.

'Your car is bigger and looks better going up to the hotel,' said Antoinette thoughtfully. 'Now, you can collect Dilys and Josette first and bring them here, and then they can come up with Ruth, because her car is lovely. I like a BMW, don't you? We don't want the hotel people thinking we're riff-raff.'

Shay looked at his mother. 'Seriously?' he said. 'You're worried about what the hotel staff think when we drive up?'

'Of course,' said Antoinette.

Shay bit his lip and he thought of other birthdays. 'Mum, do you know what I got you last year for your birthday?'

'Yes.' She beamed at him. 'That voucher for a

538

Clarins facial and a lovely face serum to go with it.'

'Do you know who came up with that idea and who actually went to the shops and bought it all?' Shay went on.

Antoinette's beam faltered.

'Cassie did. Like she buys everything for everyone. Like she makes sure you have the loveliest Christmas present each year, and she remembers that you like Rive Gauche and gets it for you. Like she knows you love Lindt chocolates and only buys them for you at Easter. The bunnies allegedly come from the girls but it's actually Cassie who goes out and buys you Lindt Easter bunnies.'

'And what does that mean?' said Antoinette, looking annoyed at this point.

'That means that the person who thinks so much of you in my home is now alone. You have never appreciated what she has done for you and neither, it seems, have I. And it means that you apparently don't care a damn about her because *not once* have you asked about Cassie, or worried about us getting back together, or indeed thought of inviting her or the girls to your party.'

'Well, I have been busy . . .' blustered his mother.

'And I've been stupid,' said Shay. 'I can't believe I have wasted so much time on a birthday party. I'm leaving.'

'But tonight, what about tonight, it's my sixty-fifth birthday party?' wailed Antoinette.

'You're going to have to cope on your own,' said Shay. And then he went upstairs to pack.

Cassie wasn't in work. He knew because he planned to go there first but had rung Belinda to check. She wasn't at home, either. Panicking now, his final port of call was Coco.

'Oh Shay, she's here, at Pearl's, and—'

'Perfect, keep her there,' said Shay, not wanting to hear another word, and hung up.

How could he have been so foolish? Cassie had been right all along.

At Pearl's, Shay rang the doorbell and Coco answered the door.

'We've found our mother,' she said joyfully.

'Right,' said Shay, who really didn't give a damn either way. 'Where's Cassie?'

'In there with Pearl . . .'

Pearl was lying on her couch with Daisy attentive beside her.

'I should call the doctor, Pearl,' said Cassie. 'You've had a shock. You need your blood pressure taken. I don't know why you don't have one of those blood pressure things.'

'Does Peter have one?' asked Shay, shocking Cassie as he arrived.

'Yes,' said Pearl weakly.

Shay kissed Pearl lightly on the cheek, patted Daisy, and then took his wife into his arms.

'I am so, so sorry, my darling,' he said. 'I love you and I'm never going anywhere again.' He kissed her and Cassie kissed him back. 'Except to run over to Peter's and ask to borrow his blood-pressure machine.'

'What?' said Cassie, but he was already gone again.

'Thunder,' said Pearl, managing to smile through her tears. 'Always means something.'

Peter arrived with a portable blood-pressure machine and a worried look on his face. He took Cassie's place by Pearl's side.

'Darling,' he said, 'you're going to be fine.' He quickly took Pearl's blood pressure. 'One eighty over one ten,' he said. 'Hospital for you, my love.'

My love? Cassie mouthed the words at her husband, who grinned and grabbed her hand.

'Love is not only for the young,' he whispered.

The hospital kept Pearl in for observation but seemed impressed by her general good health.

'You're her husband?' the doctor said to Peter, who replied: 'No, fiancé.'

'We'll keep her in overnight, hooked up, but she should be fine to come home in the morning. It's more precautionary.'

'Fiancé?' whispered Cassie to Pearl when the doctor was gone.

Pearl smiled and held tightly on to Peter's hand. She couldn't speak anymore. But her family knew she'd never lie to them about something so important. She would never have done what Jim had done. Never. And yet he was her darling son and she could understand his pain.

Still, there would be no more secrets from now on.

'Yes, fiancé,' she finally said, looking tremulously up at her granddaughter. 'No more secrets,' she said.

CHAPTER 25

LONDON

Sitting in the small London hotel, where Mari appeared to know the manager who'd sat them in a tiny private room upstairs, Coco didn't know who was more nervous: her sister or Mari, who looked utterly stunning and dressed with such exquisite flair that Coco wanted to inquire as to the vintage of every one of her pieces of clothing. She knew that this was hardly the time or the place, but she kept staring at Mari. She looked familiar, so beautiful, like a model from an Ossie Clarke spread in *Vogue*.

'It's like an intervention in reverse,' Mari said nervously as they waited for Elsa and her friend, Anastasia, to appear.

'She might run straight out the door,' said Cassie. 'I still think we should have told her.'

'You don't understand,' said Mari in her cut-glass accent, 'your mother thinks she doesn't deserve the joy of seeing you ever because she was a drunk.'

'You can't call her that!' said Coco, shocked and furious.

'Course I can,' said Mari. 'I was one too, and

a junkie. We're both one day away from going right back there. We use those words so we don't forget. That's what being an addict in recovery is about: one day at a time.'

'I thought that was a corny old saying,' muttered Cassie.

'Not corny at all,' said Mari. 'Honestly, I'm going to have to teach you everything. We all have a chance to make it up to people we've harmed in the past and your mother never had the chance to make it up to you two, so she has never really forgiven herself. I don't know how she's stayed sober all these years with that pain inside her, but still, she's very strong.'

'What does she do exactly?' asked Cassie as they waited.

Mari grinned. 'You really won't believe it so I won't tell you, I'll let her tell you, but you'll be very proud. You should be proud of her for all she's achieved in her life, and getting sober is one of the biggest things. Without that, you'd never have the chance to see her.'

'Is drinking genetic?' asked Cassie suddenly.

Mari angled her beautiful head and stared hawk-like at her. 'It can be,' she said slowly.

Cassie felt herself pale under that stunning gaze.

'Your mother is an incredible person to talk to about that,' she said. 'She's looked after so many people during their first sober years.'

'I'm not saying . . .' began Cassie. 'It's just things have been tense . . .'

'Don't tell me, look inside and ask yourself for the truth,' murmured Mari.

'It's her, it's got to be her.' Coco's voice interrupted them and the three women turned.

Cassie and Coco saw a tall, slender woman walking into the hotel, holding on to the arms of an older lady with white hair. The younger woman was in her sixties, certainly, but with chic, short hair shot through with only a little grey and a white flash of hair rippling from her forehead. She had angled dark brows like Coco, beautiful cheekbones, midnight dark eyes, and an elegance about her despite the casual jeans and crimson coat she was wearing.

'Over here,' said Mari, and both women looked over.

The woman who had to be Elsa stopped dead. She let go of the other woman and both hands flew to her mouth.

She saw herself in those two younger women: one with long curling hair dressed in pretty vintage clothes; the other, taller with shorter hair, with Elsa's own eyes and a slightly wary expression that suddenly dissolved into tears.

'Coco, Cassie . . .?' she said.

Coco was transfixed but Cassie felt overcome with emotion. *This* was the woman she remembered, even if the hair had been longer and streaky then, and the clothes different, but this was her mother.

Her mother. The person from her dreams as a child. The person she'd never been able to replace.

She ran to her and put her arms around Elsa. The scent – *that* scent – filled her nostrils.

'I dreamed of this,' she murmured. 'Your perfume, I searched for it everywhere . . .'

'Guerlain's Jicky,' said Elsa, one arm around Cassie and the other held out to her baby, who wasn't a baby anymore.

'Mum?' said Coco tentatively, and then the three of them were holding each other, clinging on as if they would never let go.

'I told you it was a good idea,' Mari said proudly to Anastasia. 'I think we can go.'

When Mari smiled and waved goodbye, Cassie led Elsa to the couch to sit down and the three women sighed at the same time.

'I need tea,' said Cassie.

'Coffee,' said Coco.

'The anaesthetic has turned me totally off both,' said their mother. 'But Earl Grey I can manage.'

'I love Earl Grey!' said Cassie.

Elsa wanted to touch them, to trace the contours of their faces the way she had when they were children, and yet they were grown-ups now and she was still scared. This was all so tenuous. Any word might make them bolt, like nervous, unbroken horses.

'Elsa, Mum – I'm not sure what to call you,' Coco said, taking her mother's hands. 'I don't remember you, so this is easier for me than for Cassie. She's had a tough time lately.'

Elsa wanted to hold her older daughter by the shoulders and pull her into her embrace, but she was too anxious such a move might be too soon.

'Cassie is married and has two daughters—'

'Oh, can I see them – pictures, I mean,' said Elsa. 'Sorry.' She was shaking. This might be all she'd ever have of her daughters, this meeting. They might leave and never return. She must go slowly and be grateful for anything they gave her.

Cassie smiled for the first time. 'Of course.' She took out her phone and the three of them wriggled closer as Cassie scrolled through her photo album.

'Beth's going through the tricky teenage stage right now,' Cassie said, 'but she's a wonderful girl, so strong and loving.'

'So beautiful,' breathed Elsa, touching the phone as if it was a priceless ancient scroll.

'Here's Lily, who's thirteen.'

Again, Elsa's fingers touched the screen. 'Lovely.' She couldn't help it: she began to cry. 'I am so sorry,' she said. 'This is all my fault.'

Over their mother's bent head, Cassie and Coco looked at each other.

'Nothing's ever that simple,' Cassie said. 'We both know that. Now that we've found you, we're not letting you go again. Why don't you tell us about your life?'

The story took them through tea and coffee, then a taxi ride to Elsa's house, where her daughters wandered around touching everything, tears in their eyes as they saw the precious pictures of them their mother had kept in her bedroom: several of Coco as a tousle-haired baba, Cassie as a baby, then a toddler, then as a serious little girl in her school uniform.

Coco cried when she saw the letters sent back from their father: a fat wad of them, clearly read and sobbed over endlessly because they'd been folded and refolded so many times, and had water marks on the paper.

'I never knew he was that bitter.'

'It's my fault,' Elsa said. 'My fault. I take responsibility.'

When Elsa felt weak and needed painkillers for her surgery pain, the sisters lay on her bed and the three of them talked some more, with Coco getting up to make scrambled eggs on toast and more tea, and Cassie going around the house turning on lamps, closing curtains, making up the fire in the small sitting room.

Coco talked about Jo, darling Fiona, and the wasted years when she and Red could have been together.

'Pride, stupidity, not listening,' she ticked them off.

'And fear of abandonment,' said Elsa sadly.

'Listen!' Coco took her mother almost roughly by the shoulders. 'We have you back now. We can go two ways, Mum – into the mire of who did what to whom and whose fault it is, or forwards. Do we blame your mother for being schizophrenic and putting fear in your life so you found solace in drink? Do we blame our father for not being able to let go of his pain and do the right thing for us? If we keep searching for someone to blame, we will never stop!'

Cassie began to laugh – the old Cassie's laugh. 'Meet your feisty, passionate daughter, Mum,' she said. 'Coco Keneally, crazy lady. Did I tell you that she jokily wanted me to bitch fight my mother-in-law? No?'

Even Elsa giggled.

'It's just a phrase,' said Coco. 'I didn't mean to run round and whack her with your handbag . . .'

And suddenly they were all laughing, nobody was walking on eggshells, Elsa was muttering that she'd have to bring 'bitch fighting' into her practice, Coco was saying it should be all the rage for getting rid of anger issues.

Cassie grinned. 'Wait till we get you back home, Mum,' she said, 'and get the whole family together, including Red – who you will love – and Lily, Beth and Shay—'

'And Fiona, my baby, and Jo,' added Coco.

'And Pearl,' finished Cassie. 'Pearl wanted so much to come because she feels so guilty.'

'She feels guilty?' said Elsa.

'She thinks she didn't look after you properly. You know Pearl. Anyway, Peter, who she is marrying in a few months, insisted she wasn't well enough to travel.'

'I always loved Pearl,' said Elsa, her eyes growing misty. 'I'm so happy she's happy.'

'She's going to be the most fashionable

seventy-nine-year-old bride ever,' Coco said. 'And talking of weddings, you're going to have to come to mine too.'

Elsa examined her cuticles. 'You both might go home and decide you don't want me in your lives,' she said slowly. 'We are all getting carried away with the happiness of the occasion now but you have a lot to work through. I left and, for whatever reasons I didn't return, so it's not that easy for me to slip back into the family now. You will go through anger and resentment towards me; you will have to. I have hurt you enough. I want to be in your lives but . . .' How could she say that she was no longer sure if she could be strong enough to face their hatred?

'I've wanted a mother all my life,' said Coco.

'I've wanted my mother back all my life,' said Cassie.

The two sisters held hands and looked at each other. They'd talked endlessly about just this. They knew there would be difficult times: there's been so much pain, so much time had gone by, and Elsa would always be a slightly different mother from the ones who'd grown up with their daughters, the ones who'd helped with homework and comforted over lost boyfriends.

'We know it won't be easy,' Cassie said. 'But can we try?'

Elsa could no longer see, but two hands reached towards her with tissues. Two hands touched her comfortingly.

'Let's try,' her daughters said.

EPILOGUE

SIX MONTHS LATER

E lsa was wearing a turban: a beautiful silken thing from the 1930s with an exquisite marcasite brooch pinned to the front. The turban matched the flowing, long-sleeved dress that swirled around her figure and hid the fact that she was mildly bloated from steroids because of an infection she'd picked up as a result of her immune system being so diminished.

Pearl, who wasn't much of a woman for jewellery, had found an old glass bead necklace in her drawer and was putting it carefully around Elsa's neck.

'That doesn't hurt you, does it?' she said, afraid the glass beads would scratch the skin already fragile from chemo.

They were all experts in chemotherapy now, thanks to Elsa's illness. Coco had bought special cancer-skin-sensitive shower gels and creams in honour of her stay, and Cassie had sourced an amazing organic rose facial oil, which had made Elsa nearly cry with happiness at their kindness. All this from two daughters she'd thought never wanted to see her again.

'No, the beads don't hurt at all,' said Elsa, staring at her mother-in-law behind her in the mirror. It still felt incredible to her that Pearl, particularly, was so welcoming.

'I behaved so very badly all those years ago,' Pearl had said to her that first night Elsa had come back to Delaney Gardens. 'I wanted you to go, I wanted you gone out of the children's lives because I thought you were a danger to them. I didn't think about how badly it would affect both of them in the future – and I didn't think about how devastating it was for you. I am ashamed that I never looked for you afterwards to see where you were or how you were doing.'

'I *was* a danger to them,' said Elsa. 'I agree, there might have been better ways to help me face what I was doing, but perhaps not. I hadn't reached my rock bottom, I didn't realise how much I was throwing away. Nobody could stop me drinking. If there's one thing I've learned over the years, it's that nobody but you can decide to put down the glass or the drug.'

'But you're here now,' Pearl said and stroked one of Elsa's arms through the long-sleeved dress.

Elsa caught one of Pearl's hands. 'Thank you,' she said. 'Thank you for letting me back into this family. And I love Peter. I am so happy for you.'

'I am very lucky,' Pearl said, and her face looked serene. Their wedding had been a tiny affair with Father Alex in his element, happier even than when he'd been able to present the cheque to the school for the parish's fundraising week for Africa.

'Two special occasions this week,' he'd said after the ceremony, when everyone was in Pearl's house. 'One: we fulfilled our obligation to those less fortunate, and two: I have married two of the most wonderful people in our parish.'

Pearl hadn't wanted her wedding to overshadow her granddaughter's, and today was to be a grand, Delaney Garden's affair, the wedding Coco had been dreaming of for years.

'Oh my goodness, ladies, you both look beautiful!' said Coco, arriving into her old bedroom in a froth of antique lace. She may have not have been able to coax Cassie into vintage for *her* wedding, and Pearl had worn a pale blue modern gown with a flowered hat for hers, but for her own nuptials, Coco had gone all out. She was the very vision of a 1930s bride with a creamy Brussels lace veil and a headdress made of incredible filigree silver trails twisted into wildly random curlicues. Her richly dark hair had been persuaded into thirties' movie-star kiss curls around her beautiful face and there were flowers along with diamanté pins in her hair. Her dress was elegant: ivory silk and lace with a sheer high bodice that skimmed her creamy throat, highlighting the softness of her décolletage underneath. Delicate kid dancing shoes finished off the look. She was a voluptuous bride, rather than the perfect rail-thin version of the thirties with their held-down bosoms, and she looked wonderful.

'You're not supposed to be worrying about how *we* look, sweetie,' laughed Pearl, turning to admire her stunning granddaughter.

'It's fabulous, isn't it?' said Coco, without a hint of narcissism, because she was referring to the dress and not herself. 'If Phoebe hadn't worked so hard on it, I'd be dressed in rags, because really, when it came into the shop, it was nothing but a fragile reminder of a dress. She tweaked and patched and sewed tiny slivers of lace on top of other bits of lace until it's like a mermaid's dress now: exquisite lace and embroidered scales on top of one another. But we knew it was the one. I touched it and I knew it was a happy dress, that I could marry Red in it.' Her face assumed the rosy blush that emerged whenever she said his name. Entirely aware of this and determined to go back to her normal colour, she raced on. 'Phoebe is a genius and I don't know how Ian managed to create this tiara.' She reached a hand up to touch the headdress.

'He loves working with metals, doesn't he?' said Pearl, moving closer to examine the amazingly twisted filigree wires laced with crystals and pearls, with little whorls set at the perfect angle for flowers to be pinned into them. 'It's ingenious.'

'Yes.' Coco peered into the bit of mirror left over and sighed. For once in her life, she didn't feel as if this was all too good to be true. This was good and true; miracles could happen.

Fiona, dressed as a thirties flower girl and looking

mildly put out not to have been allowed to incorporate bright purple into her ensemble, even with much cajoling of the soft-touch Coco, marched into the room. Jo had put her foot down about the purple. The immoveable force that was Fiona met the immoveable force that was her mother, now nearly entirely recovered from her stroke and, thanks to her brush with near-tragedy, living life with vigour. Jo won.

'Coco,' Fiona said now, ignoring everyone else because she was on an important mission, 'Red is on the phone and he wants to know what to do about the courier and the champagne he sent round to the house, because the courier company rang up and said you'd sent it away.'

Coco shot an anguished glance at her mother. 'Erm, tell Red we are not a champagne house today,' she said in a high voice.

Elsa smiled at her daughter – she could barely believe she was able to look at her own beautiful daughter on her wedding day! – and said: 'Don't worry, Coco. I've gone twenty years with plenty of temptation in my face. It's my job not to drink it, not your job to hide it from me. Have your champagne, honey. Peter has got some lovely elderflower cordial for myself and the other non-drinkers.'

Elsa knew that her other daughter would be joining her on the elderflower cordial.

'How do I tell people I'm not drinking?' Cassie had asked, who had given up alcohol for a year because she was determined that wine o'clock would not destroy her the way it had destroyed her mother.

'Don't say anything,' said her mother. 'Your life: your choice.'

'Gosh, well, tell Red to send it back then,' said Coco.

In the other upstairs room, Cassie was fiddling with Lily's headdress.

'You are going to have to call Ian,' she said. 'I can't do this. I am no good with flowers or girlie stuff.'

'Yes you are, Mum,' said Beth, surprising them all. 'You just don't do it. I don't know where you got the idea that you're not good at girlie things. Just because you can change a tyre doesn't mean you can't be girlie. You can be a feminist and still wear lipstick, you know. They're not mutually exclusive.'

Cassie stared at her daughter for a moment and then burst out laughing.

'Thank you,' she said, delighted at both the sentiment and the fact that her clever, darling elder daughter knew words like 'mutually exclusive' and was interested in feminism.

Shay roared up the stairs: 'I need help down here! I've opened some wine but someone needs to bring it upstairs. I'm sure I'm not allowed to see all you visions of beauty. Plus the dogs are going insane and I can't leave them or they'll totally trash the place.'

Fiona raised her eyes to heaven. 'Some people just don't know how to handle dogs,' she said, sounding so much like her mother that everyone laughed. She marched out of the room, calling: 'Lily, dog duty.'

'My headdress isn't fixed,' complained Lily.

'Come on,' said Fiona impatiently. 'I can do it later. I am very good with headdresses.'

Downstairs, Shay had opened two bottles of wine and was simultaneously trying to stop four dogs from entirely wrecking Pearl and Peter's beautifully organised house. Peter was outside overseeing some final flower deliveries.

'Girls, can you please get the dogs off the cushions?' he said.

'Doggies,' said Fiona in her best stentorian dog-training voice, 'kitchen, *now*. Treats!'

Daisy, Apricot, and Cassie and Shay's two rescue spaniels, King and Charlie, followed her excitedly. *Treats* was a word they knew well. And Fiona was very good at giving treats.

'It's all in the way you say it,' she explained to Lily, raiding the cupboard where the doggie treats were hidden.

Fiona loved spending time with Lily. Lily was one of the few people who let Fiona boss her around – well, apart from Coco, who was putty in Fiona's little hands. Red, whom Fiona adored entirely, liked to tease her by saying she'd have to stop bossing Coco around once they were married.

Fiona loved that. 'As if!' she'd say, sounding like a teenager.

Her mother was back to not letting anyone boss her around. Now that her leg was not wobbly anymore, Jo was determined to be in charge of her life, so Fiona was stuck with telling the dogs and her beloved Apricot what to do, as well as twisting Coco around her little finger.

Jo was still getting her hair done in the dining room and the noise of the hairdryer could be heard blasting alongside loud conversation from Ian and the make-up artist.

'You really could go into business with those headpieces,' the make-up artist was saying. 'I love your work. They're perfect for weddings: so easy to fit on and work flowers through them. Genius.'

'Nah, I'm still in college,' said Ian. 'I want to learn it all and then decide what I want to do. Headpieces are just a hobby at the mo.'

'But you could make a *fortune*,' the make-up artist went on.

Ian shot her a withering gaze. 'I am so not into avarice,' he said dismissively. 'There's more to life than money.'

In the O'Neill house on Longford Terrace, Myra was back from the hairdressers and was watching as one of her daughter-in-laws applied a faintly shimmering pale lilac eyeshadow to her eyelids.

'Is this my colour?' she said anxiously, one eye half-open as she peered at herself in the mirror. 'I don't normally wear anything shimmery. I don't want to be looking like mutton dressed up as lamb.'

'Myra, will you relax? It's already looking lovely. I'm good at this,' protested Alix, who had several years of beauty college behind her before settling down to have her two children.

'I want to look perfect. You know they're having a make-up artist at the house and everything,' added Myra, still not convinced.

'You could have gone over,' Alix reminded her. 'Coco offered and Red said he'd hire one here.'

'I don't hold with that sort of thing,' said Myra, who knew she'd feel anxious until the priest had said 'amen', the register was signed and it was all over.

'Besides, you're not doing badly, Alix, just not so much purpleness,' she added.

'Fine,' said Alix resignedly, who knew there was no point mentioning her trophy for make-up application in college.

Upstairs, in the bedroom he'd shared with Dan and Mike for so many years, Red was thinking that he was glad he'd chosen to leave for his wedding from his own family home. He could have had his pick of any of Dublin's swankiest hotels, but somehow it seemed right to be leaving Longford Terrace to marry Coco, when she was getting ready in Delaney Gardens, just around the corner. He knew she was probably already wearing the spectacular dress she'd been giving him endless hints about.

'It has to be a surprise,' she'd say mysteriously, any time he tried to get more information.

'If it's a surprise, stop giving me hints,' he pointed out.

'Oh, I so want to share it with you,' she'd sighed in exasperation.

'Crazy woman!' Red had said and pulled her close. 'How did I manage without you to drive me mad for four years?'

'I can drive you mad for a long time to come now,' said Coco, nestling against him.

Red allowed himself to think briefly of when he'd get to take off the glorious, much-hinted-at dress that night and smiled to himself. There had been a mention from Phoebe of stockings. The thought of Coco's curves in stockings was enough to make him want to cancel the whole party afterwards and drag her off to a hotel like a caveman.

'Hey, lover man,' said his brother Dan, popping his head round the door. 'Can I run through the best man's speech with you? I don't want to put my foot in it anywhere 'cos I know you will kill me, so can we talk? Might wipe that sappy smile off your face!'

Cassie looked out the window to Delaney Gardens where the garden had a small marquee with bunting, balloons and flowers strewn all over the place. Coco, who'd worked very hard, had wanted fairy lights attached on to everything that didn't move.

Please let it not rain, she begged frantically the night before.

'Those lights aren't suitable for outdoors, you know,' said Cassie, stalwart of many, many functions in the open air.

'None of them?' wailed Coco. 'Oops. Pray harder for no rain. You see, I wanted to do it myself and didn't want you to have to work at my wedding. It's hard enough with your new business without having to do all of this yourself too.'

'I'm not on my own,' Cassie reminded her. 'I've got Belinda and Kenny working with me.' She smiled. 'It's so nice not being shouted at in the morning anymore.'

'Red says he'll put all his Irish business your way,' promised Coco. 'The Keneally sisters stick together.'

'I think learning that you're marrying Red is what made Loren back off with her wild threats to sue us,' Cassie said. 'Plus the round-robin email where everyone who left said she'd bullied us all the time and if she decided to sue, we'd counter-sue for constructive dismissal. That doesn't look good on any events company's CV.

'Tell me, 'Cassie went on, 'did you sort out the seating plan so that you know where to put Aunt Edie so she can do minimum damage?'

'Red says he has a sweet, churchgoing widowed uncle on his father's side. He was captain of his golf club, so he'll do nicely. I'm putting her beside him.'

'But she might get angry because she's not close enough to the action,' Cassie pointed out.

'Oh, don't worry – she couldn't get any closer to the top table unless she was sitting on the cake,' said Coco. 'I don't want her shrieking at me for the next twenty years.'

Coco suddenly saw that the bathroom was free and raced into it. Taking out her mobile, she rang Red.

'Hi darling,' she said.

'Hi beautiful,' replied Red. 'I was thinking about you wearing stockings . . . Are you?'

'I might be,' said Coco saucily. 'But we are going to a church, remember. No groping.'

'Right, no groping,' repeated Red. 'None at all?'

'Perhaps in the car on the way back here,' said Coco, relenting. 'I love you.'

'I love you,' said Red.

In her perfect *eau-de-Nil* house, Edie dithered over which diamond brooch to wear. She hated dithering; it annoyed her so much in other people and she couldn't bear such behaviour in herself either. But the right impression was important today. She wanted the O'Neills to know they were marrying into a substantial family. Just because Pearl had never had two ha'pennies to rub together, and her verandah was still made out of those old packing cases that got painted blue every summer, didn't mean that the other branch of the family hadn't done well.

Edie was determined to wear her little mink jacket to demonstrate this. She'd thought of wearing a lemon short-sleeved sheath dress, but then decided her lower arms might look crêpey and decided there was nothing worse than a lady of her vintage showing off crêpey arms. It had to be long sleeves, she decided, even though it was a fabulous day for May and the weather forecast was for a marvellously sunny day.

'Wear what you feel like,' Pearl had said in exasperation when they'd had this discussion. 'Nobody's looking at your arms to see if they're wrinkly or not, and if they are, do you really care for the opinion of those sort of people? As I said, wear what you want. You're beautiful.'

A lifetime of being thought of as Pearl Keneally's sharp, harsher and much less pretty younger sister reared up in Edie's mind like a wild horse. Nobody had ever said she was beautiful, not even Harry.

'No, you're the beautiful one, everyone always said so,' said Edie, stung. 'Even Harry never said I was beautiful, so don't make fun of me.'

Pearl looked at her sadly. 'Harry was a good man but he had a roving eye, and there was nothing you could have done about that, Edie. Even if you'd been Rita Hayworth, he'd have been off. You were always so beautiful and elegant, so perfectly turned out. You made him, you made that business flourish, and he loved you. If he hadn't, he wouldn't have come back.'

'What do you mean?' asked Edie, too upset to

realise that Pearl had known about Harry's peccadilloes after all.

'He loved you and so do I. Plus, I think you're beautiful,' said Pearl simply. 'You're my sister; I'll always love you. Stop worrying about if you're showing too much wrinkly arm and wear what you want to Coco's wedding. She'd want you to be happy. I want you to be happy. I'm sure that Harry, sitting up there chatting up angels, wants you to be happy too, so if you happen to catch some dashing gent's eye, you'll do it in your lemon yellow faster than in that dull beige dress that'd make anyone look like they'd been embalmed.'

Edie couldn't help herself: laughter burst out of her. 'Pearl, you're dreadfully irreligious, you do know that?'

'And you can be terribly po-faced, Edie, but I love you all the same.'

Phoebe and Ian took a moment from fixing head-dresses on to people to sit out in the sun on the front step and breathe.

'We must have been mad to go into fashion,' Ian said, face still triumphant from how wonderful everyone looked in his amazing headpieces.

'Mad,' agreed Phoebe, smiling at how proud he looked. He was such a darling. So talented, and not just at fashion either. Right at this moment, his mother – handsewer extraordinaire – was in the McLoughlins' house with Phoebe's mother discussing the whole McLoughlin organic hand-dyed and handmade craft range.

'It can't be like any old craft range,' Ian had said when he explained the idea to Phoebe. 'Not just lavender sachets, etcetera. No, you need a USP.'

'Is that like a UFO?' teased Phoebe.

'We can't have her involved in the business,' Red had said, amused.

'No bullying,' Coco had intervened.

'I am not bullying. I am giving them the benefit of my business acumen,' Red said.

'And seed money!' said Phoebe in a loud whisper. 'He can say what he likes.'

Ian and Phoebe had designed the range: hand-dyed linen bags for laundry and travel, herbal sachets, and all quirkily embroidered with words like 'lingerie' or 'knickers', depending on the market. Red and Ian, who was proving to have a fabulous business brain, were already thinking along the lines of luxury bed throws and cushion covers, and three potential premises in an industrial estate in Bray were currently being looked at.

The McLoughlin farm's sheep had been sold, although the hens and the ducks remained.

'They're pets,' Kate had told her daughter. 'Besides, Prince needs something to herd or he'll go mad.'

Ethan and Mary-Kate were astonished to hear that their mother would be earning money, and had already asked if they could buy paint and do up the inside of the house.

'A salary for definite,' Red had said gruffly, before mentioning the sort of money that made Kate and her children gasp.

'You are a kind man,' Coco had said, kissing him.

'How long has it taken for you to figure that out?' demanded Red.

'It will work out, won't it?' Phoebe asked Ian now.

Ian gave her his *I am a genius* stare and then laughed. 'Course it will, you daft maggot. How can it not with us behind it.'

They had to leave for the church in half an hour. The house was chaotic with laughter and joy, so Elsa – who wasn't used to so many people around her all the time, unless she was in a television studio – went into the back garden for a moment's peace.

She sat down on a bench that looked hand-carved and wondered if it had been there all those years before. She thought it might have been. She might have sat on this very bench with Cassie and hugged her as a little girl, with Pearl's old roses nodding their heads peacefully in the sun beside them.

She still felt nervy about returning home. No matter how much they all wanted it to work, she'd been gone a long time and her daughters had been through so much since – plenty of it because of her absence.

'Pearl said you were out here.'

It was Cassie, looking elegant and beautiful with her hair piled on top of her head with tendrils snaking down around her cheekbones. Her gown was the sort of thing Cassie never normally wore. It was fitted close to the body and Cassie had been quite shocked to see how slim and feminine it made her look.

'You look lovely,' said Elsa to her older daughter.

There was the most work to do with Cassie, she realised. Coco was so full of joy about getting married, but Cassie had endured more pain, Elsa knew.

It was Cassie who'd been the grown-up when Coco was small, Cassie who'd taken care of her sister and protected her from all harm. Elsa could see it in their relationship: the way Coco turned to Cassie all the time, showing her things, smiling and asking questions.

Coco had really had two stand-in mothers: Pearl and Cassie, while Cassie had only had one and the memory of another one who'd abruptly left her.

Cassie sat down beside Elsa on the bench.

'Do you hate me?' asked Elsa. 'I could understand if you do. It's all right to hate me. What we feel deeply inside isn't always what we think we ought to feel, but you have to honour your feelings. There are no good or bad ones, just what we experience.'

Unexpectedly, Cassie laughed. 'I'm glad I know where my desire to fix people and my over-analytical brain comes from,' she said.

Surprised, Elsa smiled. 'I want you to feel what you need to feel . . .' she began again.

'Elsa, I have been overanalysing my feelings about you for my whole life,' she said. 'Everything that happened in my life, I wondered if it happened because I didn't have a mother or a conventional upbringing. I have my husband back, my family back and my mother back. Right now, I have had enough of analysing.' She turned to face Elsa, which was difficult on the tiny bench. 'And I believe that you can't analyse me because I am your daughter.'

'Not professionally,' agreed Elsa, beginning to smile, 'but I can't help myself.'

'Let's make a deal.' Cassie took Elsa's hand in hers. 'Let's put off the analysis till after the wedding – but if we see someone with a particularly weird hat or an odd tic we need to discuss, we can analyse the heck out of them. Deal?'

'Deal,' said Elsa, smiling.

'Now, I have to round up the troops and get everyone ready. Are you OK out here?'

'Perfect,' said Elsa, and she was.

When Cassie had gone inside, Elsa looked at the house with its cheerily painted walls and the south-of-France blue verandah hung with tea lamps and flowers, and let the pain go. It had been such a long journey but she was here now and she could be happy. She'd battled to be here and she deserved it.

There might be tough times ahead but she would

be thankful for her beautiful daughters and her family and try to get through it. It was all any of them could do.

Then she raised her face to the sun and let the heat bathe her skin.

Today was all they had; tomorrow they would cope with when it came.